Graveyard Blues

Graveyard Blues

By Harriet Rzetelny

H\S
HAMILTON STONE EDITIONS

Grateful acknowledgement is made to *Alfred Hitchcock's Mystery Magazine* in which several of the characters in this book originally appeared, and to *The Bellevue Literary Review* which published two of the chapters in this book, in a slightly altered form, as a short story.

Library of Congress Cataloging-in-Publication Data

Rzetelny, Harriet.
Graveyard Blues / by Harriet Rzetelny.
p. cm.
ISBN 978-0-9801786-3-0 (alk. paper)
1. Social workers--Fiction. 2. Murder--Investigation--Fiction. 3. Brooklyn
(New York, N.Y.)—Fiction.
I. Title.

PS3618.Z48G73 2010   813'.6--dc22   2009026391

To Marc Kaminsky

and the memory of Sara Blackburn

ACKNOWLEDGEMENTS

Marc Kaminsky's support and encouragement have never waivered. I thank John Clark who asked the right questions, Danielle Ofri who insisted I dig deeper, and Sue Willis for her unlimited patience and practical help. Carole Rosenthal and Lynda Schor read the manuscript in its various stages and gave excellent feedback. Randy Shreve took a series of exquisite promotional photos. Without Wendy Shreve's encouragement and never-ending support, this book would still exist in pieces on my computer. And, of course, my deep love and appreciation to my family, Neil, Adam and Dan, who never doubted for a moment.

Chapter One

Mrs. Canover was sitting in the waiting room holding her dead husband, Herman, on her lap when Molly arrived at the office.

"How are you, Mrs. Canover?"

It wasn't really the *corpus* Herman that Molly saw, but rather the ornately embellished silver urn that contained his ashes. Molly had last seen that urn at Herman's memorial several months earlier, having attended the service as one of her last acts as his homecare social worker.

"Is that you, Molly dear?" Mrs. Canover's milky-blue eyes blinked rapidly.

"Yes, Mrs. Canover." It hadn't been a rhetorical question; Mrs. Canover's cataracts prevented her from seeing clearly.

"What time is it, dear?" Mrs. Canover asked rather pointedly.

"It's nine-eighteen."

"I thought your office opened at nine?"

Leo Stuttman, Multi-Care Home Service's director and Molly's boss had been standing near the reception desk leering down at Nilda Carillos, the receptionist. He looked up at Molly and scowled. Molly sighed, knowing she was in for another tongue lashing.

But Stuttman wouldn't say anything in front of a client, so she smiled at Mrs. Canover and said, "That's true. I'm sorry I was held up." Pushing her hair off her face with slender fingers, she added, "Let's go into my office."

Mrs. Canover was a round dumpling of a woman, in her mid-seventies, with lots of frizzy gray hair and a surprisingly unlined, pink-cheeked face. She was wearing a navy blue coat with frayed sleeves, bought during better days. As she creakingly got to her feet to be escorted to the little windowless cubicle Molly laughingly called her office, Mrs. Canover settled Herman a little more securely into the crook of her arm. As she did so, a dusting of gray appeared on her coat.

Horrified, Molly realized that Herman's ashes were trickling down the dark blue fabric. The seam of the urn must have split. She darted a quick glance around. Stuttman had gone back to leering down at Nilda who, though a single mother of three, still had a cleavage worth a few whistles and always wore low-cut tops. As Nilda had said to Molly many times, Stuttman liked them and Nilda needed the job.

Stuttman never leered at Molly. She wasn't big-breasted like Nilda, nor in the least bit flirty. Small-boned with dark, naturally wavy hair—her best feature, she thought—cut in rather long bangs across her forehead and a small, sharply-planed face, Molly never been married and had no children.

Neither Stuttman nor Nilda appeared to have noticed anything, so Molly decided not to notice anything either. She got the Canovers, Margery and Herman, comfortably settled into her one client chair and hung up her own coat on her antique oak coat rack. That and her poster of Arches National Park were her two attempts at individualizing her tiny space.

"Now what can I do for you?"

"Well, dear, I want to know when I can have that nice Mrs. Lopez back." Mrs. Canover tried a winsome smile, but it never got past her mouth. Her eyes, under the film of her cataracts, were sad and anxious. "You did say, I know you did, that I could have her back." Molly had never said any such thing.

"Mrs. Canover," Molly began gently, "I know how much she meant to you, and how well she took care of Mr. Canover . . ."

"Herman, dear," she interrupted, looking down lovingly at Herman in his urn. "Call him Herman. He never did stand on ceremony."

"Herman," Molly corrected herself. "But since he passed away, we can't go on sending you a homecare worker, especially since you're in such good health and get around as well as you do." Molly had explained this to her several times before, but Mrs. Canover simply refused to hear it.

"It isn't for me, dear. Herman still needs her. He hasn't completely passed over, you know," she added sadly.

Molly knew full well what the problem was. Not only had Mrs. Canover lost her Herman, who had been both husband and child to this otherwise childless woman, she'd lost Angelina Lopez who'd become her closest friend while they both took care of Herman through his last months. All this prolonged caregiving had taken so much of Molly's time over the past several years that her own life had kind of slipped away from her as well.

"You see," she continued when Molly didn't say anything, "the messages he sends me are quite clear. His soul is not yet at rest."

She shook the urn a little, perhaps to demonstrate Herman's state of unrest. "Mrs. Lopez was such a calming influence," Mrs. Canover was continuing, apparently unaware that Herman was slipping away a lot faster than she thought. "Please dear," she entreated, "at least until he's passed safely on."

Poor Mrs. Canover. She needed to find a replacement for both

Herman and Angelina Lopez—something or someone to get involved with.

"If you would just give me her telephone number, dear, I wouldn't have to put you to all that trouble."

"You know I can't do that." Giving out personal telephone numbers is a real no-no in homecare.

Mrs. Canover readjusted the urn on her lap and went on as if Molly hadn't said anything. "I know if I explained the situation to her, she would be more than willing to come back and help Herman pass over peacefully."

"What makes you think that Herman's spirit is troubled?"

"Well, I hear him. The noises and the banging—they go on all day and night."

"Noises and banging?"

"He's trying to get out; I just know it, dear. He bangs on the door, the walls, the pipes and sends me all kinds of messages. He's so unhappy."

Once again Molly thought she knew what the problem was since she had encountered this kind of thing before in elderly people who lived, grieving and alone, with no one to talk to for days on end except an occasional neighbor or busy shopkeeper. Mrs. Canover lived in an old building where radiators knocked, floorboards groaned and plumbing banged—noises that easily became restless spirits or ominous messages when you lie awake all night with nothing to do except listen to them and think about your dead husband. Molly believed Mrs. Canover was hearing ominous noises but thought it was strictly connected to the age of the building. She couldn't have known how wrong she was.

Not having second sight, however, she considered her current options: Mrs. Canover was no longer a client of the agency, and Stuttman was clear about the need to limit her involvement to actual clients, not the widows of restless spirits.

"How about I come by later this week during my lunch time"— what Molly did during her lunch hour was her own business—"and we can go to the center together."

Mrs. Canover blinked sadly, but she didn't say no. Molly knew an offer of lunch at the senior center with its noise and its cliques was not what Mrs. Canover wanted, but it was the best she was going to get.

11

Chapter Two

With his well-tailored gray overcoat and charcoal-gray silk scarf, and his silvery hair carefully combed over his bald spot, Stuttman stood out in contrast to the physical premises of the agency he directed. These ran to glaring fluorescent lights, dirty partition boards hung with yellowing notices, and dented-steel file cabinets.

Now he stopped to glare at Molly who had just escorted Mrs. Canover out the door. "You were late again, Miss Lewin."

Molly smiled as contritely as a not-terribly-contrite nature allowed her and said, "I'm really sorry, Mr. Stuttman."

"Apologies are no longer sufficient," Stuttman said severely. "I'm going to have to write you up." He slammed out the door. Behind his back, Nilda rolled her eyes.

Molly sighed. Why he was so antagonistic towards her? Yes, she was late a little too often, but his hostility went deeper than that— paperwork not completed on time, bending the rules a little too much, not washing out the coffee pot after being the last person to use it, etc. etc. As much as she understood people, she was clueless when it came to Stuttman. Dedicated to the welfare of his clients, he was one of the few agency directors who knew the name of almost every one of them. And he had to raise the money for her salary every year as there was no line in his no-frills, mostly Medicaid-funded budget for a social worker. Then why was he always giving her flak?

"It's only because he's a little afraid of you," Nilda maintained. "Why don't you flirt with him? That's all he understands. Let him think he's Brad Pitt, problem solved." Nilda used flirting to get what she needed—time off when the baby sitter didn't show up, or when she had to take one of her kids to the doctor, or any of the other myriad problems that she faced as a single mom. But Molly had grown up to believe that center stage was not her natural due; she thought of herself as a fly on the wall in the lives of other people, listening to their stories, immersed in their problems. As long as a fly doesn't buzz around, nobody pays much attention to it.

Swandell Green hurried by with a stack of green file folders clutched under one mahogany-colored arm. As he swerved around Molly, she said over her shoulder: "I put a referral in your box. Cal Bruchman, the patient with ALS who lives over near the river. You know him, right?" Molly nodded. "His son, Donald, has been getting my goat," Swandell went on, "and if I have to keep dealing with that man, one of us will end up in the hospital and it won't be me." She tossed her head and her long beaded braids twirled around her face like a whirligig.

When Molly was first hired, Swandell had let her know that she didn't have time in her busy life for social workers. They couldn't take blood pressure, change a dressing or make a bed. After Molly turned one of Swandell's nastiest patients into, well not exactly a sweet little lamb, but as close to one as that miserable old woman was ever going to get, Swandell did an about-face.

Molly picked up the referral, waved to Nilda and continued on to her cubicle where she called the Bruchman apartment. Louis Kroski, Cal's home attendant, answered the phone. "Oh, hi, Ms. Lewin," he said in his husky voice. "I'm glad you called. It's a madhouse up here."

"What's been going on?"

"Everyone's fighting with everyone. Cal's son, Donald, has been storming around, threatening to put his daddy into a nursing home and evict poor Willie." Willie Cobb was Cal Bruchman's roommate and long-time companion.

"Do you know why he's suddenly doing this?"

"He's not one of God's finer creatures." Louis said dryly. "Look, I gotta get Mr. Bruchman ready for his doctor's appointment. The Medi-Van is picking him up in an hour, and you know how long it takes him to do anything. Donald is coming back this afternoon. Can you come up and maybe talk to him?"

Molly promised that she would. After hanging up, she tried to call Donald Bruchman who she hadn't yet met and ended up leaving a message. By the time she left for her appointment with Cal Bruchman, Donald hadn't gotten back to her.

The Freymont Avenue neighborhood where Multi-Care Home Services was located was perched on the Brooklyn side of New York City's harbor. Overlooking Manhattan's downtown skyline, the neighborhood had sustained an almost mortal wound when the towers of the World Trade Center came down a little less than a year and a half ago. For months after the disaster, the spirals of smoke had risen like the vestiges of funeral pyres from the site of what had been the Twin Towers, and tears still came to Molly's eyes every time she looked towards the river and saw what wasn't there.

It was now two weeks into the new year of 2003, and the city was in the middle of a January thaw. As Molly walked along Freymont Avenue, a heavy-set woman pushing a stroller anxiously looked up at the sun which was shining down brightly. Molly briefly speculated on whether this was a sign of the times. Ever since the events of 9/11 anything and everything was scrutinized as a potential for disaster. Warm weather would invariably lead to melting ice caps and bring on the final deluge. Snowy weather would strangle the city and lead to the deaths of countless elderly and homeless people. Disruptions in the subway due to its ancient equipment were frightening reminders of how vulnerable the city was to terrorist attacks. Molly, who thought of the city as one living breathing organism, often wondered if it would ever recover from the terrible wound it had sustained to its heart.

In the last six months, however, Molly had noticed an influx of younger, hipper people moving into this working-class, relatively low-rent area, bringing along their cafés, bars and boutiques. Freymont Avenue itself was also gentrifying, but much more slowly. The check-cashing places, Greek greasy spoons, the Wash-n-Glow Laundromat, the little bodegas still looked pretty much as they had for the eight years she'd worked here. But the Wash-N-Glow Laundromat had recently been spiffed up with a self-serve coffee bar to accommodate the new arrivals.

Right now, the neighborhood was like a patchwork quilt with the newly-painted shutters and potted plants that signified gentrification: brightening up some streets, while others still wore the peeling paint, boarded-up windows and littered yards that were the result of the neighborhood's long post-industrial decline. Molly, who would never forget the sight of those twin towers exploding right in front of her eyes, had to grudgingly admit that life, though fractured, did go on.

Cal Bruchman's apartment was in a dilapidated building, one of three four-storied brick buildings that sat on Warwick Avenue, directly across from the water. Gentrification hadn't found its way there yet. The piers that had lined Warwick Avenue, when this riverfront was one of the busiest in the world, had either been abandoned or torn down, and most of the weedy, littered riverfront sat behind barbed wire or semi-deserted grimy industrial buildings.

During the waterfront's heyday, Molly knew, Cal's building had been a gentleman's gaming parlor. There were some vestiges of the building's former elegance in the remains of the Italianate lintels above the windows, the cracked marble stairs that led to the front door and the wrought iron banisters from which the paint peeled, making the surface look like a series of oxidized flower petals. But the building had long ago been chopped up into ever tinier apartments under a succession of subsistence landlords.

Cal and his roommate Willie were among the last remaining tenants in their building. Molly entered the building, made her way up the two flights of stairs—remembering not to trip on the missing tread—and knocked on the door. Louis let her in.

Massively built, Louis's brownish-gray hair was buzz-cut in a military style—a reminder of his navy days, he'd told her. He'd retired from the service to care for his aging mother and became a home attendant after her death. It had been over three years, now, that he'd been working for Cal and Willie. According to Swandell, who didn't hand out compliments lightly, Louis was one of the best they had.

"Hey, Willie," Louis called over his shoulder. "Look who's here."

Willie sat on an old wooden chair. Rail thin with high cheekbones and salt-and-pepper hair, he had skin the color of finely polished walnut. If he hadn't told her, Molly would never have guessed that he was 86 years old. A much-used, oversized acoustic guitar was propped up next to the chair. As he saw her, he picked it up and began singing:

> *"Hey Billie Lee*
> *Ma yellow honey bee*
> *She's bowlegged and lazy*
> *Cock-eyed and crazy . . . "*

Willie's voice was worn out and scouring-pad rough, but his bony fingers slid up and down the neck with the sureness of a long and intimate relationship. When he finished the stanza, Willie stopped singing, frowned again and said, "Miz Molly." His left hand continued to move up and down the neck of the guitar, while his right hand picked out the succession of rhythmical chords that had accentuated his words. "There be trouble here"

"So I've been told."

The room they were in was hardly better looking than the building. Everything was old—the sagging couch that had once been velvet, the faded flowered armchair, the chrome-and-Formica dinette set, the ancient T.V. on its corroded stand.

By contrast, the wall behind them, which framed a window that looked out on to the river was hung with photographs that sang with life—Willie and his guitar playing with musicians such as the legendary Muddy Waters, Howlin' Wolf, Big Bill Broonzy and Sonny Terry. Molly was a big music buff—blues, jazz, opera—just about anything with soul and passion. But the blues in particular spoke to hidden, smoky places in her, clandestine corners filled with a deep, dark sadness and, at moments, unexpected bursts of joy. The photos represented a gallery full of national treasures; it gave Molly goose bumps just to look at them. She sighed to think that so few people even remembered who they were.

Louis came into the room wheeling a chair on which sat a sunken blond giant.

"Good afternoon, Cal," Molly said.

"Have to go . . . can't stay here," he said.

Molly glanced at Willie who was glaring at Cal. "I thought this was where you wanted to die. Right here. That's what you tol' me enough times."

"Yes . . . but . . ." Tears were rolling down his immobilized face. "Must . . . leave."

Molly couldn't look at Cal without getting angry at what this disease had wrought upon this once vital and handsome man. Cal had been some hunk; she'd seen a few pictures of him as a younger man, before he insisted that they be taken down from the wall. In one he was posed in the briefest of bathing suits against the Coney Island beach and boardwalk, smiling at the camera with an expression that managed to be at the same time guileless and incredibly seductive..

"And what about me?" Willie shot back. "Where am I supposed to go?" His long, skinny body began to tremble. He's really so frail, Molly reflected with some surprise. She usually thought of Cal, who was only in his sixties, as being the older one.

"It sounds like Cal wants to move," Molly said to Louis.

"That's what I don' understand," Willie said to Molly. "You'd think he was that no-good landlord, the way he's trying to get us out of here."

"The landlord has been trying to get you out?" Molly asked.

Willie glared; his eyes fierce in his narrow skull. "He been hasslin' us for a long time, trying to get us to move. Now Cal says he thinks we should move." He gave Cal a withering look. "Now what we gonna go and do that for?"

Turning to Louis, Molly asked, "Who's the landlord here?"

"Why don't you ask me?" Willie snapped. "Far as I know, I ain't gone addled yet."

"Sorry, Willie," Molly said.

"Rent gets paid to KB Real Estate Corporation. Kenneth Belloc— that's the KB—he fronts it, but Papa Skana is the money behind him." Ivan Skanov, better known as Papa Skana, was reputed to have ties to the Russian Mafia which had taken over drugs and prostitution in the area. Ken Belloc, on the other hand, was, supposedly, the upstanding head of the Freymont Avenue Business Association. "They're buying up a lot of these old buildings," Willie went on. "Trying to get people to move out so they can raise the rents and make more money."

"Ken Belloc, huh?" Louis said, looking up from a tray on which he was arranging a small bowl of cut-up Jello and a plastic tumbler of something that looked like a thin milk shake. He added a bent straw to the drink and continued, "Do you remember, after 9/11, when Belloc led a campaign to change the name of Freymont Avenue to Freedom Hill?"

"So?" Willie shot back, not willing to be deflected. "You think

16

that makes him some kind of patriotic saint?"

Louis met Molly's eyes and they both solemnly shook their heads.

"I think they're paying that no-good son of his," Willie pointed in Cal's direction, "to help him get us out."

"No . . . not Donald," Cal sputtered, the tears running down his face now red in his effort to speak. Louis put the tray down on a snack table in front of Cal and carefully placed a small towel on his lap.

Willie rolled his eyes. "You'd think the sun rose and set on that boy, the way Cal will hear nothing bad against him."

"Willie," Molly asked. "How do you know all this?"

"I've got my sources," Willie said mysteriously. "Jes' because I'm an old man don't mean I'm stupid."

At that moment the door opened and a youngish man walked into the room. "You been bad mouthing me again, old man?" he snapped at Willie.

"You been listening at doors again?" Willie snapped back.

It could only be Donald. The resemblance between him and the younger Cal Bruchman was unmistakable. Although Donald had nowhere near the height nor bulk his father had had, they both shared the same aquiline nose, jutting chin and blond hair, which Donald wore slicked back from his face. In those photos of Cal, Molly had seen a kind of joy in himself and his body, but there were no such qualities in his son. Donald wore his gold jewelry, belted soft leather jacket and gleaming boots with the pomp and precision of full military regalia. He looked completely out of place in this rundown apartment.

"My father has agreed to go into a nursing home," Donald announced, "where he can get proper care." His eyes aimed a hot burst of anger in Louis's direction. Louis shrugged briefly and went back into the bedroom.

The tears continued rolling down Cal's face as if they had a life of their own. Otherwise, his body was motionless. ALS, commonly known as Lou Gehrig's disease, was slowly destroying Cal's nerves and muscles while it left his brain intact so that he could understand everything that was said.

What was going on here? Louis was the perfect home attendant. He was strong enough to easily move Cal from the bed to the wheelchair, yet he cared for him with the tenderness of a mother.

"Is there a problem with Louis Kroski?" she asked Donald.

Donald pressed his lips together. "My father needs round-the-clock nursing care. That man is not a registered nurse, and he's only here during the day."

"I can do what he needs at night," Willie interjected hotly.

"I just bet you can," Donald retorted, his eyes once again blazing. Underneath his fair, almost dead-white skin, a muscle in his jaw

17

twitched once, like a suddenly startled creature of the night.

For a moment, Cal's eyes came alive and rested on Willie with a mixture of sorrow and pleading. His body remained motionless. Nobody had ever said anything, but Molly was pretty sure that Willie and Cal had been lovers. Now she was convinced that Cal was begging Willie's forgiveness for choosing his son over Willie and doing whatever Donald needed.

She glanced at Donald again, with a little more empathy. Behind his arrogant exterior, Molly sensed a pool of grievances that were as old and as deep as the cracks on the walls. What would it have been like growing up for a boy like Donald to know that his father was gay?

"Why don't you let me send our nurse in to do a re-assessment?" she suggested. "If she feels that your father needs more care than he is able to get from your agency, we can talk about his options at that point."

"I can see what's going on with my own eyes," Donald retorted. "I don't want either of these men," he waved his right hand grandly, indicating both Willie and the bedroom door that Louis had closed behind him, "taking care of my father anymore. Dad agrees with my decision."

"And what about me?" Willie sputtered. "Where am I gonna go?"

"You're not my responsibility," Donald said, his voice full of gleeful hatred. "Maybe you should go into a nursing home, too. Get the government to pay for it."

"Is there a reason why he can't stay here, even if your father does leave?" Molly asked. "After all, this is his home, too."

"His name is not on the lease," Donald announced triumphantly. "He's got no money of his own. He's been living off my father for years."

"It's that Belloc and his skunk of a partner, Papa Skana," Willie proclaimed. "Jes' wants to get us out. And don't care how they do it, even if they have to loose that snake on us." That last comment was spat out in Donald's direction. "Las' week, Cal was on the top of the stairs in his wheelchair, waiting for Louis, here, to carry him down. Belloc is standin' on the second floor, lookin up at him—he don't see me—and I hear him say, real mean like, 'It's a long way down those stairs, Bruchman. You could be on the bottom before anyone would know anything about it.'"

"You're just senile, old man," Donald said viciously. His fingers brushed an unseen spot of something off the bottom edge of his leather jacket. "You'd accuse anyone of anything so you can keep sponging off my father."

"Excuse me," Molly interposed.

"This is really no concern of yours, Ms. Lewin," he interrupted, turning to her with a tight smile, his voice now smooth as silk. "I'm formally ending your agency's services as soon as a bed becomes available at St. Agnes's Home."

Molly knew she should back off. Donald wanted his father to go into a nursing home, and Cal appeared willing to do it—for whatever reason. Stuttman's voice rang loud and clear in her head: "Willie is not our client. Cal Bruchman is. Case closed."

Instead of listening to Stuttman's voice, she chose to follow agency protocol to the letter and said tartly, "I'm sorry, Mr. Bruchman. You are not our client. Your father is. You don't have the authority to fire us. Only your father does."

"I don't, huh." The muscle in his jaw began throbbing again, as if his feelings were about to burst right through his skin. "I'm finished talking to you, Ms. Lewin. Let's see what your boss has to say about it." He got up, carefully adjusted the legs of his pants over his boots, turned on his heel and slammed the door behind him.

For a moment, they all stared at each other. Then Willie moved his chair nearer to Cal and began stroking his hand. "You don't want to go into no nursing home, do you?" There was a pleading tone that Molly had never before heard in Willie's voice.

"Donnie . . . I'm afraid." Cal mumbled. The tears rolling down Cal's motionless face were like thin trickles of water flowing from a sheet of melting ice.

"You hear that?" Willie barked at her. "Cal's afraid of his own son."

She nodded. "I hear it, Willie."

"So what you gonna do about him?" Willie was indignant. He was also, she realized, laying the whole thing in her lap.

"I don't know yet, Willie." She took a deep breath. "Let me work on it," she said with far more assurance than she felt. "I'll be in touch with you."

After leaving the apartment, Molly crossed Warwick Street and looked through the littered lot at the river. It had gotten colder, more like January. The wind was kicking the water up into pewter-gray ripples which crashed against the abandoned pilings. Bits of the lower Manhattan skyline loomed up through the clouds that hunkered over the horizon, blocking out the sun. Sometimes Molly swore she could make out the ghosts of the towers rising up into the mist, like those eerie phantom limbs—the non-existent legs and arms that amputees believed were still attached to their bodies.

She shoved her hands more deeply into her jacket pockets. The exchange with Donald had left her shaken, both at her own impulsiveness at overstepping her professional role, and at what she perceived as an undercurrent of real hatred in that apartment. A sudden gust spiraled a pile of old Styrofoam cups and other rubbish that had been dumped on the water's edge up into the turbulent sky. A storm was about to break. Turning around, she looked up at the windows in Cal Bruchman's apartment and shivered.

Chapter Three

The Crawfish was named after the pattern of stained–glass that sat over its double-doors. The pattern resembled some kind of crustacean that might well have been a crawfish. The bar, which used to be a working class hangout, had recently morphed into an *avant–garde* bistro catering to the young émigrés from Manhattan and other high rent districts. All that was left of the old chipped dark-wood interior was the long wooden bar and the embossed tin ceiling which had been newly painted an off-white color to match the walls where abstract paintings and notices of upcoming poetry readings now hung.

It was just after five, and Ian was sitting at the nearly empty bar waiting for her. Ian Sorenson, Assistant Professor of Sociology at Brooklyn College, was good-looking enough—nearly six feet tall with a body toned by hours in the gym; light brown hair that flopped down onto his face, hazel eyes and well-shaped features. They'd met at a fundraiser for the families of cops and firemen who had lost their lives during the 9/11 disaster. Attractive, intelligent, politically astute, reasonably well employed—he might have been plucked right off a rack of low-key, designer males of an age and outlook deemed suitable "For the Mid-Level Career Woman." He and Molly had had some pretty good sex for a while, but it soon settled into the kind of affair that filled up an evening every week or so.

"Hi, babe." Ian's tone was offhand and without much warmth. He might have been talking to any female acquaintance. Leaning over, he gave her a cheek-brushing kiss.

Molly smiled brightly, as if her smile could bring warmth and light to the increasing emptiness and loneliness she felt when they were together.

Ian, who had already started on his Grey Goose martini, ordered the white wine she liked.

"So how'd it go today?" Without waiting for an answer, he tossed back half of what was left in his glass.

Molly told him about her visit with Cal and Willie and Donald because she knew it would interest him. "Willie believes that Papa Skana is the money behind Belloc's scheme to buy up a lot of the old buildings, force the tenants out, and raise the rents."

"It's what's happening all over the neighborhood, especially along the waterfront." He frowned, his normally smooth brow furrowed at the thought of all those greedy landlords. "The City has a big development thing in the works to buy up all the vacant buildings on the waterfront and build a shopping mall—I think they have Sears and Penny's lined up as anchor stores—a new and modern industrial site, and mixed-usage housing. And you know what that means."

Molly nodded. "Mostly luxury apartments with a few lower rent units thrown in as a sop." She took a sip of her wine which lacked any oomph – just like this whole conversation, and valiantly went on: "Willie said that they are paying Donald to harass the tenants. Have you heard any scuttlebutt about it?"

"Speak of the devil," Ian said, raising his eyes to look at someone behind her. Donald? But Cal's son wouldn't incite the sudden spark of interest in Ian's eyes. Molly turned to see who it was.

A young, blond woman in a long, black leather coat had just made an ENTRANCE—Molly automatically capitalized the word. Ana Skana, Papa Skana's daughter. A familiar face around the neighborhood. Molly and Ian knew Ana from community meetings that Ana often attended to represent her father's interests, as Papa himself tended to keep a low profile. Other people in the neighborhood, it was rumored, knew her in very different ways.

Ana stopped just inside the door. She stood with one hand on her hip, raking over every man in the bar with her eyes, as if daring any of them not to look at her. Which, of course, every man did.

Including Ian, Molly thought, turning her head around to see if Ian was susceptible. His eyes sparkled; his face suddenly looked brighter, as if he'd switched on an internal lamp.

Molly turned back to study Ana Skana. Papa's daughter wasn't really pretty with her off-center nose, her rather long face and slightly crooked teeth. The attraction was in her personality. It was more than animal magnetism or simple sexiness, although Ana had that in spades – men instinctively smoothed their hair down in her presence. No, this was something else

"Ah, the Professor and the Social Worker," Ana said slipping into the empty stool on the other side of Ian.

"Ana, can I buy you a drink?" Ian asked. Without needing to be asked, the barman appeared with a glass of colorless liquid—vodka?

Ana tossed off the whole drink. Then her mouth turned up in a seductive smile aimed solely at Ian. "Is warm in here, no?" Ana's voice was low and throaty, with a hint of the harshness of her native Russian. She shrugged her coat off her shoulders, the movement resembling a pampered cat settling onto its cushion. Ian, like an adoring puppy, reached over to help her.

Feeling like a third wheel in a *pas de deux,* Molly quickly finished

22

her wine and tapped Ian on the shoulder. "I have to go. I promised myself I'd check on my brother tonight."

Reluctantly, he turned away from Ana. "Are you sure you can't stay for another drink?" Once again the polite, well-mannered Assistant Professor of Sociology. He'd never say "Yeah, well, good-bye," which was what he actually meant.

It was funny, she mused while walking to the Manhattan-bound subway, she didn't even feel that bad. This bothered her. Shouldn't she be angry at Ana Skana for poaching her boyfriend? Or at Ian for letting himself be so easily poached? What was wrong with her? There was only a deep desire to possess whatever it was that Ana had. It wasn't jealousy—Ian just wasn't that important to her; the closest Molly could come to understanding it was to compare it to her feelings when she saw a Picasso painting, or heard Pavarotti sing, or stood in the presence of anyone who had a great talent that she, Molly, simply lacked. Ian couldn't be blamed for responding as he did to Ana Skana anymore than an enthusiastic audience could be blamed for leaping to its feet and applauding wildly for a great ballerina.

Molly got off the subway at Canal Street and walked east, passing the store-front synagogues that still lined East Broadway, to her brother's block. As much as Molly loved old buildings—and she cherished them the way other people cherish their older family members because they gave her a sense of history and continuity that was so absent in her own shattered family—it was hard to love the Clinton Street building where Ben lived, a seedy, non-gentrified Lower East Side block of nineteenth century tenements.

The lock on the lobby door was missing, as was the doorknob. She put two fingers into the empty hole where the cylinder had been, pulled open the door and entered. The floor of the grimy hallway was composed of ancient mosaic tiles, so cracked and dirty that their original pattern was barely discernible. The air smelled of Lysol, alcohol and something that might have been alive once. Steeling herself, she climbed the two flights of stairs, called out to him, and he let her in.

The apartment opened into the kitchen whose single window looked out into an airshaft. The window had been painted black. Old, dried-out food containers littered the counter top. Dirty dishes and glasses were scattered everywhere, and little crystals of broken glass lay in the sink. Ben was dressed in weird layers of clothing—dirty white yoga pants peeked out from under a wine and gold caftan thrown over a faded flannel robe.

Oh my god! In the less than two weeks since she'd seen him, he had really deteriorated. She threw her jacket and bag on the crusted table, went over to the sink and began washing the dishes.

"It's okay, *Malke Liebe*." His soft voice came from behind her. He

23

had started calling her *Malke Liebe*, which was her Yiddish name while going through his Jewish mystical period. He was the only one who'd ever called her that besides her grandmother. "Bacteria are life, the universal creator, the creator of life."

"Yes, darling," she said over her shoulder. "Bacteria *are* a form of life, but these dishes need washing anyway."

Ben, at forty-six, was eight years her senior, but looked much older. Tall and bony-thin, with lots of dark, curly hair now shot with gray which up around his long, narrow head. A scraggly beard almost hid most of the deep pits left over from terrible teenaged acne. His eyes, a lovely soft brown, looked out from a place that most people never go to.

"*Malke Liebe...*"

"It's okay, Ben."

"Turn off the water," he implored. "Please. The sound bangs in my head." He grabbed his head with his hands and shook it back and forth, as if testing the ripeness of a melon.

"I'll be just a minute, Ben." When she'd finished, he was no longer in the kitchen.

Molly walked through the sleeping alcove with its unmade bed and filthy sheets, into the front room. He was sitting on the dirty brown love seat scavenged from the street on one of his long, rambling walks. The table in front of him was piled with papers and notebooks, and he was writing away like a man in a frenzy.

"What are you writing?"

He spent much of his time writing long tracts interlaced with mythological, poetical and theological references that purported to prove some of his totally crazy ideas. After 9/11, Ben wrote a seventy-five page treatise arguing that Billy Collins, America's Poet Laureate at the time, was actually behind the plot to blow the buildings up in order to prove to the world that poetry still mattered.

Silly question. He didn't look up, nor did he answer her. Bending down, she tried to read it. It seemed to be an essay on Muslims and Islam woven through with quotations from the Koran and Omar Khayyam and other references that may or may not have actually existed..

Molly stood up and rotated her neck a few times. Trying to follow Ben's crazy logic always made *her* head hurt. Yet if she didn't at least attempt to read what he wrote, she feared the loss of any ability to understand the bizarre associations in his conversations.

When they were younger, Ben had been her friend and protector, buffer against the world, fighting her fights and teaching her how to look beyond the surface and see beauty. She adored him. By age sixteen, he'd won awards for his poetry and a full scholarship to Emory College. Just before his nineteenth birthday he became convinced that their mother was sucking the life fluids out of his brain and went after her with a hammer. Later, Molly realized that the signs had been there earlier, but nobody had seen them, attributing his odd turn of mind, his esoteric discourses and bizarre beliefs, to his brilliance. Since then, there had been several more psychotic episodes. Between them, he managed to live as a somewhat functional, oddly brilliant, but always reclusive eccentric, a kind of semi-life, made possible by modern pharmacology. He usually maintained a certain level of basic cleanliness. Except when he was starting on one of his down-hill slides.

"How have you been?" As soon as the words came out of her mouth she realized how ridiculous the question was.

Ben's eyes turned up towards her with the sharp, bright look that meant he was turning her words over in his mind, wrestling with their deeper meanings. .

"Been," he said. "Past participle of the intransitive verb 'to be.' To exist. To have actuality, reality, life. 'Been,'" he repeated. "Yes, I would say I've been. As to whether I am now . . ." He shrugged, glancing around him. Then he brought his eyes back to her face. In them was a look of pure anguish.

It was as though he had reached out and tapped on her heart with a small mallet, the kind the doctor uses to test your reflexes. Oh god! What was happening to him? He never showed much emotion, so while suspecting what this anguish meant, she couldn't ask him because he couldn't answer in words that she would understand. Molly and her brother were cut off from each other for the time being, as much by her sanity as by his madness.

As the shared language of feeling was inaccessible to them, she stuck to the concrete. "Are you eating? Sleeping?"

He shrugged.

"Are you taking your pills?"

He moved his head in one of his strange gestures, something like the sharp, thrusting movement of a bird's head. "Were pills God's answer to the agony of Abraham and the suffering of Job?"

She fluttered through the apartment like a moth, looking here, looking there, finally locating them on one of the kitchen shelves. The vial, dated over a month ago, was three-quarters full.

"Ben, you promised me you would take your pills."

"They shoot guacamole in through my ears."

"Who shoots guacamole in through your ears?". What did he mean? He didn't answer, probably because he couldn't. The medication could be making him feel dull—a sensation that he hated—as though someone was filling his head with a dense, thick substance. He would rather have his crazy thoughts than no thoughts at all. She should really urge him to take his pills, but so empathized with his need to retain some

25

vestiges of life and vitality that she didn't have the heart to do it. Maybe his medications could be changed again.

"Ben, do you want to go out for a walk?" It would do them both good to get out of there for a while.

He shook his head. "The sounds of the street slice through my skin. And man can only take so much vision before he, too, burns up."

There was almost no food in the house, so she went out to do some shopping for him, nodding in passing to Marushka who was standing on the stoop. One of a large tribe of gypsies who lived on the first floor of Ben's building, Marushka was the mother of several grown children who Molly knew. The gypsy dressed in low-cut blouses and full skirts that twirled around her legs, and her face wore the remnants of an old beauty like a tattered shawl of once-fine brocade. Marushka was often out on the stoop when Molly visited Ben and occasionally the two women would pass the time of day.

A sign on Marushka's front window had a picture of the palm of a hand divided into numbered sections with the words *Know What the Future Has in Store.* These words were also on the apartment door with the addition of, *Please Knock and Enter.* Molly often had the impulse to do just that. It wasn't as if Ben's future was unknown to her, the only question was when it would happen. If someone could predict the exact timing of Ben's upcoming melt-down, she could make plans and prepare for the inevitable. It was the not knowing that produced this state of indecision and paralysis.

Should she ask Marushka for a reading? Laughing at herself Molly thought: Nobody, not even the best psychiatrist in the world, could answer that question. So she walked on instead to the little deli-market on the corner and bought some cold cuts, a roasted chicken, a loaf of bread and a bag of apples and brought them all back, showing him each item as she took it out of the bag. It was unclear whether or not Ben even heard her. After leaving again, the little knot of anxiety that lived in her like a piece of grit at the center of a pearl had grown a little larger.

It was after nine when she got home to her little studio apartment in Manhattan —one large room with a tiny bathroom barely bigger than the toilet, midget sink and stall shower that were crammed into it. An efficiency kitchenette took up the wall space next to the bathroom door. It had been her maternal grandmother's apartment, and Molly had moved in while in social work school to care for Bubbe after she had broken her hip. Sleeping on a fold-away bed, surrounded by Bubbe's walker, commode and other medical supplies, Molly felt like an addendum in an already overcrowded space. Pam Littlejohn relieved her for a few hours a day so she could go to class. Molly always associated the tall, straight-backed, Jamaican home aide with the squares of paper towels that Pam would rinse out after use and hang all over the tiny kitchenette. Pam and Molly argued about this, and Pam's many other waste-not-want-not schemes, like an old married couple. But when Bubbe suddenly died a little over a year later, it was Pam, not Molly's mother, who held onto Molly at the graveside and wept with her as they watched the clumps of dirt falling onto the coffin. Molly's mother stood to one side like a stony cliff, impervious to this new grief or to the feelings of anyone else, much less her daughter's.

Molly, knowing she could never move back home, had been wise enough to get herself onto her grandmother's lease before Bubbe died and so found herself with one of the last rent-controlled apartments in Manhattan, a fact for which she was extremely grateful since, as the old joke went, "Relationships come and go, but a rent-controlled apartment is forever."

A mountain of mail was piled up like dried autumn leaves on Molly's tiny table. Now, pushing it all aside, she threw down her keys, her bag and the mail she'd just picked up. Culling out the important stuff, Molly added the rest to the pile. The answering machine was blinking. Ignoring it, she flung her jacket over the back of a chair and opened the mini-fridge.

Inside: a head of wilted lettuce, half a container of dried-out rice from a Chinese take-out order and two cans of diet soda. There should be a frozen dinner in there, but the tiny freezer compartment was so encrusted with ice that only a blow torch could get at it.

Wasn't that typical, buying all that food for Ben and nothing for herself? Why didn't she defrost her refrigerator, stock it with food, sort though the pile of papers, and hang up her clothes? Why did Ben count more in her life than she did? Or Ian, for that matter? Molly plopped down into the one beautiful piece of furniture that she owned—an antique oak rocking chair with delicately carved arms and a curved back.

Maybe the psychiatrist at the aftercare center could help. But who was the current psychiatrist anyway? They flitted in and out of the center like fireflies on a hot summer evening. The last one, who'd prescribed the medication that had apparently shot guacamole into Ben's ears, was undoubtedly gone now. He had been a young, well-meaning Pakistani who viewed Ben's rambling discourses as a symptom that needed to be extinguished. He didn't understand that these discourses were all that remained of Ben's once fine mind. Wipe them out, and you leave him with nothing but his illness. Yet without medication, Ben gradually lost the ability to function.

Molly walked over to her collection of CD's and vinyl discs—the one area in her apartment that was carefully dusted, arranged and catalogued—selected an old Lester Young record and put it on the turntable. She'd recently contemplated buying an IPod, but the thought of transferring her entire collection onto it was much too daunting. With a sigh, she sank back into the rocking chair and closed her eyes.

The pure, unadorned sound of Lester's sax in "These Foolish Things Remind Me of You," recorded in 1945 after he came out of military prison where he'd spent a year for drug use, was like a crystal-clear stream flowing directly from his sax right into her heart. It was as though she and Lester shared an intimacy so deep it went beyond words. An intimacy she couldn't seem to achieve with any man. Except one, maybe, and that relationship had ended in disaster. There certainly had never been any with Ian Sorensen, even back in the beginning when the sex was still good. And how sad was that?

Back and forth, back and forth, she rocked and listened to Lester until she finally fell asleep.

Chapter Four

Molly woke with a painful crick in her neck from spending the night slumped over in the rocking chair. The rain was streaming down the window. She thought about calling in sick, but, after a minute or two, stumbled into the tiny kitchenette to start the coffee brewing. While it finished dripping, she forwarded through the messages on her machine. None from Ian.

Bits of last night's dream came back—the World Trade Center, collapsing just as it had that terrible day as she'd stood by the river and watched it happen. Would she ever stop seeing it? Dreaming about it? How could those buildings have simply disappeared? Every time the thought came into her mind, Molly had the feeling that she could simply disappear herself, right through the floor boards, down into the earth.

Arriving at the office a little early for once, she headed into the staff room for another cup of coffee. Nilda was sitting at the big Formica table talking to Manny, the porter, night security man and occasional escort for the nurses who had to go into high crime areas. Manny, who'd never met a lady he didn't like, was anywhere from fifty to seventy with a full head of iron-gray hair and the massive, barrel-shaped chest of the chronic asthmatic. At that moment he was wearing a soft, dreamy smile which meant he was chatting up Nilda. But as the chat was taking place in Spanish, Molly couldn't comment on his technique.

"Holá Manny," Molly said. "How's it going?"

"Ah, Señorita Molly," he answered, winking at Nilda. "Not too bad. Nilda, here, has just been telling me about this big landlord who wants to empty a bunch of low-rent buildings and put up some shopping mall."

Oh, come on Manny, Molly thought. Men don't wink like that about shopping malls. "Actually, he wants to sell the land to the City which plans a big development thing on the waterfront here—shopping mall, industrial site, luxury housing, maybe a few units of affordable housing."

"Affordable housing," Nilda scoffed. "Is that what they call it?" She opened the tiny fridge, took out a yogurt, pried the cover off and stared into it as if hoping it would turn out to be something deliciously decadent. "They put up what they called 'affordable housing' in my sister's neighborhood." She stuck a plastic spoon into the container. "Eleven hundred dollars a month they wanted to charge her for a two-bedroom apartment. Sonia only makes twenty thousand a year. You do the math."

"She gets too serious," Manny nodded his bull-like neck in Nilda's direction. "Why don't you relax a little?" he said to Nilda. "I'll come over, bring some beer, take your mind off your problems. You'll feel better."

Nilda licked the creamy mixture off the spoon and flashed her eyes at Manny. "I don't got time to take my mind off my problems. I got three kids to feed, homework to check and laundry to do." Lowering her lids her lids, she let a small smile curl around her mouth. "You wanna come over and do some laundry? Then maybe I'll have time for some beer."

Manny snorted. "Spanish men don' do laundry."

"Don' I know it."

Their eyes met and some message passed between them. For a moment Molly saw Ana Skana and Ian Sorenensen as she'd left them at the Crawfish last night and wondered for the thousandth time why some women found it so easy.

"Used to be this neighborhood didn't need the City to bring business into it," Manny said, his eyes still on Nilda. "Used to be so many factories around here. Remember the big paint factory on Polanski Street, Nini?"

Nini, huh, Molly thought. Someone must be doing somebody's laundry.

"I was a little girl then," Nilda said with a smile. "When they had that thing going full steam the whole neighborhood used to smell like it was getting a new paint job." She scraped the final bits of yogurt out of the container and flicked her tongue around the spoon.

"That was the last of the big ones," Manny said, watching her with hungry eyes. "They close down, nothing came in to take their place. And that don't even take into account the jobs there used to be on the docks"

"Yeah," she nodded. "Even when the unions weren't hiring no Spanish, my brothers could always pick up something there. Now, nothing." She looked at her watch and said, "Well, better get to work."

After waving to Swandell who had just come in, Molly dutifully made her way to her cubicle and got right down to the Medicaid re-certifications and other paperwork that had been growing on a corner of her desk like a malevolent fungus. Just before noon, she pushed the piles of paper away and, remembering her promise to take Mrs. Canover for lunch at the senior center, decided it would be a good idea to pave the way first, to ensure Mrs. Canover's acceptance by the regulars, or the poor lady would never go back.

Molly slipped into her rain jacket and left the office for the four block walk to the center. The rain had stopped, but it was still overcast. The misty clouds gave the streets a silvery quality, and the newly painted facades on some of the older buildings stood out like glittery new stones in old tarnished settings.

Nothing could have helped the Henry J. Kronin Senior Center. A long, rectangular concrete-block structure, it was and would remain one of the world's ugliest buildings. Molly had never learned who Henry J. Kronin was or what he had done to merit naming this eyesore after him, but the final naming had been the result of a fierce battle between the descendents of the Irish, German and Eastern Europeans immigrants who had all come over in the early years of the last century.

Inside, the lunchroom was bustling. Alice Manning, the doyenne of the center, was sitting with David Scheunfeldt at a table at the far end of the narrow room, right near the steam tables. This was a choice location in a place where location was everything. Tables were as hotly fought over as any in the most "chichi" restaurant. Center members who were relegated to the tables near the entranceway found themselves eating cold food by the time they maneuvered their way down the entire length of the room.

Alice caught sight of Molly and waved at her. Alice was short and plump with fruit-colored hair that changed according to the season. In the spring, her curls sparkled like the color of ripe strawberries and raspberries; in July and August they were tinted a pale peach; by the fall they were the color of purple grapes; and in the winter, as she had once told Molly, she brought a little sunshine into her life by dying her curls the color of Florida's best orange juice. The two women had met when Multi-Care was providing homecare to Alice's late husband, and had grown very fond of each other.

Molly waved and walked through the dining room to Alice's table. Since it was January, Alice was sporting hair the color of a Sunkist orange. She reached up and gave Molly a kiss. "Darling, I see you, I see my dead husband's face; may God watch over his soul."

David Scheunfeldt, a burly man with a bulbous nose and a few wisps of gray hair covering a bald, freckled head, winked at Molly and asked Alice, "Does she look like your late husband before or after he died?"

Alice made a dismissive gesture in his direction. "He doesn't change. For forty-five years I've known him, and he still doesn't change."

Molly sat down next to David Scheunfeldt who smiled. "Let me get you something to eat."

"Thank you, Mr. Scheunfeldt."

"Always with the Mr. Scheunfeldt." He turned one hand up. With the other he patted her arm. "It makes me feel old. Just call me Dave."

"Dave." She smiled back. "But no, I'm not hungry at the moment."

Dave dug into a plate of meatloaf covered with sepia-tinted gravy that reflected the fluorescent lights on the ceiling. When he finished swallowing he smiled again and said, "Did you know, my dear lady, that this very building was once a big commercial bakery and I worked here as a baker?"

"I think you did tell me that."

"It doesn't matter," Alice said to Molly in an audible whisper. "He'll tell it to you again."

As if he hadn't heard Alice, which maybe he hadn't since he was a little deaf, he went on: "The oven ran the length of the building, my dear lady, and a long conveyor belt inside of it moved the loaves along. By the time each loaf made the trip back and forth twice, from one end of the building to the other, it was baked."

"She's heard the story already, Dave," Alice said loudly.

"I don't mind," Molly said. "A good story is always a good story."

"See, Alice?" Dave said with another wink in Molly's direction. "This is a young lady of discernment."

Molly grinned and thought how comfortable she felt with these people and in this place, as if they were the family she should have had. During her early twenties, Molly had gone into therapy, spending most of the sessions discussing other people in her life with empathy and compassion. But when it came to herself she fell mute, unable to talk about the deep psychic bleed that began on the day that Ben was first hospitalized. It wasn't for lack of wanting to talk; she just didn't know how. It was as though the event happened in a time before words, a place where no one had yet invented a language that could fully or adequately express the depth, the myriad catacombs, and the reverberating pain of that experience.

The one good thing that came out of it all was the therapist's suggestion that Molly go to social work school. Which she did, only realizing much later that it had all been about learning how to make Ben sane again, as if there existed, somewhere, a body of knowledge and skills to be used for restoring lost lives. She soon learned better, but did come to understand a little more about her own particular talent—or maybe it was a need—for involving herself in other people's problems, and found the voice necessary to become a really good client advocate. After graduation, she drifted around for a while, working with teenaged mothers, homeless people and families at risk until she'd taken what was supposed be a temporary job working with old people and found her home.

"Alice," Molly said, "I need to ask you a favor."

32

"Anything for you, darling."

"Do you know Margery Canover?"

"I know her," Dave said. "She lives in my building. Poor lady. She's never been the same since her husband died."

Molly nodded. "It's been very hard on her. Especially being alone so much now, she's starting to hear knocks and bangs at all hours of the day and night." Molly leaned forward so as not to be heard by others. "That poor lady thinks it's Herman's troubled spirit. She really needs some friends."

"'Herman's troubled spirit, my *tukhas*," Dave said hotly. "A *tukhas*, for those of you who don't know, is what you sit on," he added. "What she hears is that bastard landlord, Belloc, or that Gestapo goon he sends over, trying to get us to move." His whole body bristled with indignation. "I hear it too, day and night, just like she says. It sounds like the ceiling is going to come crashing in. And that's when he not standing in front of your face, threatening—not by words, mind you, he's too smart for that—what's going to happen to you if you don't get out."

"Have you ever complained?" Molly asked. There could be no question now. Here was a real pattern of harassment.

Dave shrugged. "I complained, yes, but I'm just an old man."

"Well," Molly said, "you're confirming what I've been hearing from some of my other clients." Including Margery Canover, Molly realized, despite what poor Margery believes about Herman's passing. "I'm thinking that it's related to a plan by the City to develop the waterfront."

"Yeah, I heard about it. Another shopping mall." Dave sniffed contemptuously. "This Belloc is trying to get us all out so he can sell the property to the City and make a pretty penny." Angrily he pushed his empty plate to one side and transferred his contempt to a small dish of canned fruit salad. "What I wouldn't give for a nice piece of strudel like my Goldie, may she rest in peace, used to make. The bakery used to sell us workers day-old bread and rolls at half-price, but who could eat the bread they made here? You'd pinch a loaf, it would jump back at you from all the air they beat into it."

Alice cut him off. "Enough already, Dave. That was a long time ago."

"Every Friday morning Goldie would be out in the kitchen by five-thirty in the morning to start the week's baking," Dave went on, ignoring her. "Of course, by then I'd be long gone. I had to be at work by four a.m. to fire the big ovens up—we used coal when I first started working here." His massive hand, gnarled like a burl on an old tree, played with the slice of white bread that had come with his lunch. "I first hired on as a stoker." He shook his head. "How times change."

33

Alice waved dismissively. "And if they didn't change you'd still be making fifteen dollars a week and Goldie would still be adding water to the soup so there'd be enough." She turned to Molly. "So, you want me to take Margery Canover in hand? Introduce her to people? Make her welcome?"

Molly nodded.

The talk at the table went on, but Molly, who'd suddenly remembered something, was only half-listening. "Dave," she said at the first convenient pause, "you mentioned a Gestapo goon that Belloc sent around. Do you know his name?"

Dave shook his head. "No."

"Why did you call him 'Gestapo?'"

His faintly yellow eyes opened in surprise. "What do you mean, why? Already the younger generation doesn't know who the Gestapo was?"

"Were you just using it as a general term," she tried to explain, "or was there something specific about him that reminded you of the Gestapo?"

"He's the real Gestapo. Hitler would have been proud of him." His massive hand suddenly closed around the slice of white bread, crumbling it into a pasty ball and throwing it onto his tray.

"What do you mean?"

"Blond hair, the leather jacket, the boots." Dave's lip curled. "The Aryan race—he's one of that kind."

Donald Bruchman!

Chapter Five

Manny was leaning against the door of Molly's cubicle when she arrived at work, still bleary-eyed from too little sleep.

"You been working with Mr. Bruchman, right?"

She nodded.

"I talked to Louis Kroski late yesterday—he came in for his pay check." Manny reached for a pack of cigarillos bulging out of his shirt pocket and then let his hand drop. The staff room was the only place in the office in which smoking was allowed. "He says that Bukka is back again."

"Bukka?"

"Yeah, Willie's grandson, or maybe it's his great-grandson. He's a junkie. Was living in a squat over near the projects after he broke up with his girl friend, but they tore it down and so he's back, hitting on the old man for money. "

"Donald must love that," Molly muttered.

"Yeah. Louis said he could see the smoke coming out of Donald's ears." Manny shook his head and frowned. "I don't want to tell you your job, Ms. Molly, but if I were you, I'd get over there fast. Something gonna explode in that place."

Louis let her in. Behind him, Willie was playing the guitar, and a young man with corn rows was sitting across from Willie looking bored. Cal was propped up in his electric wheel chair. He grimaced into his version of a smile.

"Manny told me there was more trouble here yesterday," Molly said to Louis in a low voice.

Louis ran his hand over his close-cropped hair. "That was some afternoon. They don't pay me enough for this." He put on a fleece-lined denim jacket that had been draped over a chair and picked up a pile of dirty bedding. "Donald is the reason why I could never be a good Catholic. As far as I'm concerned, he's a poster boy for a woman's right to choose." Shifting the laundry to one arm, he reached over with the other and grabbed a bottle of detergent. "I'm glad you're here. I need to go drop this stuff off at the Laundromat, and I don't like to leave him alone, especially when that junkie kid is around."

"How is Cal?"

"When that bastard son of his leaves him alone, he's much better."
Raising his voice, he said to the two older men: "Ms. Lewin is here, and
I'm off to do the laundry. See you in a little bit." He slung the bag over
his shoulder and clomped off down the stairs.

Willie looked up from his guitar and said gravely, "Mornin' Ms.
Molly." He looked tired and worn-out. "This here's my great-grandson,
Bukka." Keeping his elbow on the body of the guitar, his fingers
gestured towards the young man. "Bukka, this here's Ms. Lewin, Cal's
social worker."

Bukka nodded indifferently. Maybe nineteen or twenty, he was a
few shades darker than his grandfather and dressed urban chic—baggy
pants, black satin tee shirt, sneakers without socks, and one gold earring.
His eyes, in constant motion, were like two beads of water jumping
around on a hot stove.

"I heard there were some problems here yesterday," Molly knelt
down in front of Cal. "How are you?"

"Good." His throat muscles tightened to enable him to pronounce
the word, but his breathing was even and regular.

"That no-good son of his thinks he owns the place," Willie said
disgustedly. "All dressed up in his leather and his gold chains. Thinks
he can tell me who I can and can't have visit me in my own home."

"He's giving you grief about Bukka staying here?"

Willie nodded. "Cal don't mind. Cheers him up to have a young
person around, don't it Cal?"

"Fam'ly . . . good," Cal said.

Willie started playing again, a syncopated rhythm in which he used
the guitar mainly as a percussive background to the words he was
singing.

"I have a recording of Blind Gully doing that one," she said.

Willie's face lit up, like the sun suddenly appearing from behind
storm clouds. "Blind Gully," he said almost reverentially. "Now I ain't
met no young person for over forty hears even heard of him."

"It's sad, isn't it, Willie?

"Time was when everybody up and down Highway 61 knew who
Gully was." A small smile played around his lips. "I was Gully's lead
boy, did you know that?"

Molly shook her head, awed once again by this old man—a piece of
living history.

"I started running with him when I was 'bout ten years old, stayed
with him for over nine years. We must've traveled every mile of that ol'
61—on foot, from Memphis to New Orleans." Willie pronounced it as if
it were one word, "Nworlins," with the accent on the -or. "We'd come
into a town, and I'd lead him over to a busy corner. Didn't take long for
the people to come round. He'd start to play and I'd pass the cup." He

shook his hand as if it still held a cup. "He was one of the great ones."

"You're not too bad yourself," Molly said.

"Can't do much pickin' anymore. Arthritis won't let me. But Bukka now," he gestured towards the young man, "he's the real bluesman in the family. Play us something, boy, let the lady hear what you can do."

Bukka shrugged, took the guitar from his great-grandfather's hands and wrapped his fingers lovingly around the neck.

"How 'bout the one Gully used to do," Willie said. "You know, Cellar Door Blues."

"Been a lotta songs written since Gully died." Bukka's annoyance bore witness to a long-standing struggle between them.

Willie glared at him. "I taught you them songs before you could walk; you took your first steps to 'Hey Billie Lee.' Now they ain't good enough for you?"

Bukka shrugged again, gave Molly a quick glance, and began to pick out some opening bars, and for Molly, everything dissolved away into his music.

> *Blues hangin' out my window*
> *Blues sittin' on my cellar door*
> *So much blues round here baby*
> *Never see daylight no mo'.*

Though his voice was smoother and less strident than Willie's, it was still powerful, evoking deep sadness and loss. The guitar playing that circled behind, around and between the lyrics was something else, though—aggressive, scornful, bitter, sad, angry, lonely—and technically brilliant.

"Wow!" Molly said when he finished. The kid seemed so unformed, so inarticulate—how did he learn to play like that?

For a brief moment Bukka smiled. It was, to Molly, as if he'd stepped out of a dark forest into a sun-drenched meadow. A scowl immediately replaced the smile; the sunlight disappeared as quickly as it had come. "Nobody likes this old-time stuff 'cept him. He's stuck in the past." Bukka tossed his head and handed the guitar back to the old man.

Willie, who had been watching him with the kind of hungry love Molly had seen on her mother's face when Ben, still in his glory days, came home with a poetry award, took the guitar and rested it on his lap.

"I like . . . it." Everyone looked at Cal as if they had forgotten he was there.

"I see where he gets his talent from," Molly said.

Willie shook his head. "Not from me, he don't. That's not to say I wasn't good in my time, but good ain't nowhere near to great. Blind Gully was great. And Bukka here . . ." He waved in Bukka's direction, who looked down at the floor. "It's like it come straight from Gully, passed through me like I wasn't even there, and went direct into him."

"Why's he always layin' all that Gully shit on me," Bukka complained. "Them times are gone. People don't want to hear this stuff no more."

"You be only half the man Gully was, that'd be something," Willie snapped. His gnarled fingers caressed the guitar, stroking softly up and down the curved wooden sides.

"That's a beautiful instrument," Molly said thinking how much she'd love to own one just like it, though it would be wasted on her; she could never do more than strum a few chords.

"This ol' Gibson," he said softly. "Gully bought it off a bluesman who had his arm crippled in an accident and couldn't use it no more."

"Gully's dead sixty years, Gramps. A lotta life happened since then. A lotta music, too." Bukka grabbed the guitar back from his grandfather and went into a riff that Molly recognized as one of John Coltrane's. It was Coltrane, and at the same time, it was more than Coltrane. She never knew it was possible to play an acoustic guitar like that!

But Willie was not to be sidetracked: "Paid the bluesman two dollars for it. Couple years ago some white boy offered me over five hun'red for it. Probably worth close to a thousand by now. Wouldn't sell it, though." A smile flashed on and off.

Bukka rolled his eyes and handed the guitar back to his great-grandfather who went on: "Most of 'em back then used a steel-body National. It could give you some sound—that was before amps and such. But not Gully. He liked the wood 'cause he said it sang along with him. 'Sides which, Gully didn't need no 'lectrification. Him and this here Gibson, when he got it goin', was powerful enough all by themselves to shake the walls of them jook joints." He played a few bars of an old blues. "Gonna be Bukka's someday."

"No stoppin' him once he starts," Bukka grumbled. "Rest of us might as well not be here." Once more he took the guitar out of his great-grandfather's hands and started jamming some syncopated, rap-type rhythm—complex, intricate, sophisticated and again so unexpected coming from this half-formed kid.

Willie watched him reverently. "Ain't nothing' he can't play. Just like Gully."

At that, Bukka stopped, shook his head and thrust the guitar back into Willie's hands.

The way they pass that guitar back and forth is like alternating current, Molly thought, a symbol of the charged feeling that flows between them.

The door suddenly opened and Donald strode into the room, followed by Louis staring daggers into Donald's back.

"That little parasite still here?" Donald barked, his eyes ripping Bukka apart. "Well, not for long." He turned to his father, puffing his chest out as if he'd just won a long coveted prize. "St. Agnes has informed me that a bed has opened up in their nursing home. They're ready to admit you today. Pack a bag for him," he commanded Louis. "Whatever he'll need for the next day or so. We'll move the rest of his stuff once he's comfortably settled."

Tears gathered in Cal's eyes and his throat made convulsive movements.

"Mr. Bruchman," Molly said, knowing that she should stay out of it but unable to do so. Donald Bruchman got her so angry that all good intentions went out the window, "You don't have to go into St. Agnes's unless you want to."

"Yes . . . go . . . Donald."

"He don't wanna go, can't you see that?" Willie begged.

"He just said yes," Donald stated gleefully. At that moment he looked like a sleek elegantly-dressed ferret about to pounce on an undernourished mouse. He must really hate his father, she thought. "Dad wants to live in a clean, well appointed home. Not one that's falling down around his ears, like this one. He knows St. Agnes is the best place for him."

"Look, Mr. Bruchman," Molly said, trying to get back her rational self, "this is kind of abrupt. Older people don't make these kinds of transitions very easily. Why don't you at least let him make a visit first, see the place, give him a little time to get adjusted. You would want to visit a place, see what it looked like before you moved into it, wouldn't you?"

"Of course, Ms. Lewin," Donald said evenly. "I'm not a heartless person. But if my father doesn't accept this bed today, it goes to the next person on the list. That's the way nursing homes work. I didn't make the rules."

"He don't have to go at all." Willie was almost crying. "He's got a good home here."

Bukka looked from Donald to his great-grandfather and rose to his feet. "Time for me to split," he said. "Later, Gramps." The door slammed behind him.

Louis was standing back with one hand on his hip. "Well, Ms Lewin," he said. "If that's the way it is, Mr. Bruchman is going to need transportation to the home." Pointing to Cal's wheelchair, Louis added, "He can't walk there by himself."

Their eyes met. Louis was trying to tell her something. Oh, smart man. "We'll have to arrange for a Medivan," she said, "Your father needs a specially trained person to carry him down the stairs."

"So go ahead and do it."

Molly picked up the phone and dialed a number that was posted on the wall. "My name is Molly Lewin. I'm a social worker with Multi-Care, and I need to arrange transportation for one of our clients to go into a nursing home. There's a bed available today. How soon can you get here?"

She listened for a minute, trying to keep from grinning, and then said, "You'll have to explain that to his son. Let me put him on."

Donald grabbed the phone and said, "I'm Donald Bruchman." As he listened, the muscle in his jaw began its strange dance again, and his fair skin gradually got redder. "What do you mean you don't have any vans available at such short notice" he exploded. "The bed is available today. We have to get him there now." He listened some more, then slammed down the phone.

"You both knew this!" The force of his rage made his slight body tremble, like a sudden wind shaking the branches of a slender tree.

Molly shrugged and said in an expressionless voice: "Sorry, Mr. Bruchman. Transportation for the elderly is a real problem in this city. There aren't enough Medivans for all the people who need them. Some of our clients have to wait days for an appointment."

"Well, there's more than one way to skin a cat." Snapping open his cell phone with his thumb, Donald announced, "I'll call my car service."

"As she told you," Louis said, pointing at Molly, "it takes a specially trained person to carry your father, who is very heavy, down those stairs. No car service driver is going to be able to do it. I have to help the Medivan drivers a lot of the times."

"I wasn't speaking to you," Donald said imperiously. "But since you apparently *are* trained, you can just carry my father down the stairs when the car gets here."

"Sorry, Mr. Bruchman," Louis stated with no regret in his voice. "My back is out today. I can't manage it." Molly, who had just seen him sling a large bag of laundry over his shoulder, didn't say a word.

"I'll carry him myself," Donald declared as if he were announcing he intended to carry Old Glory into battle. "You just pack his bag."

"Whatever you say," Louis retorted and turned towards the bedroom.

"Oh, Louis," Molly interjected, "you'd better include a separate package of adult diapers for Mr. Bruchman." At Donald's look of surprise, she explained: "Your father tends to lose bladder control when he gets excited or stressed, and getting him down those stairs is a real ordeal for him, even when Louis does it."

Donald glanced down at his expensive leather jacket and sharply creased slacks. "I don't believe a word of this," he said through clenched teeth. "You're both in collusion to stop me from moving my father out of here."

"I'm just trying to help make this as painless as possible," Molly countered in her most reasonable voice.

"Oh no you're not!" Donald shouted. "I know what you two are up to. I'll be back tomorrow *with* a car *and* a trained driver. St. Agnes's will hold the bed if I make it worth their while. I want his things packed and my father ready to go. And if you two do any more to stop me, you'll be hearing from my lawyer." With that, he stamped out of the apartment.

"Well, I don't know what that did for us." Louis grinned. "But it sure felt good."

Molly smiled impishly. "Yeah, I haven't enjoyed myself so much in a long time." Then she bit her lip, not wanting to imagine Stuttmans' reaction if he ever found out about it.

Unfortunately, Cal had not enjoyed this as much as she and Louis. His face was wet with tears. Molly sat down next to him and took his hand, massaging it gently. "I'm sorry you got upset, Cal. It takes some time to arrange these things, which I don't think your son understood." Well, that was somewhat true. Louis brought over a box of tissues and Molly wiped Cal's eyes. "Cal, if you really don't want to go into St. Agnes's, Donald can't force you to do it."

"You don' . . . unnerstand." It broke Molly's heart to watch him struggle to get the words out. "Don . . . ie always angry." He stopped and caught his breath again. "Didn't give Donnie . . . he needed me . . . wasn't there."

"Are you saying that you weren't there when Donald needed you and that's why he's always been so angry?" She continued to stroke his hand to help him relax.

Cal jerked his head up and down.

"So you are willing to go into the nursing home, even though you don't really want to, because it's something he needs you to do for him?"

"Ol' man . . . die soon."

Throughout the whole exchange with Donald, Willie had been slumped into his chair, his hands resting loosely on the guitar which sat on his lap. Now his fingers began pulling at the strings, twisting them until they yowled with pain.

"What about me," he cried. "Don't you care what I need?"

"We had . . . years," Cal began, and then stopped, unable to continue. His eyes were full of anguish, and Molly could only imagine how trapped Cal must feel because of his inability to explain it all to

41

Willie, and to ask for Willie's forgiveness.

"Willie," Molly said softly, "I think Cal needs to rest now." Louis nodded, grabbed the handles of Cal's chair and wheeled him through the doorway, closing the door behind him.

"What am I gonna do, Ms. Molly?" Willie wailed.

"Well, you might have some rights under the Domestic Partner laws. Under the Stabilization Laws—and I think these buildings are rent stabilized—if Belloc wants you to move so he can demolish the building, he has to give the tenants moving costs. I might be able to get you a lawyer who's worked with some of my other clients pro bono."

"Don't want to move, Ms. Molly," Willie cut in. "Cal and me, we've been together in this place more years than I can count." He shut his eyes. Behind him, the gently undulating line of gray between river and sky mirrored the waves of almost palpable grief that emanated from his body. "Long as I stay here, Cal's still with me. Anywhere else, he be gone."

Chapter Six

The next day started with a call from Louis Kroski. He'd gotten to Cal Bruchman's apartment at his usual starting time of nine-thirty, but no one answered his repeated knocking and banging.

Molly felt a *frisson* of alarm. Where could Willie be? He was always there to let Louis in. As she went into the file room safe to get the spare key the agency kept for each of their clients, her anxiety increased. Willie was an old man; he could have fallen, or be dead for that matter.

Willie was there all right, stretched out flat on the floor, his chest moving up and down. But he was the lesser of the problems.

Cal Bruchman was slumped over in his wheelchair. Half of his head was caved in. The half that was left was dark-red with clotted blood and little gobs of red-tinted oatmeal.

Oatmeal? At first the thing made no sense. Then realization sank in. Cal's fragile skull had been hit so hard that parts of his brains had leaked out. She quickly turned away, trying to control the nausea rising up into her throat. Her body began to feel colder and colder until she couldn't stop shivering.

Louis, standing behind her, was saying something, but the words sounded like they were coming from very far away. He turned her around to face him and said, several times, "Molly, I need you to stay with me here, okay?"

More than the words, the feeling of his hands on her skin, were like a safety line to sanity. Then his fingers were gone and his disembodied voice said, "I'll be right back." A moment later he was draping a blanket around her. The shock was evident in his eyes, but he appeared in control of the situation and this was very reassuring. "Just don't look at him. Look at me. Okay?" Dumbly she nodded. "Keep looking at me," he repeated.

"How is Willie?" It was her voice, but it, too, sounded like it was coming from miles away.

"Well, he's not dead." He sat her carefully down on a chair, facing away from what was left of Cal Bruchman. "I want to check on him. Just sit there for a minute. I'll be right here. I'm not going anywhere."

Closing her eyes, she tried to take deep, regular breaths. A sudden image burst into her mind—Ben, in a psychotic rage, going after their mother with a hammer. Cal's mutilated head is what her mother's might have looked like had Ben's hammer actually connected. Another wave of nausea hit her, and it took every ounce of resolve not to leap up and run out of the apartment.

She deliberately erased the picture from her mind. In the background Louis was speaking to 911. Then he was beside her again. "Willie's okay. I think he's just passed out."

Time went by as if in a dream. Two uniformed policemen galloped up the stairs, took a brief statement and said that the detectives would want to talk to her further. The EMS people appeared and reported that Willie was passed out drunk. At some point, the CSI team must have come because there they were, but she had no memory of seeing them arrive. Louis wanted to take her home. Not wanting to be alone, she asked him to take her back to the office. The detectives could talk to her there.

But Nilda's horrified exclamations of "Oh my god!" and "You poor girl!" along with the cups of hot, sweet tea she thrust into Molly's hands, and Swandell's insistence on checking her pulse and blood pressure every ten minutes (or so it seemed) irritated and annoyed her instead of calming her down. She needed to act, and no one would let her get up.

"Ms. Lewin."

Molly's head snapped around. At first she couldn't believe it. If Elvis himself had suddenly walked into the room, it wouldn't have been more disconcerting.

Big, sandy-haired, a physique that had once been good when he was a lot younger than he was now. Rumpled grey suit. Icy blue eyes revealing nothing.

"Detective?"

"I'd like to ask you some questions. Are you up to it?"

"Let's go into my office."

She could feel Nilda's and Swandell's eyes following them, but it was the detective's broad back that was the focus of their attention, not her.

He lowered himself into her client's chair and she collapsed behind her desk.

"I understand you found the body."

"His name was Cal Bruchman." Her voice sounded thin and reedy. "He was a person before he became a body."

"I'm sorry. I don't mean to be insensitive."

"Oh no?" she fired back with eyes that were blinking rapidly, still adjusting to the actuality of him. "We haven't seen each other in, let's see . . ." She mumbled the names of the months while counting them on shaking fingers, "one year and four months and the first words out of your mouth are, 'I understand you found the body.' What do you have in your veins, Detective, ice water?"

He took a deep breath, well-remembered anger darkening his eyes. "Look, Molly, I said I'm sorry."

"You don't look in the least sorry." she snapped.

"I am, Molly, I really mean it." The anger was gone, replaced by a deep sadness, also well-remembered, that made his big shoulder appear even heavier.

Steve. Back again. That's all I need. She breathed deeply for a minute. Calm down, Molly.

Wariness was replacing the sadness in him. Wariness—and something else, something that reminded her of why she'd felt such a strong attraction to Steve when they'd first met during a series of burglaries, since cops were not usually her cup of tea.

Molly remembered sitting on a bench outside the courtroom, anxiously waiting to give testimony against the home attendant who was on trial as he came out of the courtroom. During the investigation he'd been very much the polite, impartial and very competent detective, and had never treated her as anything but a potential witness. At that moment, quite unexpectedly, he came over and sat down next to her. "First time, huh?" he'd said gently. "It's difficult when you're not used to it. But you'll be fine."

Steve had known without her having to say a word. In fact, much of the attraction back then, and the reason she'd accepted that first dinner invitation and continued going out with him, was based on her belief that he *did* know her—not only physically, but all the broken pieces of herself and her life that could never be talked about. Steve had a way of listening with a kind of empathic attentiveness that Molly interpreted as his ability to hear the silent words hiding behind the ones actually spoken. Later, after he disappeared, she wondered if that was just something she needed to believe.

"Apologies are easy, Detective," she said now, still determined not to let him off the hook.

"This whole thing must be very hard on you," he said softly, the wariness receding just a little. "First finding that poor man, and then me showing up."

"Yes, you." They looked at each other for a moment, circling the ring. "When did you transfer into Homicide?" she asked.

"About a year ago." He stopped, and when she said nothing further he went on, "Do you want my partner, Detective Ortiz, to continue this later on, when you're feeling more up to talking?"

But she didn't want Detective Ortiz. Up close Steve's big body appeared leaner, the sandy hair bleaching into white along the sides. His face looked haggard as if he hadn't slept for weeks.

"What happened, Steve? Why did you disappear on me like that?

Didn't I deserve at least an explanation?"

He leaned back in her client's chair and sighed. "You're right, Molly. I should have at least called. I just want you to understand that it had nothing to do with you."

"That's a standard line, Steve and you know it. 'It isn't you, it's me.' It's the line men use when they want out of a relationship."

"Look, now is not the time to get into all of this. I'm investigating a homicide. I know you're upset, but I'm assuming you want to help me find out who did it."

She did. "Just give me a little time to get back to myself."

"Maybe you should go home."

"No. I don't want to be alone at the moment."

"Then why don't I call you later. If you are still here and up to talking about Mr. Bruchman, I'll come back. Otherwise, I'll stop by your apartment." A corner of his mouth twitched--almost a smile. "You're still living in the same place, right Molly?" She nodded and he rose up from the chair. "You knew him, Molly, and I need all the information you can give me about his life—his relationships, possible enemies, who might want him dead—you know the drill."

"Okay." Molly looked down at some papers on her desk and heard the door close behind him.

Oh god! I don't want this to be happening again. Well, maybe it wasn't happening—at least not from Steve's side. Because who really knew what Steve was thinking? Certainly not her. An image of Cal as she had just seen him flashed into her mind. Steve was back because of a murder. And that was that

But memory has a life of its own. Other images came flooding in— that first dinner with Steve, when he'd asked her to tell him a little about herself—a question she never knew how to answer because it had the potential to open up all of those areas in her life that couldn't be talked about. Instead, she began to sing the first line from that lovely aria from *La Boheme* where Mimi tells Rudolfo all about herself: *"Si, Mi chiamano Mimi."* Her voice had sounded so soft and clear. Without batting an eye, Steve responded, *". . . ma il mio nome è Lucia."*

It blew her away.

"What's the madda?" he asked in a broad Bensonhurst accent, "ya think cops don't know opera? Whadiya think I am, a Philistine?"

Molly burst out laughing. He'd grinned a lop-sided grin of total joy, like that of a kid who finally cracks his mother up with one of his jokes, and she responded with equal joy—a feeling so rare in her life that it almost made her cry.

In the midst of these thoughts, the door opened. Stuttman. "How are you doing, Molly?" Once again she forced herself back from the dead, or at least the gone. "It was pretty awful."

"Louis told me." Stuttman had been out of the office when she'd come back with Louis. Now, he sat down, took a handful of pencils from the jar on her desk, laid them out and carefully arranged them according to their size. Molly understood this ritual as a sign that he was really upset. Whatever issues existed between herself and her boss, Molly respected the fact that he knew his clients much better than other agency directors did and genuinely cared about them.

"Do the police think this was a burglary, or what?" he asked.

"I don't know." It was amazing that questions about how Cal had come to be murdered hadn't even occurred to her. "Have they said anything to you?"

"Well, they haven't really talked to me, except to ask a few general questions."

He frowned—Stuttman was a man who liked to know everything that was going on. "Louis said that the fire escape window was broken, drawers were open and appeared to be rifled—things like that." He selected a pencil from the array on her desk and studied it carefully. "You were in with the detective for a while, so I thought he might have given you some idea of what they are thinking."

Does he know about my prior relationship with Detective Carmaggio? Molly thought. I wouldn't put it past him. Very little gets by Leo Stuttman. "He didn't reveal anything to me, either. Except that he wanted some information about Cal's life, enemies, that sort of thing."

"Which would lead one to believe that they aren't completely buying the burglary story."

"I guess not." Then who? Who? Certainly not Willie. Donald?

Stuttman placed the pencils neatly back into the jar and left. Who might have wanted to murder Cal? But Molly's mind wasn't ready to go there. Instead it went right back to Steve. She would not, Molly decided, let herself idealize him. That relationship had way too many other, painful sides.

On their third date they had gone to a little dimly-lit pub a couple of blocks from her apartment, where two television sets were tuned to sports. The place was crowded, so the only table they could find was a little too close to one of them for Molly's comfort.

Someone switched it to an action movie. Two guys in army uniforms were running through jungle foliage, trying to escape the bullets of an unseen sniper. Steve idly glanced at it and quickly turned away. In that instant his eyes went dead, as though something formerly alive in him had suddenly disappeared.

The familiar feeling of loneliness mixed with dread that this evoked caused her to push her plate away and chatter into the empty space,

47

grasping at anything that might get them—get *her*—through this. Slowly he struggled to bring himself back. It was like watching the gradual emergence of an image on a developing Polaroid photo.

"So," he said, picking up the conversation as if he had never left it. He glanced down at her barely touched food. "Don't you eat?"

She wanted to ask Steve what had just happened to him, but was unable to say a word. Here she was, a social worker, trained to navigate nuances of feelings with people, and she felt as though someone—her mother, maybe— had taped her mouth shut.

Thinking about it now, she should have gotten up and walked out then. It would have saved her a lot of pain. The second time it happened, they'd been listening to a classic radio station which began playing an anti-Viet-Nam war song. Once more his eyes went blank and he was gone. This time, she insisted on knowing what had happened, and he'd explained that he had PTSD, a legacy from his time in Nam and was having a flashback, He had no control over them; the past simply came up and wiped out the present. His marriage had broken up because his ex-wife couldn't put up with the flashbacks or the nightmares, or the bursts of anger or the resultant drinking which he couldn't always control either.

"I've been carrying that whole goddamned war with me, like a stone around my neck, ever since I got back," he'd told her. When he would go through a particularly bad bout, he'd literally disappear from Molly's life for a week or two. But he always came back . . . until that last time.

The night started out as one of the many; he'd drunk too much to be able get it up. They were in her studio apartment, naked on the pull-out bed. He wanted to make love, but nothing was happening. Molly tried everything a girl could do to help. Impossible. She'd have been happy to cuddle or talk about anything else instead, but he would never do that, nor would he ever say anything about whatever feelings of failure or shame that Molly believed he must have had. He'd simply get out of bed, put his clothes on and leave.

Watching him pulling on his shorts, she experienced the familiar sensation of sadness and loss that this silent departure provoked in her, but this time it was so intense that she cast around for something—anything—to make him stay. The first thing that popped into her mind was to ask, "Do you play gin rummy?"

He turned around with his shorts half on. "You mean cards?"

"What other kind of gin rummy is there?"

"You wanna play cards?"

"I bet I can beat you."

"I bet you can't."

She got out of bed to look for the one pack she owned, which she couldn't find even after rummaging through every drawer and closet in her little studio apartment. Turning around to apologize, she found him watching her with his lop-sided grin.

"I'd offer to help," he said. "But I wouldn't give up this view of your ass for anything in the world."

Molly grinned; then saw the familiar red-and-white box peeking through one of the piles she'd pulled out of her underwear drawer. Thank god! She threw the cards onto the bed, then shoved him down on top of them and pulled his shorts off. "If you're gonna see mine, I'm gonna see yours," she announced.

So they'd played gin rummy sitting naked in the middle of her bed. Towards morning, after she'd won three games in succession and he'd accused her of cheating, he pushed her down on the pillow and mumbled, "Okay, enough of this bullshit." He began kissing her, and this time everything worked.

That was the night of September 10th, 2001, and the last time she'd seen him until this morning.

Chapter Seven

Had her office suddenly turned several degrees colder? Shivering, Molly got up and put on her coat. I must still be in shock. Back in her chair, Molly pulled the ever-present stack of paperwork towards her, determined to push away the events of the day and get some work done.

Impossible. Images—of Cal, of Steve, of Ben—kept circling around her head like birds massing before a storm. Around two in the afternoon she left the office and walked three blocks along Freymont Avenue to the Acropolis Coffee Shop and settled into a cracked leatherette booth near the window. Maybe food would do her some good as she'd forgotten to eat. Hettie, the bubble-shaped waitress who had been at the Acropolis forever, was behind the counter talking with five or six men all wearing grease-spotted uniforms or flannel shirts. Hettie's Coterie, Molly had named them. Any time of the day or evening they could be found sitting at the counter, hands wrapped around their coffee mugs, talking and laughing with her.

"So," one of the men said in a loud voice, "did Quentin's Eagle come in for you last night?"

"Quentin's Eagle?" Hettie made a sound like *Tsa* and moved her meaty shoulders up towards the heavens. "More like Quentin's Turkey. At this rate, I'll have to take my Florida vacation in New Jersey."

Hettie nodded towards Molly, picked up the coffee pot and a menu, and made her way across the room as if she were on the last leg of a long and arduous journey.

Molly ordered a tuna fish sandwich. While waiting for her food, she closed her eyes and sank into the warmth of the place, letting herself just relax and stop thinking.

"Ms. Lewin, er, Molly?"

She looked up to see the well-manicured, almost delicate hand of Ken Belloc extended out from the sleeve of his expertly-tailored suit. Raising her head even further, she saw his round, freshly-shaved face with its tiny, dimpled chin smiling down at her as if she was the person he had been waiting all morning to run into.

Keeping her hands around her coffee cup, she nodded. He took this as an open invitation and slid into the booth across from her.

"I wanted to tell you how sorry I am to hear about Cal Bruchman's murder," he said, apparently deciding that her refusal to shake hands with him was mere oversight. "I understand you found the body." She took a deep breath and nodded. "How awful that must have been for you. He was one of my tenants, you know."

"Yes, I do," Molly said with a sigh.

"I hear somebody broke in through the fire escape window." Ken smiled sadly. "Those old buildings are so unsafe. Especially the ones on Warwick Avenue, along the river."

They wouldn't be if you maintained them properly, she thought.

"Aside from lack of elevators and ancient wiring there's no security. So easy to break into. I've been fighting a losing battle with those buildings for years. The City's archaic rent stabilization laws don't allow us enough in income to pay for basic maintenance, much less to modernize them and make them habitable for our tenants, especially the elderly." It sounded to Molly like a canned speech.

Hettie plopped down the plate with Molly's sandwich in front of her. She gestured with the coffee pot resting in her other hand, but Molly shook her head no.

Although they knew each other from her work with some of his tenants, Ken never went out of his way to be particularly friendly to her. So why he had he approached her now? "What will happen to his roommate Willie Cobb? I don't believe his name is on the lease. Do you intend to evict him?"

Ken raised and lowered his expensively-suited shoulders. "I don't want to be responsible for what can happen to a man of his age, alone in an unsafe apartment."

"Well, I'm quite worried about what will happen to him if he loses his home. As you know, there are hardly any low-rent apartments left in this neighborhood."

"It's a little too soon to talk about that, wouldn't you say?" His eyebrows went up, as if surprised that she would even mention it, as Cal hadn't even been buried yet.

"It's never too soon to be sure that you have a roof over your head."

"If that turns out to be a problem, Molly, uh, I'm sure we can work something out." His eyes darted around the room and he said, almost in a whisper, "I might be willing to offer him some moving money, say five thousand dollars as compensation."

She was about to answer that five thousand dollars would barely cover Willie's move and a month's rent and security in any decent building when she noticed that Ken's normally smooth brow was wrinkled and he was clenching and unclenching his hands. Ken Belloc was very worried about something that had nothing to do with his tenants.

Suddenly, Ken suddenly stood up and slid out of the booth. Molly turned to see what had caught his attention. Ivan Skanov was standing inside the door.

Ken joined him and the two men sat down at one of the tables, away from everyone. What was *this* all about? The Acropolis Coffee Shop was not the kind of place that Papa Skana generally frequented.

Papa Skana's sloping forehead and narrow face would not ordinarily make him prepossessing, but he was definitely the Alpha male in that duo. He leaned across the table, punctuating his sentences with a closed fist. It looked like he was laying down the law about something. Ken Belloc, on the other hand, seemed to have shrunk and was hunched down in his seat, nodding submissively. Since Papa was speaking in a low voice, it was impossible to hear what he was saying.

Molly was so caught up watching the two men that she didn't see Manny, the porter, until she heard him call her name.

"Hey, Manny," she called back. He ordered a container of coffee at the counter, came over with it and slipped into the seat across from her, dumping a bag labeled 'All-Rite Hardware' on the seat next to him.

"One of the stalls in the ladies bathroom is backing up again." He pried the lid off the container and blew on it. "What is that you ladies are always putting down those toilets to get them to back up the way they do?"

"Do you want me to go into detail, Manny?"

His laugh turned into a coughing fit. "No, gracias," he said after thumping his chest a few times. "Spare me. Besides, those toilets are probably older than you and me put together and they're tired; they just don' wanna work no more."

He grinned, but his eyes circled the diner. Manny was another one who didn't miss a trick, Molly thought. "I was talkin' to Louis Kroski a little while ago," he said. "Tol' me how bad it was this morning. Sorry you had to be there to see it."

"Thanks, Manny. It was no picnic, I'll tell you that. But Louis was wonderful. He took charge of everything, called the police and the ambulance."

"He's a good boy, Ms. Molly. These last couple months, he's earned his salary twice over with everything he's had to go through with those people."

"What do you mean, Manny?"

"You know. Since Mr. Bruchman's son turned up."

"You mean Donald?"

He nodded and sipped a little of his coffee. "Been about two, three months now, Louis was telling me. Before that, the old man could have been dead for all his son cared about him."

"So Donald starting coming around just about the time all that talk began about developing the river front."

"That's right Ms. Molly. It was just about then that Donald showed up, starts throwing his weight around. You tell that detective about it."

52

So that was the reason Manny had come into the coffee shop instead of helping himself to the free coffee that was available in the staff room. He knew about her prior relationship with Steve, just like he knew about everything. And he wanted to make sure that he passed this information along. She wondered why Louis hadn't told them himself.

They sat in silence for a few minutes as Manny slowly drank his coffee and watched her out of the corner of his eyes. It looked like Donald really was involved in harassing the elderly tenants into moving. Could he have had a hand in his father's murder also?

"I hear the lease on this place is up and they're going out," Manny said, drawing his forefinger across his throat. "Some fancy little café will come in here that charges two-fifty for a cup of coffee. Or three-fifty for *café con leche*—that's coffee with milk. Those yuppies can call it *latte*, but it's still coffee with milk."

She shook her head in commiseration. Another piece of the neighborhood about to be erased. And what will happen to Hettie and her coterie? Molly sighed. Why did the fate of this neighborhood, this little greasy spoon, this waitress, matter so much?

Glancing out the window, Molly saw a black Lincoln town car pulling over to the side of the curb. Papa and Belloc got up and left the diner. The driver opened the back door of the Lincoln and Papa's daughter, Ana, emerged. She and Ken exchanged a couple of words, and Ken walked off.

"The lovely Ana Skana," Manny said, following Molly's gaze. "*La Puta.*"

Calling Ana a whore didn't quite fit what Molly knew about Ana. Whores had sex for money. Molly wasn't sure what Ana's criteria was for who she had sex with, but Molly didn't think it was money. Certainly, Ian Sorensen, an underpaid Assistant Professor of Sociology, was unlikely to be able give Ana cash or expensive presents—at least as far as Molly knew.

Hettie came over with the check. For a moment the three of them watched the Skanas. Papa seemed to be having another one of his heated discussions, this time with his daughter. But unlike Belloc, Ana was no submissive sycophant. Her black leather coat was open, and she was standing with one hand on an aggressively thrust-out hip and gesticulating with the other as she answered him back.

"You see those two together so much," Hettie said dryly, "you'd think they were married."

"Nah," Manny said. "The married couples I know hardly spend any time with each other, outside of weddings and funerals. Those two carry on like high school sweethearts." There was some talk around the neighborhood about Ana and her father being involved in some kind of an incestuous relationship, but Molly didn't believe that.

"I'm surprised he hasn't broken her face," Hettie declared.

Manny looked at his watch. "Well, that ladies room is waiting for me." He took a cigarillo out the pack, tapped it on his sleeve and slid out of the seat. "See you later, Ms. Molly."

Mollie paid her check and left the coffee shop a little behind Manny. To get back to the office, she had to pass the Skanas who were still arguing in Russian, which she couldn't understand. Just as Molly was about to walk by them, Ana stopped talking and turned to her. "That old man, you found him, right?" she asked in a voice which always sounded to Molly as though it was coming out of a grater. Papa pulled his daughter's arm and gestured towards the waiting Lincoln with the other hand

"Yes, I found him," Molly said.

"He was an old, sick man. He shouldn't have to die like that." Ana shivered a little, pulling herself out of her father's grasp and wrapping her coat firmly around her body.

"I couldn't agree with you more, Ana," Molly said, trying to keep the surprise out of her voice. The two of them had barely ever spoken to each other.

"So, do you always walk away and leave your man to another woman?" There was nothing sarcastic in Ana's voice. She sounded truly curious.

Since Molly had never pondered such a question, she shrugged noncommittally.

"How generous of you." Ana concluded.

Determined not to be baited, Molly decided on honesty. "As far as I can see, no woman can steal a man who doesn't want to be stolen."

Ana gave a little laugh, low and throaty. "And no woman lets a man be stolen if she really wants him badly enough, eh?"

Once more Papa touched his daughter's shoulder. She turned towards the driver, brushing his arm with her breast as she moved. Without a change of expression, the driver carefully helped her into the car. Papa shot Molly a look out of unblinking, light-gray eyes that told her absolutely nothing, and followed his daughter into the car.

What was that all about? Molly thought on her way back to the office. It seemed to be no secret to Ana that Molly wasn't all that interested in Ian. So Ana had no need to gloat, nor play catty girl games. Molly shook her head. She could come up with no answer to the mystery of Ana.

Steve called soon after she returned to the office, and about forty-five minutes later he was sinking into her client's chair, pushing it back to give his long legs room to stretch out. If anything, he looked more tired and haggard than when she'd first seen him that morning.

54

"So, was it a burglary?" she asked.

"I'm asking the questions here, Molly." His voice had that flat, cold, take-charge sound—his cop voice.

"Okay, Steve," she said, rolling her eyes. "What do you need to know?"

"Can we start with some background?" He took out his notebook and flipped to a fresh page.

"He and Willie have been living in that apartment for over fifteen years." She glanced at the open case file on her desk. "I know you've probably spoken to Louis, so just stop me if you know this stuff already."

"Don't worry, Molly." His voice was a little less official, a little warmer now. "Everyone sees things a little differently and I learn something new from each person." He shrugged. "If nothing else, I get corroboration, always a good thing."

Steve was a superb interviewer, every bit as good as herself. So the best thing would be to just tell him everything, and let him decide what was relevant and what was redundant. Molly pushed the file away. It was all there, in her mind. "Willie was an itinerant musician and Cal was some kind of a construction worker. He developed ALS—that's Lou Gehrig's disease—about three or four years ago."

"I know what that is."

"Cal is the lessee of the apartment which is owned by a landlord named Ken Belloc." She stopped to see if there was any sign that he recognized the name. His face showed nothing. "I believe Belloc is fronting for a real estate development scheme backed by Papa Skana."

"Ivan Skanov?" Steve looked up, his eyebrows raised in surprise. "He's branching out into real estate development?" So, she knew some things that he didn't. "Who told you all this?"

"Willie did." Apparently Louis, who knew all about it, hadn't told Steve. "I don't know where he got his information, or even if it's true. But I saw Papa and Belloc together just a little while ago. Belloc seemed worried and scared."

"Scared?"

"I don't know what's going on between them, or what it's about. What I do know is that the City wants to develop the whole waterfront area. If Belloc and company can get the old rent-stabilized people out and sell the land to the City, they stand to make a killing."

"You think Belloc and/or Papa Skana had something to do with this homicide?"

"I don't know," she admitted. "I do know that a number of old people who live in his buildings are being harassed."

"Harassed? How?"

"Well, so far its been knocking and banging on the walls and pipes at all hours of the day and night, threatening insinuations, stuff like that. Talk to Dave Scheunfeldt." She gave him Dave's address and went on: "Willie thinks that Cal's son, Donald, is working for them. And Manny, our porter who knows things before they happen, tells me that Donald never bothered with his father until about two months ago when he suddenly turned up and started making trouble. It could be a coincidence."

"Coincidence?" His voice turned the word into a question which he then proceeded to answer. "As an old timer once told me, 'Coincidences in a murder investigation are as rare as a three-legged dog'."

"Well, coincidence or not, it seems to me that if Papa was behind the deal, he'd be using his own Russian goons to do the strong-arm stuff."

"Not necessarily. Papa likes to keep up the illusion that he's just a business man." He grinned a little of his lop-sided grin. "You know, drugs, money laundering, contract killing, those kinds of businesses." Just for a moment their eyes met, and her mouth turned upward a bit in a matching smile. "Although he hides it all behind legitimate all-hours clubs, real estate, a couple of limousine service," he continued, serious again. "Besides, he knows we're watching him and he may not want to tip us off that he's involved, if he is." Steve turned to a fresh page in his notebook and wrote something down. "I'll check it out."

"A day or two before this all happened Donald had been pressuring Cal to go into a nursing home." Molly leaned forward, her brow creased. "This desire to get Cal into a nursing home—which means out of the apartment—seems to have come as suddenly as Donald's appearance on the scene. Makes me wonder what's behind it."

"Playing devil's advocate for a moment, a lot of sons have got real hard-ons for their fathers."

"That's probably true in this case, which could be partly motivating whatever other machinations he's been up to. There doesn't seem to be a lot of filial love on Donald's part."

"What do you mean?"

"I believe that Willie and Cal were more than just roommates. Which might explain why he's so angry at Willie as well."

"You mean they were homosexual?"

"Willie came close to admitting it yesterday. He's never talked about it before. But that's true of a lot of old gay couples. They never came out of the closet because they lived through the time when homosexuality wasn't as accepted as it is now. They've always been discreet, referring to each other as 'my roommate,' never as 'my lover.'" He nodded, understanding. "There used to be some beefcake photos of Cal on the wall. He was some hunk." It all seemed so sad and senseless. "But that all happened so long ago. I would think that if he was going to

56

murder his father because of it, he would have done so already."

Steve turned his big hand over in a questioning gesture. "So this desire to get his father into a nursing home came on suddenly. How did the deceased feel about it?"

"I think he was ready to go, if his son wanted him to."

"Oh?" He raised his eyebrows and flipped back in his notebook. "That's not what your home aide, Louis Kroski, told me. According to him, Cal was afraid of his son and didn't want to go into the nursing home."

Molly ran her fingers through her hair and thought over everything she'd seen and heard in that apartment. "Well, Willie insisted that Cal was afraid. But in all fairness, I'm not so sure it was fear on Cal's part. It was more like guilt. He admits that he hadn't been a good father to Donald, and that by going into the nursing home as Donald wanted him to, he could atone for some of his past, uh, neglect."

"He said this?"

"He doesn't, I mean didn't, have the ability to articulate the words, but when I talked with him yesterday that's the very strong feeling I got."

"But you can't be certain."

"No," she said thinking back to her talk with Cal . . . was it just yesterday? "But I repeated back to him what I thought he was saying, and he affirmed it."

"So Donald wouldn't have had to murder his father in order to get him out of that apartment."

"Donald wouldn't necessarily have known that. This conversation took place after Donald had already left."

"I've talked to Donald and he is quite positive that his father was ready to go into the nursing home."

"He would like to have you believe that, but I'm not so sure that *he* really believed it." For a moment, it felt so much like old times, the two of them sitting across from each other, having a conversation that was a real meeting of the minds. Why couldn't it have lasted?

"Donald thinks Willie did it out of anger," Steve was going on, "because Cal was moving out and leaving him without a place to live since his name is not on the lease. But no weapon was found. Can you see an old man like Willie, having just killed his lover in a fit of rage, having the presence of mind to run downstairs and throw the weapon into the river?"

Molly shook her head. "And Donald's wrong. I told Willie that I thought he did have some legal rights to stay in the apartment, or that I could at least get him some moving money and that I could probably get him a lawyer."

"How about Bukka, Willie's great-grandson?" He readjusted

himself in the chair, stretching out his long legs. "We looked at him. He's got a few priors—drug possession and stuff like that."

"But what's his motive? If Willie loses his home, so does the kid."

"He has an alibi—of sorts. He says he was jamming at an after-hours club that night, and several people saw him there. But there still could have been enough time for him to do the old man." He glanced at Molly again, uncertain how she would take his choice of words but she'd finally got her mind in gear and her emotions on hold. "Unfortunately, we haven't got any forensic evidence that ties him, or anyone else, to the crime."

"Have you spoken to Willie?"

"I tried to, but he was in another world. Do you think he's a little, uh . . . ?" He tapped the side of his head with his finger.

"He's usually sharp as a tack," she said slowly. "But with what he's just been through. . ."

"Anything else you think I should know?"

"I can't think of anything. But if I do, you'll be the first to know." It all seemed so easy again, to be talking to him like this. "Can I ask you something?"

"You can ask."

"Are you sure Cal wasn't killed during a burglary?"

"We haven't ruled it out. The fire escape window was open, a couple of drawers were pulled out and things were messed around, but I've seen a lot of burglaries in my time, and this one didn't fit the picture. The TV wasn't taken, and there was a jewelry box with some gold cufflinks in a nightstand drawer which hadn't even been opened. Why kill him and then just leave all that stuff behind? Unless he heard Willie coming home and ran out. That's one of the things I want to ask Willie—when he comes back to himself—if he comes back to himself."

Steve put his notebook into his pocket. "Well," he said slowly as he rose to his feet, "thanks for your help." He dug a card out of his jacket pocket and held it out towards her. "If you think of anything else . . ."

Anything else? Was he kidding? The coldness of that statement jolted her right back into feeling mode. Jumping up, she thrust herself between him and the door. "Don't think you're getting out of here just like that."

Chapter Eight

For a moment it looked as though Steve would side-step her and go right out the door; and perhaps he meant to. Instead, he stopped, a little embarrassed and asked in an overly aggressive voice, "What do you mean, just like that?"

Molly didn't answer. Steve minutely examined her antique coat rack with its collection of jackets, sweater and umbrellas. Looked at his watch. Finally he sat back down and sighed. "Okay, you win." His jaw tightened as if this was the last thing he wanted to talk about, but he took another deep breath and said, "You know I have Post-Traumatic Stress. I came home from 'Nam with it."

She sat back down and nodded, remembering the bleakness of those moments when he'd simply disappear, right in front of her eyes..

"Post 9/11 it got very bad again. It was like I was reliving that whole goddamned war. I was in no shape to be in a relationship with anyone.

"Why didn't you tell me?"

"You're a fine one to ask that question. What did you ever confide in me? You knew all about my ex-wife, my kids, my job, and I know next to nothing about you. All you ever told me was that your parents are dead and you have a brother somewhere who is out of touch."

A rush of heat ran all the way up into her face. She'd been so sure—no, had so needed to believe—that he knew who she was without her ever having to put it into words, that she'd never asked herself how *would* he know?

"Did we ever have a real relationship?" he went on relentlessly. "That's the question women usually ask. With us it was all one-sided. We dated, I know that, we had some fun. But what do I really know about you?"

It felt just like he'd stripped the skin off her body. She was desperate to say something in her own defense, but couldn't assemble her thoughts in any coherent way—and now, goddammit, she was crying!

"I'm sorry, Molly." His voice was gentler but still held a tinge of anger. "I told you I didn't want to get into it."

It was awful to feel like this—condemned, ashamed, exposed. Grabbing a tissue from the box on her desk and blotting her eyes, she breathed deeply a few times, working to get herself back under control.

"I asked you to tell me," her voice was shaky "and you did." A couple of deep breaths. "I don't know what came over me. I guess I was more upset than I thought about Cal Bruchman's murder. I'm all right now."

He'll get up and leave, Molly thought, but he didn't. Their eyes met; and she saw something powerful, and very unexpected. It was as though one of the stone faces on Mount Rushmore suddenly came alive and looked back at her. The whole thing was so unnerving that it left her without anything to say in return. So she scrambled around for anything handy—fortunately her desk never lacked for unfinished paperwork— chose a folder at random and opened it.

"So that's that?" he said. When she still didn't say anything, he got up and said, "Well, thanks again for your help."

The sensation was exactly as though someone punched her in the chest—the feeling of loss was that deep and painful. "Steve," she blurted out, surprised at the words even as they came out of her mouth, yet knowing that if he walked out of her life again, just like that, it would be unbearable, "uh, you doing anything for dinner tomorrow night?" Tonight she'd have to collapse into bed.

"I'm not so sure that's a good idea, Molly." The moment, for Steve, was over.

"We don't have to talk about the case."

"You're dammed right 'we don't have to talk about the case'" he said, mimicking her tone which had sounded like an old-fashioned schoolmarm. "Technically, I shouldn't be talking to you at all, outside of these formal interviews—you may be called to give testimony if this thing ever goes to trial."

"After what you put me through," she asserted, "you *owe* me a dinner." It felt as though she'd just taken a step off the curb, against the *Don't Walk* sign, right into oncoming traffic.

For a while Steve sat and regarded her with his cop's face—no expression. Then he sighed again. "Well, maybe I do owe you a dinner. But I'd just as soon not eat in Brooklyn. Let's meet at that pub on Third Avenue where we used to go. Remember?"

Molly nodded, absurdly pleased that *he* remembered.

"What time?"

"How about six?"

"Okay." He got up. "But I might have to cancel. You never know how things break on a case like this."

"Any excuse, huh?"

"Look, Molly," he said flatly. "You know what it's like."

She was already regretting her impulse. What was wrong with her? A healthy person would never want to speak to him again, much less ask him out to dinner.

In no mood to sit and do any paperwork, Molly went out into the reception area. Stuttman's office door was open. Apparently he'd been waiting for Steve to leave because he immediately beckoned her inside. Unlike the windowless cubicles the staff were confined to, Stuttman's office had real walls, curtained windows and was roomy enough for a desk, a small conference table and a leather couch. The walls were covered with plaques honoring Stuttman for notable achievements, such as the Henry J. Kronin Senior Center Man of the Year, and photographs of Stuttman with local politicians and other Brooklyn biggies.

Stuttman waved Molly into a red leatherette chair in front of his desk and sat down in his own real leather chair. "I understand you've just spoken to Detective Carmaggio. What's their theory of the murder?"

Murder? Molly's mind, still spinning like a pinwheel in a gale after her conversation with Steve, had forgotten all about what had brought Steve back into her life in the first place.

Slowly, she brought her attention to the crime that had been committed. "I don't think they have a theory yet. They're looking into every aspect of it."

"Could it have been a burglar?"

If murder had to happen on his turf, Molly realized, Stuttman would much prefer it to have been committed by an anonymous burglar. Unfortunately, it might just land a little closer to home. "You know about the waterfront development project, don't you?" Stuttman nodded. "Well, there's been some talk about Ken Belloc, who owns a number of those buildings along the waterfront, harassing the tenants to move out."

"And the police think that this somehow led to Cal Bruchman being murdered?" His voice was outraged. "Ken Belloc isn't capable of anything like that. He's a true patriot."

Molly almost snorted out loud. Ken Belloc had garnered that reputation in the weeks following 9/11 by spearheading the drive to change the name of Freymont Avenue to Freedom Hill—"The Great Freedom Hill Battle"—as Molly later named it. Building on an upsurge of patriotic feeling in the neighborhood, Ken Belloc and his Business Association decided that Freymont Avenue should be rechristened Freedom Hill. Since most of Freymont Avenue ran through an area of Brooklyn that was flat as a board, this seemed to Molly a bit of a misnomer. But not so to Ken and his supporters. In a neighborhood with so many factions and with feelings running so high, sides were drawn and tempers flared.

Ken had done some research and announced that the word Freymont was actually a bastardization of *Freimont*, the name of the old Dutch- German settlement—*frei* being German word for free, and *mont*

61

being the word for mountain or hill. Maybe there was a hill once, Molly told Nilda, but there wasn't one now.

Beth Trebold from the local Historical Society, who didn't like Ken, maintained that Freymont was actually an Americanization of *Vraimont*, from the French word *Vrai*, meaning truth or certainty. According to her research, a parcel of rich riverside land had been given to the French nobleman, the Comte du Beque, as a reward for his help during the American Revolution. He named this estate Vraimont in honor of the Declaration of Independence: *We hold these truths to be self-evident.*

Ken had taken out ads in the Brooklyn Weekly News to promote his view—*Our Freedoms are mightier than the terrorists who seek to destroy them. Support Freedom Hill*—implying, of course, that anyone who didn't support the name was anti-American. Beth, who didn't have Ken's budget, went on the local lecture circuit and spoke at the art society and ladies club meetings, denouncing the re-writing of history. Everyone took sides, including Molly who thought that the phrase, *"We hold these truths to be self evident"* were as patriotically American as any words could possibly be, and wrote a letter to the editor saying as much.

Molly thought later that the fight over the naming of Freedom Hill was probably a healthy thing for the neighborhood. It gave people something concrete to think about and to do in those dark, despairing days during which it became clear that there were to be no more survivors and the bodies of the dead were mounting up. The Weekly News finally threw its weight behind Ken's historical interpretation. According to the cynics, of which Molly was one, it was Ken's advertising dollars that influenced their decision. In the end, given the anti-French feeling and the pro-freedom sentiment of post-9/11 Brooklyn, Ken Belloc and Freedom Hill won the day. There was a big re-naming ceremony, and lots of American champagne got imbibed, but everyone continued to call the street Freymont Avenue, just as they always had.

Stuttman scowled at Molly while his hands arranged and rearranged his pencils again.

"He may be involved with Papa Skana in some way," Molly said. "I saw the two of them together at the Acropolis coffee shop, and it really looked like Skana was reading Ken the riot act."

Stuttman's lips tightened. "Well!" he declared, "Ivan Skanov we all know about. Russian mafia trash. Into capitalism big time. But Belloc?" He shook his head slowly. "I'd find that hard to believe. I've known Ken for years. He has his faults like we all do, but harassment?" He turned the palms of his hands up and raised his eyebrows. "Who told you this?"

"Cal's roommate, Willie Cobb, said that Belloc made a veiled threat to Cal, something about how easy it would be for him to fall down the stairs."

"It may not have been a threat. That building is very unsafe. Ken may just have been warning him."

"Mr. Stuttman, it's not just Cal Bruchman. Margery Canover, Dave Scheunfelt and others have experienced some kind of harassment. Dave was menaced in his own building by a man who looks just like Donald Bruchman. And both Louis Kroski and Cal's roommate, Willie, both agree that Donald showed no interest in his father until a couple of months ago, just the about the time the waterfront development deal was being proposed."

"That doesn't prove anything."

"No, you're right, Mr. Stuttman. But if the police find that Donald Bruchman has been working as some kind of enforcer, he wouldn't be doing it on his own. Belloc, or Belloc and Skana, would have had to put him up to it."

Stuttman shook his head resolutely back and forth. "I'd believe it of twenty other people I could name right now. But Ken Belloc? Never!"

Chapter Nine

There was no answer to her knock. Instead of going home and collapsing into bed, Molly had transferred to the F train and gone to check on Ben, who didn't appear to be home. Maybe he was out on one of his long rambles, but then again—the image of Cal's dead body wouldn't go away. She had a key, which she'd promised to use only for emergencies. Did this qualify? She knocked again, this time pushing on the door a little. It opened, which made her heart pound. He always kept the door locked.

The kitchen was dark, but a shaft of light from the front room was reflected on the floor. Molly walked through the kitchen, through the narrow hallway and stood in the doorway of his bedroom-cum-living room and stared at the scene inside. Ben was stretched out on the daybed with his back to her and his head on Marushka's voluminous skirt. She was on the daybed too, propped up against the wall, her face framed by her mane of rust-colored hair, like an edging of autumn foliage around a crumpled bouquet. Her neon-purple blouse was open and he had one of her still magnificent breasts in his mouth.

Molly was astonished. She thought she knew everything about him, but Ben had never even mentioned Marushka. This was not a scene a sister should be witnessing. Better to leave and quick. Unfortunately, her brother was a scavenger, and his apartment was full of old furniture and street junk. In her haste to escape, she stumbled into a bicycle with half its spokes missing that was propped up near the door to the front room, biting her lip to keep from crying out when the kick-stand hit her in the shin. Frantic, she caught the bicycle before it crashed, cushioning it with her body, and finally lowering it gently onto the floor. Ben seemed oblivious to the noise—his head was so full of all kinds of noises, Molly thought later, that this one hardly registered—but Marushka looked up. Their eyes met, Marushka's full of defiance. Molly, face flaming, disentangled herself from the bicycle and ran out of the apartment.

Instead of waiting for the bus, she walked uptown, barely aware of her throbbing shin. How could I not have known, or even suspected? Am I so naïve to really believe that Ben's mental illness had wiped out his sexuality along with his ability to balance a checkbook? How had Marushka gotten past the pervasive mistrust of people that kept Ben so isolated?

She stopped for a moment in front of Wo Yee Food Provisions to think about that. No answer came, but instead there was a surprising sense of gratitude—that Ben had a connection with somebody other than herself, and that he was getting at least a modicum of pleasure in life.

So, where does that leave me? When was last time *I* had had any real pleasure in *my* life? Certainly not with Ian Sorensen. Outside of the brief conversation with Ana Skana, he hadn't merited a thought all day. And how sad was that?

Molly started to walk again, past the old Essex Street Market, across Grand Street which started out as Chinatown and morphed into Little Italy in the space of a few blocks, up Allen Street to where it became First Avenue, her moving feet fueling her thoughts. Since 9/11, life had been feeling pretty grim. She enjoyed her work—at least the client contact part of it. And she did love her brother—of that there was no question. Of course, when he was psychotic, or nearly so, she felt overwhelmed and angry with him—for the anxiety he caused her. But she could always depend on him to be in her life, to need her care, to rely on her to interpret him to the world because no one else really knew him. Which, apparently, wasn't true.

Home at last. Molly dropped her keys and the mail on the table and slipped a Billie Holiday CD into her changer—one of her last recordings, made near the end of her life. Billie's voice was gone, but the phrasing was still there, that unique way she had of twisting the words around so they came out meaning almost the opposite of what they were intended to mean. Molly had always felt that Billie recognized something about love and life that eluded most people. Things were rarely what you thought they were.

Billie was singing, as she often did, about a man who had left her. Instead of sounding sad, Billie sang the lyrics as if she'd known all along that this would happen and she'd be on her own.

Funny . . . as often as Ben had disappeared, Molly had never questioned the fact that he would always come back to her . . . in his own oddly peculiar way. But now, realizing how much she didn't know about her brother, there might come a time when all that would change. Not that there was even a remote chance that Ben and Marushka would live happily ever after—but nothing is forever. For one thing, there was so much about his illness that she really didn't understand. Maybe one day he wouldn't come back from one of his psychotic episodes. Where would that leave her?

Molly sat for a long time slowly rocking, listening to Billie. Was it only this morning that Cal had been murdered? It felt, somehow, like a dim memory. Shock. She should call Steve and cancel; after all, he was the original disappearing man. No, that distinction went to her father who walked out of the house at some point after Ben had been hospitalized and never came back.

Disappearing men . . . her life had been full of them. The CD stopped; she removed it from the player, took off her clothes and got into bed. No good would come from thinking about all that. But the mind has a funny way of going exactly where you don't want it to.

The morning of September 11, 2001 had started out as a happy one. Steve, on an early shift that day, had not woken her up before he left. The memory was so clear: seeing the imprint of his body on the bed next to her and feeling so close to him as she thought about their gin rummy game of the night before. Little did she know that in just a couple of hours, the whole world would go mad, and that ghostly image of him was all that would be left to her for a very long time.

Even now, almost a year-and-a-half later, she had no sequential memory of that terrible day. September 11, 2001 existed for her in snippets, chopped-up pieces, like a damaged video disc that kept skipping and stopping, skipping and stopping.

The weather that Tuesday morning was spectacular—cool, with clear blue skies—and she remembered entering the subway at 14th Street in Manhattan on her way to work feeling buoyant. She came up out of the Brooklyn end of the tunnel to a world gone mad. People were standing stock still in the middle of the sidewalk with horror on their faces, radios and cell phones plastered to their ears. Several people were running down Freymont Avenue as if they were being pursued by a homicidal maniac. A middle-aged woman in a dirty pink corduroy jacket was slumped on the ground, literally ripping clumps of hair out of her head and screaming that hundreds of planes were crashing into the World Trade Center. The next thing Molly remembered was running with a long stream of people towards the river. Somehow she found herself standing with Manny and Nilda at the river's edge, having had no memory of how they found each other, watching in horror as smoke and flames poured out of the towers while dark forms rained down alongside of them. The river was lit up—a blazing, smoking, dancing fire— rippled reflections, Molly decided later. The absolute shock—almost incomprehension—when she heard from someone watching the scene on a portable TV that the dark forms raining down were people. In fact, some of them were holding hands as they fell.

Another shock when the towers began collapsing in on themselves. Everyone was screaming, crying and hugging one another. Everyone but her. She'd watched dry-eyed, like a piece of stone, the shock and loss too huge for tears. For months afterwards the images of those falling people, those collapsing buildings, plagued both her waking and dreaming moments. Molly still felt like a piece was ripped from her heart every time she looked out over the river and saw only sky.

For the whole of that terrible day and for weeks afterward, the news was filled with images of cops and firemen. At first, they were running into the towers to rescue those trapped inside, and later, their faces covered in soot, sweat and anguish, they were leading shocked and haunted-looking people out of them. Still later, they were back, along with EMS workers and volunteers from all over the country, digging through the rubble, searching for survivors.

She'd tried to call Steve, leaving dozens of frantic messages for him on his cell, his home, his office. But they were never returned. She'd gone to his apartment more than once and banged on his door. No answer. Finally—a week, two weeks later—that whole period of time was still fuzzy to her, consumed with anxiety, she climbed the sandstone steps of the precinct house to talk to Steve's lieutenant who assured her that Steve was alive. He was probably working on the site with the other cops and firemen. So she went down there, joining the masses of people behind the police barricades. The anguish there was as palpable as the huge piles of rubble in the distance. Of course she couldn't find him. After that, a paralysis set in and she couldn't even punch his number into the phone. He never called nor contacted her.

Chapter Ten

Sleep didn't come easy that night and Molly woke, groggy and foggy, to a cloudy, misty morning. The clock said 8:15—late again—but cert

ainly Stuttman wouldn't have the *chutzpa* to read her the riot act after a day like the one she'd had yesterday.

He was leaning over Nilda's desk, telling her a story about something as he stared down her cleavage. But he said no more to Molly than a good morning and asked how she was feeling.

"Yesterday was a hard day, and I have felt better."

Stuttman's small brown eyes filled with concern. This surprised Molly. Up to now his only two feelings towards her seemed to be anger or annoyance. A small nod of thanks brought forth nothing in return, so she picked up a stack of Medicaid recerts that were sitting in her box, and went off to her cubicle.

The first was for a client that Molly knew well—Mrs. Mendez, an 82-year old woman who lived with a schizophrenic son who had been hospitalized several times. Mrs. Mendez, diabetic, single amputee, almost blind, adored her son and had introduced him proudly to Molly when they'd first met as "my Juanito." Juanito was a middle-aged man with vacant eyes and the perpetual fattening and flattening of lips and tongue, a side-effect of some of the early anti-psychotic medications. Older than Ben by a few years, he mumbled to himself a lot, but when prompted by his mother, he said a polite hello to Molly. To Mrs. Mendez, her Juanito could do no wrong—well, his mind wasn't always right, that she'd admit—but it was because he was sick, yes? You can't blame someone for being sick. Juanito was her treasure and she worried continually about what would happen to him when she was no longer around to provide care.

Mrs. Mendez was as different from Molly's own mother as a ripe plum is from a dried-up prune. Mrs. Mendez and Mrs. Lewin were both mothers—there the similarity ended. Molly wondered what her mother would have thought had she come upon the scene yesterday between Ben and Marushka. For a moment Molly smiled, picturing what she knew would have been the look of horror and disbelief on her mother's face. If Molly had been in denial about her brother's sexuality, her mother had been into even more denial, not only about the possibility of her son having sex with a gypsy fortuneteller, but about his entire illness. She could never accept the fact that her once and future son was never going to be the bright and brilliant poet with a life-time of accolades stretching out in front of him.

In the last few years of Doris Lewin's life, Molly's feelings towards her mother veered between angry frustration when she resisted Molly's attempts to do something—find newer medications, better doctors, more advanced treatments—and the resulting guilt at the never-ending arguments that ensued. The worst battlefield between them became whether or not to hospitalize Ben during those times when he became increasingly psychotic.

Molly slammed Mrs. Mendez's file shut and pushed her hair off her face. Why, after all this time, were those arguments still so vivid in her head? A typical scene: Molly's mother sitting at her old kitchen table with Molly standing near the doorway, trying to explain why she thought Ben needed to go back to the hospital.

"Those hospitals have never done him any good," her mother insisting. "That first one almost killed him!"

"He almost killed you, Ma," Molly answering wearily. "And himself. That's why he had to be admitted."

"When he's in a hospital, he's sick. When he's not in a hospital, he's not sick."

Go argue with that one. But Molly went on trying until the end. During the whole time her mother lay dying, she refused to talk about her son at all.

So many unspoken words hanging between her mother and herself, like dead leaves after an early frost. After Ben's first psychotic break, when a terrified Molly had let the police in and they'd wrestled Ben to the ground, cuffed him and dragged him out, silence descended upon the house. It was a silence that was to last for the nearly nine months of his hospitalization. Her mother took to her bed and stayed there. Her father, a stationery salesman who traveled a lot, stopped coming home altogether. Molly did the shopping, made the beds, took out the garbage and cooked the meals that neither she nor her mother would eat—all to atone for her betrayal and to convince her mother to love her again.

Eventually Molly, too, gave up and spent more and more time by herself, in her room, with her music collection. She took a vow of silence. Words could be like terrifying winds—gales, tornados—in their power to destroy. It just wasn't worth the risk. Unfortunately, this didn't make for many close friendships, or a particularly intimate love life, as Steve had pointed out. But she'd never felt especially lonely. When Ben was out of the hospital and not actively psychotic, she quite enjoyed him. His mind was like an old suit of once-excellent quality that has been patched and re-patched with odd pieces of material that don't quite go together, kind of like a crazy quilt. Even as a child she recognized that there was a wild beast living in him that erupted from time to time, fed by something fierce and terrible that he couldn't control. But she loved him, and he loved her. And as long as he was in her life, she didn't need much more. Or so she had thought.

Molly stared at the form in front of her. Any more paperwork would be impossible this morning. Rising from her chair, she stretched and once again walked into the main reception area. Nilda was on the phone, Stuttman was nowhere to be seen and Swandell was out. Time to check on Willie.

The door to the apartment was open but it was Donald she saw, not Willie. He was standing just outside the yellow *crime scene* tapes with his back to her. His hands were resting on the waist of his elegant leather jacket and he was watching two CSI investigators scraping samples of things off the furniture.

"Mr. Bruchman," Molly said softly, "I'm so sorry about your father. I liked him a lot."

He turned around, his slight body bristling with an anger that seemed to be as central to his internal workings as his perfectly pressed pants, carefully belted jacket and highly polished boots were essential to his surface persona. "If you hadn't deliberately gotten in my way, he would have been in St. Agnes now, where he would have been well-looked after and *alive*."

Molly could think of nothing to say that would penetrate the rage that was consuming him like a flesh-eating virus. And, of course, he could very well be right.

"I blame you and that . . . that *pervert* he was living with. If *he* hadn't been out drinking . . ." The muscle in his jaw was writhing again

"Willie?"

"If it hadn't been for that man . . ."

"Your father wouldn't have left you," Molly finished softly.

"I don't want to talk about it." He pulled a handkerchief out of his pocket and began to rub an invisible—to Molly at least—spot on his boots.

Was it only Willie he blamed? How angry was he at his father for abandoning him? Angry enough to crush his skull? Molly, who prided herself on how well she knew people, had no answer to that. Instead she said, "If you need help with anything . . ."

Donald jerked his head up. "I can take care of everything that needs to be taken care of," he asserted. "My mother and I have already arranged for the funeral which can take place as soon as they release the body."

"Your mother?"

"They were never divorced, you know, and she still considers him her husband." He threw this out as if challenging her to deny it.

Poor Willie, Molly thought. There'll be no place for him in that funeral procession. "Do you know where Willie is?"

Instead of answering, he pressed his lips together and then said in a voice wiped clean of resentment: "Now there's something you can do, Ms. Lewin. That man needs to be out of here so I can close up the apartment. Any help you can offer will be appreciated."

Apparently he had decided not to antagonize her further. "It may take some time," she said, not wanting to unleash his anger again by mentioning her efforts to keep Willie in the apartment.

"The rent is paid up to the end of this month. I'm sure you can find him something else by then."

"Do you know where he is now?"

Donald shrugged, a very eloquent shrug that said very clearly that he didn't know and he couldn't care less. "I'd look in the nearest saloon."

She finally located Willie in Lonnie's Riverside Bar, a local hangout that hadn't yet been gussied up for the newcomers, and wouldn't be, if Lonnie had anything to say about it. Willie was sitting alone in a back booth with the guitar in his hands. A glass half-full of something amber-colored rested on the table in front of him. A Miller High Life sign was slowly rotating from the ceiling behind him.

"Willie?"

There was no recognition in his eyes. He was gone.

By the time Molly returned to the office, about five o'clock, Steve hadn't called to cancel. So she put her jacket back on and took a slow walk to the subway. The clouds were back, the wind had picked up and the temperature had dropped even further. If he stood her up tonight . . . not wanting to think, she turned her attention to the people on the street, many of whom were the newcomers to the neighborhood. Mostly young, they seemed impervious to the cold, striding along in fashionably flimsy coats or short jackets, their cell phones glued to their ears, as if the world outside them was a million miles away. Rootless they appeared to her, almost like urban nomads in the way they migrated from place to place, in search of the next low rent or ultra-hip neighborhood. In comparison to them, she must appear stable—the same apartment for over fifteen years, the same job for eight. At the moment, though, she felt as rootless, as unconnected, as she imagined them to be. Like a tree that's been overturned in a storm. Emotional overload, she diagnosed herself. All systems down.

At Union Square, she changed for the L line which would take her to Third Avenue. Being so preoccupied, she missed the stop and got off at First Avenue instead. No point crossing the platform for a return train, which would involve paying another fare. So she decided to hoof it and walked up First Avenue where she had a sudden flashback of walking up the avenue in the days and weeks following 9/11. Back then, every lamp post and building wall had been plastered with posters of the missing—those who had been inside the World Trade Center on that never-to-be forgotten day. She remembered some of their names and faces so clearly after all this time because she'd passed them at least twice a day for months: *Missing since Sept. 11. Maggie Brian. Last seen on the 98th floor of the South Tower. Her children want her back . . . Missing: Ernesto Vega, since Sept. 11 . . .* The Gallery of the Dead. Once again she remembered frantically trying to reach Steve during that time, especially before learning that he wasn't one of the missing.

The pain of being completely cut off from him had felt like the days after Ben's first hospitalization, after the police had twisted the hammer out of his hand, wrestled him to ground and taken him away. She'd been desperate to see her brother, to reassure herself that he was okay and that her call to the police hadn't caused his death. But no one would say a word to her about where Ben was, and whether or not he was still alive. It was as though he'd been wiped clean off the face of the earth.

Molly turned left onto East 20th Street and walked up to Third Avenue, the westerly wind blowing through her as if she had no more corporal substance than the tattered photos that had hung for so long on those walls.

The pub somehow gave the impression of being smoky even though the smoking ban had been in place in New York City restaurants for some time now. Steve was sitting on a stool at the long wooden bar. His big shoulders were hunched over a half-empty glass of clear, carbonated liquid. He was watching a news program on one of the TV sets. Images of dead soldiers in far away places flickered on the screen. Molly sat down on a stool next to him and he turned. She expected now to see that far-away look—the PTS thousand mile stare. Instead, she saw fury.

"Three more kids blown up," he said, jerking his head up at the TV. "The army sends them out on patrol in vehicles that don't even have armor plate." He breathed deeply for a few minutes, calming himself by force of will. "I gotta get away from that TV set." They walked to the back along dark, wood-paneled walls and found a booth. Only a few people were scattered around the place. Candles in little glass holders on the tables barely produced enough light for them to see each other.

"What'll you have, Molly?" he asked after they'd slid in opposite each other. "White wine still your drink of choice?"

She nodded, pleased that he remembered. "What are you drinking, Steve?" She gestured towards the glass that he'd brought with him. "It doesn't look like beer."

"Yeah, well, it's club soda for me these days."

"That's good, Steve."

"I don't know how good it is . . ."

There was an awkward pause. He was right. They'd never done much of the kind of talk that revealed the hidden hurts, fears, vulnerabilities—and he, the smoother talker, was as guilty as she. Sure he told her stories about his family, but they were nothing more than that—oft-told stories. They'd both backed away from anything deeply meaningful, and now there didn't seem to be anywhere to begin. "So," she said, slipping into the easiest thing for her, which was to ask a question, "how are your kids?"

"My kids?" He cocked his head to one side. "Dee Dee is in college studying marine biology and male physiology." Molly laughed. "It's not funny," he admonished. "It's a good thing she's down in Florida while she's doing it, because otherwise I'd be guarding her door with a shotgun. I know what I was like at that age, and I don't suppose those boys are any different." He took a sip of club soda made a face. "I hate this stuff. Even after all this time, I still crave the good old taste of alcohol."

"Are you in AA?"

"I have been. Not at the moment. "

Still not sure where to go with this, she continued on with his kids. "And Sean?"

His face darkened. "Sean is over there, you know."

"Iraq?"

"Yeah. He enlisted after 9/11 and got sent over when the war started." Steve's blue eyes flickered briefly, like a fire that suddenly flares up and then dies back down into smoldering embers. "He went to Iraq to destroy the weapons of mass destruction and capture Bin Laden," he said darkly. "They sold him the same bill of goods that they sold me when I went to 'Nam, only then we were routing out Communism, and now we're routing out terrorism. But the weapons of mass destruction somehow snuck under the fence and migrated to Iran and North Korea, and Bin Laden is alive and well and living in Saudi Arabia." He lifted his big shoulders and let them drop.

"I'm sorry, Steve." If she reached over and touch his arm, would he stiffen, or push her away? Afraid of the rebuff she sat stiffly on her side of the flickering candle until the waiter appeared with her wine.

"Here I am, talking about me again," he said with a wry grin, after the young man placed the glass on a little cardboard coaster.

"It's okay, Steve." The wine, pale green like the first shoots of grass in the early spring was cold to her tongue.

"No, it's not okay. I accuse you of not confiding in me, and then I don't shut up. " A corner of his mouth turned up. "Now it's your turn.

I'm not saying another word." He clamped his lips together. For a moment neither of them said anything while she fought to keep her mind from going blank again.

"And don't talk opera," he added. They'd spent a lot of time during the period they'd been dating talking about opera, which he had grown up with, his family having owned old 78 rpm records of the greats— Beniamino Giglio, Caruso, Schipa. In the area of Italy where his father came from, whole families used to follow the opera stars the way American's follow sports players. Molly, who loved almost every kind of music except the over-produced sound of the now current pop-scene, found it a neutral and mutually enjoyable topic of conversation. It wasn't going to work now.

Not wanting to raise the subject right then of Steve's own disappearing acts and failures of communication, Molly sipped her wine and cast about wildly for something to say. "It's really hard for me to talk about myself," she ventured. Nothing. He wouldn't open his mouth. Out of desperation she said at last, "You're a skilled interviewer. Why don't you ask me some questions?"

She watched him consider it and make his decision. "Okay. Why did you invite me out for dinner tonight?"

Why? A moment of weakness, immediately regretted after he left. No point in saying that. Nevertheless she was determined for once in her life to speak honestly to a man. So, consciously bypassing her internal censor, she let it all come out: "I'm feeling a bit lonely because I've discovered that my schizophrenic brother who has been the one person I've loved for my entire life and who barely talks to anyone other than me, is having a sexual relationship with a red-haired gypsy who has bazongas as big as watermelons."

He laughed so hard he almost fell off his seat.

"It's true!" she yelped.

"I know it's true," he said when he was able to talk again. "At least I know the part about the schizophrenic brother is true. The gypsy with the bazongas I didn't know about."

"What do you mean" Molly couldn't believe what she was hearing. "You know about Ben?" He nodded. "How could you know?"

"I'm a detective," he shrugged. "I detect."

"Don't give me that bullshit!" Outrage exploded through her like a canon charge. "Tell me! Now!"

"Calm down, Molly," he said, making shushing gestures with his hand. "It's not a state secret."

"Oh, oh, oh, there you are so wrong!" she sputtered. "It was a state secret in my family—I spent my whole life making sure it stayed that way—and you're not leaving here until you tell me how you found out about it."

74

He must have realized she meant it, because he said, "I pulled his sheet."

"You did what?"

Steve had the good grace to look a little embarrassed. "He's in the system, you know. A couple of arrests for disturbing the peace. All those non-voluntary hospitalizations where the police had to be called in."

"You bastard!" she yelled, shooting up from her seat as if she were heading straight through the ceiling. "You spied on me!"

"Come on, Molly," he pleaded. "This is post-9/11 New York City, for god sakes. You think people don't do this all the time? I have a buddy, a retired detective, who makes a good living out of investigating potential partners for women who know nothing more about these men than what they say on the internet."

"I can't believe what I'm hearing!" Heads were turning in their direction but she was beyond caring. Her emotional wiring, already on overload, had ignited and was burning beyond her control.

"It's true," he said, trying to explain. "I'd never met anyone like you before, and I didn't know what to make of you. I still don't. You got under my skin." His face turned bright red, but he plowed on. "That doesn't happen to me very often. But you're like a chameleon. Just when I think I got you pegged, you turn into someone else. You talk about blues and jazz with an encyclopedic knowledge one minute, and the next minute you're talking opera like an Italian. You're all serious one minute, funny as hell the next. You're one of the brainiest women I know, but you play gin rummy like . . ."

"And this gives you the right to invade my privacy and spy on me?"

"I don't like things I can't understand. You were so evasive about yourself that I couldn't help getting suspicious. I can't help thinking like a cop."

"Well, go think like a cop with someone else!" Another thought hit her. "Am I in the system?" The word 'system' sounded like something dredged up from the bottom of a sewer.

Steve shook his head.

"Then how did you know Benjamin Lewin was my brother?"

"I pulled all the Lewins, and looked up the next of kin. I didn't even have to go very far. You popped up under 'B' for Benjamin."

"That easy, huh?" She thrust her arms into her jacket, snatched up her bag and maneuvered herself out of the booth.

"Molly, wait . . ."

"Go to hell, Steve!" Her legs were shaking so much that it took every ounce of strength she had to make it out the door.

Chapter Eleven

Another night of dream fragments. One occurred near morning: *Cal Bruchman, slumped over in an office chair near Nilda's desk, his skull shattered into tiny, bloodless pieces. Molly stands in front of him, facing the office, shielding him with her naked body. Stuttman, leering, runs his hands over her bare breasts. She's paralyzed with shame, unable to move. Somewhere above them, Stuttman's disembodied voice declares, "I'll have to write you up for this."*

Awake now, feeling dirty, disgusting, violated. You don't have to be Sigmund Freud to analyze that dream. Molly burrowed under her quilt, trying to will her mind to go somewhere else. It did—back to the pub and Steve's words: "I pulled his sheet. He's in the system, you know."

Rage again, but this time it came from realizing that the secret she'd given up her life to protect rated no more than a couple of lines on some police report. It was as if she had been given the job of guarding some powerful virus mutation that could potentially destroy the entire city, only to find out it was a strain of the common cold.

No use staying in bed. To calm her nerves, she slipped a CD into the changer and made some coffee. The lovely, lyrical Intermezzo from Mascagni's *Cavalleria Rusticana* soared through the speakers, evoking lush Sicilian hillsides covered with fragrant vineyards on a sun drenched summer day. It was just the accompaniment by which to erase several un-heard messages that had come in from Steve after she'd gotten home last night.

She'd never been to Sicily, had no idea whether the hillsides were indeed lush or covered with vineyards, and in the opera, the Intermezzo comes as the calm before the storm, the lull before murder and terrible tragedy unfold.

Molly stood in the shower for a long time trying to wash away the bits of dream and operatic tragedy that still lurked around the corners of her memory. After toweling herself vigorously, she pulled on a shapeless black turtleneck sweater and loose khaki pants, surveyed herself critically in the bathroom mirror, and added a silver pendant and some matching earrings bought on a trip to Mexico many years ago. Accessorize, even if you look and feel like hell.

Late again. She opened the office door to hear Nilda's eager voice:

"So, you two are back together?"

"What are you talking about?"

"Oh, Molly, come on, you don't have to play coy with me. Steve Carmaggio has called you three times already since the office opened."

"He's working on Cal Bruchman's murder, as you know." Molly said in her calmest voice. "He probably thinks I have some vital piece of evidence that he needs."

"No way." Nilda shook her head. "He didn't sound like he was working on anything, except trying to talk to you."

Oh god! Why can't he just leave me alone?

Nilda sighed and said in a thick Spanish accent, "Okay, don' tell me. I'm just the little Puerto Rican receptionist . . . ."

At that moment the phone buzzed. Nilda switched to her natural voice. "Multi-Care. How can I help you?" She listened, then grinned and flashed her eyes at Molly. "Ms. Lewin is right here, sir. I'll connect you."

"I'll take it in my office." Damn Nilda! She's enjoying this. "Tell him to hold on."

I just won't pick it up. He can hold on all day for all I care. But she knew he wouldn't let it go, so it might as well be now.

"Hey, Molly, I'm really sorry about last night."

"What are you sorry about? That you *told* me you spied on me? How about the *fact* that you did it? Are you sorry about that? Do you know how that feels? Just like being raped."

"Molly, let me try to explain. I was just coming off the booze, and feeling very paranoid—even more paranoid than I usually feel. I couldn't get you out of my mind, so I started to, sort of, find out things about you. You were like a puzzle that I had to solve."

"Why didn't you ever call and ask me? You could have found out all about me first hand."

"I doubt it, but that's beside the point. The truth is I wasn't in any shape to be in a relationship. Not for a long time, and by then it seemed too late. What else can I say?"

"Nothing, Steve" As usual, Something about the sadness in his voice caused her own anger to dissapate. "There's nothing else you can say."

"Look, Molly, let me make it up to you. At least let me buy you the dinner I never got to buy you last night."

He'd walked out of her life without a word and then spied on her, she reminded herself. He was paranoid, a barely-dry drunk.

"So what about it?"

"I don't know . . ."

"C'mon. The worst that can happen is that I'll get you so angry again that you'll throw something at me. That's a hell of a lot more entertaining than eating alone."

"You know, it's going to take me a long time to trust you again."

"Is that a yes?"

"I guess so."

Click. Damn! Why can't I stay angry at him?

Her mother came vividly to mind as Molly had seen her during one of their last visits—was it three years already? It was just before the pancreatic cancer that Doris Lewin never had diagnosed put her in the hospital and eventually killed her. Molly had walked in angry, ready to do battle because her mother would not discuss hospitalizing Ben, or changing his medication, or whatever. Her mother was sitting in the dimly lit kitchen in that run-down apartment in Sheepshead Bay where time had stopped for her after Ben had had his rampage with the hammer. A game of solitaire was laid out on the table and she was bent over it.

Molly could still see the hopeless misery in the heavy, downward curve of her mother's neck and head, the despairing slump of her shoulders as she sat over her game. It dissolved Molly's anger, making her want to cry instead. Picturing it now, Molly realized she'd never been able to sustain anger in the face of such desolation and grief.

Sighing, she turned to her notes from the past couple of days and realized she'd promised Mrs. Canover to take her to lunch at the senior center. Molly picked up the phone.

Of course Mrs. Canover, who was, apparently, the only person in the neighborhood who hadn't heard about Cal Bruchman's murder, had more excuses than a centipede has legs: "I didn't sleep well. My back is hurting. I have to wash my hair."

Mrs. Canover would never agree without a little push, so Molly said firmly, "I'll come by at eleven-fifteen, and we can decide then." She'd justify it to Stuttman by claiming to be taking an early lunch.

On the dot of eleven-fifteen, Molly was climbing the steps to Mrs. Canover's apartment. The building, on Warwick Avenue, was a few doors away from the one in which Cal Bruchman had lived and died, and was in a similar state of disrepair. The lovely Italianate façade had long cracks running down it, the hallway looked as though it hadn't been painted in twenty years and the stairs squeaked like frightened mice.

Mrs. Canover answered the door in her housedress, her filmy blue eyes full of anxiety. "I don't think . . ." she said before Molly even entered the apartment.

"Today is Thursday," Molly said brightly, plopping down on a overstuffed chair in the living room, "and I know that the center serves chicken, one of their best meals." The room was exactly the same as it had been during those last months just before Herman died and she'd been visiting on a regular basis. Antimacassars lined the backs of each chair and sofa. The surfaces of the heavy dark-wood furniture were covered with crocheted doilies on which stood lamps and china shepherdesses and a few photos in frames. One picture, a black and white posed portrait of a girl who resembled Margery Canover herself, stood on its own doily on top of the buffet. Mrs. Canover's only daughter Polly had died in an automobile crash ten years ago.

And the same beautiful oil paintings still covered the walls. Bouquets of flowers and bowls of fruits, so real and alive you could almost smell the aroma emanating from the peonies and roses, or taste the succulent juices that would spurt out of the peaches or the grapes should you be able to pluck one out and take a bite. Herman painted them, Mrs. Canover had said proudly. Herman himself, in the midst of his slow, painful dying, would smile shyly when Molly would praise them, his eyes lighting up for a brief moment before the pain and the medication would take him away again.

Mrs. Canover reluctantly sat down on the couch across from her. "I don't know . . ." she began hesitantly.

"I'll go with you," Molly said reassuringly, "and if you don't like it, I'll take you right home."

Mrs. Canover made no further protests, but didn't look happy. She allowed Molly to help her up and together they went into the bedroom to pick out a suitable dress. The bedroom was another paean to Herman's memory. One devil-may-care photograph of him in a military uniform stood on the walnut dresser; a few others in which he looked older and somehow sadder, sat on the night tables and on the big wardrobe. His pajamas were carefully laid out on one side of the bed; his slippers on the floor. When Mrs. Canover opened the closet, Molly could see that more than half of it was full of his suits, shirts and shoes. His urn stood in its own ceremonial spot—the top of the small TV that faced the bed.

"He hasn't passed over yet, poor soul," Mrs. Canover said sadly. "Last night he gave me so many signs and signals of his distress." She looked around the room and said, "I want him to know, dear, that until he's ready to pass over, he'll always have his home."

Everything of Herman's was kept perfectly preserved, perhaps to stave off Mrs. Canover's absolute loneliness once it was all gone. What will happen to her if Belloc and Skanov are successful in forcing her out of the home that she and Herman shared? Molly couldn't bear even to contemplate it. In the meantime it was necessary to help Mrs. Canover make the transition to life without her husband.

By the time they got to the senior center it was already twelve-thirty, way past the time the members lined up for lunch. But Alice Manning was true to her word—Molly had given her a call just after speaking to Mrs. Canover that morning—and had saved her a seat at the choice table.

David Sheunfeldt greeted his friend and neighbor, gallantly helped her negotiate the steam table and got her settled with her tray. But David's eyes were troubled, and he soon left Mrs. Canover to Alice Manning's ministrations and pulled Molly aside.

"I heard what happened to that poor man in 419. You found him, no?"

Molly nodded, in no mood to talk about it anymore, but sensitive to the fact that the center members would want to. It was better they get accurate information from her than rely on the vagaries of gossip.

"It must have been terrible for you, my dear lady," Dave shook his head sadly. "I didn't know him, except I saw him in his wheelchair when the Medivan came to pick him up or drop him off. Was it a burglary?"

"The police are investigating."

"You mean they don't think it's a burglary." His lips narrowed. "It was Belloc or that Gestapo goon he employs. So he's emptying apartments now by murdering people."

"Nobody knows how it happened yet."

"And to add insult to injury, Loraine Brenner had a heart attack last night."

"Loraine Brenner? I don't think I know her."

"She lived upstairs from me, a great friend of my dear wife Goldie, may she rest in peace."

"What happened?"

"Her daughter called me from Nevada. She couldn't reach her mother and was worried. I have the key, so she asked me to go in and check up on her. I did so, and what I found . . ." He closed his eyes briefly, as if to blot out the terrible sight. His lids were intercrossed with tiny blue veins, like miniature rivers. "The poor woman was on the floor. Her breathing sounded like the old elevator in the train station on Atlantic Avenue. I dialed 911 but she died before they came." Two tears started down his face.

Molly took his hands. They were as cold and dry as a branch on an old tree. "I'm so sorry, Dave. It was just as terrible for you to find her like that as it was for me."

"It's that Gestapo thug again. The people they can't get to move, he's frightening to death. He killed her as sure as if he stuck a knife into her breast." Dave gave Molly's hand a squeeze and took a handkerchief from his pocket.

"How do you know it was him?"

"He was in the building last night. I saw him when I was downstairs with the ambulance. Of course, right after that, he left. But it will start up again—the knocking, the banging, he even has a radio in the hallway with that bass thing turned up so loud your head could explode which he plays for most of the night." Dave wiped his eyes with a handkerchief. "I'm an old man. How much time do I have left? Why can't he let me die here in peace with my friends around me?" His mouth was trembling and new tears were forming.

"My Goldie, may she rest in peace, I met her after the war ended. She came here from the camps, you know. She had the number tattooed right here." He tapped the inside of his wrist with two fingers. "She never talked about it, but those camps never left her. She always kept a suitcase packed in the closet, in case she had to leave in the middle of the night. I used to say to her, 'We're in America, Goldie. Why do you need this?' But she would never let me unpack it. Over fifty years we were married. On the day she died it was still in the closet, packed and ready to go." He wiped his eyes again. "She knew, my Goldie. May she forgive me for doubting her."

Married fifty years, Molly thought. Her own parents barely lasted twenty, and it didn't look as though it would ever happen for her at all, especially if she kept picking the wrong men. She sighed, bringing her attention back to the present. "Dave, I don't know if it will help, but I will tell the police about it."

He took her hands again and said with a trembling voice, "Anything you can do, my dear lady."

Chapter Twelve

Margery Canover agreed to stay if Dave would walk her home, so Molly went back to her office, determined to make a dent in the endless paperwork by completing travel vouchers, monthly statistics and other such things. But her brain still refused to concentrate. So, yet again, she went into the reception area to talk to Nilda.

"I didn't see you come in, Molly. Louis Kroski is in the staff room, asking for you. I told him you'd be back soon." Nilda grinned. "I read your horoscope for today, Molly. It said you will be irresistible to men. First this Steve, now Louis . . ."

Molly shook her head. "Get real."

"Horoscopes never lie," Nilda declared. "Besides, he likes you. I can tell."

"I don't know where you come up with these things, Nilda."

The phone buzzed. Nilda smiled knowingly and plugged in.

Molly made her way around the cluster of desks and partitions to the staff room. Louis was sitting on a green plastic chair, reading a magazine which he folded it up and stuck in his carryall when she entered and sat down. "Hi, Louis," Molly said. "You wanted to see me?"

"How're you doing?" He was wearing a blue plaid flannel work shirt over a pair of khaki chinos.

"Well, aside from a few bad dreams, I guess I'm doing okay." That was true, Molly realized. Since this morning, she'd managed to push the terrible scene of Cal's murder into some mental back room.

"I was up visiting Willie this morning, to see if he needed anything." Louis ran a meaty hand through his close-cropped hair. "Saw Belloc in the building with a suit-and-tie man, but not too expensive, kind of better-brand, off-the-rack."

"What are you trying to tell me?"

"This guy—well he might as well have been wearing a sign— was from one of those City agencies like HPD or something like that. "

"You can't know that."

"How much do you want to bet?" He ticked it off on his fingers. "He wasn't dressed smart enough to be one of Skanov's mob; he wasn't high-level, like a Deputy Mayor; he wasn't dressed like a contractor who Belloc might have suddenly hired out of the goodness of his heart to make repairs on the building."

"Okay, okay."

"He and Belloc were smiling and shaking hands." Louis made a face. "If ever I saw two wanna-be deal makers in action that was them."

This time it was Molly who frowned. "You mean . . ."

"Yeah, that's exactly what I mean. I don't know precisely how it works, but it happened to a friend of mine. The landlord wanted the tenants out, but they were gonna fight it. Next thing you know, the City comes in like some god dammed hit man and condemns the building. Just like that. The rest of the tenants make whatever deals they can and get out. But my friend still thinks he can fight it—he's one of those guys who believes he's a lot smarter than he is—and he's digging his way through reams of rules and regulations—gonna be his own lawyer, you know that kind of idiot. Well, he hasn't even gotten to page eight hundred and sixty or something like that, when the Marshall is banging on the door and he finds himself and all his belongings out on the street."

"Yeah, I saw it happen to an ex-client over on Rotterdam Avenue." Molly could still feel the anger in the pit of her stomach when she thought about it. "You know those buildings they demolished for that Sports Stadium that they still haven't built." Running her fingers through her hair, she considered what Louis had just said. "Condemning a building like that is usually a last-resort kind of thing; the City doesn't like to be perceived as the heavy, driving poor, old people out of their homes into the night."

"But if someone is offering some underpaid city employee enough money . . ."

"Like Skana, you mean."

"Well, he's certainly got the bucks." Louis shrugged contemptuously. "Belloc is probably just doing his dirty work."

"I'll ask Howie Markowitz about it." Howie was a well-connected lawyer who Molly had gotten to know through his father, who had Alzheimer's disease. She'd found an excellent aide to care for the elder Mr. Markowitz, and when that was no longer enough, she'd helped to get him into one of the better nursing homes. Out of gratitude for all this, Howie occasionally took on a case for one of her clients, pro bono. He was the lawyer she was hoping would represent Willie, should Belloc actually try to evict him. "Howie might know some scuttlebutt."

"I'm worried about Willie." Louis rubbed his lower lip with a thick finger.

"Belloc was talking like he's willing to give Willie some moving money." Molly glanced at the coffee pot. What was left in the carafe looked like dark-brown swill. "Maybe Howie can get him to actually come through and put something down on paper."

"Willie's dug in his heels." The tone of Louis's voice echoed the look of concern on his face. "He says he won't leave, they'll have to take him out feet first. And Donald wants him out now. It's real personal with him. And he can make life pretty miserable for Willie."

"If he tries anything, I'll talk to the police about it. That's about all I can do. Willie is not a client of the agency, as Stuttman never ceases to remind me. I'm already overstepping by going this far."

"There's something else." He folded his hands and dropped his eyes to his lap. For a moment he looked exactly like little boy who knows he's done something bad and doesn't know whether or not to 'fess up.

"What?" When he didn't say anything, she added in a mock-stern voice, "You'd better tell me."

"Well, it's gotten a little, uh, sticky."

"What happened?"

"Let's just say, it became a little physical between Donald and me." He raised his eyes. There was a hint of a smile in them.

"Louis! For God's sakes!"

"Actually, he swung first. I know how to fight and he doesn't, so I blocked him pretty good. I didn't hit him and I didn't hurt him . . . well, maybe just a little." The smile transferred itself to his mouth, and he immediately wiped it off his face. "Thing is, he's threatening to sue the agency."

"You're going to have to tell Mr. Stuttman about this."

He nodded, contrite. "I know. I'm only bringing you into the picture because I don't want Donald hurting Willie because of my actions."

"What were you even doing there? Once Cal Bruchman was dead, you should never have been in that apartment. Especially with Donald just looking to make trouble."

"I read the rules and regulations. But, you know, you work in somebody's home for three years . . ." Louis shrugged and in that gesture Molly saw all the feeling in the man that went beyond words and job responsibilities. "I became, like, very fond of Willie. He's got no one now but that junkie great-grandson of his who's less than useless—when he's not making music, that is."

Louis got up. "I'd better go see Mr. Stuttman and then I've gotta go find myself somewhere else to work."

After he left the staff room, Molly sat for another minute trying to put her mind in order. Useless. Anxiety about Willie and what Donald might do to him in retaliation wouldn't go away. She went back to her cubicle, grabbed a form from the drawer and left the office. If Stuttman says anything, I'll tell him I'm doing an assessment on Willie to see if he needs any services.

Instead of going straight into Willie's building, though, Molly crossed the street and stood for a while looking at the water. The wind was whipping the pewtery surface of the river into tiny wavelets. Life at the moment felt choppy, with barely understood undercurrents pushing her along. It was a strange feeling for a person who was as resistant to change as she was. Shoving her hands deeper into her pockets, she turned around and crossed the street again.

The apartment door was open, the crime scene tape gone. Donald was nowhere in sight. Willie was sitting on a chair in the living room, guitar in his hands, singing the blues.

Oh, lord, lord
Devil creeps round my door
Makes me love you baby
Know its wrong for sure
Oh sweet loving' man
You got 'a hold of my soul
When I'm with you baby,
Jes' want more o' your jelly roll.

The river light coming in from the window behind Willie bathed him and the photos that hung on the wall with a silvery sheen, like a film of tears. As he sang the words to the song, the fingers of his left hand pressed the strings into the neck and then rolled them around so that each note was twisted and squeezed into a gut-wrenching sound that almost broke her heart.

Molly cleared her throat. Willie looked up with an expression that Molly, after all her years working in the field, still found hard to reconcile with being old. No man had ever felt that way about her, not even Steve. How could they? You have to get into each others' hearts in order for that kind of relationship to develop, and who had she ever let in besides Ben?

She smiled shyly and said, "Good morning."

After a moment, he nodded. "Mornin', Miz Molly."

"Louis tells me that you and Donald were at it again."

He shook his head back and forth. "Weren't me who Donald swung at. I told that little piss ass he'd have to take me out feet first, and that's what he'll have to do. Ain't nothin' more to say."

She pulled a chair close to him and sat down to be at eye level. "Why is Donald so down on you, Willie?" She knew the answer already, but also knew that Willie needed to talk about it. "It's something else with him, something more than just wanting to deliver an empty apartment to Belloc, isn't it."

Indecision was all over his face: to tell or not to tell. But, as Molly surmised, it was important that he have another person understand him and his life. She gave him an encouraging smile and said, "Tell me, Willie."

Willie sighed once and said, "He always blamed me for taking his daddy away from him and his mama." His eyes darted to her face to see how she was taking this. "Cal was still living with his family when we met. It weren't long after my son was born, that's Bukka's grandpa, that I found out what I was and knew I couldn't change it, but Cal was still goin' this way and that 'bout it. I wasn't his first, and I wasn't his last, neither."

For a moment his eyes watered. Straightening his back as he must have done many times in his life, he continued: "Lookin' the way he did, and being that much younger 'n me, I guess I couldn't blame him none. And he always came back to me." Once again his hands caressed the guitar as if it was his long-time lover, as he must have caressed Cal. A pang of loneliness hit Molly so hard, she felt as though the wind rattling the windows was blowing right through her.

"But anyway," Willie went on, "'til I came along, he never quite made the break, you understand what I'm sayin'?"

Molly nodded, becoming once more the fly on the wall.

"It wasn't like it is now. Nowadays, as long as you stay away from them Catholics and them Baptists and them Born-Agains, most folks look the other way. But back then . . ." His face grew stormy, and Molly could only imagine what must have happened to him. "Specially for a black man. That's why I came up North."

"So Donald thinks he has a score to settle."

"Cal always felt bad about leavin' them like that. Tried to send 'em some money when he had it. But Donald's mama 'ud always send it back. She'd never accept anything that 'issued forth from perversion,' is what she'd say. Must've been some kinda Baptist herself. Or maybe one of those white religions like Lutheran. Don't think she was a Born-Again. But anyway, that's probably why Donald thought Cal didn't want him no more."

Willie's hands, resting on the strings, picked out a series of minor chords, slow and keening, like the bells that ring for men lost at sea. He began to sing: "There's a man goin' 'round takin' names. He took my mama's name . . ." Stopping, he added softly, "and Gully's and Smokehouse Brown, and Pete Johnson and Charley Patton and just about every one else I ever knowed and loved. Thought he'd be takin' mine way before he ever got to Cal."

"I'm sorry, Willie."

"I should'a been there that night, instead of out drinkin'." He wiped the tears from his eyes with a dirty handkerchief he'd pulled out of his shirt pocket. "Maybe I could have protected him."

"Willie," she said firmly. "You couldn't be here all the time. You needed to have some time away; all caregivers do."

Willie's fingers continued to run through a series of minor chord progressions. What is it about minor chords? Molly thought. They're only a half an interval lower than major chords, yet a major chord is a marching band and a minor chord is a funeral dirge.

"I never minded taking care of him. When you . . ." Willie's face got darker than it already was.

"When you love someone." Molly said it for him.

He nodded. "When you feel that way, you wanna do it. Can't think 'bout nothin' else anyways. That's why I should'a been there."

"If you couldn't have gotten away for a little bit," Molly argued, "you might have gotten sick yourself. Then what good would you have been to him?"

"I know, Ms. Molly," Willie sighed. "That's what Louis tells me. But my mama always tol' me that drink don't do nothing but bring a man to a bad end."

"You feel guilty about having been out drinking?"

He didn't respond directly. Resting his hands lightly on the guitar, he said: "My mama now, she was a god-fearin' woman. Was always goin' to church. Used to take me along, too." Slowly, his hands began to stroke the guitar, as if he was pulling the strands of his memories out of it, one by one. "She always used to warn me offa white women. 'Jest you listen to me,' she'd say. 'Ain't nothin' worth nothin' in no white woman.' I'd be maybe eight, nine years ol—she died when I was ten." His voice rose in timbre as he mimicked her. "'They know how to paint their faces and wear fancy clothes, but not one of them knows how to wash and iron the clothes that's on their back, and that is the living truth. Who you think been doin' it for them all their natural lives?'" He stopped. "Beggin' your pardon, Miz Molly, that's my mama speakin, not me." Then he grinned slyly. "Never warned me off no white *men*, though. Maybe best if she had."

Molly grinned back at him.

The door opened and Bukka came into the room wearing the same satin tee shirt and baggy pants he was wearing the first time Molly met him. He dropped a paper bag on the table and took out a couple of beers, offering one to Willie who propped the guitar against the wall behind him and took it. Bukka popped open the other one.

"Hi, Bukka," she said.

His eyes came back from someplace deep inside his head and he gave her a slow smile. He'd taken a recent hit. Willie was looking at him with that same hungry love she'd seen before, but this time it was tinged with something else—anxiety? anger? So many kinds of love, Molly thought, and only one word for it all.

Bukka stared at the beer in his hand as if he couldn't remember

87

what it was and said, "Gonna take me a little nap," then disappeared into the bedroom, closing the door behind him.

"Willie, I don't know exactly how to say this, but . . ."

"Yeah, I know, Ms. Molly." He popped the top and took a long swallow. "I got eyes in my head. Don't want to be thinking that all that music I gave him sits in a bucket with so many holes. But what am I gonna do? Besides, he's all that I got left."

"I know how it is to love someone with so many broken pieces," Molly said softly.

Willie looked at her in surprise, so rarely did she offer any personal information about herself, even when asked

Aware that a line was crossed that shouldn't have been, she changed the subject. "I know a lawyer named Howie Markowitz who owes me a favor." No need to mention her conversation with Louis for now because at this point it was pure speculation. "I'm going to put in a call to him. He'll advise you about your rights to this apartment."

"Don't want no lawyer," he grumbled.

"Willie, listen to me. Information is power. Howie works for a big law firm, Stiegel, Lowe, Myers and Donleavy, but he won't charge you anything."

"They think the more names they got, folks will think they're somethin' worth somethin'. But they be wrong. The more names they got, the more people they got to hide behind."

"You need someone on your side. Just talk to him, and let him help you."

Willie frowned. "We'll see. But I 'preciate it."

"Do you need anything else?"

"Louis brought me some food and some other stuff when he came by. He's a good boy."

"Yes he is," Molly agreed wholeheartedly. "Willie, has the detective investigating Cal's murder spoken to you yet?"

"Some policeman been by to talk to me." Steve? "Told him 'bout Donald, but . . ." He shrugged. "Ain't much he can do, less he finds out Donald did it. And as much as I don't like the little bastard, I hope for Cal's sake 't weren't him."

"If it wasn't Donald, then who was it?"

"That is the question for sure, Miz Molly." He picked up the guitar again and started a rhythmic chord pattern running up and down the frets. It sounded like short bursts of machine gun fire. "You find out, you come and tell me."

Chapter Thirteen

The Japanese restaurant on Lexington Avenue where Molly and Steve met was called Honshu. After work she'd gone home to change, selecting a crimson-red sweater—to reflect the color of the anger that she should have been feeling—and a pair of dove-gray slacks more in tune with the sad, muted quality of her actual feelings.

Steve, too, had changed out of his usual working clothes and was wearing a dark green cable-knit sweater over an off-white shirt and black slacks which looked particularly good on him. He helped her off with her jacket, hung it up and then gave the hostess his name, so Molly knew he had gone to the trouble to make a reservation.

"So how's it going, Molly?" he asked after they had been seated and given their menus.

"Not too good."

He waited with questioning eyes, but she didn't say anything further. "So tell me," he said at last, "did you know that Honshu is the largest of the Japanese islands?"

"No, I didn't know that."

Molly buried her head in the menu and stared unseeingly at the selections until his voice broke through: "Eventually the waiter is going to come and take the menu away. Then what? Shall I buy you a newspaper?"

She looked up. "You could have asked me what was wrong, or why I'm not feeling too great."

"I guess I know what's wrong. I just don't want to go into it all again because what else can I say about it?" A deep sigh. "I apologized, isn't that enough?"

The waiter came over and they both ordered the regular sushi and green tea.

"Are you going to make me jump through hoops?" he asked with a tinge of annoyance after the waiter left.

"Look, I'm not angry anymore. I wish I were. And I certainly don't want to make you do anything you don't want to do." It was his turn to say nothing, and after a moment she asked, "Shall we just cancel the order and leave?"

On the far wall was a traditional pen and ink drawing of a Samurai warrior, sword in hand. He studied it for a while and then sighed.

89

"I'll try to explain this one more time," he said wearily. "After that, it's up to you. If you still want to leave . . ." He glanced again at the warrior and plunged in. "As I said, 9/11 hit me really hard and I went a little . . . well, it brought up the whole 'Nam thing again, big time. I couldn't sleep. I was having flashbacks day and night. And I started drinking more and more just to numb it all out." Two red spots appeared on his cheeks. "I didn't call you at first because I didn't want to subject you to any of it."

"Okay." It surprised her to see how embarrassed he was. "But I still don't understand what made you spy on me?"

"I told you why. I couldn't figure you out. And I didn't spy on you, as you call it, until way later, when I was trying to get my life back together and deciding whether or not to call you again." The waiter brought over two delicately shaped cups of tea. Steve took a sip and made a face. "I've been sober for well over a year and still crave alcohol almost as much as I did on the day I stopped drinking."

"It still doesn't explain why you did it."

"I don't know how to explain it exactly, but it has to do with trust."

"Are you saying you don't trust me?" Anger surged up again. "I may not have told you the whole story, but I never lied."

Steve took another sip of tea sip and closed his eyes.

"Look, Molly. You gotta understand something about cops." His eyes opened, but once again he could have been miles away. "I started out right after the Academy as a uniform working the Seven-Five in Brownsville. Now, you work that area as a white cop, you're completely alone, in hostile territory. You're a white target in a black world. And if you get into any trouble, there is nobody who is gonna lift one finger to help you. So you gotta have a partner you have absolute trust in to watch your back, or you're not going to survive.

"My first partner back in the Seven-Five was a guy named Pete Lenniger. A real stand-up guy and the kind of partner you could trust with your life. As a matter of fact, he saved my bacon plenty of times. His wife, Rhoda, pestered him into taking a job with the Port Authority Police because she didn't want him working the streets. But we stayed good friends." He stopped and rubbed his temple. "I don't want to talk about this."

"I know you don't, Steve," she said. "But I want to understand."

Wiping all the expression from his voice, he went on: "The Port Authority cops were first responders when the Trade Center was hit and a lot of them died when the buildings collapsed. A week or so later I went down with Rhoda Lenniger to identify Pete's remains. Not that there was much to identify." There was a small hiss, almost a gasp, as the breath moved in and out of his chest. "They showed us a charred hand with a ring on one of his fingers. It was Pete's hand wearing Pete's ring."

In his eyes was an agony so intense that tears sprang up in her own eyes.

She clasped his hand, wishing she could simply reach across the table and take him in her arms. "I'm so sorry, Steve."

"I took it real hard, Molly. I started having these dreams again, like the ones I had when I first came back from 'Nam. Or perhaps they were memories. It's hard to tell sometimes. But they were so real." The dreams—or were they memories—flooded into his eyes the way a river will suddenly overrun its banks. "I'm back in 'Nam," he said softly, "walking through a village after we've bombed the shit out of it. It's dead silent. Even the birds are gone. Burnt up. We come to a charred field, and it's lined with the blackened skeletons of trees. And hanging from the branches are body parts—arms, legs, skulls—just hanging there like some kind of bizarre fruit."

The life behind his eyes disappeared again; she might as well have been sitting there by herself. An image of a small, stunted creature, neglected and alone in this field of death, suddenly came up from somewhere deep down inside of her. She blinked a few times, but the image wouldn't go away.

"You are such a goddamned good listener, Molly," she heard him saying, "and that's the problem." The grief had made his voice husky. "I didn't come here to tell you all that. What I wanted to tell you is that after identifying Pete's body I fell apart. Like I said, I started drinking till I passed out, so that I wouldn't have those dreams or flashbacks, or whatever the hell they were. The Department gave me a choice—go into rehab and counseling or leave." He shrugged. "Well, here I am so you know what choice I made, though god only knows why. It is much harder than dying would have been."

He stopped and took another sip of his tea. Molly stayed silent. She was shaken, thrown off balance, as much by the image she'd just had of herself as by his story.

"I thought about you, Molly, I really did. But I was in real bad shape. I needed a good person watching my back. But I didn't know if you were that person."

"What do you mean?" she asked, fighting to keep her voice steady.

"Even after I found out about your brother, I still didn't know who the hell *you* were, so how could I know whether or not you were that person? You don't talk." He shifted sideways in the narrow booth to give his long legs more room to stretch out. "About yourself, that is. You're a great conversationalist about mostly everything else."

What words could ever describe the image she'd just experienced?

"You know how many people have crazy mothers or alcoholic brothers—take my sister, Connie, for example. She and my mother went to ALANON, and she'll tell anyone who'll listen what a time my family had with me. And with you being a social worker and all." He added wryly, "I can't say as I fully get you now. But I'm in somewhat better shape myself—not that I'm perfect, you understand. I still get angry way too fast, and I don't think the flashbacks and dreams will ever go away, but I don't have them as often. And I'd like to see how things go with us." A corner of his mouth turned up. "As I said, I really like the way you play gin rummy and all. But it's your call."

The waiter arrived with their sushi. Molly looked at the raw fish with repulsion and pushed the platter away. "Steve, I don't know how to do what you want me to do. It's true, I don't talk about me; it all lives in my head and in my feelings, but not on my tongue. I can tell you that when I was ten years old, Ben went after my mother with a hammer and I called 911."

The memory flooded up with a rush which almost knocked her backwards. "There's nothing else I can say about it. In many ways you're much better at talking about this stuff than I am. I didn't see my brother again for long, long time. My mother became depressed. My father left." Her shoulders rose and dropped. "End of story. Ask me to tell you more, and the words just disappear."

Suddenly that lop-sided grin split his face. "That's like the perp who finally confesses, 'I shot her, okay?' and when you ask him why, he says, 'because I had a gun in my hand, that's why."

She had to laugh at that. "Really, Steve, it's the best I can do at the moment."

"I should introduce you to my sister, Connie. She'll teach you. She's read every self-help book on the market, watches all the talk shows like Dr. Phil and Oprah. She can talk you upside down about any problem, tell you exactly why anyone does anything. A kid goes after his mother with a hammer? Hey, it's his inner child acting out."

"This is different," she said, hurt by his tone. "Ben has schizophrenia."

"I know it's different, Molly. I don't mean to make light of it." Steve poured soy sauce from a little green pitcher into the tiny dish and added a dollop of wasabi. "But you're a social worker *and a* woman. Don't you come with hard wiring that makes you want to talk about everything?"

Molly studied the green wasabi swirling through the darkness of the soy sauce. Very much like her feelings—struggling to break through their dark and bitter-salt world. "It's not that I want to keep anything from you." Trying to find the words to explain it to him, but they just wouldn't come. "I guess we're both damaged, Steve."

Again, the lop-sided grin. "Well, I'm glad we've got that settled." Deftly, he picked up a piece of sushi with his chopsticks. His hand

92

hesitated in mid-air. Dropping the sushi and chopsticks back onto the plate, he covered her hand with his own. "Please, Molly," he said gently. "Try. Give me credit for *some* understanding."

It was the touch of his fingers on hers—the sheer physical bulk of them—that allowed her feelings to evolve into words. Taking a deep breath, she said: "My mother was, well, *she* couldn't talk about anything, either. Especially anything about my brother. She'd fly into rages if I even referred to it. So I shut up."

Steve nodded. "I know about rages, that's for sure."

"It wasn't until much later that I learned silence was the only way I could avoid her wrath and keep both of us safe. She was so full of grief that sometimes I thought she'd explode." Molly looked up, met Steve's eyes and realized how well he really did understand. "It's a hard habit to break, silence."

"I know about that, too," he said. "It took me I can't you how long until I could talk about that goddamned war and what happened to me over there. I remember that first group session at the rehab center." He stopped suddenly. "I'm doing it again."

She smiled. "It's okay, Steve. This talking stuff is going to take me some time, and I'm out of words for now." His hand was still covering hers. Under her sweater, her nipples hardened as she remembered those large, strong fingers stroking them the last time they'd made love.

No. It had been enough of a rollercoaster ride for one evening. She wasn't ready for that one. Changing the subject, she said: "I know I'm not supposed to ask, but have you made an arrest?"

"Not yet." He withdrew his hand, dipped the piece of sushi into the sauce and ate it. "Although I am liking Donald for it. He doesn't have much of an alibi, and he sure did hate his father. Problem is, forensics hasn't come up with anything that definitely puts him there at the time of the murder, and no witnesses have come forth to say they saw him."

"Well, I have a witness who puts Donald on Warwick Avenue in a building right near the one Willie and Cal lived in on the night Cal was murdered." Steve's eyes lit up. She went on, happy to be able to give him something useful. "According to Dave Scheunfeldt who, as I told you, lives in a building a few doors down from Willie, Donald was there banging and making all kinds of noise in an effort to intimidate the elderly tenants into moving out. Only, one of them had a heart attack and died." She frowned, more angry than sad. "Maybe Donald took a break, walked over and killed his father." Although it was really Willie he hated, not his father. Or so he says.

Steve made a note in the little book that he always seemed to carry, and Molly continued: "Even if he didn't kill his father, can't you indict somebody on reckless disregard for human life, or an action that causes someone else's death, or something like that?"

"It would be a hard case for the D.A. to make, especially if Donald has a good lawyer, but we might be able use it as leverage, maybe to get him to implicate Belloc in the scheme If nothing else, perhaps I can put the fear of god into Donald and get him to stop harassing those poor people."

"I'd love to see that, but I'm really worried about Willie. Donald is trying to get him out, and he's refusing to leave the apartment, and I'm afraid Donald will hurt him." She picked up the chop sticks again, this time managing to actually to pick up a piece of sushi, but soon put it down, unable to actually put it into her mouth. "Willie is such a frail old man, really. He has no place else to go that he can possibly afford. Why can't Donald just leave him alone?"

Steve didn't even bother to respond to that question with words, but he smiled at her. "You really care, Molly. I like that. Sometimes I feel so jaded and cynical about everything that I wonder what ever happened to that part of me. But I promise you I'll have a talk with Donald." Glancing at her plate he said, "You didn't eat anything."

"I'm not hungry at the moment."

"Are you sure? It's good stuff."

Molly shook her head back and forth. "Not tonight."

"You don't eat any better now than you used to."

"I remember you were always telling me to 'eat, eat.'" She smiled at the memory. "You must have had a mother who said that to you."

"She said that to everyone else." He grinned his lop-sided grin. "Getting *me* to eat was never much of a problem." Steve signaled for the check and waited while the waiter packed up the sushi. "Let's get out of here."

Outside on the street, he turned towards her with a questioning look. "So, what now?"

He was just waiting for her to ask him home and into her bed. In the restaurant, Molly had been certain that she wasn't ready to make love with him yet. But the understanding he had conveyed was like a magnet that drew her closer to him. She felt comforted by his solidity, happy that he worried about whether or not she ate. It would be wonderful to just sink into him, the way she would sometimes collapse onto a grassy field on a hot summer day in the country, feeling the solid earth under her body, knowing it would hold her and she would never fall off. A part of her knew that this made no sense—he was more like a leaky boat than the rock-solid earth. But she took his arm and said, "Let's go back to my place—if you can stand me and my messy apartment, that is."

They didn't say much during the short ride back to her apartment. Once inside, she threw the packed up sushi into her little fridge and quickly cleared the clutter off the surfaces by throwing everything into the closet.

94

"You know," he said as he took his jacket off, "since I stopped drinking I can actually have a sex life. We don't have to play gin rummy this time, unless you really want to."

She didn't. He lead her down onto the bed and slowly undressed her. She could feel her nipples tingle and then harden again as he kissed them, and the slow throbbing starting up between her legs. *It's been so long, so long.* The thought was like a blues refrain going 'round in her head. *Oh sweet loving' man/ You got 'a hold of my soul.* She could see Willie Cobb's face as he sang those words. Had she ever let any man get a hold of her soul?

Steve had put on a condom and was inside her now, moving to her rhythm; sounds came out of her throat that were like the finest blues singers on earth. *Rock me daddy/ Rock me slow/ Rock me daddy/ One time 'fore you go.* Something exploded inside her and she was picked up like a rock by an avalanche, only there was no fear, just the wonderful, wild feeling of letting go and finally being able to fly.

Chapter Fourteen

Steve was standing in her little kitchenette brewing coffee when Molly woke up. An old jazz riff was playing in her head and she half rose onto one elbow and smiled. He was wearing pants but no shirt. The size and solidity of his body, so strong and substantial in that too-small space caused such a surge of happiness that she wanted to sing.

"Hi," she said.

He swiveled his head around. "You know Molly, besides not having any milk for this coffee, you don't have a drop of food in here, aside from last night's sushi, of course. Not a slice of bread, not a box of cereal, nothing."

"It's nice to see you too, Steve."

laughing, he came over to the bed, bent down and kissed her on the lips, a long, friendly good morning kiss. He straightened up, then stretching like a lion or a panther, he said, "So, I guess we're going out for breakfast."

"If that's what you want to do."

That was what he wanted to do. Molly took a quick shower and they were soon seated in a booth at a little coffee shop on First Avenue eating eggs and bacon. To her surprise, she hungrily ate everything down to the last piece of toast.

Steve was watching her and nodded as if affirming something to himself. "So now I know what it takes to get you to eat."

She crumpled the napkin and threw it at him.

After breakfast he left to do his "stuff." "Snow is in the air," announced the weather lady on the coffee shop's TV and, indeed, the sky was clouding up, but nothing could dampen Molly's spirits—or so she thought. On her way home she stopped into a little superette and put a quart of milk, a loaf of bread and a box of cereal into a basket, then added some cold cuts, a jar of mustard and a tomato. Back in her apartment, the little light on her message machine was blinking. Two new messages.

"The vermicelli that the devil sends down upon the earth is but a representation of the evil in mankind." The voice was Ben's. The second message was also Ben. "The evil demons enter through the drainpipe, the walls, the windows and burrows into my brain. My eyes are black with the vision and smell of evil."

Oh god! What was he talking about? What kind of new delusion was this? Or had something terrible, something evil, really happened to him? Molly's earlier happiness was gone as if a huge eraser had descended from the heavens and wiped her memory clean. Her telephone number was on the wall next to Ben's phone, but he rarely used it unless he was in dire trouble. What could be happening to him?

Molly threw the milk and cold cuts into the refrigerator and flew out of the apartment. Sitting on the M-14 bus that would take her to the Lower East Side, Molly was shocked to realize she'd hardly thought about Ben since the night she'd seen him with Marushka. Of course Cal Bruchman's murder and Steve coming back into her life had preoccupied her. But this was unheard of! It was as if now that he and Marushka were having a sexual relationship, Molly could let Marushka worry about him for a change. This was a new and different feeling, made odder still by the fact that Marushka didn't know that Molly had anointed her Ben's keeper.

It was even colder when she got off the bus and the sky was now the same heavy gray color as the pavement. Since it was Saturday, gangs of kids were whooping and hollering up and down Ben's block and she had to step lively to avoid a collision.

Marushka was nowhere in sight. Molly quickly ran up the creaking stairs and knocked on Ben's door. No answer. This time she had to use her keys. The door opened into pitch blackness and the musty odor of dust, garbage and dirty dishes.

Flipping on the kitchen light switch, she saw the black walls start to move. Ugh! Then she let out a whoop of laughter. Ben was being literal when he talked about evil vermin or vermicelli which the devil sends down upon the earth. Cockroaches had been coming in through the walls, the windows and the drainpipe and were bothering the hell out of him.

Worried about some strange new delusions and the symbolic meaning behind his message, it had never occurred to her that Ben was saying exactly what he meant—in his own unique way. She could call an exterminator, but that would mean arranging for Ben to be somewhere else when he came; Molly could just picture her paranoid brother's reaction to a strange man invading his apartment and spraying poison down his drainpipe and into all the cracks and crevasses in his kitchen and bathroom.

Molly walked through the apartment, flipping the lights on and off as she went. Not that she expected him to be home—he tended to go on his long rambles in the mornings—but anything was possible. Ben was known to sit in the dark during some of the worst of his times when he couldn't tolerate the sensation of light. The place was a mess, with clothing, papers, books, empty cans scattered all over everything—he tended to eat from cans when his delusions got really bad because he thought that there was less chance that a vacuum-sealed Campbell's soup can could be tampered with by those who were out to get him. But it didn't look any worse than the last time she'd seen it. For that matter, her apartment didn't look a hell of lot better.

Molly left the apartment without having come to a decision about what to do. On the wall over the mailboxes there was a sign: "Extermination Services Provided by No-Pest, Inc." After being bounced through several menus, she finally got through to a live person who, realizing she would pay through the nose for the emergency service, agreed to send an exterminator later that day.

On her way out, she glanced at Marushka's door and saw the sign: *Know What the Future Has in Store. Please Knock and Enter.* Impulsively, she did just that. A little boy with huge brown eyes answered her knock. He called out over his shoulder, and Marushka appeared wearing a brightly flowered wrap which hid little of her voluptuous figure, and gold mules through which peeked green-painted toenails. Marushka waved the child away and asked in her raspy voice: "You want a reading?" She recognized Molly and said, "Oh."

"I'm looking for my brother, Ben," Molly said brightly. "He left a message for me, but he isn't home. Do you happen to know where he is?"

"Why would I know?" She took a pack of cigarettes out of her pocket, shook one out and lit it from a cigarette that was burning in an ashtray behind her. "He does what he wants."

"Marushka," Molly said with much sincerity, "please know that I'm glad for whatever happiness my brother finds with you. He hasn't had too much of it in his life."

Marushka regarded her as she might a skirt or a jacket being considered for purchase. Then she stepped back so Molly could enter. The door to this apartment led not into the kitchen, but into a small front room. Heavy material covered the windows and the lighting was very subdued. A twin pair of leather car seats on the floor served as couches. Two very ornate floor lamps with tarnished metal bases and tasseled shades sat next to them. In the center of the room were a wooden table and three chairs. Another, smaller lamp sat in the middle of the table. The lamp was turned on and the bulb, painted red, cast a strange, devilish light over everything. The doorway into the next room was hung with long strips of multi-colored beads. On the wall was a poster, another large drawing of the palm of a hand; in the reddish light, it appeared to be bathed in blood.

"I threw the cards for him," Marushka said after they both sat down at the table. "I know you won't believe, but I have the gift. Not all gypsies have it, although they'll tell you they do. But I really do."

"What did the cards say?" Molly felt a catch in her throat.

Ridiculous, but she was ready to believe that Marushka had some insight into Ben that she herself didn't. Maybe his relationship with Marushka was a sign that the slow, steady decline of the past couple of months was miraculously reversing.

Marushka took a deep drag of her cigarette. "Do you really want to know?"

Molly nodded.

"It is not good."

Molly's heart sank. The smoke curled around Marushka's head and rose in a lazy spiral towards the ceiling. Well, you don't have to be a psychic to come up with that answer.

"I wish I could get him to take his medicine," Molly said. "He's much better when he does take it." Irrationally, she was again hoping that this woman had some special influence with Ben.

As if she'd read Molly's mind, Marushka shook her head back and forth. "I can only tell you what the cards say. I have no power to change anything." Lighting another cigarette, the gypsy took a long drag. "People come in here wanting hope. I throw the cards, and I study their palm. And often I tell them what they want to hear." She shrugged philosophically. "But I know myself that the cards never lie."

"I kind of wanted them to say something else," Molly said with a weak smile.

Marushka studied her for a moment. "You are a social worker, right?"

Molly nodded.

Marushka got up and gestured with her hand for Molly to stay. She disappeared behind the beaded curtain. Returning with an envelope in one hand and the card Molly had given her in the other, she unfolded the letter that was inside the envelope and handed it to Molly. "I don't understand this. My daughter usually explains these things to me, but she's living in New Jersey now. Read it, please, and tell me what it is."

Molly peered at the letter which had a strange red cast to it because of the painted bulb. It was headed: "City of New York, Department of Health and Human Services," addressed to Niclos and Marushka Petulengro and was an explanation—of sorts—about why their food stamps were being discontinued.

"Niclos is your husband?" Molly asked.

Marushka hesitated—Molly could sense that she didn't like revealing personal information to anyone—then said, "Niclos is the brother of my late husband." Molly took this as an acknowledgement of the fact that, as the sister of Marushka's lover, it was okay for her to know about this familial relationship.

"Well, the City thinks you are a couple, so don't tell them you aren't. It will only confuse them." Marushka smiled at that. Her teeth

99

were stained brown and in her smile was a harshness that Molly thought might be a condition of her life. Knowing what the future holds might not be all that much of a comfort.

"I think you can appeal this." Molly explained exactly how the appeals process worked and what Marushka had to do. Then she wrote it all out for her. "The administrative judges who handle these appeals are often more lenient than the clerks who are trained to look for reasons to reject."

"Thank you," Marushka said.

"And here," Molly took a small rectangle of cardboard out of her bag, "please take my card with my phone numbers." On the back of the card she wrote down the number of her personal cell phone. "In an emergency."

Marushka carefully placed Molly's card in the envelope along with the letter. She smiled again, a smile of conspiracy, as if to say that by sharing family secrets, Ben's sister had been made a member of the Petulengro family. Molly, who knew Ben much better than Marushka did, wished it could be as simple as that.

Before leaving the building, Molly went back upstairs to see if Ben might have since come home. He hadn't.

Outside it had gotten colder still and a few flakes of now were starting to fall. Molly shivered. Oh Ben, she thought, winter's back now with a vengeance. It you don't come in out of the cold soon, what's going to become of you?

Chapter Fifteen

The parked cars, garbage cans, lamp posts and mailboxes were glistening with a layer of white by the time Molly got back to her apartment. It still smelled faintly of Steve, and for a brief moment last night flooded back, causing her to smile. But the image and the feeling of pleasure the memory brought up seemed far away, as if she had stumbled upon an old photo of a relative she hadn't seen in years. After putting away the rest of the groceries that were scattered all over her kitchen table, she sank into her rocking chair and closed her eyes, once again immersed in the tight little world of Ben and herself where nothing and no one else had any real relevance.

Pink Floyd was the band that most mirrored this frame of mind. She poured a glass of wine, found the old vinyl disc and slipped it onto the turntable. Sinking back into her chair and sipping her wine, she listened to the long instrumental opening to **Wish You Were Here,** the great lament to the band's first creative light, Syd Barrett, the once-shining star, the lost crazy diamond, who slowly went insane as the rest of the band helplessly watched.

Out of the void comes one long, sustained tone—time in suspension—overlaid by a sprinkle of crystalline molecules, the random riff of a saxophone—bits of matter floating around in space. The universe waiting to be born. *In the beginning there was chaos.* Not the state of utter confusion or disorder that the word was commonly held to mean. But the purer meaning of the word: the infinity of space or formless matter before the beginning of the ordered universe, before existence, before feeling and thought; before words. Molly sipped her wine and let the images float in and out of her mind. After a long while the formlessness was pierced by the cry of David Gilmour's guitar, like the cry of a newborn bringing life into the universe. This moment always consoled her: if infinity could give birth to one universe, why not another? An alternative universe, a universe that resembled ours, but not quite. Where *up* could be *down.* Or *out* could be *in.* And crazy could be sane. Because it was there, in this alternative universe, that she'd found Ben's heart right inside her own.

The ring of the telephone brought her back into the here-and-now.

"Hi, Molly." Steve's voice resonated through her telephone. "I'm calling because I don't want you thinking that I'm the kind of man who loves 'em and leaves 'em."

"Going by past history, what else could I think?" It was supposed to sound playful, but it came out sounding sad and mournful.

"I've reformed. I went to AA and saw the light."

"I'll bet."

"So, how's it going?"

How would her morning activities play to the cop from Brooklyn? "I don't know whether you're ready for this," she began.

"Molly, if its one of those 'I don't think we're right for each other' things then, no. I'm not ready for it. Anything else, give me a try."

"Okay." She swallowed several times.. "Here goes: My brother left me a crazy message about evil vermin, or vermicelli that burrows into his brain which the devil sends into the world through his drainpipe." It all sounded so jumbled and insane to her, what could it possibly sounds like to him? Keep it light, Molly, just keep it light. "So I went running over and guess what?"

"His plumbing had backed up?"

"You're close," she said, amazed that he got it—almost. "His kitchen was infested with roaches."

"Of course," he laughed wryly, "vermicelli is Italian for 'little worms.'" He stopped and said, "I won't laugh, Molly, if you don't find that kind of stuff funny."

"Actually I do, when I'm not feeling overwhelmed by it. It's one of the reasons I love him. I just never thought anyone else would find it funny. You seem to be able to interpret his crazy language pretty well."

"I question witnesses like your brother all the time. After a while you get to understand their strange associations and it even makes a weird kind of logic. I was talking to one homeless guy who was on the scene when a woman got whacked. He tells me he didn't see anything because the plumbing in the building was broken and he had to go fix it. Now this guy is definitely not someone you'd trust with your pipes, so I'm thinking he doesn't want to be a witness. But then I notice he's holding himself near his crotch. So I nose around the outside of the building a little and I find a pool of bloody urine which turns out to be his. He was telling the truth—his personal plumbing *was* broken."

She laughed; it was so-o-o Ben. "I'm going over this afternoon with an exterminator. I'm just hoping I can get him out of the apartment long enough for the exterminator to do his job."

"Good luck, Molly." He laughed.

"By the way, Steve, did Louis Kroski, Cal Bruchman's homecare worker, tell you he saw Ken Belloc and what looked to him like someone from one of the city agencies talking together in the lobby of Mr. Bruchman's building? He got the impression there was some kind of a deal going down."

102

"He didn't, no. He'll barely say two words to me." Steve sounded exasperated. "I'd almost think he'd done it, or was involved in some way, if everybody didn't tell me how fond Louis was of Cal Bruchman. Besides which, his alibi checked out."

Molly laughed. "You suspect everyone, don't you."

"Until they prove themselves innocent, yes." She could almost see his lopsided grin right through the telephone. "I'd love to see you tomorrow," he went on, "but I promised my daughter Dee Dee who is up from college that I'd come over and visit her. So let's see what Monday brings; if I can get off at a reasonable time, how about taking in a movie?"

"Okay, what movie shall we see?"

He wanted to see the latest hi-tech thriller and she pushed for the foreign film at the Fine Arts Cinema. Because she was so happy to be arguing about it like any normal couple, she gave in and agreed to see the movie of his choice. "But you owe me. Next one we see together is the most artsy art film I can dig up. And don't bring a book."

It was about two in the afternoon when Molly got to her brother's apartment. The snow had suddenly stopped and was melting into puddles under a bright blue sky. She'd told the exterminator to get there at two-thirty, figuring that a half an hour would be enough time to get Ben up and out.

But Ben wasn't cooperating. "Go away!" he shouted after she'd knocked for a while. The chain bolt on and he wouldn't open the door.

"Ben, please let me in," she pleaded. "I need to talk to you."

"Poison control. Call poison control. The minions of the Evil One come up through the wall and pound on the door. They call themselves a sister."

It went on like this for a while. During the entire time, nobody in any of the other apartments even opened their door to see what the disturbance was all about. I could be breaking into his apartment with a blow torch, Molly thought, and not one person would come to his rescue. All the lightness she'd felt when talking to Steve on the phone earlier was gone; once more it was just she and Ben, alone together, in some surreal scenario from which there was no exit.

Molly finally had to give up in defeat. Despite the gulf of unshared language and thought that existed between them, Molly was convinced that Ben was tuned into her on some deeper, intuitive level, knew she was planning to let some stranger into his home to spread poison around, and would have none of it.

At two-thirty on the dot, the exterminator showed up. He was a balding little man in a gray uniform with "Hank" stitched in red above the pocket.

103

"Look, I'm sorry, Hank." Molly said. "He won't open the door."

Hank shook his head in dismay. "You wanna get a handle on your pest problem, ya gotta have regular maintenance."

"I know, Hank. I explained to your boss that this might happen. I can't always predict what he's going to do."

"People. Go figure 'em." Once more he shook his head. "You can always predict what your basic insect or rat is going to do. He's gonna eat and procreate, eat and procreate." Taking out a large, gray-tinged handkerchief, he blew his nose. "I've been in this business for over twenty years. I know them pests like I know the back of my hand. Eat and procreate. Eat and procreate."

"Well," she said. "I wish people were that simple."

Molly finally shepherded him down the stairs. They parted on the sidewalk. She took the bus home and spent the next several hours trying to read through a pile of professional publications that had accumulated over several months, while wondering what to do about her brother and the devil's vermicelli.

Towards evening, she returned to Ben's apartment. This time, thank god, he was out. Molly went down to the corner Bodega and bought a can of bug spray. Keep it simple, she reminded herself. It's the only way it ever works with Ben.

He still was out, so she managed to spray his kitchen and bathroom fairly thoroughly. Afterwards, she swept up the dead bugs and piles of other litter, putting it all into several green garbage bags and leaving a note taped to the wall that said: *Your sister Molly was here and took the vermin away with her. She also took out your garbage.* Locking the door behind her she left the building.

Chapter Sixteen

Sunday. Determined to clean up her apartment, Molly regretfully took a rain check on a brunch invitation from a friend who she hadn't seen for a while. After straightening, sorting, dusting, scrubbing and then hauling several bags of trash down the stairs, she collapsed in front of the TV set, falling asleep at some point in the middle of a movie about Bruce Willis being, well, Bruce Willis.

"I could have used a lot more weekend," Nilda said at the office the next morning after the two had exchanged greetings. "I never got to the laundromat like I planned. So this morning, when Jaime announced there were no clean clothes, I told him he could help out a little and do it himself." Jaime was her eldest—a teenager through and through. "And do you know what he said?"

The two women answered in unison: "Spanish men don't do laundry!"

"So, did you see the new boyfriend this weekend?" Nilda asked, after they both stopped laughing.

Well, why not. Molly grinned and said, "I don't know how long it's going to last, and I hate to get my hopes up about these things . . ."

Nilda rolled her eyes. "Don't worry. Nobody would ever accuse you of that."

"But for now. . ." The color suffused her face again, along with a little shy smile. "Just don't spread it around. I don't want to jeopardize the investigation into Cal Bruchman's murder."

"Cross my heart," Nilda made the sign of the X across her well-endowed chest. "I'm really glad for you, Molly." The switchboard buzzed and Nilda turned towards it, saying over her shoulder, "Oh, I just remembered. Mr. Stuttman wants to see you in his office as soon as you come in."

Molly glanced up at the clock: 9:20. "What does he want me for? To tell me he's writing me up yet another time for being late?"

She stopped in her cubicle to hang up her coat and made her way between the labyrinth cubicles to Stuttman's office.

Stuttman waved her to a chair near his desk and said abruptly, "I spoke to Ken Belloc. He disclaimed any knowledge about the harassment of his tenants." His shifted some papers around and lined them up, *clap, clap*, against the desk. "I absolutely cannot believe that he could be behind such a thing."

"But *someone* is harassing those tenants," Molly retorted. Should she tell him Louis's story about the possible fix that he saw going down between Belloc and someone from one of the City agencies?

Before she could say anything, Stuttman's eyes shifted from her face to her body, looking at her in a way that made her want to put on the heaviest sweater she could find. "I understand you are, uh, friendly with one of the investigating officers," he said as if asking how much she would charge to party.

She was right. No secrets here. By now, it was probably on the Internet.

He plucked a pencil out of his pencil jar—actually a mug with the words *Freymont Avenue Association* stenciled across it—and tapped the eraser against his desk blotter. "If those tenants are really being harassed, maybe you can ask your, uh, detective friend to look into it. Unofficially, that is."

He should only know I've already done that, Molly thought. But she nodded. "Mr. Stuttman, I know that Ken Belloc is your friend and you don't want to think badly of him, but it really does seem that he is fronting for Ivan Skanov and the Russian mob—or he's involved with Skana in some way."

"Lower your voice, Ms. Lewin." Snatching a quick look over her shoulder, he whispered, "I really don't think that it's a good idea for us to be talking about any of this here. We have a lot of Eastern Europeans working for us—Russians, Poles, Ukrainians. Everyone knows that they all stick together."

"Mr. Stuttman!"

"Just ask your detective friend to look into it. If there is a pattern of harassment, the police are the ones who should be dealing with it."

"Whatever you say, Mr. Stuttman."

"And you are not to repeat this conversation to anyone, including any of the other staff members. Is that clear, Ms. Lewin?"

"Yes, sir." It was all she could do not to click her heels and salute before leaving his office.

A batch of case files on her desk needed notes written for them. But since the day of Cal's murder she'd been unable to do much paperwork, especially not case notes. Writing them was a long, tedious process in which the substance of every home visit to a client, every telephone call with or about the client, and any agreements or plans that were reached, either with or on behalf of the client had to be recorded in detail. So she picked up the phone and put in a call to Howie Markowitz, surprised that it only took speaking to one secretary to get through to him.

"Hi Molly" he said in his clipped voice from which, he'd told her, he'd worked very hard to remove all vestiges of a Brooklyn accent. "How's business?"

"Way too good, I'm afraid."

"You mean there's too many people getting old and sick."

"Well, if they weren't, I'd be out of a job." She paused to smile at herself. "How's your father doing? Has he organized the patients in the nursing home yet?"

"Just about." Howie chuckled. "Seriously, though, his short-term memory is getting worse and worse. He can't remember what he had for breakfast, or anything that happened past the 1950's, for that matter. He's living back in the days when he was hauled up in front of the House Un-American Activities Committee. Back then, he didn't name names on principle. Now, he couldn't remember those names even if he wanted to. Except for McCarthy. That's the one name he does remember, and he's still as angry at him, and as irascible about it all as he was fifty years ago."

Molly laughed. "He was quite a guy, your father."

"Yes, old Red Ronald Markowitz. Quite a guy." The bitterness in Howie's tone was palpable. "Unfortunately, being the son of old Red Ronnie is not helping my goal of becoming a partner in Stiegel, Lowe, Myers and Donleavy, council to Brooklyn's *crème de la crème.*"

"They don't appreciate the sons of old lefties?"

"That's a joke, I take it." He sighed. "Well, Molly, you didn't call to hear my problems. What can I do for you?"

"You know the big development project that's supposedly going up on and around Warwick Street, next to the waterfront?"

"I've heard tell."

"I have several clients who live in some of those old buildings. I've heard some gossip that there's a deal going down with someone from one of the City agencies, maybe HDP—Housing Development and Preservation—for the City to declare those buildings unfit and demolish them."

"Do you know who owns the buildings?"

"The tenants pay rent to Ken Belloc's Real Estate company."

"Well, that could mean that Kenny is just the managing agent."

"He as much as told me that he owns the buildings." Molly decided not to mention the possible Skana connection. If Belloc was really fronting for Papa, Howie would be onto it soon enough. "Are the rumors true?"

"I don't know, Molly. But I'll look into it and get back to you."

"Thanks, Howie."

After hanging up, she pulled a pile of folders towards her, opened the first one and wrote a couple of sentences. Then she pushed it away, and went into the staff room for a cup of coffee.

"They finally completed the autopsy," Steve said on the phone later that afternoon. "There was a back-log, they told me, so they couldn't get to it sooner—that shoot-out in Bed Stuy and the kid that went on a rampage at that school in Red Hook—all high-profile cases with lots of bodies."

And the death of an old man is not a high-profile case, Molly thought. So it gets bumped to the back of the line.

"And," Steve went on, "surprise, surprise. Cause of death was blunt-force trauma to the head."

Blunt-force trauma to the head. A hand—whose hand?—picking up something lethally heavy and bringing it down hard on the fragile skull of an old man who couldn't defend himself. The thought enraged her. Don't go there, Molly!

They agreed to have a quick bite after work and then go to the movies. After the show they stopped in for a cup of coffee at a little hole-in-the-wall place on Second Avenue where the pastries, like the offices of Multi-Care, looked like they'd seen better days.

"So what did you think of the movie?" Steve asked, making a face at the coffee which was no better than the pastries.

"It wasn't a movie that required any thought, Steve."

"Yeah, yeah," he scoffed. "Well, I don't care what you say, but I liked that female scientist."

"You mean the blond who wore those skin-tight outfits that barely covered her tits?"

"Yeah, that one."

"When does she have time to be a nuclear physicist," Molly mused, "with all that clothes shopping to do? The woman had on a different outfit in every scene."

The lopsided grin lit up his face again. "You're just jealous because . . ."

"I wouldn't try to finish that sentence if I were you."

"You're probably right." He took a bite of his Danish and frowned. "To tell the truth," he said with a small sigh, "I didn't watch much of it. I had other things on my mind."

"What's wrong?"

"I'm worried about Sean." Steve pushed the plate away and said, "I haven't heard anything from him for over a month."

"Wouldn't you have heard if something was wrong?"

Steve shrugged. "Maybe, maybe not. He's with the army's Special Operations Forces—that's the army's version of the Navy Seals or the Green Berets—which means I don't know exactly where he is, nor do I hear from him very much. But his mother and I usually get some kind of a communication every three or four weeks letting us know he's okay."

Steve's fingers closed around the Danish, crushing it. "This is the longest it's ever gone."

"It must be really hard for you. I know I'd be crazed if it was my kid."

He took a photo from his wallet and handed it Molly. The young blond man in uniform looked a lot like Steve must have looked before the years, the war, the job and alcohol had done their work.

"He's a good looking kid, Steve. As a matter of fact, he looks a lot like you."

"Yeah, so everybody says. And he's so much like me, too. Which makes it worse." Steve stared at the picture for a moment. "I know what I went through in 'Nam," he mumbled, "and I keep thinking he's gotta be going through the same thing."

Suddenly his face went blank, as if a light had gone out.

He must be having a flashback. "Where are you Steve?" she asked softly, not quite knowing whether or not to touch him, or hug him, or what.

After a few moments, he took a deep breath and brought himself back into the room.

"Tell me what just happened, Steve. And don't say it was just a flashback."

"Fair enough, Molly." Briefly, his eyes rested on the photo of his son. Then he blinked a few times and began: "A week or so after I first got to 'Nam we were ambushed bad. Half the guys I came over with, guys I'd been talking to just that morning, were lying there dead." His body went totally still; then he went on in a hollow voice: "I'm all broke up. This sergeant, Mason T. Buffet his name was, from Alabama, he takes me aside and says, 'Boy, I'm gonna teach you a little something about survival.' I still remember his words like they were engraved on my brain. 'You don't want to get close to anyone here,' he said. 'You don't want to know what towns they come from, you don't want to know about their girlfriends, their mothers, their kids. That way when they die, you won't feel anything.'"

Molly put her hand on his arm and gently squeezed it.

"It was good advice then, Molly." There was a kind of lost anger in his voice. "It got me through that goddamned war."

"And now?"

"He's my son, Molly. Like Pete Lenniger was my friend. " Something in his voice sounded just like David Gilmour's weeping guitar. "You can't go through life without letting yourself feel anything—you might as well already be dead. That's why I stopped drinking. But sometimes, like now, I wish I could go back to the old way."

Molly's hand was still on his arm. He covered it with his other

109

hand. It was so much larger than hers that again she felt secure, at peace, as if she were snuggling into her blue-and-white comforter on a cold winter morning and nothing bad could happen to either of them. This is crazy. It's like I'm two separate people. One of me knows he's so tightly wound himself, he couldn't possibly offer security to anyone. The other one—God help me!

"I gotta get out of this head," he said. "Let's go back to your place."

They joined the stream of people and walked down Second Avenue. When they entered her apartment, Steve looked around at the shiny, uncluttered surfaces.

"You didn't have to do this for me," he said dryly.

"Don't let it go to your head."

He sat down at her kitchen table while Molly brewed some fresh coffee.

"So I talked to Donald today," Steve said after Molly brought the coffee over and sat down opposite him. "He's a real punk, that one."

"What did he say?"

"I knew if I simply tried to warn him off the harassment bit, he'd just blow me off and I wouldn't get anywhere. So I ask him to come down to the station house with me to answer a few more questions about his father's murder. Throw him off balance a little."

"And he came?"

"Yeah," Steve shrugged. "I can be pretty persuasive if I want to."

He got up and opened her refrigerator. "You bought milk, too." Shaking his head in wonder, Steve poured some milk into his coffee and took a sip. "Now, like I said, this guy's a real punk. And punks like him are cowards. So I get him in the interview room, just the two of us, and I let him see me locking the door. And I say to him, 'I'm not really here to talk about your father, Donald.'"

For the briefest of moments Molly felt sorry for Donald Bruchman. Then she thought, why is Steve telling me this?

"I give him a moment for that to settle in, then I look at him real hard and I say to him, 'I got a thing against little shits like you who threaten helpless old people.' At first he tries to deny it, but I tell him I got witnesses who'll ID him.

"Now I can see the guy's shittin' his pants. He tells me if I touch him, he's going to file a charge of police brutality. I say to him, 'What I'm gonna do to you, it's gonna be to your insides. You'll never be able to prove a thing. This is just between you and me 'cause I don't like you.'.

"He's dying there. I could smell the fear coming off him like it's sweat on a hot summer's day. He starts telling me he never laid a hand on anyone, and I should be out investigating the murder of his father, and he's not going to say another word until he talks to his lawyer. I tell him that's okay with me because I don't give a shit what he has to say.

"By this time I'm right in the little punk's face and he's shaking so hard he couldn't talk even if he wanted to. He starts to get up from the chair to get away from me, and I push him down, maybe a little harder than I should've, and tell him he's not going anywhere until I say so. When I see that sinking in, I back away a little 'cause I don't really want to hurt him and say, 'I'll make a little deal with you, Donald. You promise me right now that you'll stop harassing those old people, and you get to be able to eat your next meal without vomiting.'"

Molly listened to this with a growing sense of unease – not on Donald's behalf; she'd sicced Steve on Donald to do just what he'd done. But this was a side of Steve that she didn't really want to know about.

He was watching her with a kind of cynicism that told her he could read her thoughts. "I should have just done it and kept my mouth shut, huh?"

Rising, he went over to her music wall and leafed through her collection. In a moment the studio was filled with Pavarotti singing *Che gelida manina*, one of Puccini's most passionate arias.

"Take off your clothes." It was the same tone of voice he'd used on Donald Bruchman.

"Oh no," she retorted. "You don't get to talk to *me* that way." She smiled slyly. "*You* take off my clothes."

The hint of a grin; then he bowed his head, knelt in front of her and began unbuttoning her sweater. Between Pavarotti's glorious voice which washed over her like the fragrance of a thousand flowers and Steve's hands exploring her breasts, her body started to heat up as if it were a lit stove. He made love to her with an intensity and force that could have been scary had she not known it was all about Sean. I wish I wasn't so goddamned empathic, she thought just before she fell asleep.

When she woke up, just before dawn, Steve was gone. A note on the table said, "I have to get to work early. I'll call you later."

Chapter Seventeen

Steve didn't call, nor did he pick up his phone or return her messages. He's busy, Molly told herself, trying to calm her sense of déjà vu. He may have caught a new case. The first few days on any investigation were critical, and in the past he'd told her not to expect to see him during that time. But, then, how long does it take to make a phone call?

Late in the afternoon Molly made a home visit to a client who lived out near the Expressway. Gentrification hadn't proceeded this far, and the two- and three-story mix of run-down residential and industrial buildings hunched down together in the gloom like prehistoric animals awaiting extinction. It was past quitting time and dark when the visit ended. But she decided to make a detour to Cheap Chuckies on Van Guilder Street, adjacent to the Expressway, to buy inexpensive storage bins and closet organizers before going home. The presence of Steve in her life had reactivated her nesting instincts, and she vowed this time to keep her apartment organized.

Van Guilder Street was known locally as the Runway because of the prostitutes who strolled up and down ready to service the homeward bound drivers who could easily zip off the Expressway, have themselves a quickie, and then zip back on again.

Molly was half-way up the block when she noticed a familiar-looking figure leaning against a car and walked over to check it out. The "lady," if you wanted to call her that, was wearing a low-cut electric blue one-piece body stocking with the word "Da" embroidered across one prominent point and "Mour" embroidered across the other.

"Da Mour, huh?" Molly said, raising her eyebrows.

"Yeah, I'm a friendly sort," Da Mour said in Louis Kroski's voice. "I like people to know my name." There was no trace of embarrassment on Louis's face which was covered by several inches of make-up.

"Louis . . ."

"Please, call the lady Da Mour when she's dressed to the nines, dressed so fine, walking the line," she said in what must have been Louis's "femme" voice—a breathy parody which was part sex kitten and part drill sergeant.

Molly couldn't stop staring. A big, blond bouffant wig that sported masses of puffy curls sat on Da Mour's head. On her feet were white patent leather high-heeled boots decked with tassels and fringes. Draped over the whole ensemble was a long white fur coat. Since Louis was built like a truck driver, the whole effect looked like something out of a weird, psychedelic trip.

Another drag queen, this one a somewhat less flamboyant brunette, sashayed towards them on five-inch spike heels, looked Da Mour up and down, and said, "Darling, I don't know how you pee in that thing." Then she batted her eyelashes and said to Molly, "You like doing it with the ladies?"

"Butt-out, Pamona," Da Mour said in Louis's voice. "This is a friend of mine from my day job, when I used to have one."

"Any friend of Da Mour's . . ." Pamona big, red, pouty lips turned up at the corners. "Hey, honey," she said to Da Mour, "did you hear about Roxanne?"

Da Mour shook her head back and forth.

"She died of an overdose about two weeks ago. They did an autopsy and do you know what they found?"

Molly and Da Mour both looked at her expectantly.

"*She* was a she!"

"What?" Da Mour exclaimed incredulously. "I don't believe it!"

Pamona's head bobbed up and down several times. "Roxanne was actually female. She had a pussy, ovaries, a uterus, no cock, scars from several abortions, the whole shmear."

"Roxanne was one of the most campy and outrageous TVs around," Da Mour explained to Molly. "She appeared at all the drag balls-- she was even voted Queen one year, wasn't she?"

This last was directed at Pamona who nodded. "I thought it was a conscience vote, because they hadn't selected her the year before when they should have."

Da Mour nodded in agreement. "Do you remember her dress the year she didn't win?"

"Honey, who could forget?" They both paid a brief silent homage to this immortal creation, whatever it was.

While they were talking, a continuous line of cars paraded past them. Windows rolled down, catcalls, whistles and a variety of derogatory remarks floated through the air. Every once in a while, one of the queens would respond in kind, but mostly they reacted by displaying themselves even more suggestively, or doing an exaggerated imitation of a model's languorous walk. Sometimes a car would pull up to a particular drag queen and the bargaining process would begin. Then she either entered the car, or she and the potential John would shout insults at each other before going their separate ways. One such heated exchange was going on right in front of them, and Molly found it distracting.

Da Mour noticed Molly's expression and said, "Look, let me buy you a drink"

Molly grinned. "I've never been picked up by a drag queen before."

"There's a first time for everything, Ms. Molly. Besides, I'd like to talk to you."

Da Mour steered her into a joint a few feet from the Runway. Half bar and half cafeteria, it was lit by low wattage fluorescent lights and had a list of specials taped to the greasy hood above the steam table. The paper these gourmet delights were written on was so yellow and speckled, they could've been from last month or last year. A No Smoking sign hung over the bar, but nobody was paying any attention to it.

Da Mour led her to a chipped Formica table. "So, I'll get us something to drink. What's your poison?"

"Let me pay." Molly opened up her bag. "You're unemployed at present."

"Your money's no good here. I invited you."

"Okay, I'll have a coke." Molly watched her swinging hips as Da mour walked over to the bar which had a series of deep notches along its wooden lip, as if someone had attacked it with a hatchet. It gets weirder and weirder, she thought.

Da Mour came back with a small bottle of coke and a dirty glass, along with another glass that contained what looked like whiskey or scotch. After sitting down and working her arms out of the fur coat, she reached inside the top of her body stocking, pulled out first one pointy foam cup and then the other and plopped them both on top of the table, where they sat like two miniature snow-covered mountains.

"They were starting to itch."

Reaching back into her coat pocket, she took out a pack of cigarettes, shook one out and lit it up. She leaned forward, put both elbows on the table and inhaled. It was a totally masculine movement. Louis Kroski was back in charge.

"I hope you don't mind," he said. "I never smoke or drink when I'm on a job, but since you already found me out . . ." He took a few drags while Molly stared at the falsies sitting on the table. "I only come here when I'm not working," he explained as he ground the stub of his cigarette out against the bottom of his tasseled boot and dropped it on the floor. He had decided, Molly thought, to come clean. "And I don't usually let anyone pick me up because I'm disease free and I intend to stay that way. But where else is a cross-dresser going to find a little company in this part of Brooklyn?"

Louis lit another cigarette and sat for a while, looking Molly up and down. What the hell was going on?

"I'm not really gay, you know."

114

"I'm getting that idea."

"It's hard for a heterosexual cross dresser to find understanding women."

"Are you making a pass at me?" She was not about to encourage such suggestions from a fellow employee—or even an ex-employee—especially one who was wearing a Dolly Parton wig and parked his falsies on the table.

He smiled a little and shrugged. "I apologize, Molly." His earrings, long cascades of rhinestones, tinkled and twinkled as he moved his head. "When I'm dressed *femme,* things come out of my mouth that I wouldn't ordinarily say."

"Okay, Louis." Molly smiled back. "Did Donald press charges?"

"Oh, that." Louis dismissed Donald with a wave of his hand. "He complained to Mr. Stuttman all right. But afterwards, Donald let me know it was all a misunderstanding and that he is not pressing charges." He tilted his head slightly and gave Molly a questioning look. "Somebody got to that man."

Molly said nothing.

"Okay. Don't ask, don't tell. An old Navy motto predating Clinton by at least two hundred years. But I can't see Stuttman reassigning me to anyone else, so I'm still out of a job." Tipped up his wig a little, he scratched his head. "I must have an allergy. All this stuff is making me itch like crazy." He took another drag from his cigarette and slowly blew the smoke out. "I want to talk to you about something. I've been visiting Willie, on my own, just to see how he's doing."

"The agency doesn't encourage that, you know, Louis."

"Yeah, I know. But besides Donald, I get a little worried about that great-grandson of his, Bukka. He's been hanging around the apartment ever since he broke up with Ana Skana."

"Bukka was going around with Ana Skana?" Molly found this hard to believe.

"Yeah. You know who she is, right?"

"I sure do," Molly said emphatically and narrowed her eyes. "Did Willie tell you this?"

Louis nodded. "Everyone says that Papa loves his daughter even more than he loves the joys of being a full-fledged capitalist entrepreneur. But Willie told me that *she* likes dark meat." The red-painted lips turned up. "Especially dark meat that plays jazz guitar. All those Russians just love American jazz."

Well, Ana likes white meat as well. However, her run-in with Ana over Ian Sorensen was none of Louis's business. Molly examined the glass Louis had brought over with the coke, put it down and took a swig from the bottle. "Whatever else you might say about Bukka," she said, remembering what he could do with that guitar, "he really is an incredible musician."

"But Papa wasn't having it. According to Willie, he *convinced* her," Louis said this with a particular emphasis that made Molly shudder to think of some of the measures a man like Papa could have taken to convince someone, "that Bukka was not for her."

"This might open up a whole new angle on Cal's murder," Molly mused out loud. "Maybe Papa murdered that poor old man to let Ana know he meant business. Did you tell the investigating detective about it?"

"I wouldn't tell that Detective Carmaggio anything," Louis declared, jerking his head up and to the side which caused the cascades of rhinestones to jingle and jangle. "He thinks that because I do woman's work—that's what he believes being a home attendant is—he can strong-arm me? Well, let him think again."

"Did he say that?" she asked incredulously.

"No, he didn't use those words exactly, but I could see how he felt."

"Wait a minute!" she exclaimed. "Wouldn't Papa have murdered Willie or Bukka rather than Cal?"

"He could have been killing two birds with one stone," he shrugged. "Do away with the leaseholder and reel your daughter in at the same time. At any event, it puts Skana right in the middle of it."

"Would you object to my telling the detective?"

Louis smiled slyly, "That's why I'm telling you. He's your boyfriend, isn't he? Or so I've heard."

Molly let out a sharp exhalation. "I can't believe this! Does everyone in Brooklyn know that I'm dating Detective Steve Carmaggio?"

"Is that a yes?"

"Look, Louis, I don't want my private life to be the subject of gossip and speculation."

Louis smiled a very sweet smile. "I can't say as I think much of your choice in men, but then I'm not one to talk. Be assured that those who haven't heard about it already won't hear it from these lips. And I'd just as soon you not tell anyone where you found this girl today."

Her face must have been showing how upset she was because he said: "Honey, that's the way life goes. Gossip is meat and drink to people. You can't get too uptight about it." He rose and slipped his arms back into the fur coat. "So, you'll make sure that the Neanderthal Man knows about the Ana Skana connection?" Molly nodded. "Putting my own personal feelings aside," he said as he scooped the two white cones off the table, pushed them back under his body suit, and wriggled them around until they were adjusted properly, "I really want to see them catch the bastard that did this to Cal."

"So do I, Louis. So do I."

Chapter Eighteen

"I don't know why you aren't returning my calls," Molly told Steve's voice mail when she returned home. "How much time does it take to just leave me a message and tell me you're busy but you're thinking about me, or something?"

She made a sandwich from the cold cuts that were supposed to be part of her new-found domesticity and plopped down on her rocking chair. After two bites, she put it back on the plate and placed them both on the little end table. Country Western, that's what I need to hear tonight, she thought and went over to her music collection, pulling out an old Red, "Big Daddy" Hawkins CD. *You've got an ice cube for a heart, my honey/And I can't melt it down.* When it comes to love gone bad, nobody sings it like a good ol' boy.

Maybe it was Red's country twang backed by the maudlin instrumental arrangement that caused her mood to shift. Is it really love gone bad? He doesn't call me for a day and I think the worst. Since when have I gotten so clingy?

"Steve, I'm assuming you're still working on Cal Bruchman's murder," she said after once more waiting for the beep, "even if you're too busy to call me, or have gone into hiding, or to Florida, or something. I don't know if this has anything to do with anything, but Louis Kroski told me that Willie's grandson Bukka was going around with Ana Skana, Papa Skana's daughter and it wasn't making Papa any too happy. Could it be that he decided to do something about it?"

His voice sounded so tired and dispirited when he called her at work the next day that she immediately abandoned the plan made during her shower that morning to have it out with him. "What's wrong Steve?"

"Molly, can you take the rest of the day off?"

"What happened?"

"Sean was listed MIA—Missing in Action."

"Oh, God! Steve, I'm so sorry." She desperately wanted to touch him, know through her skin that he was all right.

"They're not saying he's dead, which is a good thing—I have to keep telling myself it's a good thing—but they don't know where he is. He was part of a Special Forces Reconnaissance Team that went down in a plane that was trying to rescue another team of Navy Seals who got captured by the insurgents. They've found the plane and four bodies, but Sean and two others are missing. They think they survived the crash,

117

and got taken prisoner by the rebels. But they don't know for sure. And one of the known rebel fortresses in the area got bombed this morning so if he did get captured, he may well be buried under several tons of rubble."

She knew what he was thinking: Pete Leninger's hand and the smoking pile of concrete, glass and steel that used to be the World Trade Center.

"I'll take a personal day.".

"I have a few things to finish up here, and then I'll pick you up at the office."

"The tongues around here have enough to flap about. I'd rather meet you at the Acropolis coffee shop on Freymont, near the subway station."

Molly was sitting at the counter, half-way through a cup of coffee, when Steve's car pulled up at the curb. Throwing some money on the counter, she ran outside.

Steve leaned over and opened the door. She slid in and put her arms around him. For a moment they sat without speaking. Then he pulled away, made an illegal U-turn and headed towards the highway.

They traveled east, first into Queens and then picked up the Long Island Expressway. He said they were going out to his family's summer house, on the north shore of the south fork of Long Island, overlooking Great Peconic Bay. Then he lapsed into silence. Molly tried to say a few comforting things, but nothing penetrated through the cloak of desolation and grief that covered him until finally, as had happened with her mother's silences, Molly withdrew into herself in defeat. They drove the last twenty miles without saying a word.

The difference between this side of Long Island and the famous south shore beaches, like Amagansett and the Hamptons where she'd spent an occasional weekend, is striking. The south shore is lined with scrub oak and long stretches of sand dunes and battered by the unbroken swell of the Atlantic surf. But the side of the north fork that overlooks the bay is rocky and dotted with little tree-covered coves which must have been shady in the summer. Now, in January, it was deserted and windblown. The snow, which had all but disappeared in the city, was piled up along the side of the road and still clung to the leafless branches and bushes.

He turned the car into an empty parking area along one of the little coves. The snow had not been cleared from it, and the tires crunched through the pristine whiteness, leaving long mud-covered tracks in their wake.

They walked along the pebbly beach. The wind, which made tiny ripples along the otherwise calm surface of the water, blew right through her as if she were one of the leafless bushes. She hadn't dressed for the beach in winter when setting out for work that morning, and she hunkered down into her jacket and felt the melting snow seeping into her shoes.

"I can't stand this not knowing!" They were the first words Steve had said in what seemed like hours. "It's such a helpless feeling." Two gulls, crying their Banshee wails, circled over their heads like emissaries from the grave. "Especially for me. I find missing people all the time. But when it comes to my own son, there's not one single thing I can do." He turned with a jerky movement and smashed his fist into a "Protect This Fragile Environment" sign.

The sound of it reverberated right through the blowing wind. He flexed his fingers and began rubbing them with the other hand. Gently, Molly took the hurt hand into her own and kissed it. "I don't know what to say, Steve. The usual stuff I tell my clients who are hurting feels lame and clichéd, somehow, when it's someone you care a lot about."

He nodded. "And even if he's alive, I know what we—and they— did to prisoners in 'Nam. Which doesn't help."

Still flexing his fingers, Steve brushed some snow off a large outcropping with the other hand, sank down onto it and pulled her down next to him. His eyes went from pained to hollow—one of those thousand mile stares that went along with his flashbacks.

"I remember my top kick when I first got to 'Nam," he said after a while. "He wanted us to know what they did to *our* prisoners, so we wouldn't feel too guilty about shooting into a downed man. We had to do that because they'd play 'possum and if we didn't make sure they were really dead, one of them could suddenly jump up and shoot you."

He stopped for a moment, his face gray; the sound of his breath moving in and out of his chest like a muted version of wailing wind. "I was just an eighteen-year old kid from Our Lady High School in Brooklyn. Nothing ever prepared me for shooting into dead or dying bodies— that wasn't how John Wayne or any of those movie heroes ever did it—and the top kick knew that. He took a bunch of us new recruits down to a tunnel where they'd found six of our guys hanging from the wall. They were all naked and . . . mutilated." He closed his eyes briefly. "They'd all been executed. 'That's what they do to our prisoners,' he told us. And believe me, for a long time after that, we didn't take any prisoners, either." Steve looked at her to make sure she understood exactly what he meant. "You see something like that, it stays in your mind forever." He pressed the fingers of his left hand into his temple as if he were trying to force down all the horror that lived in his head. "I don't know how I'm going to get through this, Molly."

She sat shivering—from the cold, and from the story he had told her and the anguish it brought up in her—remembering those lonely, dark times after Ben's hospitalization and even after he came home with that same vacant-eyed stare that was so familiar in Steve, feeling her mother's grief like a thick gray pall hanging over the house. She'd retreat to her room and turn on her music. But the time would always come when she had to open the door and face it again.

"You just do, Steve," she said. "You just get through it." Her arm went around as much of him as could be reached. "Besides, you have me now. You're not alone."

They walked back to the car and drove two blocks to a boxy gray shingled house with a long porch that stood in a little grove of mixed green conifers and leafless hardwoods. The snow crunched as they negotiated the path and went up the wooden stairs to the front door. Steve took a key out of his pocket, unlocked it and they went inside. By now it was late afternoon and the thin, weak sun slanting in through the kitchen window didn't do much to dispel the cold, damp feeling in the house. He took her into the living room, pulled down a hand-crocheted throw from the hall closet, and settled her on the couch with the blanket over her before going down to the basement, to turn on the electricity, he told her. In a moment he came back up and switched on a couple of lamps. Then he laid a couple of pieces of wood, some tinder and crumpled newspaper on the fireplace grate, struck a match to it and in a few minutes, flames were leaping up the chimney.

"*Voilà!*" he said with an attempt at brightness. "Light and heat."

The room was simply yet comfortably furnished with what looked like everyone's castoffs—an old plaid-covered couch on which she was sitting, a couple of over-stuffed rocking chairs, a big, scuffed-looking Lazy Boy that didn't match anything else, a long coffee table carved out of half a log. And photographs, everywhere.

He noticed her looking at them. "The Carmaggio family," he said, "all of us, in every stage of development from pupa," he pointed to a very pregnant woman who was a little darker than Steve, with a more classically Italian nose, but who resembled him otherwise, "to old age." The last photo he pointed to was of a well-dressed older couple, sitting at a table in what looked like a catering hall. "My mom and dad," he said. "At my niece's, Kimberly's, communion two years ago."

Molly thought back to the barrenness of her own home. No photographs on display. There was an album, but it sat in the closet and contained BD—Before that Day—snapshots—mostly of Ben from babyhood to his high school graduation, and a couple of her as a baby and small child that had been thrown in almost as an afterthought. All visual recording of the Lewin children stopped when she was ten. There were no pictures of her high school graduation—there wouldn't be one of her senior prom because she hadn't attended it— none of her graduation from college or social work school. If one looked at the pictorial record, her entire family ceased to exist the year Ben had his breakdown.

"We used to call this place, 'The Cottage'," Steve was saying, "until the Kennedys came along; then we called it 'The Compound" because that's what they called their estate in Cape Cod. I spent my summers here as a child with my brothers and sisters, and later Sean and Dee Dee spent their summers here with all their cousins."

For first time since he picked her up that morning, his face relaxed and he smiled a little. "This is where I learnt how to sail as a kid, and where I taught my kids to sail. Sean was like a little fish—my father was convinced that his grandson was spawned in the sea—we could never get him out of the water." For a moment he looked like the young father he had been when some of the pictures of that little blond boy were taken. "I wanted to come here because this is the place I feel closest to him."

Steve collapsed onto the couch and she put her arms around him again, wishing she had some magic words for him, wanting to make his pain go away; feeling lost and helpless, utterly helpless.

"If they find him . . . dead." He could barely get the word out and hurried on, "If that happens, my dad and I intend to bury him in the little graveyard up the road which overlooks the bay."

"Oh, baby," she said, "I hope to god it doesn't come to that." Then she added, "What about your ex-wife? Doesn't she have some ideas of her own?"

"She can't even wrap her mind around the possibility of Sean not being alive," he said angrily. "She's still convinced they're going to find him alive and well—she never did live in the real world—so I haven't been able to discuss any of this with her."

Living in the real world—was that always the prize people made it out to be?

Molly moved the blanket over the two of them and snuggled into him. His large body was comforting, protecting her from all the fears and uncertainties that waited for them in the real world beyond the door. For a while she was able to mute both his grief and her helplessness and feel secure.

Molly must have fallen asleep because the next time she noticed the fire it had burnt down. Steve was staring straight ahead; he looked as though he hadn't moved. Feeling her stir, he said, "It's getting late. I'd better find you some place to eat before we head back to the city. I can't have you starving to death on me. "

She reached up and kissed him, happy to be back, however briefly, to their old teasing ways. "Come on now, Steve. I may be a little on the thin side, but do I look like I'm starving to death?"

He moved a little further back from her running his eyes up and down her body and said, "It depends on who's doing the looking. To

121

me, you look just fine. But my mother's answer to that question would be, 'Yeah, you do,' and she'd be heating up the gravy and putting up the water for the pasta by now."

They found an open fish and chips place that looked out over the bay. There was no one else in the place but a bored-looking counterman and someone in the back called Wally. Steve studied the beer offerings, but ordered a coke, as did she. Unfortunately, the fish and chips tasted like they had seen better days, so neither of them ate very much. Nor did they talk much. Steve sat staring out at the water, and she too fell silent and gazed out the window with him.

A wooden pier, empty of boats and extending from the foot of the restaurant, creaked a little as the wind blew it back and forth against its moorings. The bay itself was almost as desolate, the curving shoreline dotted by leafless trees and the spiky branches of barren bushes. No boats were out on the bay either. Just the wind blowing across the darkening water—invisible, ceaseless.

They made the trip back to the city mostly in silence. She wanted him to come up, but he wouldn't. At least he'd wanted her with him during this pilgrimage, she consoled herself. She selected a CD and slipped it into her changer. The somber notes of Prokofiev's haunting elegy, *The Field of the Dead*, poured from her speakers. Molly had recently seen the movie Russian movie *Alexander Nevsky*, for which the music was written, at a retrospective. Sung by a contralto woman's voice, the song accompanied a young woman in the long skirt and shawl of that long-ago time as she made her way over the corpse-lined snow. The woman was searching for the body of her lover, slaughtered in a battle between the non-Western Russian peasants, the good guys in this movie, and the hooded and very scary-looking Knights of the Teutonic Order, the Christian invaders of that time. It's funny how history keeps repeating itself, Molly thought. Listening now to the low, sorrowful voice—*I shall fly above the field of death*, said the translation—her feelings slowly began to seep through. Please, Molly begged whatever universal forces were at work—her version of God—please, let Steve's son come home to him alive.

122

Chapter Nineteen

Once again, Steve wouldn't pick up his phone or return her calls. It wasn't until the middle of next morning that she finally got through to him.

"No," he snapped in answer to her question regarding news about Sean. "Nobody can tell me where in the hell he is. How could they? No one in our supposed intelligence units out there speaks Arabic. Can you imagine? Dumb! Dumb!" She could just picture him hitting his head with the heel of his hand.

"Steve, I . . ."

"Look, Molly," he sighed, "I know you're just trying to help. Everybody keeps asking me if there's any news, and god knows they mean well, but it drives me crazy because I don't have any answers for them. Believe me, Molly, when I know, you'll know."

"Steve, let me take you out for dinner tonight. I promise I won't ask any questions."

"Thanks, Molly, but no thanks. I'm not up for any company."

As soon as she put the phone down it rang again—Howie Markowitz inviting her out for lunch. She accepted and then sat for a moment, thinking about Steve. Yesterday, she'd felt so close to him; today, it was as if it had never happened. Now you see it, now you don't.

Now you see it, now you don't. You were supposed to *want* to see the person you were dating. She had been supposedly dating Ian Sorensen, but hadn't wanted to see him enough to even try to tell him off after the episode with Ana Skana. As a matter of fact, she'd barely thought about him since leaving them together in the Crawfish. It's true, a lot had happened since that evening, but even so.

Maybe the issue was caring. Other than enjoying the reasonably good sex they'd had at the beginning, she'd never cared that much about Ian. But Steve, she didn't doubt for a moment, *did* care about her. Yet he didn't want to see her. The whole thing made her head ache.

Molly opened up a case file, determined to get back to her paperwork. Instead, she rubbed her forehead with three fingers and contemplated the word *dating*. It conjured up movies and malt shops and senior proms—a kind of innocence that she couldn't remember ever having experienced in any of her relationships with men—and certainly not with Steve. Any innocence she might have felt about dating was lost the day Ben went after their mother with a hammer. She'd been so blindsided by it. How could she ever trust any man again?

For a moment Molly felt a surge of anger that brought on a flurry of neatening—straightening the folders on her desk, re-filing those she'd completed during the days before the murder, re-adjusting her poster of the Arches National Park which tended to slant to the left. As did the whole cock-eyed building. As did her brother, for that matter. Smiling at the image, her anger dissipated. Ben had had no control over what he'd done; at least he loved her and always had.

Dating. Such a pallid little word—one that had nothing to do with her relationship with Steve. She'd met him during the investigation of a crime and almost lost him when two towers exploded. There had been good moments since they'd started seeing each other again, but on the whole Molly felt as though she'd jumped into a wave-tossed ocean without ever having learned how to swim.

Lunchtime came. She threw on her jacket and, without a word to Nilda and Swandell who was standing by Nilda's desk, ran down the stairs. Molly could almost feel the eyes of the two women staring at her back, perplexed.

The wind was blowing, the temperature was dropping and the people on the street were hunkering into their coats. Molly saw the bus coming along and she hopped onto it. As the bus continued down Freymont Avenue which wound its way like a river of asphalt through several miles of what used to be distinctly different neighborhoods, she looked out the window and wondered what would become of it all. The old neighborhoods well remembered from her early days at Multi-Care— the Latino area with its bodegas and Santerias, the Polish kielbasa and pirogi shops, the Jewish kosher butchers and matzo bakeries, the *salumnerias*, those Italian delis smelling of garlic and basil with glass cases full of fresh-made sausages and mozzarella cheese— were fast losing their ethnic flavors as the rents went up and old stores were replaced by little boutiques and cafes that were indistinguishable from each other and marked the arrival of the urban nomads.

Molly mourned the passing of these neighborhoods, the disappearance of the city that she knew and loved. She pictured the old neighborhoods as precious containers, each preserving some of the history and culture that a particular immigrant group brought to this country. It was a rich mix. Soon there would be nobody left to remember except for a few old people who sat out on chairs and stoops on a warm summer evening and told their stories of the way it used to be. And when they were gone, what then? And why did it matter so much to her?

Molly was meeting Howie at Rumson's, a restaurant that was

halfway between her office and the Heights which was now, as it had always been, the upscale Freymont Avenue neighborhood where sea captains and rich industrialists once built their mansions overlooking the harbor. Rumson's billed itself as serving *eclectic cuisine* which, as far as Molly could tell after the waiter came over with the menus and the wine list, meant fabulously expensive food.

Howie was delighted to help her select just the right wine from the just as fabulously-priced wine list, discussing vineyards with her as if he had been born a grape grower instead of Red Ronnie's working class son. They both ordered the *plat du jour*—a duck dish with a name that Molly couldn't pronounce but Howie could.

"So tell me, Howie, what have you found out?" Molly asked as they sipped their wine, which was really very good, Molly had to admit.

Howie sat back, ran his fingers through his wiry salt-and-pepper hair and regarded her for a moment. "You know, Molly, I would have cancelled this lunch if I wasn't really grateful to you for helping me out with my father."

"Why?" she asked, surprised.

"Because I can't really talk about it." He picked up the wine list which was still on the table and began studying it. "Do you know about this vintage?" He pointed to a wine that was far more expensive than the one he and Molly were drinking and which she had never heard of. "I've bought up a few cases and put it away. It's like an investment but better because, if nothing else, you can always drink it."

Molly had no intention of letting him off the hook that easily. "Why can't you talk about it?"

He leaned in towards her and, as if he were leaking state secrets, said *sotto voce*: "I think you're in over your head with this one, Molly. It's much bigger than a few of your clients and their housing situation."

"I think I figured that out already." The waiter brought a basket containing chunks of dense bread and a saucer into which he spooned some red-pepper-flaked grated cheese, added olive oil and whisked the cheese and the oil together with a miniature wire whisk. "I know Skanov is involved in this," she said after the waiter walked away.

"I really can't say anything about it." Howie grabbed a hunk of bread and dipped it into the oil. "Nor can I do anything for your clients because Stiegel, Lowe, Myers and Donleavy who happen to pay my salary have just been retained to represent one of the principals in this deal." He chomped down on the hunk of bread, as if to cut off anything he might inadvertently let slip.

"So, the son of the champion of the working class is representing a reputed Russian Mafia member, or overlord for all I know, who wants to throw some poor old people who worked hard all their lives out of their homes and into the street," Molly allowed disgust to fill her voice. "All for a little filthy lucre. How ironic is that?"

"You sound just like my father." Howie bristled. "Both of you are living somewhere back in the last century. And neither of you really understand anything."

"What don't we understand?"

"That it's all about the deal. The bigger the better."

Rumson's interior had tin ceilings and was shaped like an oblong with a bar down one side. It had probably once been a grocery store or a TV repair shop. Now, as it filled up with the lunch-time crowd, the noise level was increasing. Molly had to bend forward to hear what Howie was saying.

"I like you, Molly," he went on. "You've got a good heart."

"You say that as if you are diagnosing me with a chronic, debilitating condition."

Howie smiled. He had very white teeth and Molly wondered if he'd had them done by his dentist. "It's a nice quality," he acknowledged with a flick of his hand, "but it leaves you out of the game."

"What game are you talking about?"

The waiter came over with their orders. The *plat du jour* looked pretty—three slices of duck breast very elegantly draped around four baby asparagus spears which were in turn spiraled around a tiny morsel of puree of "roasted root vegetables"—and tasted okay but not quite spectacular enough for the price. Steve would have had some choice comments to make about it, Molly thought.

Howie cut a slice of duck into tiny pieces. "The game is no longer the Capitalists versus the Workers, like my father would have you believe." He transferred one of the miniature morsels from his fork into his mouth and swallowed it. "The working classes aren't even on the playing field anymore and haven't been since the days of the old Brooklyn Democratic Party machine with its ward heelers and bosses."

"What does this have to do with anything, Howie?" He was trying to deflect her from any further talk about this specific deal, and she was just as determined not to let him do it.

"Those old bosses were unbelievably corrupt," Howie went on as if he were giving a lecture to a civics class. "Nothing got done in the City without them getting their cut. But the working classes also got *their* cut of the pie, which they don't today. "

"How do you figure that?" Molly asked, interested now despite herself.

"Those bosses were truly democratic. They spread it around. You were out of a job? You go to your local ward heeler[1] who gets you a gig on the big sewer or road construction project, as long as you help get the

---

[1] An old-time district leader who worked for the political party in power.

vote out for the Democratic machine candidate on Election Day. You were sick and couldn't pay your hospital bills? Same deal. But once the machine was gone, the working class was out of the game."

Howie swallowed another morsel of duck. "The only ones who get anything now are the very poor who at least get welfare and Medicaid, and the rich who can contribute to a candidate's campaign fund or his favorite charity, or pay off some poor shmuck of a City official to throw his influence in the right direction. It's all about the deal, and who's got the power, the influence and the money to put it together and make it work. It's what oils the wheels of the City and makes it run. You watch what's going to happen at Ground Zero. Everyone is all idealistic now, but in the end, it will all be about who can put together the best deal."

"So what about this development project, or deal, as you call it?" Once more he shut his mouth again. "Talk hypothetically, Howie. It won't go any farther than me, but I'd really like to know what my clients are facing."

"I'm sorry, Molly. Besides the information being privileged, if it should ever get out that I said anything, it's not just my job that could be in danger." With the forefinger of his left hand, he made a slicing motion across his neck.

"I get the feeling that you don't approve of these people any more than your father would."

"My father was an idealist. I'm a realist."

A woman with purple hair who was sitting at the bar shrieked with laughter at something her male partner said. "Oh, no! You can't really mean that. It's like, so . . ." The rest of her sentence was cut off as she buried her face in his sleeve. Howie and Molly had finished eating. He pushed his plate away and looked around as though he were about to ask for the check.

Oh no, Molly resolved. You're not getting away so fast. "People who call themselves realists are actually cynics who don't believe anything can change. If you don't believe anything can change, it never will. At least idealists fight for change, and often bring it about. Think Rosa Parks, Gandhi, Martin Luther King."

Howie's eyes flashed. "Do you know where my father's idealism got us? Living in a slum, which my father called a working class neighborhood, with me going to a blackboard jungle-type school where I got beat up regularly." He exhaled sharply through his nose—an expression of extreme disgust. "He was so stuck in that goddamned ideology that he didn't see—or didn't *want* to see—what was going on under his own nose, to his own children. Those people hated him, and he didn't have a clue."

"That must have been very hard on you, Howie."

"I survived." He shrugged. "But don't give me ideology. I can't

127

stomach the word."

The waiter came over and Howie asked for a pot of coffee.

"So let's be realists," Molly said. "What about the poor people who are being forced out of those buildings? They can't afford to move anywhere else. What's supposed to happen to them in a world where everything is about the deal?"

"They can hire their own lawyer, which is what they should do."

"Yeah, Howie. And pay with what kind of money?" When he rolled his eyes, Molly toned it down: "Ordinarily, the law stipulates that the tenants are entitled to a stipend and compensation for moving expenses—that's if the landlord wants to demolish the buildings. From what I've been told, though, Papa Skana—or whoever the developer in this deal is," she added as Howie started to look daggers at her, "has a fix in to get the City to condemn those three buildings along Warwick Avenue as unsafe. As I understand it, once the buildings are condemned, the City is required to demolish them if the landlord refuses to make any repairs?"

Howie nodded.

"So what happens to the tenants in that situation? Does the City compensate them?"

"The City isn't in the tenant compensation business. These deals are put together by private interests."

"Why can't something be worked out?" Molly persisted. "However much it would cost Skana, or whoever the developer is, to compensate those people is chicken feed compared with how much he stands to make from the deal. Why is he so dead-set against it?"

The waiter deftly maneuvered around the tables with a tray holding a silver coffee pot, two cups and saucers, a little pottery creamer and an assortment of sweeteners. With the tray balanced on one arm, he set out the cups and saucers with his free hand, poured the coffee and placed everything on the table as if he were serving high tea.

Howie added cream to his coffee. "You really don't get it."

"What don't I get?"

"You're just thinking of this in terms of those three buildings." He sipped some coffee. "You have no idea how big this deal is, and how many acres of land are potentially involved here—land that is now being under-used." Glancing around as if fearful of being overheard, he went on: "Look at the ten blocks of waterfront property just along Warwick Avenue. Besides the parcel of land that those three buildings are on, there's a junk yard that sells used auto parts, several factories that barely produce anything anymore, a couple of other struggling businesses and some low-end residential properties."

"These are people we are talking about, Howie. The owners of those struggling businesses, the tenants who live in those low-end buildings, they're people. As long as you objectify the whole thing and talk about 'parcels of land' and 'low-end residential properties' you can simply avoid thinking about all the people who get swept away in these deals."

Howie waved her notions away as immaterial to the argument. "They'll find someplace else. There's still a lot of undeveloped, low-rent areas in Brooklyn."

"I still don't understand why they can't be compensated, Molly said earnestly. "It's not like nobody is going to make any money off this deal. Doesn't it bother you at all?"

"Look, Molly," Howie said as he topped off his coffee from the pot. "Let's say, hypothetically, it's Skana or someone like him we're talking about. And just for your information, he isn't the only property owner who is involved in this deal. But guys like Skana are newcomers. They come from a country where only the most brutal survive, so clawing their way in comes naturally to them. You don't show your cajones by paying off a lot of old people who are too scared to make any trouble for you. And believe me, Molly, he's got to show that he's tougher than anyone else because the other players don't want him in the game. They don't like him, they don't trust him, and they know that he is a killer. But if he's ruthless enough and shows them he can play the game better than they can and make more money, they'll respect him. 'Cause that's what they respect. Money."

He poured a little cream into the cup and stirred it. "When I was a kid, my father would put me to bed by singing Earle T. Foley songs instead of lullabies."

"The Hobo Poet. I have some of his records. They never came out on CDs." Molly took a sip of her own coffee. "He used to perform at rent parties and union rallies back in the thirties and forties."

Howie nodded began to sing in a nasal twang. "'*I've learned a lot in my long life, as through this land I roam/A poor boy robs your dollar bills, a rich man steals your home.*'" You don't get rich in America by pulling a gun and robbing some poor schmuck."

"You go after people's homes instead, and you hire Stiegel, Lowe, Myers and Donleavy to help you do it," Molly snapped. "And what about you? If you're really representing Skana in this deal, aren't you helping him aim the gun?

"Look at it this way, Molly," he went on as if he hadn't heard her. "Do you know how much money the City is losing by letting that prime waterfront real estate sit around with nothing on it but ancient housing and small businesses that barely pay anything in taxes?" Howie signaled for the check. "That real estate represents potential tax revenues, a substantial amount of it that benefits all of us. Once the waterfront is developed those taxes will go to provide essential City services like

129

sanitation, police, mass transit."

The waiter glided over with the inevitable little leather folder. "Tell those tenants to hire their own lawyer," Howie he plopped his credit card down without even opening the folder. "There's a Brooklyn Law School advocacy group that might take it on."

"Howie," she tried again.

"No, really. I've already talked too much."

Once out on the street, he put a hand on her arm and said softly, "Forget what I just said about contacting the advocacy group at Brooklyn Law School. Better you should stay out of it altogether." He leaned over and gave her a peck on the cheek. "Guys like Skana play by a different set of rules. They're brutal and vicious and will stop at nothing. And I wouldn't want to see you get hurt."

He held her by the shoulders for a moment, studying her face as if he were seeing it for the last time and wanted to memorize her features. Then he leaned in close to her again and said into her ear, "But you didn't hear any of this from me."

Chapter Twenty

No call from Steve that night, nor the next morning. In the office, Molly threw herself into the paperwork piled up on her desk. Later on she made a home visit to an 82 year old client whose case was about to be closed because he kept firing all the home attendants. He was as adamantly against accepting help after Molly's visit as he was before. She left feeling defeated.

Once on the street she glanced at her watch and thought, well, it's almost lunchtime, and I'm in no mood to eat. I'll stop by and visit Willie instead. The winds were gusting up as Molly made her way towards the river, and a few snow flakes whirled around her head like tiny ice dancers .

Turning the corner onto Warwick Street, there was Ana Skana, walking toward Willie's building. Ana's blond hair was blowing around her head and her long, black leather coat was whipping around her ankles.

A moment later, Bukka came out of the building, stood stock still and watched Ana approach. Molly might have well not even been there for all the notice he took of her.

Slowly, Ana sauntered up to Bukka, her hands on her hips. Upon reaching him, she said something indistinguishable, took Bukka's arm and together they walked up the block in Molly's direction. Ana was looking at Bukka with a smile on it that went clear back to Lilith, or perhaps even earlier to Circe, the evil enchantress. And Bukka, poor mortal that he was, could no more resist it than could Ian Sorenson, Assistant Professor of Urban Affairs at Brooklyn College.

As they came almost abreast of each other, Ana turned and met Molly's eyes, raising her own eyebrows slightly, as if asking a silent question.

What does Ana think I know that she doesn't? Molly thought. But she nodded and said, "Good morning."

"Not too good, I don't think."

"You mean the snow?"

Ana lifted her shoulders dismissively and said in her husky voice: "This is not snow. In Moscow, we have snow. For days and weeks, it doesn't stop."

So what did she mean? Before Molly had the chance to ask her,

Bukka growled, "Come on, Ana. He gonna be finished playing by the time we get to the studio."

Molly found herself surprised that Bukka was still there. His slight body, shivering in the blowing wind, seemed inconsequential next to Ana's very vivid persona. In fact, there was something almost shadowy and insignificant about Bukka altogether—until you put a guitar in his hands.

"Ah, yes," Ana said. "We go now." She turned to Molly and once more gave her that silent, questioning look.

I will never understand her, Molly concluded as the couple continued up the block. But seeing Bukka and Papa's daughter together started her mind working in another direction.

Molly climbed the stairs to Willie's apartment, and knocked on the door. "It's open," Willie called. He was sitting on a chair in front of the TV with a glass half-full of something amber resting on a on a small table next to him. For once the old Gibson was no where in sight. He turned bloodshot eyes at her.

"Ms. Molly," he nodded. "Turn that thing off, will you?"

"Hi Willie." She pulled a chair over, turned the TV off and sat down across from him. "How are you doing?"

He shook his head sadly and took a sip out of the glass.

"I saw Bukka outside with Ana Skana," she said. "I thought they had broken up."

"That boy's got a soul full of blues and a head full of grits."

"She's a pretty seductive lady."

"I wouldn't know," Willie shrugged. His words weren't slurred and he didn't seem drunk. "Even when I was going 'round with women, before I found out what god made me, I always followed my mama's advice and stayed away from white women like that. They be poison to a man."

Molly couldn't agree more. "Willie," she asked, "did you learn about Papa Skana's involvement in Ken Belloc's real estate scheme through Bukka?"

"Don't know 'bout no *involvement*," he said, mocking the word she had chosen, "but it's Papa's money, sure enough. That Russian slutsky," he made a face "tol' Bukka and he tol' me."

"Do you think that Papa Skana could have arranged for Cal's death, as a warning to Bukka, to stay away from his daughter? Or to you, to keep him away?"

"If it were a warning," he said angrily, "didn't do much good. And if that ol' man thinks I got any influence over what that boy does or doesn't do, he got another think coming. It's probably more that he wants me out of the building, thinks he can get me out if Cal ain't around."

Pushing the whole topic of Skana away with his hand, Willie got up from the chair, went over to a battered wooden desk that sat in the corner and rooted through one of the drawers. "Look at this, Ms. Molly." It was a letter. As she unfolded it, he added, "I wrote to the great B.B. King hisself. Played back-up for him in Memphis, in the old days and he still remembers me."

The letter was signed with a scrawl that could have been B. B. King, or any other name starting with a B, expressing much affection for Willie and offering to arrange an audition for Bukka with his manager. It was dated last year.

"I could'a set it all up for him, made him famous. But he don't want it. " The anger pulsated through Willie's bony body like a flash of live electricity. "I'm an old man. I traveled so many miles, with Gully and without him, seen so much that'd make a man weep." Tears started running down his face, as if his memories were more than his body could contain, and he collapsed back into his chair.

"Blues live in my belly," he said as if it was a mark of pride. "Ain't got it much in my hands no more, but once it's in your belly, it don't ever leave you. All I wanna do is make sure it don't all die with me." Like many old people, Willie's moods changed so quickly from anger to tears and back to anger again, as though they were powered by a toggle switch that kept flipping back and forth.

"I'm sorry, Willie. I know how much this all means to you."

"I'm giving him the 'ol Gibson when I die, I tol' him. What he does with it after that, ain't nothin' I can do about it."

"Guess not, Willie."

"Funeral is tomorrow." Willie's voice was flat, as if he were telling her he was going out to pick up some milk.

"Do you need help getting there?"

"What planet you living on, girl?"

Of course. Molly should have remembered. Donald had made it very clear that Willie would not be welcome at Cal's funeral. This was the sad fate of many long-time gay couples whose relationships were never officially recognized. When one of them died, the family often swooped in and took over, leaving the surviving partner to grieve alone.

"I'm sorry, Willie. Cal's death has upset me so much that it's thrown me a little off my track."

She heard a noise outside the door and in a moment Louis Kroski dressed in jeans, a denim jacket and a knitted watch cap entered the room. He was carrying two plastic bags full of groceries.

"What are you doing here, Louis" Molly demanded angrily. "If Stuttman finds out, he'll throw a fit."

"Let him, Molly. I couldn't give a shit."

His point was valid, but she was in no mood to apologize to anyone.

133

He watched her scowl at him for a moment. Then, with twinkling eyes, he asked, "How do you hide an elephant in a cherry tree?"

She took a deep breath and let the air out in a soft sigh, trying to will herself into a better mood. "I don't know. How?"

"Paint his balls red."

Molly burst out laughing.

"That's what I like to see. A little smile. A little laugh." His face took on an is-everybody-happy kind of look. "You can get too damn serious, Molly. You know that?"

"I've got a lot of things on my mind."

Louis unpacked the groceries quickly, turning to put things into the refrigerator and onto the pantry shelves. Molly stood watching him for any sign of Da Mour lurking within and finding only the strictly masculine movements of a typical blue-collar guy. Now you see it, now you don't. Do you ever know who anyone really is?

Willie had gone back to his drink and his TV set. So when Louis was finished he said to Molly, "Let me buy you some lunch."

"You're without a job at present, Louis. Allow me . . ."

"No, no," he cut her off. "I'm working temporary late-night security at *The Crooked Peg*." This was a local club that had had some problems recently with substance-fueled fights between the patrons. "Besides which, a gentleman always buys the lady her lunch."

"Now you're a gentleman? You're confusing me, Louis."

"Join the club," he mumbled.

They left Willie's building and crossed the street to the river. The wind had died down and sky was dull and overcast. The snow flakes floating around hadn't yet decided whether or not to become a proper storm. The concrete and glass buildings across the river, without any sun to light them up, appeared as dreary as the sky and the pewter-gray water. A few gulls circled overhead and two pigeons alighted on the fence. One jumped onto the ground and looked up at them beseechingly.

"Someone around here feeds them," Louis said. "They're spoiled."

They stood a while longer, each lost in thought. Molly, shoving her hands deeper into her pockets, finally said, "I saw Bukka and Ana Skana outside Willie's building before I went upstairs to visit him. If Papa was supposed to have broken them up, nobody told them."

"I know. I've seen them together, too." He grinned slyly, looking a little more like Da Mour as he did so. "I think Ana Skana enjoys playing with fire"

"Most of the time, Bukka seems more like a pile of burning embers than a raging fire."

"It's not Bukka, I'm talking about."

"What? Oh, you mean Papa."

"Whatever it is between those two . . ." Again, the sly grin. "I'm just glad I never had a daughter."

Molly laughed. "I could just see it, Louis. Most little girls compete with their mothers. But your daughter . . ."

"Okay, okay, I get the point." A gull landed on top of the fence and cackled so loudly, the pigeons flew away. Molly and Louis both laughed.

"We've been thinking that Papa had Cal murdered," Molly said, serious again, "either through Donald or someone else, to get Willie out of that building. But none of the other tenants seem to be getting bumped off, except one poor lady who died of a heart attack. Do you think the murder was more personal? Maybe Papa had Cal killed as a warning to Bukka, or to Willie to keep his great-grandson away from her?"

"I don't think Papa would bother with a middle-man. If Papa really wanted to get Bukka away from his darling daughter, he'd go straight to the source, and it would have been Bukka who turned up dead."

"Wouldn't Ana be pretty angry at him if he did that?"

Louis nodded. "He lets her get away with a lot, but nobody ever crosses Papa Skana for long. She may play with fire, but I'm not sure she wants everything to go up in flames." Another gull landed next to the first, and they watched them for a few minutes as Louis thought something over. "You think that Donald is really Papa Skana's contract killer?" he asked.

"I don't know what to think." Molly shivered. "It's getting a little chilly here. I never did like the cold." They turned away from the river and started walking.

"So what's bothering you, Molly," Louis said as they turned the corner onto Leyton Street, "if you don't mind my asking? You look like someone who has lost her best friend."

When Molly didn't respond, he said, "It's that Neanderthal cop, isn't it." Louis put a broad hand on his heart and tapped his chest—pitter-pat, pitter-pat. "He's giving you a hard time."

"I'm just being silly."

"I don't know you all that well, Molly, but you don't strike me as a silly person."

"Two nights he doesn't want my company, and I'm already thinking the worst."

"And I don't see you as particularly clingy, either. So if you're thinking the worst, there must be a reason for it."

Molly was filled with gratitude for the unquestioning way he accepted her feelings as having some basis in fact. "I lost him once, already, on 9/11."

"What do you mean?"

"We were together on 9/10 and come 9/11, he's gone. The whole thing hit him really hard. He lost friends and colleagues in that disaster.

135

And now I'm afraid he's going to disappear again."

"Why would you think that?"

"He's just had a son go missing in Iraq."

"Losing a son—that's hard, Molly, or so my mother used to imply every time I'd get dressed up to go out in a hot little something. Maybe you just have to give him some time."

"Maybe," she said, unconvinced.

Louis pulled his watch cap off with one hand and rubbed his closely-cropped hair with the played fingers of the other. "I think I must have developed some rash from that damn wig," he said morosely.

"Louis, how did you ever end up in the navy?"

"I guess I wanted to prove to myself that I really was a man."

"You told me that you were straight."

"Yeah, I never wanted to sleep with men—at least not most of them—but wanting to wear women's clothing confused the hell out of me."

They'd stopped in front of a partially-renovated three-family house on Leyton Street. It sported spanking-clean beige siding and peacock-blue shutters. Glancing up, Molly noticed that the roof was sagging. Mutton dressed up as lamb.

"Molly," Louis was saying, "do you think I just woke up one day and decided to put on women's clothes? I've been living with this stuff since I was five years old. That's about when I started putting on my mother's lipstick and walking around in her shoes. You try growing up as a cross-dresser in a working class neighborhood in Brooklyn."

She laughed wryly. "I couldn't even imagine it."

"I used to think I had a split personality. I was a football player in high school, a guard—I was never fast enough to be a quarterback. I loved the game, all that physical contact," a quick, impish smile, "but as soon as a game would be over I'd want to run right home and put on a dress. Is that a split personality or what?"

"Louis, I know what a split personality is—technically it's called Dissociative Identity Disorder—and you aren't one. In a real split personality, the left hand doesn't know what the right hand is doing. You do."

"I'm glad you have so much faith in me. You ready for lunch?" There was a slight bit of Da Mour's flirtatiousness in the way he asked the question.

The sky had become even grayer and snow was whipping around. Molly shivered again. I don't think I'm up to even a minor flirtation with a man who dressed in stiletto heels and a blond, bee-hive wig, she thought and glanced at her watch. It was past the point where she could make any reasonable claim to a continued lunch hour.

"I'm going to take a rain check, Louis."

136

Chapter Twenty-One

Dave Scheunfeldt, pushing an empty shopping cart in front of him as if it were a baby carriage, called out to Molly. She stopped as he crossed the street, which he did by putting his hand up and then waiting until two cars came to a complete halt.

"Good afternoon, my dear lady," he said a little breathlessly.

"Hello, Dave."

The warmth in her voice caused the old man to smile. "I'm on my way to the store to buy a few things before the snow really hits."

"Is this supposed to be a big storm?" she asked, remembering to speak a little louder as he was a bit deaf. "I didn't watch the weather this morning."

"Oh yes" Dave nodded, his head rocking back and forth on his brawny neck as if it were on a spring. "They're predicting four to six inches."

"Well, it's winter in New York," she said lightly. "We have to expect that it will snow."

"For you, it's snow. For me it means I'm stuck in the house." He let go of the shopping cart with one hand and pushed up his pants leg to show her a huge purple bruise in his shin. "I'm not steady enough to go out in the snow."

"What happened, Dave?"

"I'm climbing up a little step stool that I've climbed up a hundred times before, when suddenly, something in the head goes tipsy-turvey and next thing I know, I'm on the floor." He tapped the offending part of his body with the heel of his hand. "Twenty years ago, I never thought about my head, except to complain about all the hair that fell out of it. Now, I watch what goes on inside it like it was a soap opera. 'What's going to happen to you today?' I ask it. 'Will you remember where you put your keys? Or the name of that friend that you've been sitting next to at lunch every day for the past ten years?' It's like The Perils of Pauline—that's a soap opera way before your time, my dear lady. A serial, we called it then. Only it was in the movies, not on TV. Every week you would leave the poor girl in some terrible situation, like tied up on the train tracks, and you would come back the next week to find out what happened to her. That's like my head."

Molly was laughing. "Dave, I doff my hat to you. Most of the younger people I know wouldn't be able to cope with what you cope with on a daily basis—legs that give out, a head that doesn't always work right."

"Blood pressure that shoots through the roof every time I see that Belloc or his Nazi *shtarker*, that means, for you, hooligan, dear lady." he finished. "Which reminds me, he hasn't been around lately. Do we have you to thank for that?"

Dave looked at her expectantly. She smiled and said mysteriously, "I have my ways."

He grabbed hold of the shopping cart with both hands and they walked together for a little ways.

"Tell me Dave, have you seen the doctor about that dizzy spell?"

"If I went to the doctor every time I had a dizzy spell, she'd be spending more time with me than she does with her husband. I met her husband once, and he wouldn't like it."

"I think you should have it checked. Perhaps your blood pressure medication needs to be adjusted."

"Maybe after the snow has gone," he said with a shrug.

He won't go, Molly knew. The older people she worked with seemed to be of two types when it came to health care: one group were either on their way to the doctor, at the doctor, or had just come home from the doctor. The other group needed to have a certified heart attack before they would even contemplate going to the doctor, and then they might just decide it was indigestion and still not go. Dave Scheunfeldt stood squarely in the second camp.

They had reached the corner of Layton and Freymont Avenue. Gentrification, big time, was taking place in the buildings around this particular corner, but the block was in flux. An abandoned loading dock stood next to a fake-vine-covered wine bar named The Purple Grape. Two doors down, an old brick matzo factory abutted a kitchy little wood and stained-glass bistro called Cathy's Caravansary.

Dave stopped walking and eyeballed the little bistro. "I don't see any camels," he said dryly.

"Excuse me?" Molly asked, a little confused.

"Do you know what a "caravansary" is, my dear lady?"

"I give up," Molly answered, happy to play along. "What is a caravansary?"

"A caravansary is like a hotel or an inn with a big courtyard where caravans can park their camels." He took one hand off the shopping cart and made a sweeping gesture with it. "Have you ever seen a camel in Brooklyn?"

"No," Molly answered with a straight face. "I can't say that I have."

"So why do we need a caravansary?"

She burst out laughing again.

"It's not funny," Dave scolded her. "This store used to be a little market where I could always pick up a container of milk or a loaf of bread. Since we got a caravansary, I have to walk five blocks more, to the big supermarket near Cooper Street. So I'd better be on my way because I must be back home before the snow comes."

With old-world courtesy, Dave extended his arm and they shook hands. He turned one way on Freymont Avenue and she turned the other. This is why I loved my job, Molly thought. Yeah, she dealt with a lot of sickness and grief, but then there'd be a Dave, or a Mrs. Canover clutching poor departed Herman, or Alice Manning with her fruit salad hair and her sly humor, and Molly would feel rooted again, attached to the generations, the ebb and flow of life, secure in a place that was so much larger than Steve and herself. Why did it all have to change? Freymont Avenue was supposed to be the place to where her heart could always come home.

Back at the office, she tried Steve again. To her surprise, he picked up.

"So, what's going on with you?" she asked. "It couldn't be that you haven't been getting my messages."

"I've been up to my ears in work," he said flatly.

"No, no, no," Molly said. "That's my line. I'm the one who finds excuses not to talk about things. You're the talker. Only you aren't talking."

Silence. Then: "Look, Molly, I need to take a break right now."

"You mean from us?"

"Believe me, Molly. You're the first woman in a long time I've even wanted to try having anything more than a casual relationship with. But this whole thing with Sean . . ."

"I don't understand." She wanted to scream at him, to beat her hands against the phone, the desk, the wall, but she forced herself to calm down. "When you're going through something like this, doesn't it help to have somebody close to you, to talk about it, to share it with you?"

"I can't talk about it, Molly, that's the trouble. Talking about it scares me to death because it makes it real. If he's not already dead, then what terrible things are they doing to him?" He made a choking sound. "I can't even think about it, much less talk about it."

"So we won't talk about it. We'll talk about other things."

"The problem is, Molly, I can't talk about anything else, either."

"So we'll be quiet. I'm good at that."

"Molly, you need someone who can be there for you, go to the movies with you, kid around with you, make love to you. I can't."

The sadness and finality in his voice drained away any remaining

139

anger. Tears welled up. "If you change your mind, or you just need a friend."

"I know, Molly."

She hung up and sat back feeling as if she was disappearing, melting away into the wood and fabric of the chair. It was a strange but familiar sensation and an image came into her mind of herself as a little girl, trying desperately to disappear in the face of her mother's sadness and grief.

It was after eight before Molly got home and glanced at her message machine. The red light shone steadily on with the coldness of a rock-hard garnet. Biting back tears, she went over to her music collection and slipped in a re-mastered CD of Frank Sinatra's, "In the Wee Small Hours," the heart-breaking album of unrequited love that he recorded after his break-up with Ava Gardner. At the first sad sound of the violins, a rush of grief and desolation came up with such intensity, it brought along with it a fear that if she let herself go there tonight, she would drown.

The album she finally settled on was one by the great stride pianist, Meade Lux Lewis. She needed to borrow some strength from somebody; and the pile-driver quality of that powerful left hand which kept the rhythm going steady and strong, punching back at the blues and making it kick ass, was what Molly needed now to get her through the night. At one point, she even managed to get up from her rocking chair and make herself a sandwich, eating it with the kind of dogged determination of someone lost in the wilderness, who will eat tasteless nuts and not-quite-ripe berries simply to stay alive.

So she sat, chewing her sandwich and listening to Meade Lux Lewis's *Glendale Glide, St. Louis Boogie* and *Six Wheel Chaser* until she fell into a deep sleep.

Chapter Twenty-Two

The light coming in through her open blinds told her it was morning. *When he died, I stopped dreaming.* Molly could still hear the widow of one of her late clients saying this in a grief-stricken voice, and she had always remembered it. Stumbling into the shower and letting the water cascade down her body, she replayed that last conversation with Steve until it felt washed out, denuded of any real meaning.

Afterwards, she wandered through the tiny apartment like a lost apparition, finally stopping by the window. It was still snowing. According to Megan Monahan, the weather lady on the local station, a little over four inches had accumulated and two to three more inches were expected. A snowy weekend with nothing much to do. She spent a long time sitting over her coffee, calling some friends, making a dinner date for the next evening with her old school friend, Katie Morris, and catching up on some bills. By the time Molly left her apartment to do a little shopping people were already outside with their shovels and thin pathways had been cut through the snow. The plows and sanders had been through, leaving dirt-streaked hillocks obscuring snow-covered cars. But the new snow was quickly replacing the old, and the plow, poised at the end of the block, was about to come through again.

Back in the apartment. After putting away the few items she'd bought, Molly went out again and took one of her long walks around the City, trudging through snow-covered sidewalks and over snow-stacked crosswalks, seeking out some of her favorite buildings—the elegant brownstones with their black iron railings, now topped with white frosting, along Gramercy Park, the gargoyles and lovely bits of architectural detail on what was left of Chelsea's once stylish shopping avenues—watching kids on their snow boards and sleds having fun and feeling depressed because she so much wanted to be doing this all with Steve.

Sunday morning—the air crisp and clear, the sky as blue as a mountain lake, walking morosely down Allen Street towards Ben's apartment to discuss his going back to the doctor. Kids were joyously throwing snowballs at each other. Someone had built a raunchy snowman with a carrot sticking straight out of his crotch and a homeboy hat tilted rakishly over one eye. Ben was out. It was actually a relief because Molly had no clear strategy on how to approach him. In her present mood an absolute refusal from him, which was more than likely, might throw her over the edge. Katie met her for dinner in Chinatown. Molly found herself listening to Katie's wedding plans without being able to say much herself. Something her mother had told her as a small child floated through her mind: *If you have nothing good to say, don't say anything at all.*

Monday morning - flipping on the TV to find out how the city had fared after all the snow. Megan Monahan looked so disgustingly bright and chipper that Molly was about to turn it off in protest.

A small news item caught her attention: the body of a young black male had been found on Warwick Street in Brooklyn. He had been shot two times with a small caliber gun and had died on the way to the hospital. He had been identified as Billy Keith Johnson.

Billy Keith . . . B. K. Johnson. Bukka? That got Molly's mind focused, all right. Break-up or not, she needed to talk to Steve and called his cell phone. No answer. She left a message asking if the victim was Bukka, brewed some coffee which she drank without much enthusiasm and put on her waterproof boots.

The Manhattan sanitation people had gone over the streets with a fine, snow-removing comb. Brooklyn wasn't as well dug out. Molly crunched through the dirty-gray snow that still covered the subway steps, the sidewalk and the curbs of Freymont Avenue. The office of Multi-Care, however, looked like it always did—the same fluorescent lights, the same scuffed walls, yellowing notices and gray metal desks. It remained as untouched as the inside of a thousand-year-old tomb.

"Hey, Nilda," Molly called out. "Are your kids happy that we finally got some snow?"

Nilda rolled her eyes. "Please! You'd think this was a really bad storm, the way everybody is going on about it," she said with disgust. "My kids were telling me they shouldn't be going to school today, like a little snow was going to kill them, or something. I told them, 'This is snow, not nuclear waste.'"

Molly laughed.

"My parents didn't know from snow when they came over here in the 1950's," Nilda went on. "There was never any in Puerto Rico. The first time my mother saw snow, she was eight years old and she couldn't believe it. I mean she'd seen pictures of it, but it was like fairy dust to her,"

"Hey, Nilda, do you know anything about the black kid that was found shot to death on Warwick Street?"

Nilda shook her head. "I didn't even hear about it. That detective—the one you're seeing—he should know." The look on her face said plainly that she was ready for some girl talk about him.

"Probably. I'll call him." Molly reached over and grabbed the

142

messages out of her box.

"You don't want to talk about it, huh?" Nilda said. "That means it's not going too good."

"I don't know what to say about it, Nilda," Molly relented. "His son went missing in Iraq, so he's not in a good head right now."

Swandell Green, about to rush through, stopped for a moment. "My cousin Tyrone got killed there about six months ago," she announced. "National Guard. He joined before the war ever started 'cause he couldn't find no job. His girlfriend was having a baby, and he needed some money to give to her, you know? Now we got one more single black mother raising a fatherless son. And that moron, Bush, talks about family values." She clicked her tongue against the roof of her mouth in disgust. "What the hell is our National Guard doing over there?"

"I'm sorry about your cousin, Swandell. And I ask myself that question all the time—how is ridding the world of Saddam Hussein going to protect our borders and make us safe from Osama? Things just seem to get worse every day."

The phone buzzed and Nilda reached for it. Swandell grabbed her messages and barreled off towards her cubicle. Molly continued on to her office and rifled quickly through her messages. None from Steve. She called the precinct and asked to speak to Detective Carmaggio. He was out. Did she want to leave a message? She did, wondering whether he would call her back, and went off to find Manny. He would know if the dead kid was Bukka. But even he wasn't around – probably out shoveling snow somewhere. So she went back to her office and settled in to do some work.

Steve finally called her back in the middle of the morning, while she was trying to make a referral to Protective Services for one of her cognitively-impaired clients who, she suspected, was being ripped off by his deadbeat son.

"I'm glad you called back, Steve. I just wanted to find out whether the B. K. Johnson that was killed on Warwick Street was Willie's great-grandson, Bukka."

"You heard?"

"I saw it on the news, but I wasn't sure it was him."

"Yeah, and since there might be some tie-in with Cal Bruchman's murder, the case has landed on me. So, I really should talk to you."

"Such enthusiasm." The anger felt better than the loneliness and despair she'd been experiencing all weekend.

"Just because I need to take a break doesn't mean that I still don't have feelings for you."

"Oh? Feelings like I should be on another continent?"

"Come on, Molly. Don't rattle my chain." Pause. "Meet me at Vinny's at noon. We can have lunch and I'll tell myself I'm working."

Vinny's had been in the neighborhood for years, but had recently been gussied up with fake wooden beams and etched glass lighting fixtures, to attract the newcomers, Always the traditionalist, Molly liked it better the old way—dark, beery, noisy, full of old timers and workingmen coming in for a lunch and a quick drink. That was all gone and Vinny had now added *Tuna Wasabe* and *Pasta Provencal* to his traditional burgers and pizza.

Steve was at the bar, a beer in front of him. She sat down on the next stool and when he turned and gave her a peck on the cheek, she could see from his eyes that it wasn't his first. Something clicked in Molly's brain and the whole thing fell into place. Idiot! Why couldn't he have just told me?

"You're drinking again," she said, trying not to sound as angry as she felt. "That's why you've been avoiding me, and why you need a break all of a sudden. You didn't want me to know."

"It all got to be too much." Steve's eyes looked sick, as if he was watching the Ebola virus ravaging through his body and couldn't stop it. "The problem is, back then, in 'Nam, I could block it all out. Yeah, I saw people dying around me, but I didn't know them. I never wanted to know them, so it was a lot easier not to feel anything much. I told myself better them than me. And now. . ." his voice broke. "It's not just Sean, it's like all of a sudden, I'm feeling each and every one of those deaths like it was happening right now, right in front of me. And what makes it worse, is that every one of those dead kids could be my son."

It could have been Ben, too. Her heart opened to him and she started to put her arms around him, but he shook his head slightly and whispered, "Not here. I don't want people talking about us."

He should only know. But she pulled herself back up and became the professional social worker: "Steve, from what I know about PTSD, there comes a point when the grief breaks through and you begin to feel everything that you were blocking out or pushing down before. It's a step in the healing process."

Steve shook his head again savagely. "There are some things you never heal from." He made a gesture with his hand as if he wanted to shove it all somewhere else and stood up. "Let's get ourselves a table."

Grabbing his beer mug, he walked over to a small table that had just been vacated. Molly followed, arranging her jacket on a chair back while the busman cleared the glasses away. Steve ordered a burger and fries and after a slight hesitation, she did, too, remembering the half-eaten bagel sitting on her desk which was all the food she'd had today.

"So tell me what you know about Bukka," he said after the waiter left.

"First tell me what happened." Molly was happy to drop the prior subject because it left them nowhere. "How did he die?"

"I'm the one doing the asking." He stopped and looked a little sheepish. "Okay. I guess you aren't a suspect."

"You only guess?"

"I'll make it a positive statement. You aren't a suspect." He managed a small, grim smile. "Until I find out otherwise."

She rolled her eyes. "God, you are as suspicious as my brother, and he's a certified paranoid schizophrenic."

"Yeah, well, it goes with the territory." He finished his beer in one big gulp. "I'm sorry Molly. This is not one of my better days."

"I know, Steve."

"So, the vic, uh, Bukka, was found on Warwick Street, half a block away from the building he was living in. Shot with a small caliber pistol, a Saturday night special, the ME says." He signaled for another beer. "Gun wasn't found. Probably dropped into the river. Nobody heard or saw anything." He shrugged. "So what else is new?"

Steve's voice, his whole body, gave off a weariness that Molly associated with some of her clients who had been struggling with a debilitating illness for way too many years. Well, post-traumatic stress *is* a long-term chronic illness. As is schizophrenia. What did it say about her that the two men she loved most in her life—and she did love Steve, she realized in a moment of intense certainty—both suffered from a chronic, debilitating, mental illness?

"It's pretty deserted around there," Molly said, willing her attention back into the manifest subject of the conversation. "Willie's building is one of only three that are left on that stretch of Warwick Street."

"Yeah, and the DOA was found in front of a vacant lot, away from the other buildings. So I guess it's possible that nobody did hear anything. Those little pop guns don't make much noise." The beer came and Steve polished off half of it.

"Do you think this is connected to Cal's murder?"

"We still like Donald for that one—he really hated his father and/or he wanted that apartment vacant—but we haven't come up with any evidence that puts him there."

"Why would Donald kill Bukka? I could see him murdering Willie, to empty the building—although now it looks like the building is going to be demolished and Donald doesn't have to do a thing about it—and because Willie was the man who broke up his parents' marriage, but not Bukka."

"I agree. I don't see Donald for this."

"Steve, Anna Skana was having a relationship with Bukka. I saw them together a few days ago, and it didn't look casual. I heard that Papa Skana had ordered her to drop him, but from what I could see, they were like two peas in a pod. I wonder what Papa Skana thought about that?

145

Steve thought about it for a moment. "It's a motive. Papa doesn't like to be crossed. He's on my list to talk to this afternoon anyway, in connection with Bruchman's murder." He sighed. "Problem is, we have no evidence linking Papa to any murder, and we're not likely to get it unless we get some leverage on him, or can flip someone who knows something about it, and right now we've got neither." He eyed the beer left in the mug and took a small sip, as trying to apportion it out. "Or maybe Bukka was killed for some other reason entirely, like a drug deal gone wrong."

"It can't be a coincidence that Bukka got shot so soon after Cal was killed."

"It happens. The kid was a junkie, and the sad truth is that drugs and violence are the milk and cookies of the urban life."

"I had a conversation with a lawyer friend of mine who hinted that Papa Skana was involved in some real dirty dealings. Louis Kroski claims he saw what he thought was some kind of deal going down between Belloc and someone he thought was a City employee. And we all know that Belloc is fronting for Skana." But is he? Molly had never really asked herself that question before. We've all assumed it, she thought, but what do we really know.

"I'll talk to Louis about it. As far as Skana goes, the DA's office is looking into a possible money laundering scheme involving the Russian mob. So far they haven't come up with anything they can prove."

The waiter brought over their burgers. Molly pried open the bun and looked with distaste at the pale, wafer-thin slice of tomato that drooped inelegantly over the meat. It was doubtful whether the *Tuna Wasabi* would have been any better.

"Well, none of that helps Willie." Her voice betrayed the irritation she was feeling with everything at that moment, including the burger she had just bitten into. "Junkie or not, Bukka was Willie's legacy to the world, his link with immortality. And now Bukka's gone."

Steve stared straight ahead and mumbled, "Link with the future . . ."

"I'm sorry, Steve. I didn't mean . . ."

Molly stopped because he wasn't hearing her. His hand groped past the burger, picked up the beer mug and, tilting his head back, he emptied it and sat staring into space.

Sean is right here in this room, she thought, and he won't go away no matter how much alcohol Steve drinks. She desperately wanted to say something that would make him feel better. But nothing came to mind.

"I questioned Willie this morning," Steve said after a while, making an effort to will himself back into the investigation. "He was barely coherent—crying and talking about some old guy named Gibson who, he kept saying, was gonna give it to him. I think he was trying to say that this Gibson threatened to give it to Bukka—but it came out all jumbled up. Do you know who Gibson is?"

"Gibson is the make of Willie's guitar. It's a fine old instrument, a classic. He always calls it 'the Gibson' or 'the ol' Gibson' and said he was going to give it to Bukka after he died."

"Go know." He shrugged. "I'm glad I asked you first, before I wasted a lot of time trying to find this guy."

Glancing at his empty beer mug, he said, "So, I'd better get back to work."

"I thought this lunch *was* work."

"You splitting hairs with me?" Back to his old, provocative self — or at least trying.

All right, Molly thought, I'll play. It's better than this "I need a break" nonsense. She smiled at him, the age-old smile of Circe, Delilah and Ana Skana.

Steve met her eyes. His face slowly relaxed and he said, "If I didn't know better, I'd think you were trying to seduce me."

"Your baser instincts are right again."

A tiny smile traveled up his face, into his eyes and morphed into his lop-sided grin. "You're good for me, Molly, you know that?"

"Come over for dinner tonight, Steve."

"You're gonna cook?"

There was such disbelief in his voice that she had to laugh.

"Yeah, I'm gonna cook. I'm not a Jewish princess, you know. I may not cook as good as your mom, but I did all the cooking around our house when I was a kid."

"You did?"

"Yeah, my mother wasn't, uh, into it."

"Okay. I'm willing to try anything once," he said lightly. "Seven okay?"

The check came. Steve paid it while she finished her burger. He left his untouched.

147

Chapter Twenty-Three

After leaving Steve, she'd walked over to visit Willie who wasn't home. The temperature had risen and the sun was shining. The glistening layer of melting snow on the buildings made them glow like aging actresses who come alive under the glimmering stage lights. Walking back to the office through streets slushy with melting snow, feeling deliciously floaty, she pushed thoughts of Ben and Sean and murder to the back of her mind as she planned the menu for the evening's meal.

When she opened the door, Stuttman was leaning up against Nilda's desk, his eyes fastened on his favorite body part. Reluctantly, he withdrew his gaze and turned towards her. "Nilda was just telling me that Willie Cobb's great-grandson, Bukka, got murdered last night."

"I know about it," Molly said, now well and truly back in the moment. "Detective Carmaggio is investigating and had some questions for me."

Nilda flashed Molly a quick grin.

"Well, of course you'll help the police in anyway you can," Stuttman said as if he were ordering her to salute the flag or rise for the National Anthem.

"Of course, Mr. Stuttman," Molly answered solemnly.

Stuttman pursed his lips and headed towards his office, motioning Molly to follow him.

Behind him, Nilda rolled her eyes.

Once seated behind his desk with Molly in the chair across from him, he squared his shoulders and announced, "There's something I need to raise with you, Ms. Lewin."

Oh, god, Molly thought. What have I done now?

"I must know what's going on in this agency. I'm the director here, and ultimately responsible for all decisions. How do you think it makes me look if staff negotiates deals behind my back and I don't know anything about it?"

"I don't understand."

"I saw Kenny Belloc at Councilman Czarnoski's fundraiser last night."

Well, at least Belloc wasn't out murdering Bukka..

"Apparently, you've been trying to convince him to pay Willie a stipend to move out of the apartment."

She had to cast her mind back to remember the conversations they'd had. It seemed so long ago now. "Actually, that's not true. He offered to pay Willie, but I didn't think anything was settled."

"Well, I knew nothing about it."

"I'm sorry Mr. Stuttman. . ."

"And I had to pretend I did, in order not to look stupid. And, to make matters worse, there were no notes about it in the case record."

Uh oh. Another black mark. "Again, I apologize, Mr. Stuttman. I know it puts you and the agency in a bad position."

"Apologies are not good enough."

Molly had a quick vision of her personnel file, laden with write-ups that were continually multiplying, like an out-of-control fungus. To avoid looking at him, she stared at the photographs on the wall behind his desk. No matter what dignitary he was with, under what circumstances, Stuttman himself always wore the same self-satisfied smirk on his face.

But instead of going on with his rebuke, Stuttman took the pencils out of their holder, arrayed them across his desk said with a certain amount of discomfort, "Kenny asked me stay mum about his offer of moving money. I don't know who he thought I was going to tell, but he acted as though his offer constituted an illegal act."

Okay. Here was the real reason Stuttman wanted to talk to her. He studied the pencils on his desk as if trying to make up his mind about something.. Finally he looked up and met her eyes. There was an expression in his that she had never seen. "Kenny seemed scared about something."

Molly, who knew the benefits of silence, gazed at her boss in an inquiring sort of way.

"You asked me once about Ken Belloc's dealings with Ivan Skanov." When Molly still didn't respond, he went on: "I'm really worried about Kenny."

"What do you mean?"

Silence. He was still deciding how much to tell her. He licked his bottom lip and said, "Kenny owns several other buildings in this neighborhood besides the ones on the waterfront. And most of the apartments in those buildings are de-stabilized which means he's collecting thousands and thousands of dollars a month in rents. And that's besides the buildings he handles as a licensed real estate agent. With the real estate market around here going through the roof, his business should be doing really well."

"And it's not?"

Stuttman looked down at the pencils and back up at her. "This is not to go any further."

"Mr. Stuttman," Molly said, choosing her words carefully, "I can promise not to say anything as long as it doesn't impact on the murder investigation. If it does, the police have to know."

Stuttman nodded once, his mind made up. "Kenny's problem is that he's a gambler. As fast as he makes it, he gambles it away—on the horses, Las Vegas, poker, anything. So he needs money, badly."

"And that's where Skana comes in." Well, Steve would have to know about this!

"Kenny is basically a decent guy," he said as trying to convince himself as well as her. "I can't see him trying to screw his tenants out of a little moving money."

"But Skana would."

The phone rang. He waved his hand at it dismissively and let his voice mail pick it up. Another first. Molly had never known Stuttman to not answer his phone in the middle of any conference they'd ever had.

"There's still something here I don't understand," he went on after the phone stopped ringing. "The buildings along the waterfront are all under rent stabilization. Even if Willie Cobb's legal position is questionable, if Kenny wants to get his leaseholders like Margery Canover out in order to sell the property to the City, under the law he is required to pay them a reasonable stipend for moving expenses."

"Except that, according to several people I've talked to, there seems to be some kind of fix going down."

"What kind of a fix?"

"Somebody in one of the City agencies is getting paid off to make sure the Department of Buildings declares those Warwick Street buildings unsafe. If the landlord doesn't make the necessary repairs, the City can go ahead and condemn the buildings and then have them demolished."

"How do you know this?" he said, glaring at her as if it was her fault.

Molly shook her head. "I really can't tell you. I don't want to get anyone into trouble. But my sources are pretty good."

"I don't like this." He slammed the pencils back into their holder. "I've known Kenny Belloc for a long time, and this is not his game. He doesn't know how to play it, and he's just the kind of schmuck who will end up taking the fall for the Skana, if it comes to that. Or, worse yet, floating in the river."

The phone rang again. He grabbed it, and Molly took that as a sign to leave. Back in her cubicle, she looked at her case notes, knowing she should write them up properly and enter them into the files, but it was no use. She needed to act. So the next few hours were spent making calls to other agencies and health providers on behalf of her clients, a job that had to be done in any event. Advocating, which ran the gamut of

150

requests, discussions and arguments, could almost always get her out of herself. Late in the afternoon, after hanging up the phone and promising without fail to do the case notes tomorrow, she put on her coat and boots and headed out to visit Willie again.

Willie was sitting in the same chair in which he always sat. The old Gibson was in his hands and a half-empty drink on the table next to him. He was jamming the blues. Molly knew the song was one of Blind Gully's, but couldn't remember the name. She sat for a while and listened to him as he played the basic twelve bars over and over again with different emphasis, different rhythms, sometimes going into the melody, sometimes playing around it.

"Willie?"

But he was so far gone, he didn't seem to realize she was there. So she left the building and crossed Warwick Street to look at the river.

A lonely tug was slowly pushing an empty barge. The sun was already down and the last rays turned the sky behind the buildings of Manhattan a dusty rose, like the color of old, dried flowers. In spite of all her immediate problems, Molly was feeling a bit sentimental—a beautiful sunset still had the ability to bring up these feelings—and she remembered the first flower a boy had ever given her. A perfect red rose. The boy was the barest of memories—someone that a friend had hooked her up for a school dance—but the flower had its special place in that memory. She'd kept it, drying it between the pages of a book, as if the keeping of it would somehow preserve the sweetness of that moment. What ever happened to that flower? And why did the flower stay imprinted in her memory and not the boy?

Looking at her watch, Molly realized she had a dinner to prepare and hurried back to the subway. On her way home she stopped to buy some chicken parts, onions, red peppers, mushrooms, canned tomatoes and pasta, thinking to try her hand at some chicken cacciatore. A bag of salad mix, a bottle of balsamic vinegar and one of virgin olive oil would complete the menu.

To accompany the chopping, dicing and sautéing, Molly popped an early Doobie Brothers' CD into her changer. It was a long time since she'd cooked anything of substance and, surprisingly, found it all very soothing. By seven o'clock the chicken was simmering, the water for the pasta was in the pot and the salad was in the bowl. At seven-twenty she turned the chicken off and called Steve. No answer. Between seven-twenty and seven-forty-five, the chicken got stirred at least ten times. At eight o'clock, after receiving no answer to yet another call to Steve, she turned off the chicken.

You've been stood up! she thought angrily. Okay, okay. Cool down. He's a cop, idiot. It's a dangerous job. He could be lying somewhere hurt, or worse.

At eight-thirty, Molly called the precinct and was told he was gone for the day. Could he possibly still turn up? By nine o'clock the walls of her apartment were closing in on her, so she turned the TV on and sat in her rocking chair, surfing the channels and trying to find something that would hold her attention. Fat chance!

At nine-thirty, she put the chicken and salad into her fridge and got undressed. At nine-forty-five, just as she was brushing her teeth, the lobby buzzer rang. It was Steve. She put on her robe and buzzed him in.

Chapter Twenty-Four

Steve stood just inside her door, swaying slightly like a dying tree in a stiff breeze. His eyes were red-veined, the blue in them almost completely obscured. He must have been drinking for hours.

"Steve, did you drive all the way from Brooklyn like this?" Appalled, not only by his condition, but because she'd known all along exactly what he was doing but had not consciously admitted it until just this minute.

Molly tried to get him over to the couch but he collapsed against her. She moved away and pushed the door shut with her shoulder while watching his knees slowly buckle; he was going limp, one little piece at a time. But the force of gravity being what it is, in a short time he was on the floor.

Steve's body had twisted a little as he crumbled and he was lying on his side with his head thrown back. His eyes were half open, the sandy-colored lashes framing the red-streaked oval of whites like a delicate border of feathers around an angry wound. His breathing sounded as though his air passages were semi-clogged with some sticky residue, but the regular rise and fall of his chest convinced her that unless he vomited he wasn't at risk for suffocating.

What to do? Molly's family may have been ridden with problems, but alcoholism was not one of them. Throughout her childhood, her mother had kept what Molly could swear was the same bottle of Four Feathers in the hutch with the good dishes for those occasional times when someone had to be offered a drink. Outside of that, no one in her family ever drank, except for the years before her father's desertion of them, when they did have a Seder. At those times, they would drink Manischewitz sweet wine, taking one or two sips out of their glasses before refilling them for the requisite four times. Molly had had alcoholic clients, but never one in this condition on her living room floor.

Would a shower bring him to a little? But there was no way she could lift him. Passed-out drunk like this, Steve was dead weight. She did manage to move his head to the side so that if he did vomit, he wouldn't swallow it. So she threw an afghan over him and left him on the floor to sleep it off.

For a long time Molly sat at her table, looking at him. Steve lay like a massive oak, his big body taking up most of the floor space in her tiny kitchenette. Why did she love men who were like this? Why not fall for some stable accountant who made a six-figure income and exercised regularly? What deep flaw drew her towards the emotionally mangled? Even Ian, the Assistant Professor of Economics from Brooklyn College, who occupied almost no importance in her life, couldn't leave his apartment without checking several times to make sure the windows were locked and the stove was turned off.

Molly took off her robe and got into bed. Sleep finally came, amidst more jumbled dreams. One fragment: *Ben's tenement apartment, where she was trying to put up new sheet rock to cover the gaping holes left from the fire, only it turned into the World Trade Center, and the walls kept crumbling around her faster that she could replace them.*

Suddenly awake, heart pounding. The sound of her front door closing. No light coming in the window; it must still be night. The hands on the illuminated clock next to her bed said three-thirty. Had someone entered the apartment? Then Molly remembered. Out of bed now, she walked the few feet into the kitchen. Sure enough Steve was gone.

"I hope you are okay," she said to the outgoing message on his cell phone. "Please give me a call."

Back into bed—but not back to sleep. Out of bed again, Molly put a Billie Holliday CD into her changer. The afghan which lay folded on the floor smelled so strongly of the alcohol that had seeped through his pores, it would have to go to the cleaners. She pulled the blue and white comforter off her bed and tucked herself into her rocking chair. The sound of Billie's voice evoked a visual image—a single, lonely bird slowly circling against a gray, cloudy sky.

Despite Billie's great passion for Lester Young and all her other affairs, before and after him, Molly was sure that Billie had been a lonely person. That same loneliness lived in herself, Molly thought. She'd tried to obliterate it by building a world populated by Ben and her clients, trying to pretend that Dave Scheunfeldt, Margery Canover and all the rest were really her family. For a while it had worked. But it wasn't enough anymore—*Ben* wasn't enough anymore. Rocking slowly for a long time, soothing herself back into a state of drowsiness, she finally fell asleep.

It was seven-forty-five when her eyes opened. No message blinking on the machine. She sighed. Late to work yet again.

Thank goodness Stuttman was at a meeting. Molly retrieved her messages and went to her cubicle. Still nothing from Steve, and no pick-up on his cell phone when she tried him again. He needed to know Stuttman's revelation about Kenny's gambling, but she decided not to leave it in a message. What did it matter anyway?

A home visit was on her schedule for eleven with a client named Mrs. Wilotski who was a late riser. "It was the getting up at four thirty in the morning every day of my life," Mrs. Wilotski had told Molly numerous times in a dry, cracking voice. "Hauling the coal up the two flights to start the stove, summer and winter, cooking the breakfasts, making the lunches, and getting the old man out for the six o'clock shift. I'm 83 now dear. And I'll not be getting up before ten ever again, if you don't mind." Molly didn't mind at all, and was walking up Leyton Street on her way to Mrs. Wilotski's apartment when she saw Dave Scheunfeldt making his way towards her.

"Two times in one week, dear lady," he said with a smile. "It's almost more than an old man's heart can bear."

"Oh, go on with you, Dave," Molly said, grinning back at him. "How are you feeling? Any more dizzy spells?"

"As of this moment, no." He shrugged and gestured outward with his arm. "And the snow all melted. What more could a man of my advanced years want? A beautiful lady, no dizzy spells and a clean sidewalk."

"So where are you off to?"

"I'm on my way to that fine dining establishment, the Henry J. Kronin Senior Center, for one of their mouthwatering lunches." Dave rolled his eyes heavenward. "Would you care to join me? I know it's a little early for lunch, but the line starts forming at 10:30. Already I'm going to be late. I can only hope that Alice has saved me a place."

"I'm sorry, Dave. Not today. I'm on my way to visit a client."

He shrugged. "Well, another day perhaps. And bring Margery Canover with you."

"She's stopped coming?"

He nodded. "Alice and I went over to visit her just before the last snowfall. The poor woman was sitting in her dark apartment, with that urn in her lap, and saying as how she couldn't go anywhere until Herman had passed over."

"Oh, dear. I'll get over to see her as soon as I can."

"Actually, my dear lady," Dave said, his bony fingers picking at her coat sleeve like a little chicken pecking at the ground. "You may be just the person to help me."

"Help you with what?"

"I'm trying to organize these *alte cockers.* That means old . . ."

"I know what it means," Molly smiled. "But what are you organizing them to do?"

"A rent strike."

"You're trying to organize a rent strike?"

"Don't look so surprised. I'm a card-carrying member of the Bakers Union, as it was called then. Now it's the Bakers, Food and

155

Allied Workers Union. I'm not exactly sure what kind of food Allied Workers prepare—probably they serve it at the center—I can't always say I recognize the food that's on my plate—but yes, when you don't like the conditions, you organize." He nodded his head several times. "Why should we be paying rent to that *shnorrer* Belloc? He wants our money, he doesn't want to give us anything for it. Just like a bum with his hand out." The wind had whipped up a little and Dave rearranged his cap a little more snuggly onto his bald head. "The buildings are falling apart. The heat comes up at 6:30 a.m. and goes off at 7:30 a.m., along with the hot water. My toilet has been leaking for six months. The stairs are falling apart, the paint is peeling off the walls. Complaining is like throwing dust in the wind."

"Are you getting anywhere with the strike?"

"I can't say as I am, my dear lady. Those people are too old and too scared. They are afraid of being thrown out in the street."

It could very well happen, if Papa Skana has anything to say about it. "Look, Dave, from what I'm hearing, it really seems like those buildings are going to be demolished, one way or the other."

"Demolished?" He said it as though he had just heard about the death of his best friend.

"I don't know anything for sure, but if the City does decide to demolish those buildings, I might be able to get you all some moving money." Oh my god! Why did I say that? Well, she'd have to talk to Belloc herself, shame him into it; find a way to get Papa Skana to go along with it.

What am I thinking? Do I really want to mess with the Russian mob? And even if she could, by some stretch of the imagination, get Belloc-slash-Skana to part with the money—crazy as it might be to even attempt it—they'd still all lose their homes.

Dave, who had taken her at her word, was saying, "Look, my dear lady. I would be lying to you if I didn't tell you my first choice would be to stay in the apartment where I spent so many years with my dear wife. But Goldie taught me that nothing in life is permanent. You know she was in the camps?"

Molly nodded.

He hit his head twice with the heel of his hand. "This brain of mine doesn't remember who I told what to. So what was I saying?"

"You were telling me about Goldie."

"Oh, yes. Goldie and I were talking it over last night. 'You think you're going to organize a rent strike?' she says to me. 'What are you, crazy? It's time to move on, before they do it for you.'"

"Goldie was a very wise woman."

"This neighborhood is not what it was," Dave said sadly. "The shoemakers, the dry cleaners, they're all moving out. Can't afford the rents, I guess. Maybe I can get a little room, closer to the senior center. I'll put everything on shelves so I can see where it all is, instead of now where it all hides away from me in drawers and closets and I can't find anything. There's a nice little superette down there. I wouldn't have to walk so many blocks. So yes, I would take the money and run."

They had come to the corner of Leyton and Holly Street where Mrs. Wilotski's apartment was located. He touched the brim of his cap. "Just know, my dear lady, that I have great confidence in you."

Oh dear. What had she started? Mrs. Wilotski lived almost at the other end of Holly Street. As she walked along the block of two- and three- storey shingled houses, each with its own concrete stoop, she found herself thinking about Dave and his Goldie—the way he still talked to her, asking for and getting her advice. Molly had recently attended a workshop on death and dying where the speaker, a young psychologist, maintained that this attachment to dead spouses was pathological – a way of denying the fact of death—and kept the survivors from moving on in their lives. It might be true for Margery Canover and Herman, Molly thought. But it wasn't true for Dave. Dave *was* going on with his life; he was just taking Goldie with him. The two of them were so interwoven, so much a part of each other's lives that death was just a blip—albeit a big one—in their on-going conversation.

Molly envied them this closeness. Would it ever happen for her? Probably not, if she kept loving such damaged men. Why couldn't she have had a father like Dave? Her own father hardly seemed to matter in her mother's life, nor in hers either, moving soundlessly through their existence like a white, puffy cloud or the merest wisp of a breeze. Suddenly Molly had another image of the small, stunted, creature deep inside her, but this time it was weeping and wailing for the father she had lost, or had never had.

It so unnerved her that she sat down on one of the stoops. How can you cry for someone you hardly knew? Thinking back, she came upon a memory of sitting on her father's shoulders and watching the Macy's Thanksgiving Day parade when she was six years old. He was a tall man, like Steve, but rangy, a cowboy hero. Molly had felt like the Queen of the World as she perched on those bony shoulders, high above the heads of the crowd, excitedly chattering on about the glittering floats and the huge Bullwinkle and Sylvester-shaped balloons as if it was her own, private fairyland. Ben wasn't with them; this was to be a special day, just for her and her father—the only one they'd ever had together, as it turned out. She'd come home so excited to tell her mother all about it. But Doris, who was in the middle of basting the turkey, had brushed her off with a brief, "Can't you see how busy I am?"

Molly sat for a while, her heart aching. She hadn't gone to her father's funeral, there was no reason to go—one Thanksgiving Day parade does not a relationship make—and here she was, so many years later, wishing he were sitting on the stoop next to her so she could ask him what happened? Had he ever loved her? And if so, why had he stopped?

"So, you sit on stoops and cry, too?"

Molly looked up and saw Ana Skana standing in front of her. Molly touched her fingers to her cheek and found that yes, there were tears running down her cheek.

Ana was dressed in a mid-calf light-green skirt, high black boots and a short darker-green jacket. If Ana had been doing any recent crying, her face showed no evidence of it. Nevertheless Molly said, "I'm sorry to hear about Bukka's death."

Ana tossed her blond hair back, smoothed her skirt out, and sat down on the stoop next to Molly. "Why?" Her harsh voice held no more than simple curiosity. "Did you care about him?"

"I hardly knew him. But I saw you two together and assumed, perhaps wrongly, that you cared about him."

Ana studied her for a moment and said, "Come. I will buy you cup of coffee, tea, drink, whatever you Americans like have before lunch."

Molly rose from the stoop, her home visit with Mrs. Wilotske having been forgotten. Ana took her arm and, smiling that secret, seductive *we are the only two people on this earth* smile, she steered Molly back up to Freymont Avenue and into the Beaux Bun Café.

The café was decorated like an old French bistro with a long, zinc-style counter, old wooden chairs, little round dark-wood tables and sawdust on the floor. As soon as they'd seated themselves, a waiter was at their table with menus and a smile for Ana that suggested that he was in the presence of celebrity. This was followed by a short, perfunctory smile for Molly—definitely a groupie and not worth more. Once again, Molly wished she knew how Ana did it.

"Tea is good?" Ana asked. Molly nodded and after ascertaining from Ana that tea was all they wanted, the waiter scurried away to do her bidding.

Ana shrugged her coat off onto the back of the chair, crossed her legs, leaned forward and said, "I thought Bukka would make love like he played that guitar, but he made love like a man does it alone in his bed, you know. . ." She curled four fingers around and, with her thumb straight up, made three slicing motions through the air. ". . . like that."

Molly blinked. "I wouldn't know."

"And so, because I don't waste time with men who don't please me, I tell him I do not make love with him anymore. But he tells me he loves me, as if that should be enough to make me want to let him have sex with him. And I say no, and he gets angry. And so . . ."

The waiter brought over a pot of tea and two cups and saucers. Balanced on top of the dishes was a plate of cookies that neither of them had ordered. He carefully set the plate down, if not exactly in front of Ana, than certainly closer to her than to Molly. Ana chose a cookie from the plate and took a small bite.

Molly, who didn't know what to make of these girlish confidences anymore than she knew what to make of anything else about Ana Skana decided to go for broke. "Did you kill him to stop him from beating you up, or something?"

Ana's eyes flashed; then she softened them with a smile. "I am not here to make confession to you." She poured tea into both of their cups. "I am curious. I want to find out why you simply walk away like you did from that professor and leave him to another woman."

Molly shrugged. "It wasn't that hard."

"Maybe you already know how boring he is, yes?"

Molly nodded, surprised. "You thought he was boring, too?"

"Ah, he wants is to have discussion with me about what went wrong with communism in Russia." Ana tossed her head. Her blond hair waved back and forth like a field of wheat in the wind. She pushed the sugar bowl towards Molly and said, "Tea is meant to be drunk sweet. In my country, most of the people couldn't always get sugar." Ana had already poured a liberal amount of sugar into her tea and now she lazily stirred the liquid with her spoon. "In my house there was always plenty sugar. My father made sure of that."

Molly, who thought of these ideological conversations with Ian as one of the connections that kept their increasingly fragile relationship alive, actually felt sorry for him. Ian was more of a one-note samba than even Molly herself had realized. "So communism, capitalism, are not topics that interest you?"

Ana wiped her mouth delicately with a napkin. "I tell him communism, capitalism, even democracy, is all the same. The strong always grab power, with guns or money or votes, and then take what they want."

Molly laughed. "I bet he didn't like that at all."

Ana glance at her, amused, added even more sugar to her tea and said, "He was very naïve, like a lot of you Americans. That self-important professor of sociology couldn't have survived for more than three days on the streets of Moscow."

"Your father, now," Molly said, still smiling, "there's nothing naïve about him."

"He knows how to get what he wants. And he will use whatever method makes it easiest for him." Ana finished the tea in her cup and raised her eyes to meet Molly's "And so do I." Tilting the spout over Molly's cup, Ana asked if Molly would like some more.

159

There was something so tender and intimate in the gesture that Molly almost said yes. But suddenly, remembering Mrs. Wilotski, she looked at her watch, jumped up and said, "I'd better get going. I'm late for an appointment with a client." Pulling some money out of her pocket, she attempted to put it on the table.

Ana placed a hand over Molly's—her fingers were warm, their touch almost like a caress—and said: "I take you out, no? Then I pay."

Molly looked down at their hands, and then at Ana's face. On it was that intriguingly seductive smile.

Chapter Twenty-Five

Molly managed to gracefully extricate her hand, but the memory of that touch lasted throughout the rest of the day and left her feeling that the two of them were in some kind of complicity that Ana understood and she didn't. After work, not yet ready to go home and think about any of it, Molly walked east, towards Van Guilder Street and the Runway. The weather had warmed up into a misty fog that swirled around the streetlamps. People picked their ways gingerly through melting piles of slushy snow.

Da Mour was hard to miss. Hot-pink shorts that looked ready to split their seams from the pressure of her heavily-muscled thighs. A low-cut, waist-length garment made of layers of white satin fringes. Where does she get this stuff? Molly thought. The blond, bouffant wig and the white, patent-leather boots looked to be the same ones she had worn the first time Molly had seen her. She was leaning on a lamppost, drinking beer out of a can. A faded denim jacket was on the ground next to her.

Da Mour caught Molly's eye and smiled. "You like it?" The red-tipped fingers of her free hand caressed the length of the outfit which had a few muddy spots on it. "Sometimes I like to look a little trashy."

"What makes this one trashier than that body stocking you were wearing the last time I saw you here?"

"Oh, honey, this one shows a lot more leg."

"Well, you look quite, uh, smashing," Molly said, trying to keep a straight face.

"Come on, Molly." Louis's voice. "Don't shit the shitter. I know what I look like in this stuff, but it makes me feel good and it passes the time." She gestured with the beer and said to Molly, "Can I buy you one?"

Molly shook her head.

"How about a cup of coffee?"

"Thanks."

Da Mour quickly finished the beer and threw the can into a trash basket. Picking up the jacket and taking Molly's arm, they headed to the joint where they'd gone the first time. The place hadn't undergone any renovations. They found a table and Da Mour went off to the steam counter as Molly looked around. Two guys who probably hadn't slept in a couple of days were sitting at the next table drinking beer. One was dressed Goth style in black leather with several piercings on his pallid face and a series of tarnished silver chains across his chest. The other was dressed in jeans and a corduroy jacket and had a Mohawk which split the top of his otherwise bald head like a mountain range jutting out of the desert.

Da Mour came back with two steaming mugs, a handful of small pre-packaged creamers and a couple of donuts on a tray. Slipping down onto the chair, she removed the wig and the long, rhinestone earrings and put them on top of the denim jacket which was on the seat next to her. Despite the make-up and the outlandish outfit, the close-clipped, graying hair and the totally masculine movements brought Louis back, and 'she' became 'he' again.

"Have you seen Willie?" Molly asked.

Louis nodded. "He's slipping away, little by little. Most of the time, all he does is sit and play that guitar. The same song, too. It's like he's forgotten every other song he ever knew." Two tiny worry lines like bird tracks appeared across his heavily made-up brow. "He's so old, Molly. Until the last few weeks I couldn't believe he was eighty-six. Today, he looked every bit of it, and more. I'll stop by later on with some supper and make sure that he eats."

"He's lucky to have you, Louis."

They sat in silence for a few minutes as Molly sipped her coffee and Louis nibbled a donut. The place was half-full of a mixture of transvestites, female prostitutes, working-class guys in flannel shirts, and hard-core punk and goth guys like the pair who were sitting next to them. Molly thought back to the first time she'd come into this place with Louis and how weird he, and the place, seemed to her. Now, the lipstick and false eyelashes were still obviously there, it wasn't unsettling in the way that it had been; she was able to see past it and find the old Louis, just as she'd always been able to look past Ben's odd behaviors and strange mannerisms to find the brother she knew and loved.

"I saw your boyfriend earlier today," Louis said, brushing crumbs from the fringes of his white satin top. "He's investigating Bukka's murder."

His eyes shot her a question and she nodded. "I know about it."

"I gotta tell you, Molly." He shifted his shoulders and readjusted the neckline to cover up a little more of his décolletage. "He appeared, shall we say, a lot more than two sheets to the wind."

Molly could feel the red starting up in her face again—for Steve as well as for herself and her choice in men.

"I don't mean to be out of line here," he said sincerely, "but I like you, I really do, and if you just want to talk, I'm willing to listen."

Molly sipped her coffee and thought about it. It would help to talk—although she'd have to pick her way through what and how much to say since Steve was the investigating officer in two murder inquiries. "I don't know what to do, Louis," she began, choosing words carefully. "He's really a good guy, but he's got PTSD and ever since his son went missing in Iraq, he's, well, you've seen it for yourself. He went through a bad time after 9/11, but he's been dry since then," she added hurriedly. "Until now."

"He's 'Nam, right?"

"Combat veteran."

"I just missed that war—I'm a few years younger than he is, I guess. But I heard all about those fucking jungles from some of the lifers I served with in the navy." His voice suddenly had a hard, angry edge. "It wasn't until 'Nam that they began to take PTSD seriously—so many guys came home with it. Until then, they called it combat fatigue and thought it came from a defect in character."

"Like schizophrenia," she said softly.

"I thought we decided I wasn't schizophrenic."

Molly smiled. "You're not."

"You've got a great smile." He smiled back. "But you don't use it enough. Life's just too damn tough to be so serious about it all the time."

"I know you're right, Louis. And that's exactly what I like about some of the old people I work with. Things can be really bad, but they've learned how to laugh at it. They've got a kind of resilience that amazes me."

Louis made a maybe-yes, maybe-no gesture with his head. "At least some of them do. Some of the others I've worked with . . . well, they can be pretty grim."

"Do you know Dave Scheunfeldt?" Molly went on, lost in her own thoughts for once. "He lives in one of the buildings on Warwick Street, near Willie, that's about to be demolished for this shopping center thing."

"I think I know who he is."

"He talks to his wife Goldie who's been dead a long time."

Louis raised carefully plucked eyebrows and tapped forehead with forefinger.

"No, he knows she's dead. He just talks things over with her because that's what he's always done. And she gives him good advice, too."

"What does she tell him?"

"She tells him that nothing is permanent and it's time to move on. If I can get him some moving money, he's ready to go."

"You don't look happy about it."

"I think maybe I offered something that I can't fulfill. And I try never to do that. Besides, at first he was talking about organizing a rent

163

strike, and I was, like, 'atta boy! Go to it!' But 'take the money and run?'" Molly lifted her eyebrows. "It feels like Goliath wins and David slinks away." Sighing, she stretched her neck to relieve some of the tension. "I seem to want time to stand still, everything to stay the same. I mourn the destruction of the old buildings, the old neighborhoods, as if they were members of my family."

"I think we're all in some kind of state of mourning since 9/11," Louis answered seriously. "We idealize what was, before 9/11 took it away from us, as if we all lived in some kind of Eden where everything was beautiful. But was the past ever really all that great?" He shrugged, the layers of white fringes shimmying back and forth with the movement of his shoulders. "The shit that led up to 9/11 was going on for years. Look at what happened in '93 with the first plot to blow up the World Trade Center? We just lost our ability to shove it under the rug and not think about it."

"I know you're right, Louis. But . . ."

"Okay, okay!" His red-painted mouth turned up and he swept his hand down the contours of his outfit. "Far be it from me to seek to destroy anybody's illusions."

She grinned at him, despite herself.

"Getting back to those buildings. The facades of the three of them along Warwick Street *are* beautiful, Molly. You can't get away from that. All the developers would have to do is to put some money into repairing them. They could still build the shopping center around them, or turn the buildings themselves into lofts and rent them out to small venders. It wouldn't take much. The buildings are still sound, a lot sounder than those twin towers turned out to be," he added sadly. "And they're part of Brooklyn's history. If the City knocks them down, they're no better than those terrorists."

They'd gotten off their discussion about Steve; it would help to talk to Louis about him some more, but perhaps she'd already said too much. She stared down at her coffee cup, aware of Louis's eyes watching her.

"It's not fair, asking Willie to give up his apartment after all that he's just lost," Molly said after a while.

"I couldn't agree more."

"But from what I've heard, the City is going to demolish those buildings and he's going to have to move, like it or not."

They sighed in unison, and Louis said, "I forgot to mention something Willie did tell me. He said that he saw Bukka arguing with someone he thought was a drug dealer a couple of days before he was murdered."

"Did he, or you, tell that to Steve?"

"As I said before—and no offense to you, Molly—I wouldn't tell the man his pants were on fire, and I don't care if he does have PTSD."

164

His fingers were playing with the blond curls on the wig that sat next to him, rearranging them into ever more elaborate constructions. "I don't know what Willie told him. Why don't you mention it?"

"I can't. He won't return my phone calls."

"He's still playing hard to get, huh."

She nodded.

"That just proves it." His hands stopped playing with the wig. Looking straight at her, he said, "Any man who manages to get himself a woman like you and then blows her off deserves to be strung up by his balls."

Molly laughed.

"No, I'm serious."

Louis examined his scarlet-tipped fingers. "Dammit, I chipped a nail." Snapping open a little beaded bag strapped around his waist, he took out an emery board and proceeded to carefully file one of the nails on his left hand. "So, you ready to take a break from Neanderthal Man?" He gave her a long, seductive look from under his false eyelashes. "The Eagles are appearing at the Brooklyn Academy of Music on Saturday. Are you into old rock and roll? Or we can go dancing."

She didn't want this, but also didn't want to hurt his feelings. "Louis, I really like you. I can see us becoming good friends, but . . ."

"I don't have to dress trashy," he broke in solemnly, "I know that's not your style. I'm willing to go for a simple little basic black number, maybe with a single strand of pearls."

"Louis," she said, choosing her words with care, "I just couldn't be romantic with a man who wears women's clothes. And from what I've read about transvestites, it's not something you can give up."

Louis's mouth was twitching; he was putting her on. Molly relaxed back in her chair and grinned.

"It wouldn't work anyway," he said with a straight face. "You're too small for me. I couldn't get into your underwear. My last girlfriend was twice your size and into Victoria's Secret big time—those lacey push-ups and the wispy little teddies. O-o-h! I was like a kid in a candy factory"

Molly laughed out loud. "You just like to shock people."

Cocking his head at her, he opened his eyes wide and said, "What else can a girl like me do for fun in Brooklyn?" His bright-red mouth turned up into a big grin. "Got you laughing, though, didn't I?"

She shook her head wryly and lifted her eyes up to the heavens.

"Besides, I know a one-man woman when I see one." He glanced down and said, "You haven't touched your donut. Do you want it?" An image of Steve, worrying about her eating habits, or lack of them. Roughly, she pushed the image away and gestured with her open palm, releasing her rights to the pastry. Louis popped it into his mouth. "So what are you going to do about him?" he asked after he'd swallowed the last morsel.

"I don't know, Louis." She was going to leave it there, but then heard herself saying, "Maybe he's just too damaged to have a relationship with anyone."

"Come on, Molly. Who of us isn't three feet off the cookie sheet, as my twelve-year old nephew puts it?" Once more he ran his hand with its long, varnished nails down his outlandishly-dressed body. "Look at me. And look around this room." Several of the strange assortment of punks and goths and cross-dressers sitting under the florescent lights. were very tête-à-tête, obviously coupled. "If not being damaged was the criteria for entering into relationships, we'd all be living alone on desert islands."

"I don't know, Louis. Yeah, we're all damaged, but some of us are damaged far worse than others. And I seem to pick 'em."

"Do you love him?"

At first, she was going to play it down, deny it. But the heat came up into her cheeks, giving him his answer.

"Does he love you?"

Her cheeks got even hotter. Aside from the possible dangers to Steve, it was so hard for Molly to talk on this level with anyone, let alone a man with scarlet lips and long, fluttering eyelashes. But need has a funny way of breaking through inhibitions. "He says he has feelings for me," she mumbled.

"If a guy like him says he has feelings for you, it means he's head over heels."

"Oh, come on Louis." This she was not ready to believe. "Besides, two people can love each other but not be able to works things out sufficiently to have a relationship."

"How do you know whether you and Mr. NYPD can have a relationship or not? Have you ever really tried it?"

"What are you talking about?"

"From what you've told me, every time you two run into a glitch, that's it. End of story."

"This isn't my doing." *I wasn't the one passed out drunk on the floor.* But this was not for Louis's ears. She sighed, remembering the click of the door closing during the night. It had sounded so final.

"It's on *your* head if you leave it like this. If you really love someone, you don't give up on him so fast."

Steve is a drunk. Do I really want to be running after someone like that?

Louis pushed his chair back and got up. "I gotta check on Willie and make sure that he eats his supper." He moved the wig and earrings aside and slipped into the denim jacket which looked completely incongruous over his hot pink shorts and patent leather boots. "Come home with me while I change, Molly, and then I can walk you to the subway. This isn't the best neighborhood."

"It's okay, Louis. I'll take a car service."

"You sure?" She nodded, took out her cell phone and punched in the code for the car service the agency always used.

A quick smile and he made his way between the tables and out into the night.

Chapter Twenty-Six

Willie looked as though he hadn't moved since the last time she'd seen him. Not having heard from Steve by lunchtime the next day, Molly had walked over to Willie's apartment to find him still playing Gully's same twelve bars.

"How've you been, Willie?"

He started a little at the sound of her voice, his fingers freezing on the strings. "My mama tol' me messing with you would get me in trouble." His voice dark with an anger that Molly knew had nothing to do with her.

"You mean because I'm a white woman?" Which white woman does he think I am, Ana Skana? Or someone I don't even know about?

"White women is what does it every time." His eyes were wild, full of rapidly shifting feelings. "Look what she did to that bitty boy. Got him into all kinds a' trouble."

Ana Skana, for sure. "Willie . . .?"

His face slowly smoothed out as recognition returned to his eyes. "Ms Molly, sorry, my mind was drifting. It does that a lot these days."

"I can understand that, Willie." She smiled to show there was no offense taken. "I have a question for you. Did Bukka say anything about Ana Skana, or her father, Papa Skana, threatening him?"

Willie's fingers went back to the guitar, beating out a rat-tat-tat on the strings that sounded like gun shots. His voice trembled as he sang:

If I don't find trouble,
Trouble find me
Oh lordy, lordy, trouble find me.

"Is that a 'yes', Willie?"

"If they did, he never said nothin' to me 'bout it." His fingers slid back to Gully's twelve bars and his mouth clamped shut. Either he didn't know anything else, or he wasn't gonna talk. Could either or both of the Skana's have threatened him, too? She wouldn't put it past them.

Molly shifted in her chair. "Okay Willie. Let's switch to something else. Did you tell the detective that you saw Bukka arguing with a drug dealer?"

Willie let the guitar slip onto his lap and thought about it. "Might have. Don't really know."

"Do you know who the drug dealer was?"

"What's the difference now? Nothing can bring Bukka back."

"Don't you want to see his killer brought to justice?" Her tone came out a little sharper than she would have wished.

He re-positioned the guitar, and his bony fingers returned to picking Gully's riff. "One thing you learn from growin' up black in a white man's world is that "justice" is a word means one thing to white folks and another thing to black folks. Don't put much faith in it myself."

"Humor me, Willie. Just tell me his name."

For a moment his eyes faded away and Molly thought he was going to drift off again. But he scratched his unshaven chin and said: "Don't know his real name. Street name is Ishmael. Think he was once some kind of Moslem. A lot of the brothers come out of jail that way." A thin smile cracked through the planes of his face. "Don' think he be much of a Moslem anymore."

"Thank you, Willie. So how *have* you been? Do you need any help with anything?"

"Louis been coming by. I must've done something good in my life for that boy to have been sent to me." One tear rolled down his face. "Don't know exactly what it was, but I am grateful."

He went back to Gully's riff which he toyed with for a while before segueing into an old blues, one of Big Bill Broonzy's. More tears gathered in his eyes, making them look luminous. *In the evening when the sun goes down/ so lonesome, it's so lonesome/ when the one you love ain't aroun'.*

The song so echoed Molly's own feelings, she could feel the tears behind her eyes. A wave of helplessness hit her like a big dollop of molasses, sliding down her body, making her limbs feel stuck and heavy.

"So many gone," he intoned. "So many gone. Don' know who to cry for first."

This is no good. We can't both be drowning in this well of grief. Molly took a deep breath and began asking him questions about his early life. The stories Willie told her were mostly repeats, but by entering into his life she was able, once again, to distance from her own feelings. By the time she left Willie's apartment and started down the stairs, the heaviness had lifted.

Molly's foot was just reaching the bottom landing when the door opened and Donald Bruchman walked into the building. In this entranceway of peeling paint and cracked linoleum, his fitted brown suede jacket and matching brown leather boots made him look like one perfectly manicured bush standing in the midst of a junk yard.

"What are you doing here?" he snapped. His anger seemed to have grown like a malignancy since their last encounter.

"Excuse me?" she retorted. "Since when do I have to answer to you?"

"Your agency has no clients living in this building. There's no reason for you to be here."

"Are you out of your mind?"

Donald stared at her as if she'd suddenly uncovered his deepest, darkest secret.

Wait a minute, whatever else he may or may not have done, his father has just been murdered. And there's no proof that he did it. Have a little compassion.

"Look, Mr. Bruchman," Molly said in a gentled-down voice, "I know this must be very hard for you . . ."

"I don't need your sympathy," he snarled, showing little pointed teeth, like those of a small rodent. "And I don't believe it anyway. You've been a troublemaker from the start."

"I'm trying to help Willie . . ."

"That pervert!" Donald's face reddened to the color of raw meat. "My father would still be alive if it wasn't for him." Suddenly his hand shot out and grabbed the collar of her jacket. "Why don't you just turn yourself around and get out of here!"

The little tingle of fear rippling down her back caused her to go on the offensive. "Take your hands off me!" she yelled, thrusting her arm up between her face and his to block him and then pushing out, knocking his arm away.

Donald jumped back; if he could have scuttled off, he would have. Hooray for her class on Street Tactics for Women! Molly's expression of compassion had been perceived as weakness. The moment she became aggressive, he crumbled.

"You're just begging me to knock you around a little, aren't you?" He curled his hands into fists, trying to pump himself back up. "Women like you need it. And don't think I couldn't do it."

But he wouldn't—she knew it and he knew it. Shame filled his eyes. Coming from a strict Christian home, and with a father like his, Donald must have spent his whole adolescence questioning his manhood, unable to talk about it with anyone. But, Molly reminded herself, he'd have no problems bashing in the head of a cripple, or someone who was old and weak.

Donald waved a dismissive hand at her and said, as if it had been his intent all along: "There are more important things at stake here, so I'm not going to give you the opportunity to have me arrested." Staying well outside of her reach, he hissed: "But don't think we're not going to win. And when it's all over, you're going to regret this moment. Because I don't forget."

He glared at her and ran quickly up the stairs, his boots sounding like blows on the wooden treads.

Molly's victory in this encounter had pumped up her adrenaline, making her feel all-powerful. Outside the building, still in a heightened state of exhilaration, she checked her cell phone. Still no messages from Steve. Damn him!

Resolutely, Molly marched up to Polanski Street which had been re-named to honor the influx of Polish people who'd settled in the neighborhood during the early years of the last century. The police station stood squarely in the middle of the block. Originally a massive yellow sandstone building, the soot and pollution that had descended on it over the years had turned it dingy gray. The original arched doorway had been replaced with square aluminum doorframes, now pitted from that same pollution. Fitting, she thought, pushing the doors open and marching up the desk sergeant.

"I'd like to speak to Detective Carmaggio," she announced. "I have some information about the Johnson homicide."

The desk sergeant, as Irish as they came with his white skin, up-tilted nose, green eyes and black hair—Black Irish, her father used to call them—was chewing gum. He checked her ID, but hardly gave her face a glance as he pointed in the direction of the stairway.

The detective squad room reminded her of the Multi-Care office. The same scuffed walls, yellowed posters, fluorescent lights, old gray filing cabinets and flickering computer screens on metal desks. Although there were a few women scattered around, most of the desks had men sitting behind them. Some of them were in their shirt sleeves, and some were wearing rumpled suits. Molly had never seen such a collection of alpha males in her life.

Steve's desk was piled with papers and yellow folders and littered with Styrofoam coffee cups. He was in his shirt sleeves, talking on the telephone and taking notes with a ball point pen. He looked up at the sound of her approach, said a few more words, and hung up.

"Did you intend to just disappear, like you did the last time?"

Steve regarded her for a moment as if weighing in his mind exactly what to do with her. He looked around at the other detectives who suddenly pretended to be busy, frowned and said, "Let's talk in one of the interview rooms."

This room was even scruffier than the squad room. It contained a table, a couple of chairs and a mirror on the wall. "That's a two-way mirror," she announced. "You're not going to broadcast this conversation to the entire squad room, are you?"

"Believe me, Molly, this is not a conversation I want the entire squad room to be hearing. That's why I brought you in here."

He held out a chair for her. Molly would have rather have remained standing because it made her feel more substantial. But she sat down, and he lowered himself into a chair across from her.

Steve looked like he hadn't slept in days; his eyes were shot through with red lines and the skin on his face looked pale and papery, as if the flesh beneath it was pulling away and disappearing. If he'd been drinking, she couldn't smell it on him.

Once again his very apparent suffering had the effect of muting her anger. "Steve," she began in a less aggressive tone, "I know you're upset about Sean, but . . ."

"The reason I haven't called you," he broke in, "is that I'm not very good at these 'it's my fault' conversations, especially when it happens to be dead-on true."

"Okay, I accept your apology." It wasn't clear whether or not it was meant as an apology, but Molly was determined to give it a chance. "So, I have some information to give you about Bukka and a possible reason why Belloc might be involved in a money laundering scheme with Papa Skana. Let's meet for dinner and I'll tell you all about it."

Steve was having none of it. "What part of 'I need a break' and 'it's my fault, not yours,' don't you understand?"

"Why is it that as soon as we run into some kind of glitch, or bad patch, you're immediately ready to end it?"

"Getting stinking drunk and passing out on your floor is a 'glitch?'" He shrugged, amazed. "Like I said to you Molly, I'm in no shape to be in a relationship with anyone."

The finality of this felt like the slamming of a coffin lid. "Steve," she heard herself pleading, "it's not fair. You opened up something in me that no one ever got near before. You can't just leave me like this."

"Molly," he said, looking like he wished he were somewhere else, "this is why men avoid having these conversations with women. I can barely take care of myself. What do you want from me?"

"You're just going through a bad period." Oh god! These social work clichés!

"I've been going through a bad thirty years," he corrected her. "This is just a little worse, that's all."

"I thought you said I was good for you. Were you lying?"

"Let's not get into all that. You deserve better than me."

"I don't know whether I do or I don't. The only problem is that it's you I love."

He flinched a little at the words, as if she'd cursed him.

Molly's face reddened, but she plunged on: "Getting drunk is not going to help anything."

"It's a lot better than not getting drunk," he muttered.

"Steve, I can't possibly know what it is to maybe lose a child. But that doesn't mean I can't understand. Don't shut me out."

"Molly, this has nothing to do with you." His face had that firm, set look on it that told her it was useless. She took a deep breath, willing herself not to cry. A lifetime of practice kicked in, and she was able to say in a more-or-less neutral voice: "Well, I seem to have no choice here. You want to end it, so I guess that's the way it is."

Steve eyed her uncertainly, as if he was waiting for the other shoe to drop.

"Before I walk out of here and leave you to get drunk in peace, here's the information I have for you: Willie told me that Bukka was arguing with a drug dealer named Ishmael the day before he was murdered. And Ken Belloc is a gambler who needs money and that's a possible reason for his involvement with Papa Skana. You can take that to the DA."

The relief on his face was palpable. He wasn't going to have to deal with a hysterical woman after all. This very evident relief that she wouldn't give him a hard time brought back her anger. Why was she making it so easy for him?

Molly got up and opened the door. The same rumpled bunch who'd quickly looked away when she came in, quickly looked away again. Taking it in with a glance, she turned her head around and said loudly, as if they'd just been arguing: "And next time you want to show up somewhere in drag, pick someone else's apartment to do it in."

The expression on his face was all Molly could have hoped for. The sound of the door to the interview room slamming behind her gave her the push to march out of the squad room. The tears came while she was walking back to Freymont Avenue, and she headed for the Acropolis Coffee Shop, made her way blindly past the evening waitress who she didn't know and into the cramped ladies room where she collapsed onto the cracked toilet seat cover, giving into her misery.

173

Chapter Twenty-Seven

Somebody was banging on the door of the ladies room. "Just a minute," Molly said and quickly washed her face and hands, glad that this bathroom had a paper towel dispenser and not one of those hot air things. Finally she emerged and made her way to the subway where, tired beyond belief and unable to find a seat, she clung to the pole, wanting nothing more than to go home and get into bed.

The train, lurching around a curve in the tunnel, threw Molly against a gray-haired woman with a youthful face who grabbed onto her arm. The woman's hand was shapely and delicate. They commiserated with each other about the deplorable rush-hour conditions.

For a moment Molly had a vivid memory of Ana Skana's hand on hers, and Ana's smile—enticing and seductive—but so much more. What was going on? Molly knew her own sexual attraction was to men and not to women, but Ana's smile and the touch of her hand held out the promise of a connection or attachment so compelling that in that moment, only she and Molly existed for each other.

This feeling was a powerful draw for Molly for whom such deeply emotional connections were so difficult to make. A languid warmth enveloped her. Wouldn't it be easier to have a relationship with a woman? Molly could imagine herself simply curling up and being caressed, cared for, understood, in a way that men—particularly Steve—rarely did—*if* they were willing to do it all.

As quickly as it came, the fantasy disappeared. Ana, Molly, knew, was as hard as nails. The minute she lost interest in someone, Ana threw them away as quickly as a child would toss a used candy wrapper into the garbage.

The question was, would Bukka, once enticed by Ana, let himself be dropped that easily, especially if he was high on crack or some other mood-altering substance? Molly wished she had a better sense of Bukka—aside from his incredible musical ability, he had appeared so unformed. But she *could* imagine Ana shooting Bukka as easily as she would swat a fly, if it annoyed her or wouldn't go away.

All this thinking and unfulfilled longing brought the weariness back. Molly toyed with the idea of just going home and crawling into bed. Instead, she changed for the train that took her to Canal Street.

Ben had lost even more weight since she'd seen him last. His wrists, sticking out from the sleeves of his shirt, looked skeletal. Marushka was not taking care of him properly, she thought angrily, and then rolled her eyes. How traditional of me. A woman and a man have a relationship and it's assumed that the woman then has to take care of him. Marushka had never signed on for that, she reminded herself. Ben was not Marushka's responsibility; now and always he was Molly's.

"The Major Arcana sends a message to me," he intoned in response to her question of how he was doing. Ben had part of a deck of Tarot cards spread out on the table in front of him. They were dirty and grease spotted, probably plucked from the garbage. "The choice is made."

"What choice are you talking about?"

"Fire, water, air and earth are my wand of will," he said as if it were a logical answer to her question. "I must die so that I can live." His voice sounded like one of the prophets of doom that harangued hapless riders in the subway.

It was making *her* crazy to hear him talk like that. She wanted to throw herself onto Ben's lap and tell him all about her conversation with Steve and have him get angry on her behalf, as he used to when she was a little girl, before the illness which flattened out his emotional contours and demolished his emotional connectedness had left him so cut off from her. It all felt so terrible, lost and lonely, that she began to cry.

"Ben," she said miserably, surreptitiously wiping the tears away with her fingers, "when you say things like, 'I must die so that I can live," it gets me very upset. Are you thinking of hurting yourself?"

Ben either couldn't, or wouldn't, answer the question. Instead, he got up and walked from the kitchen into the front room with her trailing along behind him. It was as though a huge pit had opened up in front of her and all the men she'd ever loved were on one side of it, she was on the other, and there was no way to get across.

When Ben got to the far end of the front room, to the windows with their rusty gates, he turned around to face her. She'd stopped, her hands hanging helplessly at her side, making no attempt to wipe the tears away. What was the point?

He stared at her blankly for a few moments, his head making little bird-like movements. Molly had no idea where his mind was, or what he saw. Then, as if coming back from a long dream, Ben's eyes slowly focused on her face. He put his hands on her shoulders, pulling her towards him, and said softly: "The eyes of a little sister are full of tears." With one hand he reached back and picked up a dirty handkerchief – more like a rag – that had been lying on the window sill and began, clumsily, to blot her face. "Tears are the river of life," he said softly. "Fire, water, air and earth—the elements—without them there is no life."

Molly wanted to hug him, to bury her face in his chest, but was

175

afraid of startling or alarming him, of losing this moment which could disappear like smoke if he felt frightened in any way. She also discarded any idea of talking to him about going back to the doctor and starting on some new medication. It would upset him, get him angry at her, and this felt utterly unbearable. She wanted to preserve this brief interlude of closeness between them, to hold it in her heart as she would a precious keepsake as a reminder of something that she'd thought was lost forever.

Since there was almost no food in the house, and Ben had taken to wandering round the apartment again, Molly went out to the corner bodega to buy groceries. Inside, on a shelf under the window, were several geranium plants for sale. Paco, the owner of the bodega, said his brother had a nursery and grew them all year round. On impulse, she bought the one with the brightest, reddest flowers and brought it back to her brother's apartment along with three cans of soup, two cans of stew, a container of milk, three bananas and an orange.

"You look like hell, girl," Swandell snapped at her as Molly stumbled into the office the next morning after yet another night of restless dreams. "What is going on with you? Is it that man?"

Molly, her nerves already on edge, had a quick fantasy of turning around and running back down the stairs. What could she say? Her emotions felt as dangerously tangled as a rapidly swirling river that had somehow gotten clogged and jammed with debris

The feeling of closeness to Ben had lasted all the way home – until she opened the door to her empty apartment and the extent of her true isolation settled upon her. No matter how meaningful she wanted to make it, the moment with Ben, as lovely as it was, had been fleeting, a brilliantly-colored rainbow that appears suddenly out of the mists during a lull in a storm. As was her brief moment with Ana.

Molly quickly eyed the reception area for a way out of talking to Swandell. But Nilda was on the phone, Stuttman was nowhere in sight, and everyone else seemed to be going about their business. Swandell, noting the expression on Molly's face, softened a little and said, "Come on, Molly. Let's go into the staffroom and have a cup of coffee."

"Swandell, I appreciate your concern but . . ."

"I know, I know," Swandell cut in. "You don't want to talk about it. You're into denial—so typical of the alcoholic and his family." She put her hands on her hips and thrust one shoulder out in Molly's direction. "You think that's going to make it go away?"

Rather than trying to explain that Swandell's way of swooping in like a predatory bird made her feel like scurrying under the nearest bush, Molly meekly followed the nurse into the staffroom and sank down into one of the plastic chairs.

"Milk, no sugar, right?" Swandell asked, handing her a cup of coffee. Drawing up a chair, she set her own cup down on the table and said, "This has got to be said, Molly. And as a friend, I'm saying it to you. You're wasting yourself on that man."

Molly's eyes popped open as she stumbled around for something to say.

"And don't ask me 'which man?' You know perfectly well who I mean, and so does everyone else. There are no secrets in this place."

"Swandell, this isn't exactly your business."

"He interviewed me yesterday afternoon about that kid's murder," Swandell plowed on over Molly's protest. "He was slurring his words and he smelled like a gin joint after a busy night, even though he was sucking on one of those breath mint things. And other people he's been interviewing here have been saying the same thing."

Oh my god! Once again shame flooded her, as much for Steve who'd hate to hear people talking about him like this as for herself, for getting involved with a man who was totally out of control and whose deficiencies were so obvious to everyone.

"Don't you know girl, that you can't have no relationship with an alcoholic?"

"Well, denial or not, I don't really want to talk about this."

"I know," Swandell said, ignoring her. "I was married to one and I wouldn't be alive today if I hadn't worked up the guts to get my sorry ass out of there."

"Steve isn't abusive to me if that's what you mean," Molly said, bristling.

"There's all kinds of abuse. An alcoholic is always cheating on you—with alcohol. You're home worrying about him, he's out catting around with his Tia Maria at the local bar."

It was so true; she didn't know what to say.

"You'll always come second, never first. Is that the way you want to live?"

Almost despite herself, Molly slowly shook her head back and forth. It certainly wasn't.

"And the self-abuse is the worst part. You never know when they're going to total the car, or fall down and break their neck. I saw it first-hand, Molly, when I used to do hospital nursing. More than half of the people admitted into the ER are there because of alcohol, even if that's not what appears on the admitting diagnosis. If they haven't had an alcohol-related fall or other accident, then they have an underlying alcoholic condition such as liver disease, or acute pancreatitis, or hypoglycemia or they're severely malnourished which affects every system in the body. Some of these guys who have been drinking for years, their birth certificates say they're in their fifties, but they have the body and health problems of a seventy-five year old."

177

"Okay, okay, I get it," Molly said miserably.

"Well, girl, I hope you do." There was real concern in Swandell's eyes. "Or else I've wasted my breath. And that is something I do not like doing."

Swandell looked at her watch. "Well, I've got a lot of work to do. I came back too late yesterday to finish writing up my nursing assessment of Willie Cobb."

"I didn't know you were doing an assessment of him!"

"You would have it if you'd read the case file. Mr. Stuttman asked me to do it, and I left a note for you. By the way, there were no current social work notes from you in the file. And, unlike your love life, this really is my business because I had to go into that apartment cold." She gave Molly a withering look. "I tried to find you to at least get some background, but you were nowhere to be found in spite of the fact there were no home visits listed for you on the schedule."

Molly's cheeks flamed. Her involvement in her own life was so intense, she'd completely forgotten about her job.

"We're supposed to work as a team here," Swandell snapped, taking a quick gulp from her coffee cup and getting up. "I don't know what's going on with you, girl. But you'd better get your act together." With that, she was out the door.

Chapter Twenty-Eight

"This is the Marble Heights Automated Telephone System," a mechanical voice said into Molly's ear. "Please listen to our menu. If you know the extension of the person . . ." Oh no. Why can't they just have a person on the other end?

Instead of getting her case notes up to date as she'd intended to do, Molly had rifled through her rolodex and then made a call to Tony Moretti. Not even sure whether he was still working at Marble Heights, Molly listened to a long list of menu options with growing frustration until she was able to locate and punch in his extension.

While waiting for Tony to answer his page, she pictured him as he looked when they'd met four years ago at a group he'd run for families of schizophrenics hospitalized in the Metro City Psych Unit—stocky, with a friendly face framed by dark curly hair already speckled with gray, although he couldn't have been more than thirty-five then.

Ben had been brought to the Unit by the police for evaluation after he'd spent several agitated days roaming the streets. As usual, as bad as she knew he was at the time, Molly had been unable to make the decision to hospitalize him. "Either you're going to call the police, or I will!" Ben's neighbor, Mrs. Giovanni, had screamed into Molly's face after Ben had chased her five-year-old twins down the street brandishing a piece of pipe and accusing them of being "the devil's spawn." So she'd bit the bullet and called them. Thinking about it now, a shudder went through her.

She and Tony had more or less kept in touch – they'd even gone out to dinner with his wife, Ilise, a statuesque blond who was site manager for a construction company. Tony had sent her an announcement—was it a year ago already?—when he made the move to Marble Heights, a small private psych hospital about forty miles north of the City, in Westchester.

"Hi, Molly." His voice sounded as warm and friendly as if they'd just seen each other. "How are you doing?"

"Not good, Tony."

"Is this about Ben?"

"Yes." There was no point in getting into all the rest of it. "I think he's talking about killing himself, but I'm not really sure."

"Is he hearing voices telling him to kill himself?"

179

"I don't think he's hearing voices, but it's so hard to know with Ben. He does seem to be getting very delusional again, but it seems to be more his crazy mixed-up thinking that's sending him over the edge."

"Has he ever heard voices?" Tony asked. "I don't remember."

"As far as I know he's never heard voices, or had any kind of hallucinations, for that matter." The Devil's Vermicelli episode had not been a hallucination; he'd actually seen the roaches. "His delusions have always been more of the fixed idea type – you know, associated with crazy thinking and beliefs."

"Yeah, that's your brother. One time, now that I come to think about it, when he was stabilized on his meds, he lectured me on it. 'I don't hear voices. That's an auditory hallucination. Only crazy people have those.'"

Molly could almost see Tony smiling as he mimicked Ben's precise, emotionless tone. "Yes, he gave me the same lecture," she said, rolling her eyes. "After he came out of the hospital that first time, he spent months reading every book and article ever written on schizophrenia and decided he wasn't crazy after all."

"What about meds?" Tony asked. "Is he taking them?"

"No. He's been off them at least a couple of months, I believe. And his thinking is getting even more bizarre and disorganized."

"How about activities of daily living? Is he taking care of himself? Eating?"

"Barely, and it's been getting worse."

"He must be very scared," Tony said, putting his finger right on the truth of it all.

It was fear that made schizophrenics like Ben violent, when they did become violent. Her brother, Molly knew, struck first to protect himself from a world that became increasingly fearful and overwhelming to him as his psychosis increasingly took over, much like being lost in the woods at nightfall without a compass as it gets darker and darker. One of her clients who had been psychotic and was now on meds described it like living in a perpetual horror movie where the danger could come from anywhere—even the most innocent children can turn into monsters in the blink of an eye.

"Yes," Molly agreed, bringing her mind back to the conversation. "He has enough awareness left to know he can't depend on his mind to make sense of anything."

"I've always liked your brother," Tony said thoughtfully. "When a brilliant mind like his develops a thought disorder, it takes on such unusual and interesting forms." He stopped. "I'm sorry, Molly. I shouldn't be talking about your brother as if he's a case study, not a person."

"It's okay, Tony. I know you appreciate him and try, always, to

180

understand, which is more than I can say about a lot of the other professionals I've encountered who need to pigeonhole him without having any idea who he is, or why he does what he does." Slowly, she rubbed her temples. "Actually, it's a relief to talk about him with somebody who knows and likes him."

"Thank you." Molly could almost see Tony lowering his head, his usual reaction when given a complement.

"Ben is certainly not your classic paranoid schizophrenic, either," she added, happy to keep talking about him rather than face the her own inability to come to a decision and act on it.

"I know."

"His thinking is too symbolic and dream-like. Most other paranoid people that I've met have got all the details of their delusions worked out.

"Yeah," Tony agreed. "I was talking to one this morning. He believed Bin Laden blew up the World Trade Center in order to kill him, personally. And he explained the whole scenario to me very logically— if you accept the crazy assumption it was based on. It all had to do with his ex-wife's brother who hated him and went to work for the CIA in order to infiltrate Al Qaida and convince them to blow up the World Trade Center at the exact moment that the subway my patient usually took to his day treatment program would be in the tunnel, just under the Twin Towers. He knew all the details, down to the exact subway schedule."

"Whew!" Molly laughed for the first time that day. "I couldn't imagine my brother coming up with a detailed story like that. He can't string two logical thoughts together. Ben was barely able to tell me his apartment was infested with cockroaches."

She told him the story of the Devil's Vermicelli, much to the amusement of Tony who laughed and said, "That's why I love your brother. Once you understand what he's trying to say, it usually makes some kind of crazy sense."

"It's trying to figure out what he really wants to say that's tough."

"I know," Tony said. "So what's troubling you about him right now?" He was too good a social worker to let her divert him for long.

"I believe he's talking about killing himself. But I'm not really sure, and that's the problem. I'm trying to get him to go for a psych evaluation and go back on his meds, but he doesn't want to do it."

"There are some newer meds out there now with fewer side effects, that might benefit him."

"I know, I know. But the side effects of the various meds he's taken over the years have been so brutalizing. I don't know how to convince him to try again." Molly took a sip of an old, cold cup of coffee that was sitting on her desk, grimaced and then said hopefully:.

"It would be wonderful to get him into Marble Heights. It's got a good reputation, and from what people tell me, it's so much more humane than the City psych units."

"As hospitals go, it's a good place," Tony agreed. "But you do know that since Marble Heights is a private hospital, we do mostly voluntary commitments, which means you'll have to get him here. City cops won't bring him."

"I know."

In the background she could hear noises and the sound of someone calling Tony's name. "Look Molly, I've got to go. If you want to bring him up here, I'll arrange for an evaluation. Just give me the go-ahead."

"Thanks, Tony. I'll let you know."

Had she really thought Tony would have some different, novel approach that would convince Ben to make the trip up to Marble Heights in Westchester? This was always the problem for which there never seemed to be any solution: How in the world could she get him up there, or anywhere else, for an evaluation?

Molly leaned forward and rested her face on her hands. She so desperately wanted to avoid another hospitalization like the last one—Ben, kicking, screaming, almost frothing at the mouth, being wrestled to the ground by five cops or EMS workers—she wasn't quite sure who they were. It was so like the first time that she could almost hear her mother's hysterical screaming in the background.

And then there was the Metro Hospital Psych Unit itself which, from the outside, looked like the Bastille. The public entranceway into the unit was through a dark, narrow corridor lined with filthy, scuffed walls that smelled like the public bathroom in a bus station. Molly swore she could hear people screaming as she ran through the hallways, frantically trying to find him. Or maybe it was Ben's screams she was still hearing. Or her mother's. Whoever screams they were, they had echoed in her head that entire sleepless night, each one feeling like a separate blade slicing through her flesh while she obsessed about what she could have, or should have done instead.

Or what she should do right now.

Chapter Twenty-Nine

For the next month or so, Molly continued to obsess about Ben, repeatedly going back and forth in her mind about what to do, like a pendulum on a clock ticking the time away but going nowhere. She checked her messages constantly in the hopes that Steve would call—hating herself for doing it, especially since it began to take on the flavor of a religious ritual, like lighting Sabbath candles or reciting *Shmah Yisroel!*—hear oh Israel!—as one of her clients, Mrs. Rothenbaum, did for so many months, sitting by her husband Sam's bedside, begging God over and over again not to let him die. And with the same effect as far as Molly could see, since Sam died anyway and Steve didn't call.

It was probably better that he didn't call, she told herself, having read enough about addictions to know that Swandell was right. Why was she wasting herself on an alcoholic who ran the other way every time the waters got a little choppy? She should find a man who could love her back, like Abelard loved his Heloise, or Dave loved his Goldie. Steve wasn't that man. And yet . . . .

She saw Ana several times on the street. The first two times, Ana gave her a sardonic smile as if she knew Molly was avoiding her, which was true. The third time Molly was walking down Freymont Avenue on her way to a home visit when a black limo pulled up next to her. Ana got out of the back seat, stepping right in front of Molly's path so Molly could not avoid her.

Ana was wearing a Russian-style hat and a long, form-fitting red coat with a black fur collar and looked as if she could have just stepped out of a Leo Tolstoy novel. She smiled hesitantly and said, "I scare you that time in the cafe, yes?"

"I thought about it for a while, Ana." The late afternoon weather had turned much colder, and Molly turned up the collar of her old navy pea jacket. "And about you. There's much about you that I don't understand."

"Understand?" Ana repeated the word as if Molly had spoken it in a language foreign to her. "A ripe apple hanging on a tree is nothing to understand. If you do not pick it and take a bite, you will never know how juicy and delicious it could be."

"You don't seem to care what tree the apple is hanging on."

Ana shrugged. "Why should I? If it is ripe, juicy, delicious, what

183

does it matter whether it is picked from this tree or that tree, yes?" She indicated each choice, first with the open palm of her left hand, then with her right. "Or whether it is a pear, or a peach or a cherry."

"Just grab it and run, huh?" Molly was surprised at how sarcastic the words sounded. Sarcasm wasn't her usual mode of communication.

"And what about you?" Ana studied her as if she had set out to unravel the threads of Molly's secret self, strand by strand. "You don't see the ripe juicy apple, the pear, or the peach," she said. "Your eyes are turned towards the dead, and you see only them."

"There's a lot of death around, Ana," she declared hotly. There was too much truth in Ana's accusation for Molly's own comfort. "Cal Bruchman, Bukka. I knew them both, and now they're dead. And the old people, the tenants in the buildings your father wants to empty—one of them was scared to death by someone your father, or your father's lackey, was undoubtedly paid to harass. Would you have me forget all about them?"

Instead of answering, Ana glanced at something behind Molly's head. Molly turned to see what it was. A large dark cloud, resembling a huge black crow or raven, was hanging a little above and behind the low-lying buildings.

"We all live amidst the dead, yes?" Ana's voice sounded harsher than usual. "We kill them and feed on their carcasses to give us life. All of us, we do this." Her eyes fastened on Molly's face and her lip curled, uncovering her slightly crooked teeth. "The difference between us is that you seek out the dead and live among them. I don't. I know the dead are there, somewhere behind me. But I look towards life, always. My father, he taught me this."

After that encounter, Ana did not approach her again.

The two murders remained unsolved. No evictions proceedings had been started against the tenants on Warwick Street. Molly and Louis went out several times for a beer. It was a surprise that she craved beer—white wine had been her drink of choice for years—until she realized that Steve was a beer drinker and the beer was a connection with him, a way to hold him in her heart in some way, or at least in her belly. After that, she consciously went back to ordering wine. Throughout this whole period which lasted about a month and a half she felt distanced from everything, as if the living essence of her had been cryogenically frozen and placed in a vault somewhere, preserved but not quite alive, until conditions improved sufficiently to warrant thawing it out.

Sometime during this period she visited Mrs. Canover. Upon opening the door, Mrs. Canover smiled a little wistfully and led the way to the table where a half-eaten sandwich and a cup of tea rested on a vinyl tablecloth that had been scrubbed so often its pattern of tiny pink flowers was barely visible. In the center of the table, to Molly's surprise, Herman's urn sat on a beautifully crocheted doily that was yellow with age. Behind the urn stood the photo of Herman in his army uniform.

"There's tea in the pot, dear." Mrs. Canover reached up into a cabinet over the sink and took out another cup and saucer. "I'll pour you a cup."

Molly accepted the cup of tea with thanks, and they sat down on either side of the table, across the mini-shrine to Herman.

Mrs. Canover turned the photo so they could both look at it and said, "Today is our sixty-second wedding anniversary."

Molly examined the photo of the young man Herman had been. Dark hair, dark eyes, regular features, looking out at the camera with a twinkle in his eye as if in it he could see the bright future that lay in front of him. "He looked like a very happy young man."

"We got married just before he was to be shipped overseas," Mrs. Canover said, her milky eyes blinking a little as they rested on Herman's face. "Yes, he was very happy—we were both so happy. I knew God would send him home to me, and He did."

Molly sipped her tea, wondering how to segue into the conversation she wanted to have. Finally she took a deep breath and plunged in: "Dave and Alice and the people at the Center miss you. They told me you haven't been back for a while."

Mrs. Canover picked up the urn and shook it a little. A small dusting of grey powder settled on the front of the pink cardigan sweater she was wearing. "He hasn't quite passed over yet, dear. So you see I can't leave him yet, I really can't." In Mrs. Canover's voice was a firmness that there was no arguing with. "I shouldn't have gone and left him those other times. He needs me here. I've been tending him all these years—that's why God gave him back to me."

Molly wished she was in better emotional shape because she had the feeling that Mrs. Canover was saying something very important, opening up a topic that she'd never talked about before, and Molly couldn't quite tune into it. Instead, her eyes went to the paintings of flowers and fruit that hung on the walls. They were glowing with life as if the painter had plucked the exact moment when the peach, the grape, the daffodil, the rhododendron blossom had reached their sublime essence and transferred it onto canvas. "Herman was a wonderful artist, Mrs. Canover."

"Yes, dear," she answered as if Molly was just stating the obvious. "He started painting after he came home from the war."

"These pictures are amazing, Mrs. Canover. Did he ever have a show?"

Mrs. Canover shook her head. "He never thought of himself as an artist. He painted, he said, because he had seen such terrible things in the war, so much death and destruction that he wanted to preserve what was beautiful in life, to tend and preserve the living, so that it wouldn't all be destroyed."

"You used the same word," Molly said thoughtfully. "Tending . . . he tended the living and you tended him."

Mrs. Canover picked up the photo of Herman and looked at it with the same reverence with which the faithful regard a beloved picture of Jesus. "He was so different when he came home," she said softly. "So sad, he'd wake up in the night screaming about the things he'd seen, the boys who were killed along side of him."

Post-Traumatic Stress, Molly thought. Just like Steve. Only then they called it Combat Fatigue. "And you would tend him, take care of him."

Mrs. Canover nodded. "And a job it was, too. I was a young girl then, and wanted to go to the pictures, or out dancing, and Herman would yell at me, 'What are you, some kind of ghoul? Dancing on the graves of all the dead?' "

"It must have been really hard for you, Mrs. Canover."

"It was, dear. But God had joined us together, in sickness and in health." She stood the photo of Herman back up on the table and sat back, blinking a little with her milky eyes. Taking a handkerchief from the pocket of her sweater, she dabbed at them. "It was the lady in the hospital who gave him a set of paints and a canvas and told him to try painting."

"The VA hospital?"

Mrs. Canover nodded.

"And it helped?"

"He'd come home from work every night and on weekends and paint as if his life depended on it."

Painting as atonement, Molly thought, looking around at the pictures hanging on the walls. Roses, dewy-sweet, lit up by the morning sun; lilies of the valley, virginal-white, shyly hiding in the shadows; sprays of forsythia—forsythia was the official flower of Brooklyn—oranges and pears and grapes bursting out of their skins.

"He'd always wash his hands before he started painting—to purge them of the blood, he'd say. But he never could, you know."

"Get rid of the blood?"

Mrs. Canover sighed and pressed her hands together. "That blood was there until the day he died."

"It was kill or be killed, Mrs. Canover. He was fighting a war." But how does a non-psychopathic person with an active conscience ever forgive himself for taking all those lives? The bible clearly says, "Thou shalt not kill." It doesn't say it's okay to kill these people, but not those. She remembered the dream Steve had recounted about the bleeding and burned limbs he saw hanging from the branches of the trees and a new thought occurred to her: How many men had Steve personally killed? Could he consciously or unconsciously believe that by taking Sean, God was punishing him for the lives he himself had taken?

Mrs. Canover was going on: "He'd work on each painting until the bottle was empty. I'd watch the level, and when it was gone, I'd know he was finished with the painting. I'd throw the bottle in the trash, open a new one and he'd be ready to start another painting."

"Bottle?" This was something Mrs. Canover had never mentioned before. "You mean he drank?"

"Well, he wasn't one of those . . . what do they call them?"

"Alcoholics?"

She nodded. "He wasn't one of those. He worked every day of his life." It was said proudly, as if working was the mark of a man; only bums could be alcoholics, "Loading and unloading the ships. And when there were no more ships to load, he took whatever work he could find. He wouldn't ever start the drinking until he came home."

"And you bought it for him?"

"Yes, I bought it for him, to make sure there was always a fresh bottle when he needed it. He couldn't paint without it."

A classic enabler, that's what Mrs. Canover was. What would Swandell have to say about all this? But in this case it seemed so right because it was an act of love and came from an understanding and an intimacy beyond words—Molly was sure that the couple had never talked about it. "So you'd know that when the bottle was empty the painting was finished?"

"Yes, dear." Mrs. Canover touched Herman's urn lightly. "Just as I know that when this urn is empty, Herman will have passed over."

"You mean that you know Herman's ashes are disappearing from the urn?" Molly asked in surprise.

"Of course, dear," Mrs. Canover looked at Molly as if she were a simpleton. "Every time I shake it, it feels lighter."

"So when it is empty. . ."

"When it is empty, he will be in God's hands." Tears gathered at the corners of her eyes.

Suddenly, Molly understood. "God will be tending him then," she said softly. "You can let him go."

Mrs. Canover nodded, dabbing at her eyes with the handkerchief. For a moment, she was completely still. Molly wondered what thoughts or memories were in her head. Finally she said, "Once I know he is safely in God's hands, we can go back to the Center, if you'd like."

Chapter Thirty

During the fourth week of February, when it seemed the cold had been going on forever, Molly attended a meeting organized by an ad hoc committee to discuss the proposed development of the waterfront. It was held in the parish hall of St. Stanislaw Church. Manny and Nilda came with a group calling itself the Neighborhood Coalition for Affordable Housing, one of the few times in Molly's memory that the Latinos, the Afro-Americans and the Eastern Europeans willingly sat on the same side of the room.

Alice Manning, her tangerine-colored hair making her highly visible in the winter-drab crowd, attended with Dave Scheunfeldt and a group calling themselves *Senior Power*, which was an action committee representing the members of the Henry J. Kronin Senior Center. Also present was an environmental group dedicated to saving the habitat of some little-known, Latin-named mollusk that made its home on the underside of the abandoned piers and forgotten stanchions. The piers were slated to be removed if the complex went up, thus putting these unlucky creatures in jeopardy.

The various groups were all having a wonderful time courting, and being courted by, the local media who were gathered outside. At the moment, Ken Belloc was making a statement to the press, his head bobbing up and down like a sea gull strutting his stuff. Neither Papa Skana nor his daughter were anywhere in sight. Molly pictured Papa hovering somewhere above the neighborhood like a circling hawk, waiting for the lesser creatures to finish with their petty concerns so he could swoop down on his prey and eat his fill.

Councilman Czarnoski opened the meeting with a speech extolling the Partnership for Waterfront Development— the name they'd given to the deal that would end up putting Willie on the street, if he refused to leave his home voluntarily. According to the councilman, The Partnership—as he lovingly called it—would bring jobs and economic growth to the neighborhood, to Brooklyn, to the entire New York City harbor. A good-looking young woman from the Mayor's Office for Economic Development did what was essentially a PR piece for the mayor on the lengths he had gone to in order to put the Partnership for Waterfront Development deal into place, all for the benefit of the community, making him sound like an amalgam of Alexander the Great,

Machiavelli and Mother Teresa.

Then Ken Belloc addressed the attendees. Since he'd become the poster boy for patriotism, at least in his own mind, he couldn't resist making reference to the terrorists who would be totally demoralized by the fact that their enemy, the Americans, were building yet another high-end outlet center. Several times during his talk, he referred to Freymont Avenue as "Freedom Hill," prompting more than a few people in the audience to look questioningly at each other, not knowing exactly what he was talking about. How quickly we forget, Molly thought.

The big surprise of the day was Leo Stuttman. He was on the committee which had put the meeting together, so Molly had expected him to be on the dais, but had not expected him to make a speech.

The speech was beautiful—a plea to include senior housing in the development plans; but more than that, it was a tribute to the importance of retaining a neighborhood's older people. He likened the neighborhood to a tree; its economic development was the new growth of branches and leaves, and the old people were its roots. Without the strong root network made up of a neighborhood's older people, there is no continuity, no history, nothing to maintain the balance of life in a community.

His speech was very well received, quoted in the local weekly and appeared in its entirety on Multi-Care's website. Councilman Czarnoski announced that he wouldn't support the project unless it contained a significant number of senior housing units.

"But that doesn't help Willie," Louis said one evening a few days after the article appeared in the paper. He and Molly were having a drink together in Vinny's. Louis was slated to go on security duty at the Crooked Peg and was wearing his bouncer uniform: black jeans, black tee shirt, black leather jacket, which he wore with as showy a style as if it were furs and wigs.

"Yeah. Even if Councilman Czarnoski gets his way and senior housing is eventually built, where will Willie and the rest of them go while the housing units are being built? It's not like there are any other affordable apartments in the neighborhood for them to move into, or in the rest of city for that matter."

"More to the point, Molly, Willie won't move. He's determined that they're going to take him out feet first and no other way."

"He's got nothing left," she said softly. "Only his home and his guitar. Everything else is gone." *Here I make my stand.* She pictured the Westerns she had seen as a kid where one settler, or a small band of settlers, having been shot at, burned out, beaten up by the hired guns of the cattle barons, or the railroad interests, or any other big money group who wanted to screw the settlers out of their little bit of land for the sake of their own development schemes, turned around to face the enemy and said, "I ain't a-goin'." Back then, in those movies, there was always a tall, flinty hero/gunfighter to stand up for the little guys and shoot it out with the bad guys while the audience cheered. When did it all get turned around? How did it happen that people stopped caring when the deal makers, the already-rich, began grabbing everything, leaving the little guy with nothing? Or did people only care in the movies?

Louis shook his head sadly and glanced at his leather-clad arm which was resting on the table. "Damn!" Dipping a napkin into a vase which held two little purple flowers, he rubbed away at a smudge on his sleeve. "Willie keeps getting frailer, Molly."

Molly let the old Westerns fade away into the sunset and nodded in agreement. "Swandell Green assessed him for potential client status, but she says he's basically in good health even if, again according to her, he's drinking himself to death."

"If I'd gone through all that he's gone through in the last few months, I'd be drinking myself to death, too."

Molly agreed, seeing him as he'd been the few times during the past weeks when she'd visited him after work— always in the same chair, the Gibson in his hands, playing the same Blind Gully riff that he'd been playing ever since Bukka's death. She kept promising herself to find the album it was on and identify the song. But because she was feeling so emotionally frozen, music no longer had the same appeal. These days she came home as late as possible and just fell into bed.

"Well," she said thoughtfully, "Papa Skana, or someone, must be delaying the plan to get the buildings on Warwick Avenue demolished, at least until the media scrutiny lessens a little and Councilman Czarnoski turns his attention elsewhere. If and when Dave and Willie and Marjory Canover are evicted, you can bet it will happen in the middle of the night, with no one around to see it."

Louis nodded. Molly had been idly watching a young woman with spiky orange hair and multi-colored eye make-up, who was sitting a few tables away from them. The orange-haired girl was flirting with a young man in a suit who was trying to look as if he was interested, but not succeeding terribly much. Suddenly, the girl rose to her feet. Tears were running down her face, leaving it mottled and covered with blotches of garish color. She threw her napkin at the young man in the suit and then turned and stomped off in the direction of the exit. He sat and watched her go without saying a word.

"Anything happening with the murder investigations?" Louis asked. He was facing the other way and hadn't seen any of the drama.

"I don't know any more than you do."

Louis raised his eyebrows. "Mr. NYPD still blowing you off?"

'I can't make you love me if you won't.' An old lyric, sung by a bluesy, soulful voice—Molly tried to place it but couldn't—popped into

her head. It was as true for the orange-haired girl as it was for her—you can't make someone love you if they won't. And yet, it was hard not to believe that Steve really did have feelings for her.

Molly sighed. "I don't know what to do about him."

Louis began to sing in a low, sultry, Da Mour voice: *"You'll always be my man/Gonna love you 'til I die."*

"You think there's a payoff in loving one man 'til you die?" Molly asked incredulously. "I saw a client recently who took care of the love of her life by feeding him alcohol day after day for fifty years. Now she sits and waits for the ashes in his urn to slowly dribble away so she can start having a life of her own. Is this what you're suggesting I do?"

"Love is never easy, is it?" Louis shook his head empathically. Molly could almost see the rhinestone earrings under the blond curls jingling and jangling. Then he smiled a seductively wise, woman-of-the-world smile. "Take it from a girl who knows."

"Other than the fact that it's never easy, what is it exactly that you know about love?" Molly said teasingly.

He leaned forward and replied in Louis's voice, "Not one dammed thing."

The day after her meeting with Louis, Saturday, Molly woke up to snow. Snuggled under her blue comforter, in a half-dream state, she watched the flakes drift past her window, and tried not to think about her brother.

After her conversation with Tony Moretti, Molly had visited Ben a couple of times to discuss his going back on meds. The first time she tried to bring up the subject, he'd ignored her. The second time, Ben's eyes blazed and he began to run around the apartment as if fueled by some internal fire, like an old steam engine, all the while yelling something about Concordia and Discordia (she was Discordia from what she could make out). But he no longer talked about dying, which she tried to believe was a good sign. Unable to take the discussion any further she went back to obsessing about him, which meant that she did nothing. In fact, she hadn't even seen him in over a week. Determined now to at least convince Ben to go back to the aftercare clinic for an evaluation, Molly went to visit him.

A blanket of snow was beginning to accumulate on the building rails, the concrete window sills, the fire hydrants and the cars parked along the street. A blanket of soft, white snow should be warm, Molly thought as she trudged along, aware of a slight sense of betrayal every time she touched snow and it turned out to be cold.

Molly could hear Ben's voice from behind his apartment door. He didn't answer her repeated knocking, so she took out his keys, unlocked the locks and entered his apartment. He was sitting on a kitchen chair, alone, facing the door. In his raised hand was a stout wooden table leg which he gripped like a club. His face, shadowed by several days' worth of beard, was covered with bruises and dried blood. On guard, he was awaiting the next assault of an unseen assassin.

"Oh my god, Ben!" Molly cried. "What happened to you?"

He continued to stare at her, his eyes rigid with fear, the table leg poised to strike.

"Ben." Gently, gently. "It's me, Malke Liebe. I'm not going to hurt you. Let me come closer, okay?" Once more the tears came; it ripped her heart into shreds to see him hurt.

Molly wiped her eyes with the sleeve of her jacket, afraid to go into her bag for a tissue because it might alarm him even further. "Ben, it really is me, Molly. Please put the table leg down."

"Genghis Khan and the Mongol hordes," he muttered, watching her carefully, the table leg still poised to strike.

Genghis Khan? What was he trying to say? Maybe he'd been attacked by a gang of Asian kids. In the neighborhood, there were several gangs who preyed on the elderly and the homeless. The thought enraged her to the point where she could have put her fist through the wall.

"What did they do to you?"

His cheek and eye began jumping as if a small creature lived inside his face.

"Ben." Calm down, Molly. Calm down. "Let me come closer. I just want to check you around and see that you are okay."

Ben, watching her warily, lowered the chair leg to his lap.

Slowly, she walked over to him and gently touched his cheek. The bruises appeared fairly recent—some of them were still oozing blood—so he hadn't been sitting there for days. Thank god!

"I'm going to wash the blood off." Molly found a fairly clean towel, wet it, and carefully dabbed at his face. "Does it hurt anywhere else?"

He didn't answer. She dropped to her knees, and he grunted as she unbuttoned his filthy shirt and examined his chest. He had a few bruises around his ribs—they must have kicked him, or maybe hit him with something. She pressed around a little while he recited in a flat, sing-song voice: "Yenking, Turkistan, Persia. The empire of Lewin strikes back!"

What in the world was he talking about? Lewin, of course, was their last name, but the rest of it made no sense.

"Ben, what is Yenking, Turkistan and Persia?"

"Where."

"Where is what?"

"Yenking, Turkistan, Persia . . . a where, a place, places, multiples of the great invasion of Genghis Khan and his hordes of Mongols."

What is he trying to tell me? Were Yenking, Turkistan and Persia places that Genghis Kahn had invaded? Unfortunately, she didn't know enough about the history of that period.

Molly pressed around some more. He winced, but he didn't seem to be in any serious pain.

"Ben, get up. Let me just see that you can walk."

He rose up from the chair with a jerky motion, still clutching the table leg, and walked with her into the front room where she sat him down on the unmade daybed. Thank god nothing appeared to be broken. If she had to get him to the hospital in his current state, it might well throw him over the edge.

Sitting down next to him, Molly breathed deeply to calm herself down. Ben was still muttering words that were unrecognizable to her, but could well be the names of other places Kahn had invaded. How could he know the names of those historical places—if that's what they were—yet not be sure who his own sister was, or be able to tell her what happened to him?

Once again any discussion about going to the aftercare clinic was out. She should really file a police report. But what good would that do? Ben couldn't give them coherent enough answers to help them make a identification. And his past experiences with the police had been so frightening that he might turn violent at the sight of them. She could just see him attacking one of the policemen and, worse, what they would do to him in return. She shuddered. No, better not call the police.

Molly cleaned him up, helped him to change his clothes, and left to do a little shopping. On her way out, Molly stopped and knocked at Marushka's door, hoping that Marushka might know who attacked Ben. The little boy with enormous brown eyes that she'd seen in the apartment once before answered her knock. He told her that Marushka wasn't home and solemnly asked if she wanted a reading.

"Do you give readings, too?" Molly asked, ready to believe, at least momentarily, that even the littlest gypsy would have the power to reveal what the future held in store for her brother.

The little boy began to giggle in the way of small children who find adults enormously funny. "I'm only in first grade, silly." He put one foot behind the other. "My aunt will be here soon."

She grinned back and went out. At the bodega, Molly bought two cans of soup, cold cuts, a loaf of bread, three bananas, and a container of orange juice. But the only thing Ben would eat was the soup after he watched her open the can and heat up the contents.

The snow had accumulated even more when she left his apartment to walk to the bus stop. What to do? As the snow flakes swirled around the window of the bus, she thought how like snow her problem was.

Every time she tried to grab a snowflake, it melted away in her hand; yet taken together, those same snowflakes turned into a mess.

The longer Ben was off his meds the harder it was for him to hold it all together and the more disorganized, vulnerable and terrified he became. If only she could have afforded to have had him followed by a good private psychiatrist with whom he could have developed a relationship over time, maybe Ben would agree to see him. But her healthcare benefits, which would cover a husband and children, didn't cover a brother. Any good private psychiatrist charged more than two hundred dollars a session, and she'd never found one who would accept the poorly-paying Medicaid that comprised Ben's health insurance. So they were both stuck with the psychiatrists at the aftercare clinic who didn't really know him. *And* Ben wasn't in any state of mind right now to trust, or even talk to, anyone he didn't know.

No solution had magically made an appearance by the time Molly got home. There was a blinking light on her message machine, and her heart gave a little leap, but it wasn't Steve. It would have been so wonderful to be able to talk to him about Ben, to not feel so alone. She paced around the apartment playing out the various scenarios regarding Ben in her head. Nothing led to any decision. Finally she collapsed onto her rocking chair and fell into a dreamless sleep.

Chapter Thirty-One

The clock on the tiny table said ten after two. Day? Night? How long had she slept? A little light was filtering through her airshaft window. It must be afternoon. Completely disoriented and jangled, she got up and put on a CD of Pavarotti singing Puccini. His luscious tenor voice usually soothed her. She settled back in her chair, but instead of feeling soothed, the passionate *Nessun Dorma* from *Turandot* brought up an intense desire for Steve to make love to her.

On impulse, Molly grabbed the phone and called him. Wonder of wonders, he picked up.

"Molly?" Caller ID—he knew it was her.

"Steve, I've missed you so much!"

"I've missed you too, Molly." His voice sounded huskier, deeper.

"My brother got beaten up." It came out with a flood of tears, passion gone as quickly as it had washed over her. Stop crying! She didn't want to appeal to his pity—never that—but was unable to control it. "I don't know what to do. I just want to talk to you."

"Molly, I don't . . ." He hesitated; then exhaled what sounded like a bellyful of air. "It will take me about forty-five minutes to drive in. Let's meet at that little pub on Third Avenue in an hour."

How drunk was he? Should he be driving? She didn't care. "I'll see you in an hour."

Steve was already there when Molly arrived, a half-full beer mug on the bar in front of him. She bent over, he reached up, and they kissed, a sweet, lovely drink of something delicious after a long drought—a little beery perhaps, but wonderful nevertheless.

"How did you get here so fast?" she said, slipping onto the stool next to his.

"The snow actually kept people off the roads. I stuck to the main arteries and it wasn't a bad trip." His eyes were red-rimmed and his skin had taken on the sallow color that Molly often noticed in people who drank to excess. Otherwise, he looked the same—lined face, graying, sandy hair, blue eyes, football-player shoulders—and Molly had a strange sensation: if she closed her eyes, she could simply slip under his skin with him and it would be like they'd never been apart.

"It looks like March is coming in like a lion in full roar," he said conversationally.

"I'm really glad to see you, Steve."

"Me, too." He touched her hand lightly and then looked up at the array of bottles lined up behind the bar as if they were ladies of the evening, congregating on a street corner for illicit purposes. She was aware of herself slowly coming out of deep mourning over the loss of him, comforted now by his solidity, the strong neck, the breadth of those shoulders.

"Let's get out of here. I'm trying to cut down on my drinking, and sitting in a bar makes it next to impossible." Steve put some money down and they left, walking down Third Avenue, towards Fourteenth Street, their arms almost touching but not quite, the snow crunching under their feet. "First let's get the unpleasant stuff out of the way," he said. "No, there's been no further word on Sean."

"Have you . . ?"

"Yes, I've contacted everyone I could think of. I've been jerked around by so many high ranking military personnel I feel like my nuts have been dipped in brass and hung out to dry. Doesn't anybody know what's going on over there?"

She rolled her eyes in commiseration.

"So, what happened to your brother?"

Molly told him about the beating. "In his mind, the whole thing is tied up with Genghis Kahn and the Mongol hordes. I want to get him evaluated and back on meds, but after this he'll be even more frightened and unwilling to go."

They had stopped in front of a little Chinese hole-in-the-wall called *Noodles and Things.* "He must have been beaten up by one of the Asian gangs.".

Marveling at his intuitive understanding of her brother's language, she asked, "Are you sure you don't have any schizophrenics in your family?"

He gave her a lopsided grin and shook his head.

"Even if I could get him to the clinic," she mused, "it's most likely that the doctor would be Indian or Asian and Ben would freak out."

"We're kind of in the same boat, you and I. Both of us have people we love who are missing in action, and neither of us know what the hell to do about it."

They started walking again. The snow had lightened considerably and the late afternoon sun was trying to peek through the drifting clouds. "Is there something—anything—you can do?" she asked.

"I have a friend in the Five—I think that's the precinct that covers his neighborhood. I'll talk to him. Maybe he can keep an unofficial eye on your brother, let old Dragon Breath, or whatever the name of their leader is, know that Ben is off-limits."

"I'd appreciate it, Steve."

They walked for a while longer in silence, past the Irish pubs, the Jewish Deli, the Asian and Middle-Eastern eateries, the Italian pizza parlors that line the Avenue. But this was no Freymont Avenue neighborhood in Brooklyn. These Manhattan eateries paid top dollar for their commercial space and catered to urban diners whose knowledge of these individual cultures ran, by and large, to their foods. Molly sighed. "Where are you with the investigation?"

"Well, we've questioned the vic's drug dealer, this Ishmael. He was seen arguing with the Johnson kid, and he doesn't have an alibi."

"The Johnson kid . . . oh, Bukka."

"Yeah. But there's nothing that ties him to it, either. We haven't been able to find the gun—it's probably in the river somewhere—and forensics hasn't come up with anything, so we had to let him go."

They stopped and sat down at a bench at the corner of a building that was set back a little from the street.

"What about Donald?" Molly asked

"We still like him for his father's murder, but same story. No hard evidence."

"And Papa? He has a motive for Bukka's murder."

As did Ana, in her own way. For a moment, Molly had a sense memory of the warmth of Ana's hands and the intimacy of her smile. Could Ana kill? If the situation warranted it, Molly had no doubt that she could. But as far a Molly knew, there was no hard evidence linking Ana to any of the murders, and Molly found herself unwilling to bring up Ana in any conversation with Steve.

"If it was Papa, he probably got one of his goonskies to do it."

"Unless he takes a special pleasure in doing it himself."

Steve stretched his neck a few times and rotated his shoulders; Molly could imagine what kind of stress he was under. "That's the problem with this case," he went on glumly. "We have motives up the kazoo. None of them have alibis worth anything—which makes me think we can't lay this at Papa's feet. If he did have a hand in this, he would have had a much tighter alibi than the one he has."

"Which is?"

At first he gave her his stony-faced look. Then he shrugged. "Oh, what the hell. You don't tell anybody anything anyway. He said he was spending the night with some Russian whore who, he knows and we know, would lie through her teeth for him and whose evidence wouldn't cut any weight with a jury, if it came to that. But I think we have to scratch Papa off, although I sure would like to get the bastard on something."

His voice sounded flat, without inflection or real interest; he was talking for the sake of talking. Molly decided to change the subject. "So what are you going to do now?"

197

"Keep going with the investigation."

"That's not what I mean."

The set of his shoulders was already stiffening—on the defensive. "What do you mean?"

"Steve," her hand touched his arm gently, "your drinking has really gotten bad. People you've interviewed at the agency are talking about it." She stopped for a moment, a little afraid of what she saw in his eyes. "While we were at the bar you said you were trying to cut back." Taking a breath, she tried for a teasing tone. "Is that like being a little bit pregnant?"

"What the hell do you want from me, Molly?" he exploded, pulling his arm away from her. "I'm doing the best that I can. What about 'I can't get through this any other way' don't you understand?"

Steve jumped up from the bench and took three large steps which took him to the curb. His arm shot out and Molly could hear the *twang* as his fist connected with a Mini-Meter Parking sign that had the audacity to be in front on him.

He swiveled back to face her, eyes infuriated. "This is exactly why I didn't want to see you. I knew you'd take this attitude. I should have followed my better judgment and never picked up that goddamned phone!"

The whole outburst scared Molly to the point where she wanted to simply take off and run down the block. In her mind's eye there was Ben, in one of his rages, completely out of control. It took every ounce of willpower to stay where she was and say to him, "But you did pick up the phone."

Steve had no answer to that one. His chest was heaving, the breath coming in gasps—which almost turned into sobs—from his throat. They were at 17th Street when he turned west, striding towards Union Squareand rubbing his knuckles as he went, with her following along behind him.

In this way they walked the two blocks from Third Avenue to Broadway and circled halfway around the little park. The snow had stopped; the sky a bright, almost iridescent blue. Kids were out with their sleds, and the street vendors were opening up for the late afternoon and evening business.

Steve halted in front of a kiosk that sold CDs and waited for her to catch up. "I'm sorry, Molly," he said with a sigh. "You didn't deserve that. And it's not really you I'm angry at, anyway. It's just . . ." He didn't finish the sentence.

"I understand, Steve. I do. I, uh, I've never loved an alcoholic before and I don't know what to do." She wished she could decipher the expression those words brought to his face. Pain? Disbelief? It wasn't happiness. But it wasn't rejection either.

"I talked to a client a week or so ago whose husband came out of World War Two like you did out of 'Nam. He drank every day of his life, and she bought it for him." There was no way to explain those paintings to Steve and what she believed they represented in the relationship between the two old people, so she asked, "Do you want me to do that?"

Now he was clearly baffled. "What are you saying, Molly? I don't get it."

"I can't stand not being in your life, feeling cut off from you. I'd prefer that you weren't drinking, but if you are. . ."

"I told you I can't take care of anyone else."

"I'm not asking you to take care of me. I just want to be with you, whatever way you are, whatever you need from me."

Steve stood with his shoulders hunched over, his eyes hooded. What else was there to say, since he hadn't responded to what she *had* said? Molly began to rifle through the collection of classical CD's, coming upon the very Pavarotti CD she'd been playing earlier that day. She pulled it out and held it delicately.

Why was Steve so important to her that she could overlook his drinking, his irritability; his repeated withdrawals from her? Was it passion? She'd thought so while listening to Pavarotti's glorious voice. But now, standing next to him, it wasn't passion she felt. Her need for this man came from a deep, deep sadness and grief, a silent grief that she couldn't speak and he couldn't speak, but that both of them shared. Ana was right.

Grief fills up the room—lies in the bed, walks up and down with me. What poem did that come from? Her brother would have known, back in the days when he was winning poetry awards and scholarships in English Literature, before madness turned his brain into something barely knowable. *No one sleeps while grief walks the room.*

Steve grunted, then took the CD from her hand and turned it over, scanning down the list of arias on the back. "*Nessun Dorma,*" she whispered, hardly aware of what she was saying.

"*Nessun Dorma,*" he repeated in a neutral tone. "No one will sleep,' or 'Never sleep' in Italian. He's singing to the Princess who he imagines to be in her virginal room, watching the stars. That's the way I always think of you, Molly."

"As a virginal Princess?" It was absolutely the last thing she would have imagined him saying. "You're kidding, right?"

"*Ma il mio mistero e chiuso in me/ il nome mio nessun sapra.*" He recited rather than sang the words. "Which means something like, 'My mystery hides within me. No one will ever know my name.' Puccini could be talking about you."

"I don't understand?"

199

"You're still a mystery to me." His eyes were looking down at the CD. "As much as I know, there's so much more that I don't know." A quick sideways glance—and then he said: "You remember the time we made love, after the sulk you pulled in the Japanese restaurant?"

"I wasn't sulking. I was angry."

"You were angry because you thought I was uncovering your deepest, darkest secrets. The Virginal Princess. Anyway, that night I felt like I was taking your cherry. Now why would I feel that?"

"You tell me." But she knew what he meant, all right. *Oh sweet loving' man/ You got 'a hold of my soul.* There was the passion again—accompanied by another rush of longing that made her want to sink to her knees. That night had been an awakening for her—the first time she'd fully opened her inner self, her soul if you will, to a man and let him possess her.

Steve replaced the CD and stepped over to a bench, carefully brushing the snow off the seat with his gloved hand before pulling her down next to him. Through their winter coats, their sweaters and shirts, Molly could feel the beating of his heart. She wanted to talk about passion and grief, but he was staring at something far off. Afraid to take the risk, she asked instead, "Why do you see me as virginal?"

"Well, there's always been something pure and innocent about you, something untouched, like the snow here." He reached over and delicately fingered the white crystals of snow piled on top of the bushes behind the bench. "Something . . . the only word I can come up with is virginal, even though I know that's not true. But whatever it is, I feel this need to take care of you, to protect you and I know that right now, I can't."

She got it then. And it was amazing the way, once again, Steve had homed into something that was so absolutely true about her—that small, stunted child, uncared for, neglected, wailing in the abyss. That part of her was so young—he called it virginal, and maybe he was right, although she felt as though it had been hidden away in a dark closet all these years. And Steve was the first man who'd ever seen it; she'd just barely discovered it herself. Molly wanted to curl up in his lap and have him make love to her, but one doesn't make love on a park bench. At least she didn't.

Instead, Molly pulled off her glove, reached over and gently stroked the side of his face. The late-afternoon stubble felt prickly. "Steve, the need to protect me, to take care of me—it's . . ." There were no words to describe it, but tears filled her eyes. "I don't think anyone has ever really felt that way about me before. But it's not really necessary. I've been taking care of myself for a very long time. I just want to be in your life, and I want you in mine."

He circled her hand with both of his. "There's something about the girl whose cherry you've taken that, well, there's a responsibility that goes along with it that's more than I can take on right now," he said quietly. "It's just the way I feel. Maybe it was being raised Catholic." Molly smiled at that. "The first girl whose cherry I took I married. And she wasn't even pregnant at the time."

"Sean's mom," she said softly. "But you divorced her."

"Yeah, I did. I don't know if I was ever really in love with her. But it doesn't mean I didn't have certain feelings of protectiveness towards her. I still do. I never gave her any flak about paying her alimony, and child support."

Molly sighed and gazed across the street. There were several restaurants overlooking the park. One of them had a big sign that said *Heartland Brewery.* In all the years spent honing her listening skills, she pretty much knew when people spoke from their hearts and when they didn't because her own heart responded to emotional truth, and there was an empty, flat feeling to what Steve was saying, as if he was just repeating words, explanations that he'd decided on long ago and had never re-examined. Something was wrong.

Play upon my heartstrings . . . was that a song? Not one she could remember ever having heard, but it somehow fit.

"Steve, you're bullshitting me."

He dropped her hand, his eyes narrowing.

"I'm not saying you know you're doing it," she rushed on. "But it's what's happening."

"What are you talking about?" he asked as if she'd just announced that his hair was black instead of sandy-blond.

"You're putting something on me that's yours, not mine." *Denial and projection.* Molly could hear Professor Goldblatt back in social work school saying the words: *This isn't my fault; it's yours—denial and projection—the alcoholic's two most commonly used defenses.* "You're telling me that the reason we can't be together is that you don't want to take on responsibility for me. Right?"

"Can't. Not 'don't want to.'" Pause. "Can't." Anger flashed in his eyes again. He was wishing, Molly was sure, that he'd never picked up the phone. "I'm sorry you have a problem with that, but . . ."

"It's not me you don't want to take responsibility for, or in your words, *can't.* It's yourself—your own feelings."

The words hung between them like an aftershock. She moved back from him, anticipating another explosion, afraid he would hit something else— maybe her.

But he didn't. Momentarily he turned his head away and took a few breaths. Then, he said in a puzzled voice, "You've lost me completely." It was because he respected her "smarts", she realized, that he was not simply dismissing her. "Say it again. But this time, put it in words that a not-too-bright person like me can wrap their minds around."

"You don't really think of yourself as 'not too bright,' do you?" Molly teased, hoping to soften her words, still not sure herself exactly how to say what needed to be said without sounding preachy or pompous.

"No I don't, if you must know the truth. But what you're saying doesn't make any sense to me. I've always known my responsibilities and lived up to them."

"You mean like showing up for work drunk? That's being responsible?" Steve jerked his head back as though she had just smacked him. Molly, hating herself at this moment, mentally closed her eyes and plunged on: "You're an alcoholic, Steve. I don't know a lot about alcoholism, but I do know this: To an alcoholic, it's always someone else's fault, never your own. You're drinking because of Sean. You're withdrawing from our relationship because of me—because of something you've decided I need and that you can't give me."

Steve turned away again and stared across the street, or across space, or across time. After a while he said, "Okay, Sean I get. I've heard it often enough in AA. I'm choosing to drink as a way of dealing with, or *not* dealing with, the loss of him." He quickly added, "But I'm not blaming him for it."

"I understand that."

"It's this relationship thing I don't get. There *is* something about you that brings out this protective side in me."

"I know, Steve." It would make it so much easier if he would just hold her and they could make love and it would all go away. Unfortunately, he didn't appear to have any such thoughts. Instead, his body was tense, on guard, afraid of hearing something else he was sure he wouldn't like.

"There is a piece of me that wants to be protected and taken care of." Molly forced herself to say the words. "And it's not pure or innocent. It's young."

Tears sprang up into her eyes again. Damn!. Where are all these tears coming from? It felt like a lifetime of tears had been building up and building up until now they were an ocean of tears, and she couldn't hold them back anymore.

But it wasn't the right time; there was more she needed to say. "Steve, like all good detectives, you understand other people pretty well, so you keyed into that very young piece of me. But it seems like you're using it as an excuse to withdraw, to isolate yourself, which is something *you* always do."

"Wait a minute, Molly. . ."

"I know," her voice shook despite herself, "because it's something I've always done." Until now. "I don't know why you have to walk out of a relationship when you start to feel too much, or things get sticky. But that's what you do."

Steve sat without saying anything, the sound of his breath as labored as if it was being forced in and out of his lungs by a bellows, the thousand mile stare that she now knew so well on his face. Then, in a voice that was haunted and full of anguish, he said, "There were so many of them, Molly, dead and dying all around me. Most of them eighteen, nineteen years old." His eyes closed and she had to strain to hear him. "Burned beyond recognition; their flesh coming off in strips; holding their guts in with both hands as they bled to death. What else could I do? God forgive me!"

Reaching over, Molly gathered him into her arms. Steve put his face in his hands and took in great gulps of air. Her heart ached for him, and for herself. Together they sat like this, not speaking, beyond words, as the sun slowly went down in a burning red ball behind the buildings.

Chapter Thirty-Two

If Molly thought things would now change between Steve and her, she was wrong. He called her the next day at work to tell her he had made the decision to go back into AA and needed time by himself to think stuff through.

"So that means we don't see each other?" Molly didn't even try to mask the disappointment in her voice.

"What am I supposed to say to that?" Frustration tinged with anger. "First, you tell me I blame you for my feelings."

"I only said that your need to break things off has to do with *you*, not me."

"Which, I gotta say, I don't agree with at all. Then you turn around and get upset with me because I don't consider your feelings? You're confusing the hell out of me, Molly."

"Steve, I . . ."

"Even AA says I shouldn't be in a relationship during the first year of recovery."

"AA says you're not supposed to *start* a relationship in the first year of recovery. We're way beyond that." There was no arguing with him, obstinate male that he was. But that didn't stop her from trying. "I know what you're going through is very difficult. But can't we just talk to each other on the phone every once in a while?"

"Difficult isn't the word for it, Molly. Sean going missing is the hardest thing I've ever had to deal with in my life, much harder then that dammed war and all those dead and dying kids." Steve's voice was full of anger—at that war, at *this* war, at all those dead and dying kids, possibly his own—it was hard to know.

"Steve," she said, not believing for a minute that he really felt nothing for all those dead boys and wanting desperately to ease his suffering, "why not ask the doctor to put you on something for a while, maybe an anti-depressive, to take the edge off it?"

"That's what the alcohol does. Why not stay on that?"

It was a half-hearted attempt to be humorous and she responded by rolling her eyes.

"I know, I know," he said as if he could see her expression. "At least on Prozac, you don't pass out on someone's floor. No Molly, I'm grateful to you, although it may take a while for me to really feel it because right now I just want to punch somebody out, only there's nobody to punch."

"Grateful? For what?"

"You got me to see that I have to deal with the situation as it is. And that means getting back into AA. No substances. And that includes Prozac. Sober means sober."

"Does sober mean we can't talk to each other?"

A big sigh. "Look, Molly. This is as much as I can do right now. I certainly don't want to make any promises I can't keep."

"Nobody's asking you to make any promises. All I want is to be able to pick up the phone and say 'Hello, how are you?' Why can't we do that?"

"Let's just see how it goes."

Before going home that evening, Molly stopped by to visit her brother. Steve had been in her mind all day. It's hard enough to think about losing a brother, she thought as she climbed the stairs. But to lose a child? How can anyone bear it?

There was no answer to Molly's knock on his door. "Ben, are you there? It's me, Molly." Still no answer. She unlocked the door with her keys and turned on a light. The kitchen, black as ever with the exception of the red geranium she'd bought him which was sitting on the windowsill, was as empty as the rest of the apartment. The knot in her stomach tightened another notch.

Coming down the stairs, she saw Marushka standing in the doorway. She was wearing one of her brightly-colored full skirts, a magenta blouse cut low over her cleavage and an open denim jacket. Lit by the low-watt bulb in the hallway, she could have stepped out of a Renoir painting, with a little Levi-Strauss thrown in.

"How is he?" Molly asked.

The two lines on Marushka's forehead deepened. "He got beaten up a few days ago."

"I know. I was here right after it happened."

"A gang of boys, Spanish, I think."

"I thought they were Asian."

Marushka shook her head. "They wear jackets with dragons on the back. That's why maybe he thought they were Asian." She took out a pack of cigarettes and lit one. "Anyway, Niclos, he chased them away." Taking a deep drag, she blew out the smoke. "I don't think they'll bother him again."

"How can you be sure?"

"He put the gypsy curse on them."

"The gypsy curse?"

Marushka nodded. "Niclos tells them that if they lay a hand on

205

your brother again, their dicks will shrivel and fall off, and their women will eat them for breakfast, like sausages links. Then he says some words in Romany." Her full lips turned up in a sly smile. "Everyone is afraid of the gypsies. It works every time."

In spite of herself, Molly laughed. Niclos's efforts in the scaring-off department might actually work a hell of a lot better than anything Steve's friend in the local precinct could dream up. "I'm really worried about my brother, Marushka."

The gypsy nodded. "It's not good. But I have your card," she added, patting her pocket. "I don't forget."

Three days later, on a chilly Thursday morning, the phone call Molly had been sub-consciously waiting for ever since that conversation finally came.

"This is Marushka." Hearing her voice for the first time on the phone, it sounded harsher than Molly remembered it. "You'd better come."

"What happened? Marushka. What did he do?"

"Just come." The line went dead.

Molly took a deep breath and dialed Tony Moretti at Marble Heights. As she waited for Tony to answer his page, she told herself that she was probably over-reacting. But there had been something in Maurshka's voice . . .

"We'll get the paperwork started, Molly," Tony said in his unflappable way after picking up the phone and hearing her go on for a bit about whether or not she could get him up to Westchester. "It'll all be in the works *if* you can get him up here."

"I haven't seen him yet."

"If he's really bad, you may just have to let the police take him in down there. Maybe after he's stabilized a little, we can have him transferred."

Oh God! Images of those earlier commitments flashed through her mind like scenes from the theater of the dammed. Not that. "I'm going over there now. I'll let you know."

Molly left a message for Stuttman on his voicemail, threw on her coat and ran down the stairs.

Marushka was standing outside Ben's building, her arms hugging her chest. She was wearing a man's jacket over a low-cut blouse and was shivering in the wintry air.

"Yesterday, he came into my apartment and started accusing me of being the devil's harlot," she began before Molly could get her mouth open. "When I yelled at him to get out, he got wild, threw a lamp at the wall, made a hole as big as a soup bowl. Now why does he want to go and do that?" Molly had no explanation that Marushka would understand.

"He's been locked in his bedroom since then. He won't come out or answer me. I don't think he's eaten. I hear him mumbling through the door. Niclos is up there."

"Oh, Marushka, I'm so sorry." Molly felt unaccountable anger—at Ben because, despite his fear and terror of hospitals, he was incapable of staying at least minimally sane—and at herself because her love was inadequate to protect him, as if love could be equated with some amulet—a cross, a Star of David, a crystal. She knew this was irrational. Chemicals were exploding in his brain and blowing out his synapses. The beating had made him more paranoid. Love didn't conquer all. But she felt as though it should. "Of course I'll pay for any damages."

Marushka followed her up the stairs. The door to Ben's apartment was open and Niclos was standing in the kitchen with a baseball bat in his hands. He watched them enter without saying anything, but his face clearly said, "You're both crazier than he is for not putting him away a long time ago." Remembering the force of Ben's terror-driven rages, she was just grateful he was there. The bedroom door at the end of the apartment was closed. She knocked gently and tried to turn the knob. It was locked.

"Ben, it's me, Molly. Please let me in."

Nothing.

She knocked again, a little harder. "I'm worried about you, Ben. I just want to see that you're okay."

"The voices are coming in through the walls." Ben's voice. "The walls are the stalls where they keep the words. Molly it's not. It's the words of the voices that say Molly, but how can you know evil from the mouth of a sister?"

His thoughts were off and flying again, into a world of their own strange associations. Her heart, hammering in her chest, sounded so loud she wondered if Ben could hear it through the door.

"Ben," she said, running tense fingers through her hair, "I don't want you to be hurt. Please just open the door."

"No. I can only live by dying."

"Last couple of days, he's been talking a lot about dying again," Marushka whispered sharply. Molly hadn't even realized the woman was behind her. Marushka's eyes looked troubled; this was no easy decision for her, either. "Niclos can break the door down. Maybe you better call the police."

I can't do this by myself again. I just can't. I need my mother. What was she thinking? Her mother had never been any help in this situation. From the very beginning, that very first time, Molly had been the one who had to do it. She thought about calling Steve—he was trained and could handle it if Ben got violent. But at the moment, not knowing

207

where things stood between them, she couldn't face even the slightest hesitation on his part.

Closing her eyes, an image came into her mind: herself as a little girl lying in her bed, it must have been BD—before that infamous day—and she must have been sick because her skin had been all hot and fevered. Her mother, wearing an apron with a brown stain on it, was sitting by the side of her bed, stroking Molly's hair.

Did it really happen? The touch of her mother's hand, pushing the hair away from her fevered face felt as if it was happening right now. Moly opened her eyes, willing herself back into the present. Get with it, girl. The past is the past. Your mother is dead and Steve has his own problems.

"I'll be back soon," she said to Marushka and went down the stairs.

Instead of going home and burrowing under the covers to try to bring back the memory of her mother's soothing hand, which is what she felt like doing, Molly started heading towards a rental agency where she picked up a car and drove back to her brother's building, pulling up in front of a No Parking sign.

Two older black men were sitting on the next stoop arguing with each other and drinking wine out of a bag-wrapped bottle. They looked up as she got out of the car. The curtain in Marushka's first-floor window flicked and in a moment she was out of her door and following Molly up the stairs. Niclos, still holding his baseball bat, was sitting on a chair in Ben's kitchen. Molly was struck again by the contrast between the black kitchen and the geranium as it sat in its small green plastic pot on the window sill. Its flowers, now deep-red, were dying, like the color of drying blood.

Midnight shakes the memory as a madman shakes a dead geranium. Another fragment of poetry that she couldn't place, that her brother would have quoted and named in the past. Why all this poetry? Was that her way of trying to stay connected to him? How sad is that? She took a yoga breath to calm herself and knocked on his bedroom door again. "Ben, it's me, Molly, please let me in."

Nothing.

"So should I tell Niclos to break the door down?" Marushka whispered.

"No," Molly whispered back. "That would only frighten him even more."

"So what are you gonna do?"

Molly thought for a minute. "There's a fire escape, in the rear, leading to the bedroom window. Maybe I can get in that way and talk to him."

She retraced her steps down to the first floor. The hallway stank from old garbage and the unwashed bodies and stale urine of homeless people who used the stairwell for shelter. The back door leaned crazily on one hinge and the rear alleyway was full of stained mattresses, abandoned furniture and discarded food containers.

Ben lived on the third floor, which meant climbing up two flights. Wondering whether the rusted, crumbling fire escape would hold her, she forced herself to think about the dozens of neighborhood burglars who used these fire escapes as their personal access ways with nary a scratch.

By the time Molly reached Ben's landing, she was filthy from the grime and flakes of rust that coated everything. Peering in the window, she could see him sitting barefoot on the floor in half-lotus position, surrounded by burning candles, like someone about to be sacrificed in a primitive ritual. It was shocking to realize how old he looked, although it was only a few days since she'd seen him last. When had his hair and beard gotten so gray? The bruises he'd gotten during the beating were fading into a yellowish-green color, intensifying the look of age. He was dressed bizarrely—always a sign of rapidly increasing disintegration—in a checked shirt and dirty striped pants. An old orange beach towel, patterned with a big starfish in the middle, was tied with a cord around his waist. He was watching the door, so he didn't see her on the fire escape.

The wooden window frame was so rotted she could easily remove it, but a metal gate covered the window. Without any real hope she pulled it and, wonder of wonders, it slid open; her paranoid brother had forgotten to lock it, another sign of his increasing dysfunction.

As she was attempting to slide the window frame out of its track, the glass suddenly came out in her hand and went tumbling down into the courtyard below. At the sound, Ben wheeled around, his face shiny with terror. They stared at each other, and for a moment Molly saw the scene through his eyes: some filthy apparition who had taken on the visage of his sister was trying to climb through his window to do god knows what to him. Oh, Ben! she thought miserably. I don't want this to be happening to you!

Chapter Thirty-Three

A stab of fear—a quick catch of breath; Molly knew full well what he was capable of. In all the years of his madness, however, he'd never tried to hurt her. At least so far. She just had to convince him that she was who she said she was.

"Ben, it's me, Molly." She tried to smile. "I climbed up the fire escape because you wouldn't let me in. That's why I look so dirty." It sounded lame, even to her.

He pulled two candles off the floor where they had been attached by melted wax and stood up to face her, a candle poised like a fiery sword in each hand.

"Ben," she said, trying to sound enticing and a little mischievous, "I have a car. Remember how much fun we used to have when Daddy would take us for car rides? Put down the candles and let's go for a ride."

"The lies shine through your evil Molly eyes," he said, jabbing at her with the candles.

Well, she should have known that lying to him was not the way to go—he was way too smart. Frantically she searched her mind for some way to calm his fears and convince him of who she was. Otherwise he might become violent and Niclos would have to call the police—to be prevented at all costs.

"Do you remember the song you used to sing to me when I was a little girl and would have nightmares?" She began to sing:

Rock-a-bye, don't you cry
Go to sleepy little baby.
When you wake, you shall have
All the pretty little horses.

His head thrust forward to peer at her. A tiny flicker of recognition must have penetrated his psychotic haze because the candle dropped down a little. It wasn't because she knew the words to the childhood song, she realized—an evil imposter would certainly know that—but because she sang it in the same atonal, off-key voice that he'd always teased her about. When was it that she had stopped singing?

"Ben, I want to get you some help, so you'll be safe. I'm worried about you and I love you. You're my big brother." As the words came out, she felt them so powerfully that it almost knocked her off the fire escape.

He was staring at her intently. She could almost read what was going on inside his head, or thought she could. He was desperately trying to hang onto whatever shred of ability he still had to distinguish what was actually happening from the agonizing fear and panic that was pushing him to believe all kinds of crazy things. Was it really Molly, or wasn't it? It must have been simply terrifying for him not to know.

"Ben, if you just come with me, I promise not to let anyone hurt you." Please let this be a promise I can keep. "If you won't come, I'm going to have to call for help."

It was never clear whether or not he understood her because at that moment a blob of hot wax plopped onto his bare foot.

He grimaced and dropped the candle. As he did, the other candle went out. Molly took this opportunity to climb in through the window. .

"Come with me, Ben," she murmured in a gentle voice, the way you would calm a frightened animal. "You can take your candles with you if you want. Marushka and Niclos are in the kitchen. I'm going to tell them to move away, and not to threaten or hurt you." The words from the crisis intervention course she'd taken flooded into her mind: Approach gently, non-aggressively but with assurance. Tell the patient what you are going to do before you do it.

Molly could almost smell the fear radiating from him, but she could also see the lines of strain on his face. He wasn't nineteen anymore; perhaps he was just too tired to fight. Whatever it was, he let her lead him to the bedroom door.

Unlocking the door, she gave him a reassuring smile and led him through the kitchen, saying over her shoulder in a calm, friendly way: "Marushka and Niclos, please move back. My brother and I are going out for a little while." A homey little scene. One brother and sister saying goodbye to another brother and sister—only one brother was brandishing a baseball bat and the other was as crazy as a loon.

Ben, the cunning, followed Molly into the hallway. His feet still bare, wrapped in the ridiculous beach towel and clutching his candle, he kept glancing behind him, watching Niclos and the baseball bat like a child watches the closet where he knows the bogeyman is hiding. Molly, the betrayer, still trying to convince herself she was doing the right thing, still telling herself that he would never hurt her, all the while continuing to murmur calm reassurances at him.

Down one flight of stairs and then the second. Everything was moving along until they got out onto the street. She never knew whether Ben had planned all along that it would be easier to get away from her once they were out of the apartment, or whether the noise and activity on the street were just too much for him, but he gave a yell and started running up the block, his skinny legs pumping as hard as they could under the flapping of his orange beach towel.

Like a fool she stood there and shouted, "Ben, come back!"

"Girl, man don' want you, find one who do. Plenty of us around." One of the two elderly wine drinkers was looking up at her with a big grin on his face. The other old man laughed, slapped his bony knee, shook his head and said, "You listen to my man here. He be tellin' you the truth. Don't be chasin' him up no street. Ain't dignified."

But chase him she did. From behind her, the sound of a motor jumped into life. A black Lincoln driven by one of Marushka's sons roared past her. Marushka had her family in readiness.

With a screech of brakes, the car pulled up with one wheel on the sidewalk in front of Ben just as he got to the corner, effectively cutting him off. The kid jumped out of the car and rounded the corner so that Ben couldn't run that way. With Molly coming up behind him, he didn't have too many options besides jabbing at the air with his candle.

Once again she approached him with gentle reassurance. Probably deciding that she was the better of the choices he had right then, he allowed himself to be accompanied back to the rental car. But his eyes watched her with low cunning.

She heard a *vroom-vroom* and saw the back of the Lincoln, now in reverse, passing them as it proceeded up the block. For a moment an image of Ben going after her mother with the hammer came into her mind, along with another sharp stab of fear. Resolutely she pushed the thought away.

She unlocked the car door, got Ben into the passenger seat and buckled him in. Her clever brother, however, had again been making his plans. By the time she got around the car to get into the driver's seat, he was out of his seat belt, had jerked the door open and was sprinting down the block.

"Some women just can't take no hint." The voice of the first wine drinker.

"Yeah," the reply came. "What you think so turrible 'bout her that he got to get away so badly, can't even wait to put his shoes on?"

The kid was out of the Lincoln and about to tackle Ben by the time Molly got around the car again. Once upon a time her big brother would've fought like the devil, but maybe he was burning out as he got older, because after she gestured the kid away and said, "Ben, you have to get into the car," he stopped and got back into the car. Had he decided she was really Molly? Who knows?

The trip to Marble Heights actually went smoothly, but all she could think about was Ben opening his door and running out onto the parkway. And then, how could she save him?

He didn't. What he did do was stare at her out of accusing eyes and ramble on about "lying sister words" and a plague of dead rats, dead frogs and dead vermin that he claimed were crawling around in his body.

As soon as they pulled up in front of the hospital, the accusation in his eyes turned to alarm. Ben had never seen Marble Heights, and she hadn't mentioned where they were going, but he could spot a mental hospital at one hundred paces anywhere on this earth.

"You go in," he said, shrinking from her with one of those rare moments of lucidity that are completely unexplainable. "I'll wait here for you."

But of course that wouldn't do. She coaxed him into the building and murmured reassurances while Tony and the admitting psychiatrist were being paged.

Marble Heights didn't look like your typical psych hospital. A low, gray-stoned structure, it sat on a beautifully landscaped lawn surrounded by trees and bushes, now in their mid-winter barrenness. The lobby and reception area were carpeted in forest green; the walls were beige with matching green and rose trim and were hung with attractive paintings. Upholstered chairs and low tables with magazines added to the air of quiet normality.

Tony was good with Ben, asking his questions in a calm, friendly way and simply accepting Ben's strange and disjointed answers. She was starting to relax a little when a short, thin, dried-up looking man came into the room.

"I'm Dr. Koster," he said.

His eyes bulged slightly, like a toad, and he tended to punctuate his sentences with a clearing of his throat which, unfortunately, gave him a slightly accusatory tone. The knot in Molly's stomach came back.

"Ehrm! And you are Benjamin Lewin?" he asked. A look of alarm came into Ben's eyes and he didn't answer. Uh oh. Not a good start.

"And you are . . .?" he asked her. She looked down at her filthy, disheveled self and wondered if he was determining whether she, too, was there to be admitted.

Before she could respond, he glanced at the papers in his hands and said, "Molly Lewin, sister."

"I apologize for my appearance," she said primly. "I had to climb up a fire escape."

He nodded as if this was a perfectly normal occurrence in the lives of his patients' families. Then he turned to the would-be patient. "Hello, Ben. I have some questions I'd like to ask you, okay?"

He paused for a minute but when Ben still didn't answer, he went on, "When were you born?"

Molly knew the doctor was trying to assess Ben's mental state, but also knew how suspicious it would sound to Ben. He didn't want people to know the date of his birth because he thought it allowed them to have power over him.

"Birth . . . the birth of vipers in the raging torrents of the mind battles." Ben watched Dr. Koster through narrowed eyes and began swinging his arms back and forth, a sure sign of his increasing agitation.

Dr. Koster stepped back a little and took a visible breath. He cleared his throat again and said, "Do you know why you are here?"

Another bad question, one she could have kicked herself for not realizing he would ask. This was, after all, supposed to be a voluntary commitment. Come on Ben, she thought desperately, say something at least halfway normal. Even as she thought it, the other half of her brain knew it was a lost cause.

Ben stared at the doctor and started to mutter. He hunched his shoulders forward and his hands became fists. Swinging them, he began pacing around the floor. This interview was going downhill fast.

Dr. Koster turned to Tony and said, "I think we're going to need some back-up to get the patient down on the unit. I'm going to radio for Code Team."

He took a small walkie-talkie out of his pocket and spoke into it. Molly decided later that the black box with its strange, crackling noises was the match that set off the tinderbox. Behind her, the Admissions people began to clear out the area: receptionist, visitors, other staff were all being herded away. The hospital was readying itself for the violent outburst of her brother.

And Ben did not disappoint them. Small, growling noises, similar to the ones made by the good doctor, came from his throat. The hair on his head stood straight up, as if his terror had set off voltages of electricity in his body which were charging through him like lightning.

As Dr. Koster backed away, he said in a low voice to Tony, "Why don't you take Ms. Lewin into your office?"

Tony took her arm. "Come on, Molly. He's called the Crisis Team. They're trained to deal with Ben. It would just upset you to see this."

"Mind vermin, rats and frogs!" Ben shouted, making a lunge for the walls, banging and kicking against them in his rage to escape. Since he had no shoes on, she was afraid he would break his toes. She wanted to run over and put her arms around him. But he was over the edge, and she had become part of the hostile, terrifying world against which he had to protect himself. And there was nothing she could do about it.

"Patient rapidly decompensating." Dr. Koster continued talking into the walkie-talkie as he hurriedly left the area. "I want seventy-five milligrams of Thorazine, I.M. . . . ." The rest was garbled as Tony pulled her away. Four burly men pulling a Reeves stretcher on which to secure the dangerous patient were running up the hall. The Four Horsemen of the Apocalypse. A woman with a stethoscope around her neck trailed after them.

Molly collapsed into a chair in Tony's office as he ran back to help the staff do an involuntary commitment of her brother. So what she'd been hoping to avoid was happening after all. Molly had seen enough psych hospitals to know that even in the most private and presentable of them, there would be no carpets and pictures on the walls of the room where they would be taking him. He would be wrapped in a "camisole"—a pretty word for a strait jacket. There would be a mattress on the floor and four bare walls. And he would be alone, screaming in rage at his demons and his terror until the medication took hold.

Molly sat staring into space, enveloped in a world of gray fog, hearing and feeling nothing. Gradually she became aware of the slanted rays of light coming in through the window. For a long time she sat exhausted, demolished, watching the late afternoon sun shine through the leafless branches of the trees that dotted the lawn. On the windowsill stood a vase of roses. The red flowers brought to mind the pot of geraniums on her brother's windowsill. *Midnight shakes the memory as a madman shakes a dead geranium.*

She shuddered, as if a cold wind had suddenly blown through the room. A small pulse started up in the corner of her eye, like the slow beat of a dying heart. The lyrics to an old blues song came into her head: *Motherless children have a hard time when your mother is dead.* During her mother's last days, before the cancer finally killed her, Molly had sat by her bedside watching the long, slow, agonizing breaths going in and out of that emaciated chest. Did she, too, stroke her mother's hair? *Motherless children have a hard time*—at least her mother would never have to see Ben like this again. Her brilliant child, her first and only son. That first time had finished her. The remainder of her years was merely a long, slow descent into actual death.

Tony came in, his eyes filled with concern, and asked if she was okay. Molly managed a small reassuring smile. The medication had taken hold, he said. Ben was quiet now and she could visit him. Did she want him to come with her? She didn't. "I'll be fine," she stated. "I've done this lots of times before." He explained where she'd find Ben, and asked again if she was okay. Molly nodded. After giving her another quick look, he grabbed his jacket and left.

Molly sat for a while longer, thinking about her brother, knowing exactly what she would see when she visited him. They would have transferred him to a bed with raised sides, like a metallic crib. He would still be in restraints, his wrists loosely tied to the sides of the bed, and he'd be lying on his back staring up at the ceiling out of vacant eyes. The quirky, sly, fearful, funny, suspicious guardian of the last remnants of his mind – her brother – would not be in that room. Her heart was breaking from the loss of him.

215

Like the geraniums, you can't bring back the dead, no matter how much you shake them. Once the medication took hold, he'd be back—at least some of him; each time he went through this, a little more of him disappeared forever. For a long time she just sat, watching the shadows on the lawn lengthen and flatten until it became so dark she could no longer distinguish their shapes.

Finally she took a deep breath, got up and went out into the hall. After the darkness of Tony's office, the sudden glare of the fluorescent lights made her blink. It was late and the area was deserted. I ought to check on him and see how he's doing, she thought. But her legs felt heavy, too tired to move. And she still had the long drive ahead of her. Another poetry fragment, one of Ben's early favorites, came into her mind. *Over the tumbled graves, about the chapel/ There is the empty chapel, only the wind's home.* Which ever way she looked, she faced an empty room. Pulling her coat tightly around her shoulders, she walked out of the hospital.

Chapter Thirty-Four

Instead of turning into the car rental lot, Molly kept going until she was over the bridge and into Brooklyn, hardly aware that she was still driving, not even knowing where she intended to go. The old blues song was playing around in her head again: *Motherless children have a hard time when your mother is dead.* She spoke the next two lines: *They ain't got no where to go. Gotta walk from door to door.*

Not as beautifully expressed as the lines of Ben's poetry she'd remembered back in the hospital. Her own poetry, the blues, jabbed a long, lonesome finger right into the truth of it. All the beautiful verses Ben had been able to quote . . . and it was those two plain-speak lines that characterized the feeling of her whole life. Molly had been knocking on other people's doors, dipping in and out of other people's lives—clients, friends, most certainly her brother—trying to make their lives her own because there was no place for her to go in this world, no real home. Even the little studio apartment had never been a home; it felt as transitory and lonely as she did herself. *Can it ever be a home if there's no mother waiting at the door to welcome you?* Molly, wanting desperately to comfort the lost and forsaken little child inside her, didn't know how to answer that question.

She'd reached the end, the last street in this little piece of Brooklyn. Pulling into an empty spot by the river, she sat and watched the roiling water and a lonely tug fighting its way upstream against the wind-blown current. For a moment, she saw the Twin Towers floating above the horizon like two long, ghostly shapes, unattached to Mother Earth. *Motherless children.* Unprotected, unsafe, blown up and destroyed. After a while she got out of the car and walked up to Willie's apartment. He wasn't home, but she had a good idea where to find him.

Sure enough. He was sitting in Lonnie's with a drink in front of him and the Gibson in his hands, jamming the blues, the bony fingers of his left hand twisting and pulling at the strings 'til the guitar sounded like it was being strangled to death. It was the same Gully song that Willie had been playing since Bukka died, but he'd morphed it into its funereal essence—a pure, unadulterated cry of anguish, loss and grief.

"Willie?"

Slowly he brought himself back into the bar and found her.

"Are you okay?"

He stared for a minute, trying to place her. Then, as if he were continuing a conversation he was already in the midst of, he said: "Gully used to tell me the blues is the blues, wherever you go. But I found that ain't so. The blues up north here is different than the blues Gully and them Delta blues men used to sing. Them blues was jook joint blues and cotton field blues. Love gone bad, you ain't got a job, your mama died—hello blues, come on in, I know who you are. Not the kind of blues they got up here."

"What kind of blues do they have up here?"

Willie shrugged, not able to put it into words. "But I figured I'd sing the blues the way Gully did," he continued the conversation he was having with himself, "and Bukka would learn 'em that way, and so them old blues'd sing on." He shook his head sadly. "I was jes' plain dumb, that's what I was. He didn't want Gully's blues, nor mine, neither."

For a moment Molly saw her mother, sitting mutely at the table, head down, shoulders sunk in silent grief. Her mother, too, didn't want what Molly had to give her. *Why couldn't you just have been happy with me?* It came up in her like a cry of anguish. She collapsed back against the leatherette seat and took three short, gasping breaths. It's the old wrong child blues, Molly thought. That's why she could never be a mother to me—you can't be a mother to the wrong child.

"Now when I die," Willie went on, "them blues will die with me 'cause there's no one left to sing 'em."

There was nothing Molly could do for Willie, nor for Ben, nor for her mother, nor for anyone. She drove back into Manhattan and dropped the car off. Then she went home and put Gully's album onto her turntable—anything to stop her own thoughts. Sinking into her little oak rocking chair, she closed her eyes and saw Willie's bony, twisted fingers on the old Gibson, and an idea began to form. It was insane, but as she continued to listen, the notion came back and wouldn't go away.

Gully was singing the song that Willie had been playing the last several times she'd seen him. "Graveyard Blues"—she remembered it now—*"Went down to the graveyard, got down on my knees."*

Gully sang from the plantations, the turpentine fields, the jook joints and Jim Crow of the rural Mississippi Delta. It was hard to understand the words because he wasn't singing for Molly's Northern ears. But unlike her mother's blues, this album came with liner notes, and the words were printed right in front of her. She read them; and she knew.

Thrusting her feet into her shoes and grabbing her jacket, Molly ran all the way to the subway and rode back into Brooklyn, back to Lonnie's. Willie was at the same table. By now his whole body was sagging. Red lines criss-crossed through his eyes and he looked like a road that had come to the end of itself and was just petering out.

He was still jamming Gully's song, his fingers in their accustomed place around the neck of the old Gibson.   Molly waited until he came around to the beginning again.   And then she sang the words that he couldn't, or wouldn't sing:

Went down to the graveyard
Got down on my knees
Killed the only one I ever loved
Lord have mercy please

His eyes jerked up, and what she saw in them told her that she was right.

"Why, Willie?" Sadness so bone-chilling deep, it made her whole body feel leaden.

He sat there for a long time, his fingers working at the strings. Then he simply said, "He killed Cal."

"Bukka killed Cal?" Molly could still hardly believe it, even while knowing it was true.

"Bukka wanted me to give him the Gibson." He dragged the words out as if he couldn't bear to speak them. "But I knew he was jes' gonna sell it to buy drugs. When I told him no, he waited until I was out of the house and then he came back to steal it. Didn't expect Cal to be there."

"Cal was never out. Why wouldn't Bukka know that?"

"Happened on the day that Bukka thought Donnie was gonna put Cal into a nursing home. Bukka had already gone before you and Louis stopped him from doin' it. Later that night he came in the window and started pulling out drawers, to make it look like a burglary, and there was Cal, lookin' at him." Willie rested the guitar on the seat, picked up his glass and finished the little that was left in it.

"Oh God, Willie. When did you find this all out?"

"Came home one night, and Bukka had the Gibson in his hand. Tol' me he'd already killed Cal for it, and now he was gonna take it."

"Why didn't he take it after he killed Cal?"

"It was jes' like it said on the news. Heard me coming in, got scared, and lit out fast. Left it behind."

"Why didn't he take Cal's gold cufflinks if he needed money to buy drugs? Oh," she answered the question herself, "Donald probably cleaned out his father's stuff."

Willie nodded. "Soon as the police would let him."

"Bukka was killed by a .22, a Saturday night special," Molly said, trying now to reconstruct what had first come to her as a flash of intuition. "You're telling me that was your gun?"

"After Cal died, I was scared to stay alone in that empty house. Bought me one of them little guns, for protection."

219

Suddenly Willie's hand shot out, knocking over the empty glass in front of him. "Why didn't I jes' let him take it?" he cried, torment twisting through his voice, his face, his body. "Was gonna be his soon anyways." His voice broke, and tears rolling down his cheeks. "Why did I have to pick up that gun and follow him into the street?"

"Because that Gibson was the last thing you had left."

Willie stared at her.

"Willie," Molly said softly, "he killed Cal, the man you loved and lived with for so many years."

"Cal was as good as dead before Bukka shot him. That boy was my only blood."

"You lost Bukka to drugs years ago. He was well and truly gone, no matter how much you tried to tell yourself otherwise."

Willie's head dropped, knowing she was right but hating it.

"And now," Molly went on, "those greedy, powerful dealmakers—those bad guys—were gonna take your home away from you." The tears were running down her face also, but she was past caring. "How much can one person lose before it pushes him over the edge?"

A small sigh escaped him, like the final puff of wind after a vanishing storm.

"The Gibson was the only thing you had left that was truly yours, and Bukka was even gonna take that."

Another mood shift. His mouth became hard; his fingers back to jamming. "I knowed that Gibson better than I knowed any person in this world, including Cal. Once, in a boxcar outside Louisville, I almost killed a man tried to steal it. And after everything I taught that boy, it meant nothing more to him than gettin' high."

"Willie . . ."

"Didn't even try to run. But it was like that time in Louisville; a rage come over me and when it was gone, he was dead." Willie's eyes were sick with watching it happen all over again. "I'm an old man. He could'a done me in easy. Was like he wanted me to kill him."

"Willie . . ." Molly struggled for the right words, not finding them, never finding them. Her body felt full of the grief and anguish and fear which had led Willie—and Ben, and Steve and god-knows how many other men—to violence.

"Cal met me, I was drifter, didn't have no home. That place," Willie nodded his chin in the direction of the river and the apartment across from it, "was the first real home I had since I left my mama to go on the road with Gully."

"And they were gonna take it away from you."

Slowly, silently, he nodded. "Bukka never understood. He didn't seem to need no home. Or maybe drugs was the home he went to at the end of the day." Willie leaned the guitar back against the bottom of the seat and sat staring down at it. Grief and desolation were cutting new lines in his face. She wanted to throw her arms around him, but knew it wasn't what he wanted or needed.

"Wasn't just Bukka I killed, you know. Was Gully, too."

"What do you mean, Willie?"

"Always hoped that Gully and his blues'd go on living inside'a Bukka. Now?" He shrugged. "It's all gone."

Once more Willie picked up the instrument, for which he'd paid such a heavy price, wrapped his fingers around the strings, and began to sing an old field song. His voice was still harsh but without resonance; his face appeared blurry, less distinct. It was like watching a slow dissolve. Without Gully anchored to one end of his life, and Bukka to the other, Willie was disappearing right before her eyes.

"*Done gone, lord,*" he sang. "*Like a turkey through the corn, lord, with his long tail gone.*"

Gone. Her mother, her father, Ben, Steve—no use kidding herself, he didn't want a relationship with her. Don't go there, she admonished herself. But the tears flowed again.

"No one could play the blues the way Bukka did without knowing what suffering is all about." The words came out of her mouth without her realizing it.

Willie stopped playing; his body went rigid. She hadn't meant to cause him anymore pain. "Maybe he's in a place now where he won't suffer anymore," Molly said. And, god help me, maybe my mother is there, too.

Willie started to play again, but the rhythm had changed. It was harsher, darker, edgier; more urban. These were Bukka's blues. Without thinking about it, Molly began singing words to his music—scat songs, jazz songs, bits and pieces of blues that she never even knew she knew. Her singing voice sounded strange to her, as if she was meeting it for the first time. But it didn't seem to bother Willie. He just followed along behind her. And so they sat there together, jamming one song after another, until Lonnie kicked them out.

221

Chapter Thirty-Five

"So when were you going to tell me that Willie killed Bukka?" Steve asked. It had been over a week since they'd last seen each other in Union Square Park. This morning, soon after she arrived at work, he'd paid her an unannounced visit and was now parked in her client chair.

"How did you know?" So much had happened since that afternoon—she could hardly begin to put words to it. She'd left Willie that day in a state of wonder at her new-found voice. But a voice demands a listener; Molly certainly hadn't found one in her brother who she'd visited several times and who mostly stared at her out of drugged-out eyes while she bit back the tears and tried to fill the emptiness with some meaningless chatter. Tony said they would gradually reduce his dosage once he was stabilized, but the brother she knew and loved had disappeared, for now.

The morning after hearing Willie's confession, Molly had gotten up determined to tell Steve about it. But as time went on she became less and less willing to be the one responsible for Willie's arrest. He was such an old man, what good would it do to punish him? Bukka had murdered his great-grandfather's life companion, had tried to steal or destroy the one thing that was left to the old man. Wasn't Bukka only getting the justice he deserved? On the other hand how could she, a woman who was a champion of the rule of law, support vigilante justice? She was glad now that Steve already knew.

"We found the gun with Willie's prints on it, buried in the cellar of his building. It matches the slug that we took out of the kid's body."

"He buried the gun? I can't believe it. I assumed he tossed it into the river."

"Come on, Molly," he answered wryly. "You should know better. Willie comes from the generation where you never throw anything away. A gun is valuable and he might have needed it again for protection, so he says. Especially since the waterfront area is so deserted at night."

Poor Willie. Had he wanted to be caught? "So how did you come to find it?"

"A homeless man we picked up on an unrelated charge gave it up as part of a deal. He'd found it when he was camping out in the basement of Willie's building. We got a warrant and uncovered it, exactly where he said it was."

"Why didn't the homeless man take it?"

"Who knows, Molly?" Steve shrugged—a gesture so familiar that she felt that no time had passed since she'd last seen him. "Some people just don't like guns. Willie admits to the shooting, but when we ask him why, all he'll say is, 'Ask Ms. Molly.' That's why we need you."

"He doesn't need me. He needs a lawyer."

"He's got a lawyer."

"What does the lawyer say?"

Before he could answer, the phone rang and Molly picked it up.

"Molly, it's Howie Markowitz. I'm representing Willie Cobb. You and I need to talk."

She sat back, absolutely flabbergasted. Then she glanced at Steve who was trying to pretend like he wasn't listening. "I can't talk now. Let me call you back."

Molly hung up the phone and grinned at Steve. "Always the cop. You knew his lawyer was going to call me and you wanted to get to me first so I could tell you something possibly incriminating."

"You can't blame a guy for trying." He shrugged again and then leveled icy blue eyes right at her. "But let's get back to the question of how long it was going to take you to report Willie's confession."

Molly, who couldn't really answer the question, went on the offensive. "Am I required by law to tell you about an alleged confession made by some frail, possibly mentally impaired old man?"

"First of all, the confession is not alleged. He did make it, and it's up to us to investigate the veracity of it. And, as a matter of fact, you *are* required to report it. As a licensed social worker, if a client confesses a murder to you, you are legally bound to do just that. You're not an attorney, and a confession of murder is not privileged."

"How did I know he was telling the truth? How do I know it now?"

"Come on, Molly. Don't give me that bullshit."

"Well, I need to talk to his lawyer before I say anything more to you about it."

"I can arrest you for obstruction of justice."

She rolled her eyes at him.

"Or I could meet you for a quick bite later, after you've spoken to his lawyer, which you're going to do anyway before you'll tell me a thing, if I know you." Steve's mouth curled up into that familiar lop-sided grin. It made her want to reach over and just hug him, but she very properly kept to her side of the desk.

"How about Vinny's?" she suggested.

"How about that sandwich shop, three doors down from there. I'm not drinking these days, remember? I can't even walk into a bar."

Molly nodded and Steve got up, bent over and kissed her on the cheek. After he left, she sat for a moment, caressing the spot gently.

223

Then she picked up the phone and called Howie back. "How did Willie find *you*?" Molly asked.

"Apparently, you had mentioned my name when you were trying to help him with his housing problem, and he wrote it down."

Leave it to Willie. "You know he can't afford your rates."

"I'm working for him pro bono."

"Will wonders never cease!" she exclaimed, shaking her head. "I thought you didn't work for the poor and downtrodden anymore."

"Come off it, Molly. I'm still Red Ronnie's son, as angry as I get with him. That last matter, the waterfront development plan, was and is a blatant conflict of interest."

"Yeah, Howie. I guess so." It wasn't worth getting into it all again.

"You know, of course, that Willie is in police custody for allegedly having murdered his great-grandson."

"I know."

"Well, he admits to it, but he won't say anything further. He keeps telling me to ask you. So, what can you tell me?"

How do you even begin to recount this story? There were so many layers and levels to it, like an old, gnarled tree stump with convoluted rings going back for generations. "The kid was a junkie," Molly said, trying to make it as simple as possible. "He was trying to steal Willie's guitar, which is very valuable. Cal Bruchman, Willie's long-time companion who was confined to a wheelchair, saw him and Bukka killed him in cold blood. He confessed this to Willie while he was in the middle of stealing Willie's guitar again. On top of it," she added pointedly, "Willie is about to lose his home. Too much loss for one old man."

No response.

Let it rest, Molly, she told herself firmly. There really *is* no point in antagonizing him.

So she went on: "Willie just flipped out. He picked up the gun, went after the kid, and shot him."

"How did Willie get the gun?"

"He'd bought it on the street for protection after Cal was murdered. It's pretty deserted around that area, especially at night."

"Okay, Molly. I'm going to discuss it with the ADA. Hopefully, he'll be reasonable, but you never know with that bunch."

"Let me know what happens."

"My friend ADA Vandenberg and I had a drink together," Steve said later as the two of them sat at a table covered with a Formica design of turquoise, silver and pink triangles. "Only I had club soda." The sandwich shop, now named *The Do-Wop Luncheonette*, had recently

224

been redecorated in an over-the-top, retro-fifties style and featured Do-Wop music on table-top juke boxes. "Vandenberg told me they're gonna plead it out. He's giving Willie a dammed good deal, especially since there's no corroborating forensic evidence that supports Bukka's confession to the old man. Sentence recommendation will be probation, no jail time."

"I know." Molly had gotten a call from Howie just before she'd left to meet Steve. Howie told her that Vandenberg who, Howie maintained, was a little prick, had begun by insisting that jail time had to be part of the deal. So Howie told him he would take it to trial on an Extreme Emotional Disturbance defense. And if that didn't work, he'd still bet that no jury in the world would ever convict an 86-year old man like Willie, once they heard his story. Besides, Vandenberg was looking to leave the DA's office and wanted a job with Stiegel, Lowe, Myers and Donleavy, Howie's law firm, and Howie agreed to put in a good word for him as long the deal they worked out didn't involve any jail time.

"I still wish it was Donald. He was such a perfect villain." Molly sat quietly for a moment, reflecting how attached she had become to Donald-as-villain. Well, he *was* a villain—he'd harassed those old people to get them out, including Willie—the man his father had loved.

Or it could have been Ana Skana, for that matter, or her father. Both were ruthless enough, in their own ways. But the real villains were those greedy deal-makers, who already had more money than they could ever spend, who sat behind big desks in fancy corner offices, and had no compunction about throwing people out of their homes just to flaunt their power and line their pockets even further. *What ain't got no heart, can't have no soul.* Another bit of blues that went right to the truth.

"I'm still sorry those buildings have to be demolished and that they couldn't have found a way to renovate them," Molly said wistfully. "Another little piece of this city's beauty and history gone forever."

Steve, who didn't see the beauty in what appeared to him as run-down, dilapidated old buildings and certainly didn't share Molly's passion for them, shrugged.

"But Stuttman tells me that they're definitely going to build Senior Housing as part of this project," she added. "And the residents of the condemned buildings—Dave, Mrs. Canover, Willie and all the rest of them—are going to get some money to help them secure interim housing. And while it won't quite make up for the loss of their long-time homes, at least they get something. Councilman Czarnoski insisted on it."

One side of Steve's mouth turned up. "I know." He took a bite out of his sandwich.

Molly narrowed her eyes at him. "Okay, what's going on?"

Steve chewed, swallowed and then said, "The Councilman would like to think it was all due to his influence, but I, uh, gave him a little help."

"What did you do?"

"This stays strictly between you and me."

"Steve, if there's one thing you should know about me, I can keep a secret better than anyone else in the world."

"Well, that's true enough," he said flatly. "I leaned on Papa Skana a little." His expression became positively smug. "I told him we had evidence that tied Ana to Bukka's murder, and that we intended to have her arrested."

"And what was this evidence?"

"Cops can always come up with something," he answered nonchalantly. "Even if it doesn't always stand up in court."

"What about Willie's confession?"

"This conversation took place before we found the gun and had any idea that Willie was involved." He chewed another bite of his sandwich; then went on: "I also told Papa that in my opinion, Bukka was no loss to anyone, and that I would make the evidence go away if he would be willing to kick in some relocation money for the old people."

"And he believed you?"

"Where he comes from, everything is bought and sold." Steve shrugged, echoing Howie. "And maybe he knows his daughter better than I do and he wasn't going to take any chances."

Maybe he does, Molly thought. "That's not what I mean, though. I'm thinking that in his world, nobody does anything for an altruistic reason and that if you do, it would make you a weakling in his eyes, and that would defeat your purpose."

"Come on, Molly. Don't you think I know that?"

"So?"

"So I set the price pretty high and, somehow, during the course of the conversation, he got the idea that, shall we say, I would dip my beak in the punchbowl along with certain unnamed others."

Molly sat back and laughed. "I don't believe you."

"When have I ever not told you the truth?" Steve asked in mock outrage. "Even when it gets me into all kinds of trouble."

They sat for a few minutes grinning at each other and slurping the remainder of their sodas up through straws, until Steve finally asked, "So how is your brother doing? I heard he was in the hospital."

Molly felt her spine stiffen. "Who told you that?"

"Whoa!" He put up his hands. "Take it easy. I haven't been spying on you. I happened to run into your friend Louis outside of Willie's building and he told me about it."

"Louis did?" That was a surprise, especially since Louis had declared he would never tell Steve anything.

"Yeah. He was real concerned about Willie and I told him I was too. We had a little more conversation about it," which meant that Steve was trying to pump him for information, "and your name came up, and Louis said he was worried about you. I asked him why, and he told me that you'd had to put your brother back in the hospital." He stopped and looked at her questioningly. "I think he's sweet on you, Molly."

She nodded absently, thinking how ironical it was that the man she loved had known nothing about Ben's hospitalization. Louis had been the one she'd gone to the next day in her misery over her brother's commitment. Louis had asked her if she'd told Steve about it, which she hadn't because of the way they'd left things. So Louis had made sure that he knew.

"He's a good man, Molly," Steve was going on in a reasonable tone of voice. His thoughts echoed her own. "You could do worse."

Molly cocked her head to one side. "So, are you saying that you want me to take up with Louis?"

"If you want the honest, absolute truth, no."

"I'm glad. Playing the martyr doesn't suit you."

"But, on the other hand, since I'm in no condition to be in a relationship . . ."

"We've been through this already," she cut him off. "You're starting to sound like a broken record. I know you think you're not ready to be in a relationship but, ready or not, we *are* in a relationship."

"Molly . . ." Steve had that tone to his voice that men take on when they are about to explain something that, to them, appears perfectly obvious to a woman who just isn't getting it.

"What do you think this is?" Spreading her arm to encompass the both of them she answered her own question, "A non-relationship?"

"Come on, Molly. You're deliberately missing the point."

"No I'm not," she maintained emphatically. "It may be different from any relationship you or I have ever had, but neither of us has ever done very well in the relationship department, have we?" Molly, surprised at the words coming out of her mouth, recognized their truth.

"It's like we both have this follow-the-dots picture in our mind of what a relationship is supposed to be, and as long as we keep trying to have *that* kind of relationship—whatever the hell *that* is—it won't ever work. We're both whacked out in our own ways. You don't like that expression?" Molly interjected at his raised eyebrows. "Okay, maybe it's a little strong. But you walk around seeing dead and mangled people in front of your eyes, and I live other people's lives instead of my own, including long-dead musicians and a brother who thinks cockroaches are the devil's vermicelli. And we're both like one of those plants—I think they're called Mimosa—touch them and they roll up into a little ball and try to disappear. So whatever kind of relationship those two people manage to have, it will never be your typical, follow-the-dots kind."

Molly stopped, having run out of inspiration and energy at exactly the same time. Steve was staring at her as if she was a meteorite that had fallen from god-knows-where and landed on the table.

"Wow!" he said, blinking a few times. "From a girl who never said anything, you've sure blossomed into as much of a talker as any man would ever want. Ever."

As Molly sat catching her breath, Steve folded his arms across his chest and said, "Okay. So, let me get this straight. You think since I'm bananas and you're bananas, together we'd make a great banana split? And this is your idea of a relationship?" Shaking his head sadly, he added: "You and Louis would never get on. He's way too sane for you."

You should only know, she thought sardonically

For a moment, as they eyed each other across the turquoise, silver and pink Formica table, Molly had the feeling that she'd stepped out of her body and was perched on the wall—along with the five-cent coke signs, the photos of big-finned Cadillacs and a young, sexy Elvis—watching herself and Steve. They might have been two weary but not yet down-for-the-count adversaries circling each other around the ring.

The jukebox, which was on automatic during this slow time at the cafe and was playing a string of fifties and early sixties hits, segued into one of the most popular of them all: teenager Frankie Lymon's eternally unanswered question, *Why Do Fools Fall in Love?* Steve lifted his glass to his mouth and, over its edge; Molly could see his eyes start to crinkle up. Could it be a smile? On the strength of it, or maybe only the hope, she let an answering smile reach her own eyes.

SOURCES:

Willie Cobb's character was shaped by my life-long interest in blues and blues musicians, and I've used written accounts of the lives of early 20th century blues musicians for authenticity. Certain authors were invaluable in helping me to understand Willie's life and times. One of the most important was *The Land Where the Blues Began* by the incomparable folklorist, Alan Lomax who traveled throughout the South during the early years of the 20th century. He tape recorded the stories and songs of the people he met. Albert Murray's memoir on growing up in the South, *South to a Very Old Place*, provided the inspiration for Willie's stories about his mother's encounters with white women. Other sources include *The Legacy of the Blues: Art and Lives of Twelve Great Bluesmen* by Samuel Charters, *Blues off the Record: Thirty Years of Blues Commentary* by Paul Oliver, and *Feel Like Going Home* by Peter Guralnick who documented the progression of rock and roll from its early roots in the blues until the publication of his book in 1971. The bits of poetry quoted by Molly are from *Rhapsody on a Windy Night* and *Whispers of Immortality*, both by T. S. Eliot who described grief and dark, lonely places of the mind far better than I ever could. My apologies to any other written sources I may have inadvertently left out.

About the author: Harriet Rzetelny is a writer, singer and clinical social worker. She has published many stories in *Alfred Hitchock's Mystery Magazine*, most featuring social worker Molly Lewin, and has been nominated for several awards, including A Derringer Award for her 2003 story, *Amazing Grace*. Her non-mystery fiction has appeared in the Bellevue Literary Review, a journal of humanity and human experience, and she was recently anthologized in *The Best of the Bellevue Literary Review*. She is married, has two sons and currently lives on Cape Cod.

9 780980 178630